CHECK MATE

MALORIE BLACKMAN

PENGUIN BOOKS

PENGUIN BOOKS

UK | USA | Canada | Ireland | Australia
India | New Zealand | South Africa

Penguin Books is part of the Penguin Random House group of companies
whose addresses can be found at global.penguinrandomhouse.com.

www.penguin.co.uk
www.puffin.co.uk
www.ladybird.co.uk

First published by Doubleday 2005
Published by Penguin Books 2017

006

Typeset in Bembo
Printed in Great Britain by Clays Ltd, Elcograf S.p.A.

A CIP catalogue record for this book is available from the British Library

ISBN 978-0-241-32409-7

All correspondence to:
Penguin Books
Penguin Random House Children's
80 Strand, London WC2R ORL

Checkmate was written as a book of Hope. It is a story that charts the fall and rise of Sephy's relationship with her daughter, Callie Rose. This book also charts Jude's attempts to groom Callie Rose into becoming a suicide bomber.

This book was written in 2004 and first published in June 2005. The launch party for the book was scheduled for 7 July 2005. Where was I on 7/7? In the West End of London, having my hair done, when four bombs exploded across the city. With the report of the first explosion, everyone in the hairdressing salon thought there must've been a gas leak or something. But each new customer brought with them more reports of explosions. That's when we knew that these explosions had to be the result of bombs. Central London ground to a halt. Roads were cordoned off. Stations were closed. I walked over a mile back to Charing Cross station to try to get home and didn't see a single moving car, bus or motorcycle. For central London that was unheard of. It was an eerie experience, to say the least.

All I wanted to do was get home, but with train stations closed and no trains running it wasn't going to happen. In a quirk of fate, my husband, who worked in the West End of London at the time, was at home, and I, who usually worked at home, was in the West End. Mobile-phone networks went into meltdown so he couldn't phone me and I couldn't contact him. I decided to start walking home until I could maybe hop on some form of public transport. But I didn't actually feel any real fear until I crossed Hungerford Bridge between Charing Cross station and Waterloo. I remember thinking, *If there's a bomb on this bridge, then none of us walking across it will stand any chance of surviving.* I still remember, to this day, the way I felt as I crossed that bridge, but what choice did I have but to keep moving? What choice do any of us have but to keep moving?

The events of that day seemed to highlight exactly the theme of *Checkmate*. I was criticized by some for writing this book in the first place. Some people didn't feel that a girl being trained to be a suicide bomber was a suitable topic for a novel for young adults. I disagreed then and I disagree now.

So here is *Checkmate*.

I hope you enjoy it.

Malorie Blackman

CHECK MATE

Also available by Malorie Blackman
for young adult readers

The Noughts & Crosses sequence

NOUGHTS & CROSSES

KNIFE EDGE

CHECKMATE

DOUBLE CROSS

CHASING THE STARS

BOYS DON'T CRY

NOBLE CONFLICT

THE STUFF OF NIGHTMARES

Anthologies

LOVE HURTS

An anthology of love against the odds from the very best teen writers,
edited by Malorie Blackman

UNHEARD VOICES

An anthology of stories and poems to commemorate the
bicentennial anniversary of the abolition of the slave trade

For a full list of Malorie's books for readers of all ages visit
malorieblackman.co.uk

Praise for Malorie Blackman's books

'Flawlessly paced' *The Times*

'Unforgettable' *Independent*

'A work of art' Benjamin Zephaniah

'A book which will linger in the mind long after
it has been read' *Observer*

'A gritty read' *The Bookseller*

Praise from the fans

'The first book to break my heart'
Kelsey Christmas @KelseYouLater

'Reading *Noughts & Crosses* was the first time
I could relate to anything I had ever read and
for that I'm so thankful'
Paige @paigeblanks

'The book that broke me and stuck with me for years'
Faye @daydreamin_star

'Made me see the world through a different lens'
Stand Agency @standsays

Malorie Blackman has written over sixty books for children and young adults, including the Noughts & Crosses series, *Thief* and a science-fiction thriller, *Chasing the Stars*. Many of her books have also been adapted for stage and television, including a BAFTA-award-winning BBC production of *Pig-Heart Boy* and a Pilot Theatre stage adaptation by Sabrina Mahfouz of *Noughts & Crosses*. There is also a major BBC production of *Noughts & Crosses*, with Roc Nation (Jay-Z's entertainment company) curating and releasing the soundtrack as executive music producer.

In 2005 Malorie was honoured with the Eleanor Farjeon Award in recognition of her distinguished contribution to the world of children's books. In 2008 she received an OBE for her services to children's literature, and between 2013 and 2015 she was the Children's Laureate. Most recently Malorie wrote for the *Doctor Who* series on BBC One, and the fifth novel in her Noughts & Crosses series, *Crossfire*, will be published by Penguin Random House Children's in summer 2019.

You can find Malorie online:
www.malorieblackman.co.uk
@malorieblackman

This book is dedicated to
Neil and Lizzy
as always.
I love you. As always.

THE HADLEY FAMILY   THE MCGREGOR FAMILY

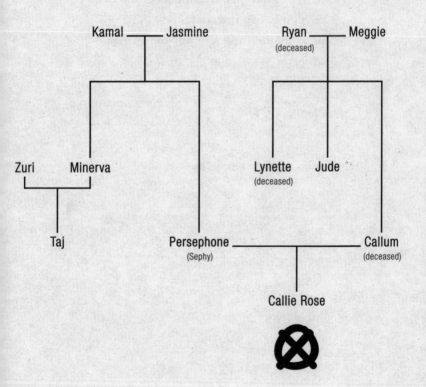

Kamal —— Jasmine   Ryan —— Meggie
                          (deceased)

Zuri — Minerva   Lynette   Jude
                          (deceased)

Taj   Persephone —————————— Callum
             (Sephy)   (deceased)

                    Callie Rose

Hope is the thing with feathers
That perches in the soul,
And sings the tune without the words,
And never stops at all.

EMILY DICKINSON

A man's character is his fate.

HERACLITUS

prologue

The General watched as his Liberation Militia commanders took their places around the imposing mahogany
dining table. He studied each of them in turn. Years of
self-discipline honed from childhood made it easy for him
to keep his expression neutral. Six men and three women
finally settled and looked at him in respectful anticipation.
Most of those around the table were older than the
General who, though in his late thirties, was the youngest
leader the L.M. had ever had.

'The room's clean?' the General turned to ask Morgan
Green, his personal assistant and right-hand man, who
sat, not at the table, but just behind him. Next to Morgan
sat Tanya, Morgan's assistant. They were the General's
retinue and he was hardly ever seen without one or
both of them in tow.

'Yes, sir. I've had the place swept for bugs and other
surveillance devices twice. We're clean.'

The General's searching gaze lasered slowly but steadily
around the room. They were meeting in the country
mansion of a Liberation Militia sympathizer who was also
a prominent Nought businessman. There were one or
two 'prominent' Noughts in most areas of society now.
One or two. A promising Nought ballerina or successful

Nought stockbroker or Nought assistant to the assistant of the Chief of Police was always trotted out and put on show for the nation's media. How clever of the dark-skinned Crosses to 'allow' the occasional pale-skinned Nought to 'make it'. Successful Noughts were a safety valve. A sop for the Crosses to point to and say, 'See! He's made it. And if he can and you can't, then that's your fault, not ours.'

Not only was the meeting top secret, it also required the highest level of discretion. The commanders had arrived at the house over the course of the previous few nights, each under cover of darkness, in blacked-out cars and only after the surrounding area had been scanned and checked to ensure they weren't being observed. It was late winter and the sky was hauntingly dark. The damask curtains with blackout lining had been firmly drawn since mid-afternoon. Two crystal chandeliers above the vast table twinkled and glittered around the candle-shaped electric bulbs, like fairy lights on a tree at Crossmas time. Each of the walls around them was decorated with oak-wood panelling. An ornate and understatedly expensive silk rug had been placed under the table, covering the hardwood floor. Portraits and landscape paintings reflecting the owner's very conservative tastes had been hung at regular intervals over the panelling.

'Brothers and sisters,' the General began in a practised tone. 'The General Election date has been set. In just over twelve weeks, the country will go to the polls. It's time for all of us Noughts in the Liberation Militia to make our voices heard like never before. Make no mistake, we are being watched. We're being watched by our L.M. brothers and sisters who have given up their freedom or, in too many cases, their lives, in the quest for true equality between Noughts and Crosses. Failure is not an option. In front of each of you is a folder containing your objectives. Each of you has a target which is to be eliminated before the forthcoming election. Some of the targets are strategic buildings, some are our enemies in prominent positions. As regional commanders, you will be in charge of the planning and details.' The General paused to give himself time to fix each commander with his piercing brown-eyed stare. 'I *know* you won't let me down. None of us in the L.M. can afford to give up this fight until we have social justice and political equality for all Noughts.'

Murmurs and nods of assent quickly stilled as the General tapped impatient fingers on the mahogany table.

'Fail-safe rules apply. None of you will know about the work of the other commanders. You will each ensure that the assignments you give your lieutenants remain the province of those lieutenants and no one else. I hope that's understood.'

'Yes, General.'

'Of course, General.'

'I'm also personally taking charge of the planning of a major event which will act as a devastating blow to the so-called authorities. It will take place the day before the election. We are all going to play our part in ensuring that this government is toppled.'

'If I may ask, General, what is this major event?'

The General turned to look at the man who'd just spoken – Jonathan Kidd, the regional commander of the South-West. Jonathan, more than any other person at the table, loved to ask questions. Inappropriate questions. Why was that? Why more questions from him than all the others put together?

'Jon, it's not our place to question the General,' Anna Tenski, the regional commander from the Mid-West, reprimanded quietly.

'No, Anna,' said the General evenly. 'This isn't a dictatorship. If Jon or anyone else for that matter has something to say then I encourage them to say it. I hope each of you feels able to express your ideas and voice your concerns to me at any time. I value your input.' The General turned to face Jon directly. 'It's better that you don't know, Jon. You're a valued member of my council and I know you and everyone else here would rather die than betray your brothers and sisters in the L.M., but what I have in mind will make every one of us fugitives for the rest of our lives. The Secret Service will leave no stone unturned in their efforts to hunt us down. Only two people will be involved in the job I have in mind, myself and one other. And it'll be carried out on that basis.'

'Of course, General,' said Jonathan, not once averting his eyes. 'I want you to know that you can count on me and all I have in any venture you propose.'

'Thank you, Jon,' said the General before turning back to face the other commanders. 'You have ten minutes to look through your folders, then I'll see each of you privately in the study to hear your initial thoughts. Analyse and memorize the contents of your folders – you will not be allowed to take them away with you.'

The General stood up. Behind him, his P.A. did the same. As Tanya, the assistant P.A., made moves to follow them, the General looked at her and almost imperceptibly shook his head. The assistant P.A. remained in her seat.

Without a backwards glance, the General headed out of the room. He didn't need to look back to know that Morgan, his P.A., was following him or to know that all eyes in the room were upon him.

'What's wrong, General?' the P.A. asked once they were safely out in the hall, the dining-room doors shut firmly behind them.

'What makes you think something's wrong?' asked the General through narrowed eyes.

Morgan didn't reply. He didn't have to. He had known the General for many years now, had even served in the same L.M. resistance cell as the General's brother. And the last four years had been spent in the General's employ. Morgan knew just about every emotional nuance the man had. He could calculate from the way the General stiffened his shoulders or linked his fingers, or the way his face would suddenly become devoid of all expression, the very depth and breadth of his anger.

After all these years, Morgan reckoned he was perhaps the closest person the General had to a 'friend'. And that was saying something, by virtue of saying nothing at all. In spite of his ability to decipher the man's moods and looks, Morgan didn't really know what made the General tick. All he knew was the General, ate, slept and breathed the Liberation Militia. Maybe that was all the *raison d'être* the General needed.

'I want Jonathan Kidd put under twenty-four-hour surveillance. I want his phone tapped and a tail put on him around the clock,' said the General.

'Why, sir?' asked Morgan, surprised.

'You know me, Morgan. I don't trust anyone. And Jon worries me.'

'Yes, sir. I'll put our best people on it,' said Morgan evenly.

'Good. You do that — and I want regular reports, understand?'

'Yes, sir.'

'You've checked out the study? It's clean too?'

'Yes, sir. I've bug-swept the entire house.'

'Good. Give the commanders another five minutes, then send Anna to me first.' The General made his way into the study. Just as he was about to close the door, he turned to Morgan with a frown. 'You know what?' he began. 'I want *all* their phones tapped. Report anything suspicious to me.' And he quietly shut the door behind him.

Morgan watched the closed door with a frown.

The General was a brilliant man, dedicated and utterly ruthless — but Morgan was growing increasingly anxious about his behaviour. If he carried on like this, it would be the General and not the Cross authorities who would bring about the end of the Liberation Militia. This new offensive the General was planning was by far the most audacious, not to mention the most ruthless, in the Liberation Militia's history. They were going to hit targets up and down the country within the same seventy-two-hour time frame. And even Morgan didn't know the details of the General's personal project. He'd put good money on it being something spectacular though. Merciless and spectacular.

Morgan couldn't help thinking that if the objective was to swing Joe Public's sympathies round to the L.M.'s way of thinking, then this was a bizarre way to go about it. But the General had moved on from trying to win public sympathy quite some time ago. His philosophy was strike, strike hard, and whilst your enemy was still reeling, strike again. Which of the General's life laws applied? Number seventeen: *The only good Cross is a dead Cross*? No, probably number eighteen was more apt. *Ask and don't get – but demand with menaces and receive with equanimity.* The General's life laws – a numbered series of rules that he lived by. He said they kept him alive.

It wasn't Morgan's place to challenge the General – he'd die before he did so.

But it didn't stop his misgivings. Morgan didn't have to wonder what had happened to make the General so single-mindedly focused on the L.M. He was one of the very few who knew. The General was without a doubt the most successful of all L.M. rulers in terms of making sure that the L.M. was never far from public consciousness. He was a brilliant tactician, that much had been proven time and time again. And he had the drive and determination to lead the L.M.

But to lead it *where*?

Sometimes such single-mindedness could be as much of a curse as a blessing. Blinkers kept you focused, but they also stopped you seeing the broader picture. Morgan sighed. He had to hold onto the belief that the General knew what he was doing. Had he been in charge then he might've chosen a less rocky route, but they all wanted to get to the same destination, didn't they?

When the General lay in bed night after night with just his thoughts for company, did doubts slink around him, whispering silkily in his ear – or was he too disciplined to let them anywhere near? Who did the General call on when he was troubled or needed somewhere to rest his head and lighten his load? The General was admired, respected, definitely feared – but he wasn't liked. Not a bit of it. Everyone called the man 'sir' or 'the General' and, in spite of their shared years together, Morgan certainly wouldn't dream of calling him anything else – at least not in front of others. The General had a number of passports and papers, each with false names and varying identities. But Morgan was one of a very select few who knew the man's real name. How long had it been since the General had been called with affection by his birth name by anyone but his mother?

How long had it been since anyone had called him Jude?

Three months later . . .

Three months interest

one. Callie Rose

These are the things I know for sure:

My name is Callie Rose. No surname.

I am sixteen years old today. Happy birthday to me.

My mum is Persephone Hadley, daughter of Kamal Hadley.

Kamal Hadley is the leader of the Opposition – and a complete bastard.

My mum is a Cross – one of the so-called ruling elite.

My dad was Callum Ryan McGregor.

My dad was a Nought.

My dad was a murderer.

My dad was a rapist.

My dad was a terrorist.

My dad burns in hell.

Every time my mum looks at me, she wishes with all her heart that my dad had lived – and I hadn't.

These facts are the only things that are mine and real. Everything else in my life zigzags around the truth. So I don't mind so much that I'm leaving it all behind. There's nothing here worth holding onto.

Nana Meggie once told me that when you die, you go to heaven and it feels just like home.

But I don't know what home feels like.

I'm not talking about the dictionary definition either, I mean the definition that comes from the heart. Not some abstract notion of what home is meant to be, but what it's meant to *feel* like. That kind of home I've never had. So no thoughts of heaven for me. I guess I'm on my way to the other place. Like father, like daughter – at least, in that respect.

Now I think about it, I've been on that journey for quite a while. And in a few hours, I'll reach my destination. But in the meantime, I have a few minutes to sit and be still and force all trace of any regrets away . . .

I did so love it here at Nana Jasmine's private beach. If the rest of the world was like this place, I'd have no need for the contents of the carrier bag on the sand beside me. A single deep breath filled my lungs with pure sea air. If only I could live for ever within that one breath. The coastline and the sea stretched on beyond imagination. But, magical as they were, it was the beach that held me. And it wasn't one of those characterless picture postcard beaches either. It was scattered with driftwood and kelp, coarse sand and rocks big enough to clamber up and over. The sea skittered away from the beach, ever-changing, always moving, never still. I could see why this place used to be one of Mum's favourite haunts.

It really was beautiful.

The sea was darker towards the horizon and the sky was at the tail end of what must've been a riotously coloured sunrise. I wanted this moment to last and last. The very air around me was charged with sadness and a strange excitement.

'Callie, you've forgotten all about me, haven't you?'

I turned to my companion. 'Of course not. I—'

'You haven't said more than two words to me all morning,' he interrupted. 'Why invite me here if you're just going to ignore me?'

I regarded him, incredibly sad that he didn't understand – but then how could he? Why did I ask him to meet me on this beach? To share the sea and the sky and the way I was feeling. To be with someone who wanted to be with me. To have a witness to my last morning. But he didn't understand.

'I'm just not in a chatty mood, that's all,' I tried to explain.

'So what kind of mood are you in?' he asked.

I shrugged, but he misunderstood what that meant. His face got closer to mine, his lips brushing against mine. Not for the first time. But for the last. I couldn't cope with it. It was too graphic a reminder of all the things I'd never have. I pulled away.

'Don't. I'm not in a kissing mood either,' I told him.

A moment's silence, then he said, 'Fair enough.'

We both turned back to look out over the sea. But the moment was ruined. I stared out again towards the horizon. But now the sea was just dark water and the sky was nothing but the careless swipes of a few colours. So what? None of it mattered. What was the point of any of it?

'Callie, what's wrong?'

I stood up, dusting the sand off my trousers. He stood up too, never once taking his eyes off me.

'Nothing's wrong. I have to go now,' I replied, bending to pick up my carrier bag.

But he grabbed my hand before I could reach it.

'Talk to me. What's wrong?' he asked again.

'Please don't do this,' I said, surprised at how close to tears I felt. I swallowed hard. It did no good. Maybe venom would dislodge what *tendresse* couldn't. 'Why don't you just go? I didn't even want you here but you insisted on being with me, like some kind of pathetic puppy.'

Harsh words to drive him away. If he walked off now without a backwards glance, then so could I. But he stood his ground, not even angry with me. I wanted him to be angry with me. I needed that.

But to my surprise, he kissed me again. And he'd never kissed me like that before – hard enough to make my heart jump around like an Olympic gymnast, but soft enough to make me want to close my eyes and breathe him in and hold onto him for dear life. At first I was too stunned to pull away, but that didn't last long. I pushed at his chest, catching him off guard so he had to step, almost stumble, back to keep his balance. And that's when I seized my chance, terrified I might not get another. I grabbed my carrier bag, turned tail and ran. Ran just as hard and as fast and as far away from him as I could. I took the stone steps of the cliff two and three at a time.

'Callie, wait . . .' he shouted after me. 'I'll see you tomorrow, Callie. Wait . . .'

I forced myself not to listen. I breathed heavier than necessary to drown out the words behind me.

Keep running, Callie. Never stop running.

See you tomorrow? All my tomorrows had become today – and today was all I had left.

Less than ten minutes later, I entered Nana Jasmine's house. Nana Jasmine rattled around alone in a huge mausoleum of a house. Her only regular companions were her Nought personal assistant, Sarah Pike, and Mrs Soames, the Nought housekeeper and cook. Nana had given Mum and me our own keys so we could come and go whenever we wanted. Mum never turned up unannounced but I often popped in, mostly after school. Nana Jasmine's house and Nana Meggie's house – where Mum and I lived – were equidistant from my school, Heathcroft High. In opposite directions, but equidistant. Nana Jasmine refused to sell her 'cottage', as she called it. It was part of her divorce settlement and she was determined to hang onto it, even though it was much too big and impossible to keep comfortably warm in winter. But Nana Jasmine said she was the house and the house was her and that's why she couldn't part with it – whatever that meant! If I were her, I would've sold it in a hurry and used to the money to make friends and have fun.

Nana Jasmine's lonely.

After her divorce from Grandad Kamal, she never even dated again – which was a shame 'cause even though she's ill, she's still really pretty and doesn't look anything like her real age. I asked her once why she hadn't remarried.

'A marriage like mine leaves scars,' Nana Jasmine replied. 'My scars are still . . . painful.'

Over the years I guess the scars had never healed. I know now that some scars never do.

'Nana?' I called out.

Usually Mrs Soames or Sarah appeared before I'd made it halfway across the hall. But not today.

'Callie, love? I'm in the kitchen,' Nana Jasmine replied, projecting rather than raising her voice. Nana Jasmine didn't believe in shouting unless there was a fire. I made my way into the kitchen – still the largest I'd ever seen.

'Hello, Nana,' I smiled as I headed towards her. I caught the way her gaze fell on the carrier bag in my hand. I clutched it tighter – noticeably tighter. Smiling, Nana Jasmine came towards me, the obligatory glass of orange juice in one hand. She kissed my forehead the way she always did and pressed the juice into my free hand. I waited for her to head back to the fridge before putting down my carrier bag.

'Thanks for coming to see me,' said Nana. 'Oh, and happy birthday! I'll give you your present before you leave.'

'You don't need to give me anything,' I told her.

It wasn't as if it was going to get much use.

'I know I don't, but I want to,' Nana said firmly.

I shrugged, unwilling to argue. 'You're looking much better today, Nana.'

It wasn't just a plastic line. Nana Jasmine's eyes were sparking and sparkling. It was a vast improvement on the last time I'd seen her.

'Thank you. I am feeling better.' Nana smiled, ever polite.

'I really can't stay long,' I told her, sipping at my OJ. 'I have an appointment and I can't be late.'

'A few minutes with me won't make you late,' said Nana Jasmine.

I watched as she poured herself a glass of sparkling

mineral water. Nana Jasmine never drank anything stronger than fruit juice and most of the time it was just bottled water. She was so practically perfect in every way, I reckon she was born with a halo and angels singing the Hallelujah Chorus around her head.

'OK, what's so urgent?' I asked.

'Drink your orange juice and then I'll tell you,' said Nana. 'You need your vitamin C.'

Anything for a quiet life. I knocked back the OJ. Nana Jasmine took the glass away from me and rinsed it out before putting it in the dishwasher. Well, at least she'd let me finish it!

'So what's this appointment you have that you can't miss?' asked Nana.

I didn't reply. I didn't want to lie.

'Is it something to do with Jude McGregor?' Nana Jasmine stunned me by asking.

The answer must have inadvertently shown itself on my face because Nana said grimly, 'I see.'

'Is that why you asked me over here? To give me a lecture about Uncle Jude?' I asked belligerently. 'Because if it is . . .'

One word, just one syllable of disapproval said against my uncle and I'd be out of the house so fast Nana Jasmine would wonder if she'd imagined my visit. I glared at Nana, almost daring her to say something, but she surprised me again by smiling. Just smiling.

'Callie, I wanted to see you on your birthday. What's wrong with that?' said Nana. 'Have a seat, Callie, love. I want to ask you something.'

Suspicious, I sat down at the breakfast bar before

17

carefully placing my bag at my feet. Its contents were too precious to be let out of my sight – even for a second. Nana sat down next to me.

'I have a couple of questions,' she said.

'Go on then,' I said sourly, which only made Nana Jasmine smile more.

'Don't sulk, darling. It's a most unattractive habit,' Nana said, her eyes twinkling. But then she glanced down at my carrier bag between our two chairs and the amusement in her eyes faded. 'Callie, d'you promise to answer all my questions truthfully?'

I considered. 'I'll tell you the truth or I won't say anything at all – how's that?'

'Fair enough. Are you a member of the Liberation Militia?'

Wow! Nana Jasmine wasn't mucking around. Straight for the jugular. I didn't answer. But then I thought, Why not? What possible difference could it make now? My life was my own – no one else's.

'Yes, I am,' I said, lifting my chin.

'I thought so.' Nana Jasmine nodded thoughtfully. 'How long have you been a member?'

'The last two years.'

'I see. When did your uncle first get in touch with you?'

'Four or five years ago. I can't remember exactly.'

Nana's look of shocked surprise was quickly masked. 'Did you . . . did you have anything to do with those terrible things that happened last weekend?'

No way was I going to answer that one.

'I see.'

Did she see? What did she see? Too much or too little?

'This appointment you're in a rush to get to – has it got anything to do with the L.M.?'

No answer.

'Very well. Don't worry, Callie, I won't pry any more.' Nana Jasmine stood up. 'Before you go, could you help me with something?'

'What?'

'I need a few bottles of wine up from the cellar. That'll give me a chance to decant my red wine properly and make sure the white is thoroughly chilled,' said Nana Jasmine.

'Is that all what you called me over for then?' I said.

'Yes, dear. And that was dreadful grammar, by the way,' said Nana evenly. 'You're . . . you're very close to your uncle, aren't you?'

Although Nana Jasmine's tone was even and non-confrontational, she still managed to sound like she was accusing me of something. I really had no idea how she did it. Her expression was carefully neutral, there was very little inflection in her voice and yet she managed to convey her disapproval of Uncle Jude in a way that left very little room for doubt. Well, I wasn't here to talk about Uncle Jude.

'I'll help bring up the bottles from the cellar but then I really must go,' I said.

'You're not going to help me prepare the rest of my lunch?'

'I haven't got time, Nana.'

'Fair enough. After you've brought up my wine, I'll

phone for a taxi to take you to wherever it is you want to go.'

I nodded. And then it hit me. This would be the last time I saw Nana. The last time I spoke to her. The last time . . .

NO! Don't think like that. Don't even think. I was going to do something worthwhile. My whole life had been leading up to this day and I wasn't going to shrink away like a coward now. Like Uncle Jude said, I was going to make a difference.

A sudden, strange, sad fatigue swirled round me like a gossamer shroud. I stood up abruptly.

Shake it off, Callie Rose. Get it together.

'Are you all right, love?' Nana Jasmine frowned.

I nodded. 'Just got one or two things on my mind, that's all.'

'Well, help me bring up the bottles from the cellar and then I'll leave you in peace,' smiled Nana. 'Give me a hug first.'

I was about to argue — why did I need to hug her before bringing up a few wine bottles? But then I remembered . . . How could I have forgotten? Nana Jasmine stood up and put her arms around me. For once, my arms didn't dangle at my sides like overcooked spaghetti. I hugged her back, breathing her in.

Saying goodbye.

Leaving my bag on the floor, I let Nana lead the way across the kitchen and down the stairs to the cellar. My bag would be safe enough with both of us in the cellar together. The cellar door was already unbolted. Nana Jasmine pulled on the handle with both hands, her lips a thin line with the effort it cost her to move the heavy door. I placed my hands beside Nana Jasmine's and opened the door with her. It didn't creak or groan. The door, like the rest of Nana Jasmine's household, was too well oiled to make any kind of vulgar protest. To squeak would've been 'bad grammar'. And Nana Jasmine wasn't into that. The door itself was solid oak, nearly three metres tall. Snaking, almost sneaking across the door from the wrought-iron hinges, was black iron scrollwork. Nana Jasmine stood to one side so that I could walk past her.

'So where are these bottles?' I asked.

'The Château D'Azonama 'ninety-five is at the other end of the cellar,' said Nana. 'Four . . . no, five bottles should be enough. Let's go and get them.'

I headed down the narrow aisle between rack upon rack of vintage wine on either side of me. The racks were lined up like elemental soldiers, with the wine bottles lying prone. But as I approached the far end of the cellar, I got the shock of my life. Someone came out from behind one of the tall racks of wine. I recognized her even before she turned to face me. I stopped abruptly. What the hell was she doing here? I'd sworn never to even stay in the same room as her again and I'd meant it. I spun round, ready to make for the door – only to stop abruptly for the second time.

Nana Jasmine was pushing the cellar door shut.

'Nana . . . ?'

'I'm sorry, love, but I can't let you do any more of Jude's dirty work,' said Nana Jasmine as the door continued to close. 'I love you, Callie Rose McGregor. Don't ever forget that.'

And in the next instant the cellar door was closed. I sprinted for the door, practically diving for the handle just as the bolts were being slid home from the outside. The sound of the bolts was more final, more resounding than the peal of funeral bells.

I was too late. Panic rose up, searing and unstoppable like erupting lava.

'NANA JASMINE, OPEN THIS DOOR!' I pushed down the large metal handle, then pushed at the door, but I was wasting my time.

'LET ME OUT!' I screamed.

Beyond the door, I could hear nothing but silence. Not even footsteps walking away from me. The door was too thick, too solid. I spun round to glare at the woman I hated most in all the world.

My mum.

This whole thing was a set-up. A ridiculous scheme to stop me from following Uncle Jude's orders.

Uncle Jude's orders . . .

A groan ripped through my body as something worse occurred to me. Here I was, locked in Nana Jasmine's cellar with a woman I despised – and my carrier bag and its contents were out there, on the other side of the door.

Out there with Nana Jasmine.

Jude versus Jasmine

two. Jasmine

I walked along the top-floor hotel corridor, trying hard to ignore the nauseating feel of my heart ricocheting against my ribs. My daughter Sephy and granddaughter Callie Rose were stuck in my cellar – an hour, several kilometres and all my hopes and dreams away. I stopped to look up and down the two-star corridor of this three-star hotel. The carpet was a mid-grey with dusty-pink swirls spaced along it at regular intervals. The walls were the same pink, adorned with indifferent paintings by long forgotten artists. I stopped in front of the best painting within eye view, and that wasn't saying much. It was a swirl of complementary colours from one slice of a DIY-store colour pie chart. Raspberry pinks collided with majestic burgundies which slammed into deep plum purples. I gave it the few seconds of attention it merited and started walking again. Each door along the corridor was light brown and distressed to make the veneer appear to be real wood. And the whole place smelled of cheap furniture polish. I could see the not-so-thin layer of dust on the skirting boards below and on the light fittings above. No doubt the hotel cleaning staff walked around with an aerosol can of cheap pine furniture polish, spraying it into the air at regular intervals to give the illusion that something more back-breaking and time-consuming had taken place. Allowing myself a small smile, I shook my head. I was doing it again – noticing those things which anyone with half a life would not.

Anyone with any kind of life . . .

I bowed my head. Time to stop my delaying tactics. I was busy doing nothing by noticing everything, to put off what was coming. I was afraid – I'd be lying if I said otherwise. I take that back. I was more than afraid. Nauseous with gnawing fear was closer to it actually. Not that I was going to back out now. That couldn't happen. Too much was at stake – Sephy and, more importantly, Callie Rose. How were they doing, locked in my cellar together? Well, they were going to be there for a while. A touch melodramatic perhaps, but needs must.

I carried on towards room thirty-one. That is what she'd said, wasn't it? Room thirty-one?

Come on, Jasmine. Don't start doubting yourself before you even reach the first hurdle . . .

The room was right at the end of the corridor, next to the fire escape. This was it. This was really it. I was about to enter a room I knew I'd never leave. A coil of anticipation twisted deep within me. I was filled with a strange and not altogether unpleasant cocktail of emotions. What should I be feeling? I wasn't sure. One last neurotic look down the corridor, a deep breath, and my hand stilled on its way to knocking on the door. The face of Callie's dad, Callum McGregor, crept unexpectedly into my mind. I remembered a time, a lifetime ago, when my daughter Sephy had been beaten up at school. Callum came round to our house to see Sephy and I gave orders that he wasn't to be let in. I remember he stood outside our gate, day after day, until Sephy went back to school, just looking up at the house. And I stood behind my curtains, watching him, wishing he'd go away. How I wish now that I'd let him in.

Oh, how I wish . . .

But it's futile to think of such things.

A recent friend of mine I met in hospital buys paperbacks and tears out each page as he finishes reading it, so that when he next opens the book it'll always be on the right page. Seems to me, my life is a lot like that. And no matter how much I might want to revisit a past page, a previous chapter, to reread it, to rewrite it, I can't. It's dead and gone. And now my book has so few pages ahead and a yawning gap behind. So many things I would do differently. So many things I would say. So many things I wouldn't say. And so many of them revolve around my daughter, Sephy. And Callum.

Callum McGregor.

Callum, who as a boy always had a ready smile – and the saddest grey eyes. Eyes old before their time. Eyes that had seen too much, too young. Each day that passed saw his relationship with my daughter grow stronger, closer, deeper, as my own connection with her waned. But then in those days the only relationship I cared about was the one between me and the nearest bottle of Chardonnay.

Strange to wonder what would've happened if Meggie, Callum's mum, hadn't come to work for me as Minerva's and then Sephy's nanny. Meggie and I were such good friends. I thought back to our true friendship, which had nothing to do with me being Meggie's Cross employer and her being a nought. But I was the one who'd snapped our friendship in two. I was the one who had fired her without a backwards glance or a second thought. I was the one who thought that her son and my daughter would separate and think no more about it, despite the fact that they had grown up together and were almost like twins in their thoughts and actions. My selfish shallowness back then makes me wince, even now.

Odd that I should think of Callum at this moment. But perhaps not so odd, considering what I was about to do. Another deep breath and I knocked on the oaken door, three sharp taps, before I could think any more.

'Just a minute,' a man's gruff voice called out.

From inside, footsteps approached. I opened my coat, my finger on the switch in the pocket of the awful wind-cheater I wore. The olive-green windcheater clashed horribly with my silver-grey trouser suit and long black coat, but no one of consequence was going to see my eclectic ensemble. The door opened. A nought man with a rough-hewn expression framing hostile brown eyes stood in the doorway. I didn't need to ask his name for confirmation. He looked so much like a leaner, meaner version of his brother, it was scary.

'Hello. May I come in?'

'Who're you?' he asked, instantly wary.

'Nemesis,' I said, trying to step past him.

He moved in front of me to bar my way. 'Jude, let me in,' I said patiently.

'Who the hell are you?' he asked again. My use of his name had obviously rattled him because his hand began to move inside his jacket.

But I revealed the inside of my windcheater first and his hand froze in front of his stomach. I knew he'd see it my way.

I smiled. 'Back up please.'

Jude stepped back. I stepped in, still facing him as I back-kicked the door shut behind me. I took in the room at a peripheral glance. It was L-shaped, a bathroom to my right with a wardrobe opposite the bathroom door and a small window adorned with lacklustre green, paisley-patterned curtains on the opposite wall. A tall cabinet with a TV visible inside was situated against the wall just up from the wardrobe. I assumed the bed was opposite the TV cabinet, but I couldn't tell from my position at the door.

'Take three steps backwards please. NO! Don't turn round. Don't insult my intelligence. Just walk backwards. Please.'

Jude did as I asked. I saw now that I was right. The bed was opposite the TV and in front of a second window there was a small circular wooden table with two chairs on either side of it. It was a typical hotel room, no doubt the clone of every other room on this floor.

'Take off your jacket please,' I asked, adding, 'Slowly. Very slowly.'

Jude did as he was told. He had two holsters criss-crossing his body, each holding a gun beneath his arms.

'Use just your thumb and middle finger to take out each gun in turn by the stock only and throw them on the bed,' I said. 'Please.'

Jude just stood there.

'Don't make me repeat myself,' I said patiently.

I stroked the switch under my thumb hoping he'd get

the point. He did. Doing as I'd requested, he removed first one gun, then the other, tossing them into the middle of the bed. Never taking my eyes off Jude, I shrugged my left arm out of my coat by hitching my shoulder up and down. The thumb of my right hand didn't move from the switch in the windcheater pocket. With my left arm free, I moved my left hand over to the switch as I shrugged my right arm out of my coat. It was awkward but do-able. I let the coat slide down my right arm until I could grab the collar with my hand. I then threw my coat on the bed over the guns. I don't like guns.

'Who the hell are you?' he asked again. 'What is this about?'

Even with the guns safely covered up on the bed, I didn't allow myself to relax. I knew better. I studied the specimen before me. The years hadn't been kind to him. Deep, permanent lines furrowed his brow and cut a groove on either side of his mouth. His lips were turned down and if they once knew how to smile, that know-ledge had been forgotten or discarded a long, long time ago. And his brown eyes – they were cold and soulless, like a doll's eyes. No, like a shark's eyes. He was tall and broad shouldered, with manicured nails gilding rough hands. His designer suit was worn self-consciously over a builder's physique.

'Sit down please.' I indicated one of the two narrow armchairs by the window.

Jude sat down slowly, his eyes never leaving mine. He reminded me of a cornered tiger waiting for its moment to pounce. My finger touched ever so lightly on the switch in the windcheater pocket. The nasty stuff it was attached to was placed in little home-made pockets all over the inside of the garment. Apart from a slight puffy bulkiness, no one could guess at what I was wearing. But I'd revealed all to Jude and he hadn't taken his eyes off me and my 'designer' jacket since. With my finger still touching the switch, I didn't feel quite so twitchy. I didn't doubt that Jude was fast – but we both knew that I'd be faster.

I sat down on the bed so that I was directly facing my adversary.

'Are you going to answer my question now?' asked Jude, trying and failing to keep the malevolence out of his voice. What a thoroughly nasty piece of work. 'Who are you?'

'My name is Jasmine Dharma Ninah Adeyebe-Hadley, but you may call me Mrs Hadley.'

Jude's eyes narrowed immediately. He might not have recognized my face – and there was no reason why he should after all these years – but he certainly knew my name.

'What d'you want?' he asked.

I smiled broadly, enjoying my dramatic moment. 'You.'

Daddy, are you watching me? Can you see me? I wish you were here to help me. Daddy, what did I do?

Mummy's going to get real stressy over this one. I still don't understand why Mrs Hoyle sent me out of the class to stand in the corridor.

What did I do?

And I've only been in her class for two days. She didn't have to send me out. D'you think Mrs Hoyle will tell Mum? I was so looking forward to moving up to the junior school, but not if it means I get sent out of the class for no reason. I want to cry but I'm not going to. Mummy says that crying is a waste of good water. I wish I could go back into the classroom. It's so boring standing out here. And there's not even anything to look at on the walls because it's the start of term. No drawings. No paintings. No pictures. No words. No nothing.

It's not fair.

What did I do, Daddy?

four. Sephy

Mrs Hoyle pounced on me the moment I set foot in the playground. One look at her pinched-in, sour-trout expression bearing down on me and my heart plummeted. She strode across the playground to where I stood chatting to Joshua and Rupal, parents who had children in the same class as my Rose.

'Miss Hadley, I'm sorry to have to tell you this, but I had to send Callie Rose out of my classroom today.'

'Oh yes?' I said with studied calm. 'And why did you have to do that?'

My face began to burn, partly from embarrassment but mostly from angry disbelief. Why did Mrs Hoyle feel it necessary to tell me this in front of every other parent in the playground? I could guess. Mrs Hoyle didn't approve of me and my 'mixed race' child.

God, how I hated that phrase! When I had first met the teacher at the end of the previous term, Mrs Hoyle had given me a startled look and a really limp handshake. Maybe she had expected Callie Rose's mother to be a Nought, not a Cross. There were mostly Crosses in Callie Rose's class, and some Noughts, but my Callie Rose was unique. At that end-of-term meeting, some of the parents who had children starting at the junior school had also given me more than one look. I had to keep telling myself that everyone who did a double take was not my enemy. But memories had made me wary of glances, askance or otherwise.

Mrs Hoyle's bloodless lips narrowed still further. 'Your daughter swore at me.'

Now I wasn't going to have that. No way would Rose swear at her or anyone else for that matter.

'Rose doesn't know any swear words, so how could she have sworn at you?'

'Forgive me, Miss Hadley,' Mrs Hoyle said, her tone super-supercilious. 'But all parents think their children can do no wrong. I assure you, your daughter did indeed swear at me.'

I counted to ten, then ten again before I could trust myself to speak. If she used that imperious tone when calling me 'Miss Hadley' one more time . . .

'I'll have a word with Rose and find out exactly what happened,' I replied at last.

'I'm not lying, Miss Hadley.'

'I never said otherwise, Mrs Hoyle,' I said. 'But I'm sure all this is just a misunderstanding.'

'Hhmm! Well, I trust it won't happen again,' said Mrs Hoyle.

Get out of my face, you old hag, I thought. And a lot more besides. But I smiled, careful to keep almost all of what I was feeling out of my eyes. And I turned away first, just in time to see Rose come out into the playground. She started running towards me, only to stop abruptly when she saw her teacher standing with me. And, even from where I was standing, I saw the light go out of her. She walked towards me, her eyes down, her shoulders drooped. One tear dripped to the ground, rapidly followed by another and another as she made her slow way towards me.

And Mrs Hoyle had done that. Not content with spoiling Rose's first week in the junior school, she'd deliberately sought to humiliate me in front of all the other parents. I wasn't going to forget that in a hurry.

'If you'll excuse me, Mrs Hoyle, my daughter needs me.'

I didn't wait for her to reply. I made my way over to my daughter.

'Rose, stop crying. Don't let your teacher or anyone else ever see you cry. D'you hear me?' I said softly.

'Yes, Mummy,' Rose sniffed.

I squatted down in front of her. 'Callie Rose – stop crying. Now.'

Rose sniffed and gulped and the flow of tears was stemmed.

'Now we're going to walk out of this place with our heads held high. D'you understand?'

'Yes, Mummy.'

'Come on then. Let's go home.' I took my daughter's hand in my own, careful not to hold on too tightly.

We made our unhurried way out of the school, without catching the eye of a single person. I didn't say a word until the school was way behind us. Then I stopped and looked down at my daughter.

'OK, Rose. Let's hear why Mrs Hoyle sent you out of the classroom today.'

Tears reappeared and threatened to wet Rose's cheeks.

'Uh-uh!' I shook my head. 'No waterworks. What happened?'

'I don't know why she sent me out,' said Rose. 'I really don't, Mummy.'

'So tell me what happened before you got sent out,' I said.

'Well . . .' Rose worried her bottom lip as she thought back. 'Mrs Hoyle was telling us the story of Chicken Licken – the one where an acorn falls on her head and she runs around in a panic, telling all the other animals that the sky was falling. D'you know that one?'

'Yes, love. So what happened then?'

'Mrs Hoyle read out, ". . . Chicken Licken ran up to the Goosey Loosey and said, 'The sky is falling! The sky is falling!'" Then Mrs Hoyle looked around a–and she asked, "What d'you think Goosey Loosey said? Hands up." So I put my hand up.'

'And what did you say?' I asked.

'What Tobey told me. Goosey Loosey said, "Bloody hell! A talking chicken!" And that's when Mrs Hoyle sent me outside.'

I sucked in my cheeks and bit the inside of my bottom lip. 'I see,' I said when I could trust myself to speak. 'Rose, "bloody hell" is swearing. And that's not the original ending to the Chicken Licken story.'

'It isn't?'

'No, love. Not even close.'

'But that's what Tobey told me.'

I sighed deeply at the mention of Tobey. Not only did he live next door to us, he also lived for the fun of winding up my daughter – and he almost always succeeded. I should've guessed that Tobey's version of 'Chicken Licken' wouldn't be the same one everyone else in the country knew and shared. Rose looked up at me, trepidation painting her expression.

'Mummy, are you going to shout at me?'

'Would you like me to?' I asked.

Rose shook her head vehemently.

'If I were you, Rose, I wouldn't be quite so quick to believe every word Tobey tells you,' I said.

When Rose heard that, her eyes went all squinty and her cheeks filled with air. It was just as well Tobey wasn't standing in front of her.

'Rose, you're puffing up like a balloon. Take a breath, dear.'

She hissed out then inhaled sharply. 'So how does the real story end then?'

'Chicken Licken and all her equally idiotic friends get eaten by Foxy Loxy for being so stupid,' I told her, all trace of humour fading.

'Oh!' Rose blinked in surprise. 'I don't think much of that ending. The fox wasn't very nice.'

'That's the way the world works, Rose,' I warned her. 'If you're naïve – which means immature, inexperienced or a bit thick – you get eaten alive.'

'Oh!'

We carried on walking.

'"Chicken Licken" is not one of my favourite stories any more,' Rose told me unexpectedly.

No, Rose. I didn't mean to upset you. And I didn't want to spoil one of your favourite stories. It's just that . . . I was just trying to . . .

I opened my mouth to show Rosie the thoughts not waving but drowning in my head. But then as usual, as always, I closed my mouth and said nothing. And the words of comfort and reassurance that I was desperate to say floundered and got washed away.

'Come on, Rose,' I sighed. 'We have to get a few things from the shops before we go home.'

'Yes, Mummy,' said Rose, subdued.

The local supermarket was about ten minutes out of our way, but I didn't want to go home and then have to come out again. We walked up and down the aisles, Rose lost in her own thoughts. I rehearsed in my head the different things I could say to make her feel better, but everything sounded wrong.

We were just turning the corner of one aisle when I almost bumped into two Cross men who were chatting away, not looking where they were going.

'Sorry,' I said, inanely. After all they'd almost walked into me, not the other way round. Both men looked me up and down, then looked at Rose. The taller one narrowed his eyes.

'Slag!' he hissed at me. 'Blanker-lover.'

And they carried on walking. Astounded, I turned to stare after them. To say that to me . . . they didn't know me from a hole in the ground, but one look at my daughter and I'd been assessed and judged. I glanced down at Rose but she was oblivious, still lost in her own world – thank goodness.

And if she hadn't been with me . . . Both men were taller and stronger and younger than me, but I would've taken them on. I wanted to rip their tongues out.

If Callie Rose hadn't been with me.

five. Rose is 7¼

I don't particularly like swinging backwards and forwards. Everyone does that. I like to twist round and round and round. That's much more fun. I like to sit with my head tilted back so I can look up at the sky and play cloud busting. I like cloud busting. Just look at that cloud! It looks just like a giant long-eared dog, racing after something I can't see. Or maybe it's running away from something I can't see. I wonder which one is right? I do like to sit on the swing and twist. I do it most afternoons after school if it's not raining. But today, twisting isn't cheering me up the way it usually does. The breeze teasing round my face has stolen all the smell from Mum's garden flowers – and I love the smell of flowers – but even that isn't making me feel any better.

The kitchen door opened. I dug my heels into the ground to stop myself swinging.

'You're horrible, you are!' I shouted at Tobey the moment he set foot in our garden. He was wearing the T-shirt Mum and me bought for his eighth birthday – the one with a photo of Tobey's pet snake, Cuddles, on it. Mum took a photo of Cuddles to a special shop where they did stuff (I don't know what!) and put the photo on a Tobey-sized T-shirt. But the whole thing was my idea.

Now I was really sorry I'd bothered. And why had Mum let him in after what he'd done?

'Sorry, Rosie. Your mum just told me off for what happened at school today,' Tobey said as he walked towards me. His mouth wasn't laughing, but his eyes were.

'It's not funny. I got into tons of trouble – and it's all your fault.'

Tobey tried to hide the smile on his face, without much luck. He smoothed his floppy, brown hair down over his forehead the way he always did. But it wasn't long enough to hide the fact that his eyes were still twinkling. 'Sorry, Rose.'

I sprang off the swing. 'You get out of my garden.'

I lowered my chin and gave Tobey my best worst look. I was so angry my face felt like it was getting smaller and more squashed up. I was so angry that my eyebrows were knitting together.

'I said sorry,' said Tobey. 'I didn't mean to get you into trouble. It was just a joke.'

'Some joke! And you should've told me. I told my teacher what you said Goosey Loosey said, and she sent me out the room for swearing.'

Tobey burst out laughing. My eyes squinched up and my cheeks puffed out and my lips were pressed together so hard, they were beginning to tingle.

'Oops!' said Tobey. 'I'm not very popular in your house today, am I?'

I wanted to say all sorts of things to him but the words just kept tripping over each other and falling down inside my mouth. Then my eyes began to prickle and itch which was even worse.

'Tobey Durbridge, I'm never going to believe another word you tell me as long as I live.' The words were meant to come out all fierce and angry but instead my eyes began to leak – which made me even more mad at Tobey. He was still my next-door neighbour but he wasn't one of my best friends any more.

'Rose, I didn't mean to make you cry,' said Tobey. And just like that the silly, smiley look on his face was gone. He looked all serious but I didn't care. Too little, too late, as my mum says.

'I don't believe you,' I snapped like a crocodile.

'Rosie, I really am sorry,' said Tobey. 'Tell you what – you can ask me to do anything you like to get your own back, and I'll do it.'

'You will?'

'Yep! Anything!'

Hhmm! I didn't feel like crying so much any more. Now the afternoon was warmer and the sky was bluer and I was in charge!

'Will you do absolutely anything?'

'Anything.'

'Eat a slug?'

'Anything.'

'Would you kiss my feet?'

'Yuk! Anything.'

'Right then. You're on!'

I looked around. Mum had planted pink and red rose bushes up one side of our tiny garden. And she regularly put horsey smelly doings under each bush. She said it was ferty-liza to help the plants grow. Time to make Tobey suffer! I was actually beginning to enjoy myself now.

'Grab a handful of dirt from under that rose bush.' I pointed.

Tobey looked relieved. 'Is that all?'

'Nope. Then I want you to eat it.'

'Eat what?'

'The dirt you pick up.'

He didn't like that – not one little bit. 'Are you serious?'

''Course. Eat dirt and then I'll know you're really sorry.'

Tobey walked over to the closest rose bush. It was covered with dark red roses but half the petals from half the flowers were decorating the ground like the rose bush had had a nose bleed or something. Tobey scooped up a handful of poopy dirt and walked back to me. My stomach flip-flopped. Yukkity-yuk! Wouldn't catch me sticking my hands in that stuff!

'Don't even think about chucking that at me,' I said in my fiercest voice.

'I wasn't going to,' said Tobey, still looking all serious.

We watched each other, then Tobey slowly moved his hand up to his mouth. He bent his head. His hair flopped forward till it was almost sweeping the muck in his hands. Was he really going to do it? No . . . Yes! His lips were just millimetres from the dirt. He opened his mouth. I sprang forward and knocked his arm down. I only meant for the dirt to drop out of his hand. But I hit his arm down and then it came straight up again like it was on a spring and the dirt went SKADOOSH – all over Tobey's face. Tobey stared at me through his mask of horsey poo and dirt and we both burst out laughing.

'You'd better wash your face before your mum sees you,' I warned him.

Tobey tried to brush himself off but all he did was rub the poopy doings into his T-shirt. It was in his hair, on his face, over his clothes – everywhere. We walked back to the kitchen, but I kept my distance. He was a bit smelly now. Actually, he was a lot smelly now.

'D'you want me to tell you the real story of Chicken Licken?' asked Tobey.

'Mum already told me. They all get eaten by a fox for being so stupid.'

'I'll tell you another story then. Only . . . it's not really a story. It's a secret – about me. And you must promise never to tell anyone else.'

'I promise.' My eyes were almost as wide as my open mouth. But then I remembered 'Chicken Licken'. I looked at him suspiciously.

'It's as true as I'm standing here,' Tobey protested. He sat down on the grass in front of me. 'Sit then. I'm not going to stare up your nose as I tell you.'

I sat down. I liked Tobey's stories. 'I'm still mad at you though.'

'Fair enough,' said Tobey. 'If I were you, I'd be mad at me too. That's why I'm going to tell you something that no one else in the whole world knows.'

'Tobey,' I couldn't help asking before he began. 'Were you really going to eat that dirt?'

Tobey smiled. 'Ah! You'll never know now, will you?'

six. Sephy

It was another one of those nights. A still, lonely night where, however much I might beckon, sleep was a stranger. So here I was again, sitting in the purple grape-skin dark, staring out at the night sky with nothing to do but count my thoughts. It was a cloudless night and very mild for the end of September. I sat by my window, perfectly still, watching the stars multiply, watching the leaves of the small, newly-planted horse chestnut tree a few metres down the road sway to their own music. All my past regrets started skirting round each other in my head, the way they always did when I couldn't sleep. Memories that grabbed hold and made me flinch and wouldn't let me go. How I wished for someone to turn to, to talk to. Someone to hold me through all my doubts and fears.

'Mummy . . .'

My head whipped round. I hadn't even heard Rose enter my room.

'Yes, treasure?'

'I had a nightmare.'

Rose stood just inside my doorway, her hand still on the door handle. My eyes were accustomed to the dark so I could make out more than her outline. Her pyjama trousers were twisted around her waist, her hair wisped up in odd angles at the front and her eyes were round and bright like full moons, but anxious. An anxiety that was only partly caused by her bad dream.

'Come here,' I beckoned, keeping my voice low and soft.

The last thing I wanted was to wake Meggie. We'd been through this so many times before. Whenever there was something wrong with my baby, Meggie insisted on sorting it out . . . to save me the bother. Sometimes we argued about it, most of the time we didn't. What would I do without Meggie? Rose walked over to me. I kept my hands at my sides.

'Want to sit on my lap?' I asked.

Rose nodded.

'Up you get then.'

Rose clambered onto my lap and put her arms around my neck. My hands fluttered like cautious birds, one to land on Rose's back, the other on her thigh. I silently inhaled. I never grew tired of the smell of Rose – especially that early-morning or late-night smell that was so clean and childlike.

'So what was your nightmare about?' I whispered.

'You promise you won't get mad?'

'Why would I get mad, Rose?' I frowned. 'It's not your fault you had a nightmare.'

'I know but . . . I dreamed that . . .'

'Go on.'

'I dreamed that Tobey turned into a wolf and came through my window to gobble me up.'

'It was just a silly dream, Rosie. Mind you, dreaming of Tobey is enough to give anyone nightmares,' I teased.

'But Mum, it wasn't just a bad dream . . .'

'What d'you mean?'

'If I tell you a secret about Tobey, d'you promise not to tell anyone else?' Rose said seriously.

My insides went warily still. 'I promise.'

'Well . . . when it's a full moon, Tobey changes into a werewolf,' said Rose.

I fought down the impulse to burst out laughing. I didn't know what I'd been expecting, but that certainly wasn't it. 'Er, I don't think so, darling. There're no such things as werewolves.'

'There are too. Tobey told me this afternoon. He said when it's a full moon, he changes into a werewolf and then he doesn't know what he's doing. He said his mum locks him in the cupboard under the stairs every time there's a full moon and keeps him there the whole night and won't let him out till morning and she stuffs cushions into the gap under the door so that when he howls no one can hear him and—'

'Whoa! Slow down before your lungs implode!'

'What does implode mean?'

'To collapse inwards instead of being blown outwards which is what *ex*plode means,' I explained impatiently. 'So Tobey told you all this, did he?'

Rose nodded. 'And he said he sometimes manages to get out of the cupboard and out of the house and so if it's a full moon, I should keep my windows closed and my door locked and he said—'

'I don't want to hear what else he said. What I do want is to wring his scrawny little neck for him,' I told her.

'Why? It's not his fault he's a werewolf,' Rose said, reproach in her voice.

'Callie Rose, the boy was winding you up – again. Werewolves don't exist. And even if Tobey was a werewolf, which he isn't, he wouldn't get past me. I'd dropkick him down the garden path.'

Rosie giggled, which is just what I'd wanted her to do – but I was only half joking about dropkicking Tobey bloody Durbridge out the house. Tobey was almost eight months older than Rose but about ten years older in worldliness. He'd regaled Rose with his nonsense stories ever since he was old enough to open his mouth and Rose swallowed his foolishness almost every time.

'Rose, I will never, *ever* let anything bad happen to you. D'you understand?' I told her, my hold on her back as light as a sigh.

'Yes, Mum.' And for the first time since she'd come into my room, Rose smiled, then yawned.

'You really must stop believing everything Tobey or any other boy tells you.'

'Yes, Mum,' Rose yawned again.

'They all tell lies, darling.'

'Yes, Mum.'

'Promise me you'll stop believing everything Tobey or any other male tells you.'

Rose's voice was so sleepily faint, I had to bend my head and strain to hear it.

'I promise, Mummy. I promise.'

'OK then. I'll put you back in your bed.'

'Can I stay here with you?' Rose asked quickly, her eyes now open.

I sighed. 'OK then. But we both need to get some sleep – OK?'

'OK.'

I smiled. 'And Rose, werewolves really don't exist. I'm not lying to you.'

'I know, Mummy,' Rose half yawned. 'You never lie to me.'

The stillness inside was back with a vengeance.

Lies by omission. Right lies for the wrong reasons. Wrong lies for the best of intentions. Lies that refused to lay down and die. Lies too old for young ears, but when did those scales balance out?

'Callie Rose, I . . .'

Rose was already asleep. What was I going to say? Did it matter anyway? Rose Hadley . . . Even my baby's name was a lie. Not what I'd promised myself, or the world – or Callum. Layer upon layer of lies. But I had to pick my moment. And this wasn't it. The full moon now bathed Rose's face in its silvery wash. She was so beautiful, her eyes closed, her long lashes sweeping down her cheeks. I stood up, carefully lifting Rose as I did so, her arms around my neck. I struggled to pull back the duvet with one hand, my forearm still supporting Rose as best I could, before placing her in the bed. I kissed her cheek and stroked her hair. I toyed with the idea of getting into bed and going to sleep myself. I could do it – I was now tired enough to be sleepy. But I headed back to the chair by the window and sat down.

Paying my penance.

seven. Meggie

'Anything else, Mrs McGregor?'

I took another quick glance around the shop, willing any items I might've missed to spring off the shelves and hover in mid-air to jog my memory.

'I don't think so, Mr Aswad,' I replied after my quick scan. 'Anyway, I don't think I could manage anything else.'

I struggled to hold up the various carrier bags in both hands to show him.

'Last-minute Crossmas shopping?'

'Last, first and every minute in between at the moment,' I sighed. 'I'm shattered.'

'I know what you mean.' Mr Aswad nodded. 'I did all my Crossmas shopping last weekend. Two hours on the bus it took me to get home. Two hours!'

I frowned. 'What happened to your car?'

Mr Aswad shook his head sadly. 'I sold it, Mrs McGregor.'

Now that surprised me. Every time I came into his shop, Mr Aswad blathered on and on about his precious WMW. I didn't even know what WMW stood for, although the nickname for the car amongst us noughts was 'white man's wheels'. Any nought with money always bought a WMW. I had to admit the car did look good – if you were into that sort of thing, which I wasn't – and definitely deserved its luxury status, along with the healthy price tag to match.

'How come you sold it?' I couldn't help asking. Mr Aswad would rather sell his shop than his car and that was no lie.

'I had to, Mrs McGregor. Not a week went past without the police stopping me and asking me to prove the car was mine. In the end it just wasn't worth it. I'm waiting for delivery of my new car but they told me I won't get it till after Crossmas.'

'What car are you getting?'

Mr Aswad told me the make of a nothing-special, ten-a-penny car which, from his expression, obviously wasn't his cup of tea at all.

Mr Aswad leaned over the counter towards me and lowered his voice even though we were the only two people in his shop. 'I was telling one of my regular Cross customers why I decided to sell my WMW and d'you know what she said to me?'

I shook my head.

'She told me the police don't do that sort of thing.' Mr Aswad straightened with righteous indignation. 'I'm telling her what happened to me practically every other day and she still refused to believe it. "The police don't do that sort of thing"! I ask you!'

The door opened, followed by the electronic chime which alerted Mr Aswad that he had a customer if he was out the back.

I turned my head. A young Cross man wearing jeans, a

fleecy jacket, rimless glasses and a single earring came into the shop and marched straight up to the counter.

'A packet of cigarettes.'

'Which brand?' Mr Aswad asked.

'Don't care,' the man said.

Mr Aswad turned and picked up the closest to hand. He told the man the price. We both watched as the man dug the money out of his jacket pocket and counted out the exact amount. The man dropped the money onto Mr Aswad's hand rather than placing it there. That was another of Mr Aswad's bugbears – Crosses who couldn't bear to touch his hand when they handed over their money, so instead they dropped it anywhere from a couple of centimetres up, to the length of half a ruler. I really didn't have time to hang around and hear the shop-keeper complain about that as well, so I decided to use the Cross's presence to make my escape.

'Nice talking to you, Mr Aswad,' I said, heading for the door.

'You too, Mrs McGregor. Mind how you go.'

His cigarettes in his hand, the Cross man scooted past me to get out of the shop first. I was obviously not going fast enough to suit him. As I stepped out of the shop, I shivered, pulling my long, woollen coat even more tightly around me, the carrier bags in my hand bumping into my body as I did so. The winter wind bit at me, making my bones ache. In spite of my coat, gloves and hat, I was freezing. It was already getting dark and the wind was try-ing to freeze my lips together. Being cold always put me in a bad mood. Did the weather match my mood? Or did my mood match the weather? Well, at least I had Jude's

Crossmas presents now. That was something after all this walking about. Another year, another plain shirt, another patterned jumper. Not that I ever saw him wearing any of my presents.

I really don't know what happened next. One moment I started to walk off, minding my own business and the next moment my legs went out from under me and I went down on my backside, then flat on my back. Mr Aswad was straight out of his shop and at my side in an instant. The next thing I knew, I was surrounded by people, all trying to help me back up onto my feet and asking the same ludicrous question. 'Are you all right? Are you all right?'

Of course I wasn't all right. I'd just embarrassed myself on the high street. Plus my backside was sore. A middle-aged Cross picked up my shopping bag and chased after my potatoes which were rolling about on the icy pavement. He packed them in my bag before handing it back to me.

'Thank you,' I mumbled, too embarrassed to look him in the eye. 'It's very kind of you.'

'Mrs McGregor, are you sure you're OK?' asked Mr Aswad. 'You took quite a tumble there.'

'I'm fine, Mr Aswad,' I told him, adding under my breath, 'My arse broke the fall.'

'Really, Mrs McGregor!' smiled Mr Aswad as he shook his head. 'And you a God-fearing woman at that!'

I stared at him. 'Bat ears!'

The crowd around me began to disappear when they saw I was now upright and mobile. Thank goodness.

'Would you like to sit down for a while?' Mr Aswad offered. 'I could make you a cup of tea.'

'No thanks. I just want to get home and have a nice hot bath,' I said.

I headed off before he could argue. Halfway up the street, I turned round to see Mr Aswad sprinkling liberal amounts of salt on the icy pavement outside his shop.

Much too little, far too late, I thought with annoyance.

I carried on home, rubbing at my upper thigh. No doubt an impressive bruise was forming already.

eight. Sephy

'Mum! Mum!' Rose ran into the room at full pelt with Tobey close behind.

'What's the matter?' I asked, looking up from my newspaper.

'The sky is having sex!' said Rose with great excitement.

'I beg your pardon?'

'The sky. Look at the sky,' Rose urged.

Frowning, I got up and opened the living-room curtains. The sky was already dark even though it was still early evening, but by the light of the orange street lamp outside, I could see myriad snowflakes swirling and twirling in the semi-darkness. The snowflakes looked more amber than white under the street lamp's glow.

'See!' Rose said, almost indignant that I'd doubted her word.

I looked from Rose to Tobey and back again. Why did I smell one of Tobey's stories behind this?

'I still don't understand,' I said carefully. 'What've the snowflakes got to do with sex?'

'You mean you don't know?' Rose said astounded. Then she grinned at me, pleased to know something I didn't. 'Well, what happens is, the sky and the ground have a big snog and have sex and the snowflakes are all the sperms hitting the ground. And all the blades of grass are the babies.'

'And where did you get that from?' As if I didn't know.

Rose looked puzzled. 'Tobey told me.'

I stood up. 'Tobey, I'd like a word with you.'

One look at the thunderous look on my face and Tobey bolted.

'I've got to go home now. Bye.'

'Tobey, come back here.' I went after him but he was out our front door and at his house before I'd cleared the hall.

You'd better run, boy, I thought sourly. You'd better run.

'Mum?' said Rose, her head tilted to one side. 'What are sperms?'

nine. Meggie

So much for my non-existent baking skills. Why was it that I could cook anything savoury, but introduce just one sugar crystal and my food became a disaster area? About the only thing I could make containing sugar which didn't go wrong was a cup of coffee. I glared down at my chocolate cake, which had sunk in the middle and was burned around the edges. It looked like a bowl. I'd followed the recipe exactly, I know I had. I couldn't take this effort into church. I could just imagine the pitying looks when my friends saw it. Maybe if I smothered it with chocolate icing and filled the middle with sweets or something . . .

Out in the hall, my mobile phone rang. I headed out of the kitchen, glad to get away from the cake, which mocked me from every angle. Digging my mobile out of my handbag, I checked for the caller ID, but there wasn't one.

'Meggie McGregor.'

'Hi. It's me.'

Just three words had my heart skipping. I took the phone back into the kitchen and closed the door, before replying.

'Hello, son. How are you?'

'Same as ever, Mum. And how're you?'

'OK, I suppose. I had a nasty fall a few weeks ago.'

'Are you OK?'

'Yeah, I'm fine now.'

'Why didn't you tell me?'

'What could you have done?' I asked. 'I was several shades of purple up and down my leg for a while, but I'm fine now.'

Jude didn't answer.

'Where are you now?' I asked.

'The Isis Hotel.'

I sighed. Jude was at his regular haunt when he was down this way, but it was still only a cheap hotel. He should have had his own home by now. When was he going to stop living out of a suitcase?

'I'm phoning because I'm going abroad tomorrow for a while,' Jude continued.

'Why?'

'Fundraising.'

'Where?'

'Anywhere where there are L.M. sympathizers. I'm following the money.'

'You told me you weren't in the L.M. any more. You told me you didn't—'

'I'm not part of the active body, Mum. I'm not a soldier. I just fundraise and work on the administrative side,' said Jude impatiently.

Relieved, I started to breathe again. 'I'd like to see you before you go,' I told him.

'I'm a bit busy . . . but OK,' said Jude.

'Where should we meet? At a pub or—'

'At the hotel. It's safer. I'll order room service,' said Jude.

He gave me his room number, then rang off. Jude didn't believe in long drawn-out conversations, whether on the phone or in person. I pulled off my apron, my thoughts now totally wrapped around my only remaining son. His prison sentence was long over but the bitterness inside still held him prisoner. If I could only get him away from his L.M. colleagues. I was convinced they were the ones filling him with hatred and poisoning his soul. I'd never give up hope of showing my son that the Liberation Militia was not the way forward. At least he wasn't an active member, so that was something, but I wanted him out of that organization completely. There had to be a way to reach him, I just had to find it. I'd never stop believing that.

And I'd never stop trying.

ten. Sephy

'I'm off out,' said Meggie, popping her head round the door. 'Don't bother leaving dinner for me.'

'Where're you going?'

'I'm having dinner with a friend,' said Meggie tersely.

I know I shouldn't've been surprised but I was. I could

count on the mittened fingers of our garden gnome the number of times Meggie went out for a meal. She was definitely not a 'lady who did lunch'. Or dinner come to that. Meggie looked around with a frown.

'Where's Callie Rose?'

'At Tobey's house.'

'So late?'

'It's not late, Meggie. I'm going to give her another fifteen minutes then go and get her.'

'Will you . . . will you be all right without me?' asked Meggie, her eyes anywhere and everywhere but on me.

Why don't you just ask me the question you really want to ask?

How long were Meggie and I going to dance around this?

'I'll be fine. Why wouldn't I be?' I challenged.

'If you need me, just phone.'

'Meggie, I'm quite capable of putting my own daughter to bed,' I said patiently.

'I didn't say you weren't. Oh, by the way, don't let her watch the TV this evening though,' said Meggie, her voice grim.

'Why?'

'There's a programme on at eight o'clock about the history of the Liberation Militia. They might mention . . .'

'I see.' Now I sounded just as grim as Meggie. Every time the Liberation Militia were mentioned on the TV, my blood ran ice-cold. I was probably overreacting; after all, Callum's name had only been mentioned in a documentary once – at least, that I knew about. That was part of the reason I'd finally decided against giving Callie

Rose her dad's surname. And that was something over which Meggie held no sway and had no say. But that didn't stop the panic rising whenever the L.M. were mentioned. I didn't want my baby to hear any of that. I didn't want my baby to know . . . Not yet. Plenty of time to tell her the truth when she was old enough to deal with it, to understand it. But it wasn't just the ashes of past sins that I was afraid of being stirred up. Each time the L.M. came on the TV, I waited with bated breath to hear Jude's name.

'Have you heard from Jude recently?' I asked.

The colour drained from Meggie's face, then a slow curtain of red began to rise, covering her neck, her cheeks. She looked away from me.

'No. Why?'

I frowned at Meggie. Why was she so embarrassed? No, it was more than embarrassed. She was lying.

'If you had seen him, would you tell me?'

'Why would I hide it?' Meggie looked me in the eye to say, 'And why ask me about him now? You haven't mentioned his name in ages.'

'He's in the L.M., isn't he?'

'Not any more,' said Meggie.

'Who told you that?'

'Jude did.'

'When?

'The last time I spoke to him.'

'And you believed him?'

'Jude wouldn't lie to me,' said Meggie, drawing herself up.

Was she serious?

'Jude does nothing but lie,' I told her. 'He killed that Cross hairdresser, Cara Imega, and he boasted about it.'

'I don't beli— That's not true. Jude says he didn't do it and I believe him,' said Meggie.

In the battle of 'he said, she said', Jude was the clear winner. I trailed in a poor, weary second.

'Besides, if he did say that, he probably only said it to . . . to . . .'

Couldn't Meggie hear herself? Didn't she hear the ridiculous excuses she was making for her demon incarnate son?

'Yes?' I prompted. 'Why would he say such a thing if it wasn't true? To wind me up? Or maybe just to rub my nose in the fact that I helped a stone-cold killer escape justice? Which reason sounds more plausible to you?'

'Jude didn't kill that girl,' Meggie insisted.

This was an entire waste of my time and my breath. 'If you say so, Meggie. Enjoy your dinner.'

I turned my attention back to the TV. Meggie stood still for a few moments, then headed out of the room and out the house. Only when I heard the front door slam did I allow myself to relax completely.

I found it very hard to relax in Meggie's house, sitting in Meggie's chair with Meggie's things all around me. And impossible to relax around Meggie. She saw everything her way and no one else's. And she didn't trust me. Not even close. But how could anyone in full possession of their faculties really believe that Jude wasn't a member of the L.M. or that he didn't have anything to do with Cara Imega's murder.

Cara Imega . . .

That name would haunt me till the day I died. For a long while, I thought that all the terrible things that happened to me after Cara's death were my punishment. The fates tearing me to pieces for my culpability. But that was before I realized that I didn't need the fates or divine retribution or any other external source to punish me. I was doing a first-rate job all on my own.

Jude was a murderer.

But by helping to hide his guilt, what did that make me?

By not coming forward when I had the chance, what was I? I already knew the bitter answer.

I stood up. Time to get my daughter. Time to lose myself in her smile and forget the past. Just for a while.

 eleven. Rose is 8½

Hello, Daddy,

How are you today? How is heaven? Sunny, I bet. It's sunny down here on Earth as well. A toasted teacake kind of day. Mummy is in the kitchen washing up and her face is shining. The sunlight glowing on and around her face makes her look like she has golden edges. She looks like an angel. Yeah! Exactly like the angel we put on top of the Crossmas tree each year. I love Mummy. And she loves me – and you, Daddy.

Isn't that wonderful?

Can you smell the soup Mummy made for our lunch? I love that smell. It smells like warm and full and safe. I bet you're jealous you didn't get any. Ha! You should've made your ghost appear when we were eating round the table. I would've given you a spoonful of soup with all the best bits in it – if you hadn't scared me too much first.

Talk to you later, Daddy.

Byeee.

 # twelve. Sephy

The dazzling sunlight was getting on my last nerve. I tugged down the blind in front of the open windows, but at first it wouldn't budge. I pulled harder until it gave. Luckily for me it didn't come off the wall, bringing down half a ton of plaster with it. I'd certainly pulled it hard enough. I stuck my hands back into the washing-up liquid, scrubbing away at the big saucepan I'd used to make our home-made vegetable and pasta soup for lunch. Scrubbing pots was like pounding pillows or beating cake mix. Goodness only knew I was getting enough practice at these things. Meggie had succeeded in winding me up. Again.

'Mummy, can I help you do the washing-up?'

I turned and smiled at Rose. 'It's all right, sweet pea, I've only got this pan left to do.'

Rose frowned at the dishwasher. 'Why don't you just stick it in there like everything else?'

'This pan's got a copper bottom and a wooden handle, and wood and copper don't react very well with the chemicals you use in the dishwasher to get the dishes clean.'

Rose's mouth turned down like an umbrella. I'd done it again. Maybe I was more like Mother than I liked to think. Rose is lucky if she can string three sentences together around my mother without having her grammar corrected somewhere along the line. 'What's cooper?' she asked.

'Copper. It's this shiny, gold-coloured metal at the bottom of the pan.'

I lifted it up to show her. Soap suds slid down its surface like giant snowflakes. Rose's eyes lit up at the sight of them. She walked over to the sink and blew a hole through the biggest mound of bubbles. The bubbles scattered in all directions.

'Rose!'

My daughter just laughed, turning her sparkling eyes up towards me. I smiled back at her, loving the sound and sight of her laughter, clinging just as hard as I could to the way it made me feel inside. Rose unexpectedly hugged me round my waist. I carried on smiling but shrugged her off, my hands still in the sink.

'Mummy, what did my dad die of?' Rose asked, leaning against the work surface next to me.

I turned away from her before she could see the look on my face. It wasn't as if it was the first time Rose had asked me that. But each time sharp fragments of dread shot through me. I started scrubbing away at the pan again, trying to frame my answer. Each time Rose asked me, I tried to say a little more, to skate a little closer to the truth. So what to say . . .

'Mum, what did Daddy die of?' Rose asked again. 'Was he sick?'

'Rose, I haven't really got time to answer all these questions now,' I snapped.

'Why not? You're only washing up.'

I opened my mouth to argue, but then closed it again without saying a word. Deep breath. Calm down.

'I'm sorry, Rose. I promised myself that I wouldn't do that.'

'Do what?'

I tried to smile. 'It doesn't matter. So what was it you wanted to know?'

'What did my dad die of?'

'Your dad was killed,' I said slowly.

Rose's eyes instantly started to leak. What the hell was I doing? She'd asked that question before many times, and each time I'd said, 'Your dad died, love. Just one of those sad things.' Then I always moved the conversation swiftly on to what Rose's dad was doing in heaven. That usually took Rose's mind off the how and why. It was . . . an evasion, for my daughter's sake.

But not today.

Quickly rinsing off my hands, I wiped them in the hand towel hanging up beside the sink. I squatted down until Rose's face was level with mine and brushed away the tears spilling down her cheeks.

'Rose, don't cry,' I said softly. 'Your daddy's death was . . . an accident, that's all. A tragic accident.'

'Was he in a car accident like Sam's dad?' Rose asked.

'Something like that.' I stroked Rose's hair, then kissed her forehead. 'But all you need to remember is that your daddy loved you very much.'

'But he didn't get to meet me. How can you love someone you don't know?'

I smiled again. Rose smiled back. I love it when she smiles at me like that. But memories made the smile inside wither away.

'Your daddy loved you when you were still growing inside me. Your daddy even loved the idea of you.'

'I don't understand.'

'Your dad was very happy when he found out I was pregnant with you. He wrote me a letter to tell me so,' I said carefully. No more lies. Just the careful truth. 'If I remember rightly, he said he was ecstatic.'

'What does that mean – *eggs static*?'

'Ecstatic. It means over the moon, thrilled, deliriously happy, overjoyed, elated, in raptures—'

'Yeah, I get the idea,' Rose said quickly before I could go through the whole thesaurus.

'Besides, you don't have to be with someone day in, day out to love them, Rose,' I told her.

I could see Rose had to think about that.

'I guess that's true,' said Rose at last. ''Cause I love Grandad Kamal and I've never met him.'

And just for a moment, my heartbeat stilled. Just for a moment.

'Can I see the letter that Daddy wrote to you about me?' asked Rose.

'I threw it away years ago,' I said.

Just a tiny lie . . . No harm in a tiny lie.

'That's a shame. I wish I'd met my dad. Not when I was a baby but when I was older – just once so I could remember him.' Rose sighed.

'So do I,' I said. 'You two would've been very good friends.'

'Am I like him then?'

Oh, Rose. Are you like Callum? How do I even begin to answer that?

I could feel my expression twist painfully to reflect what was happening to my insides.

Don't let Rosie see, Persephone. Don't let her know.

'You have the same smile, the same shaped eyes, the same way of tilting your head to listen, the same stubborn streak, the same common sense. Lots of things about you and him are the same.' I forced another smile, feeling that my face was going to crack at any second.

'Tell me some more about him.'

'Why?'

''Cause I've been thinking about Daddy a lot recently.'

'Funny . . . so have I,' I admitted. 'Well, your father stood up for what he believed was right. And he was a man who loved his family. He was very loyal to the ones he loved. Very loyal.'

'What does loyal mean?'

'Faithful, devoted, will stick by you, dedicated—'

'Yeah, I get the idea, Mummy. Did you love my dad?'

Some kind of bird was singing outside. I wondered what its song meant – if it meant anything at all.

'I don't mind you being soppy,' Rose teased when I didn't immediately answer.

'Yes,' I said. 'Very much.'

'Did Daddy love you?'

Oh God . . .

'He used to, before he died,' I managed to reply.

'Well of course it was before he died,' said Rose, unimpressed. 'He can't love you *after* he's dead, can he? Silly!'

'I don't know.' I kissed Rose on the nose. 'Maybe love lives on, even after death. Maybe it's the only thing that does.'

'So I'm really like him?' Rose asked again, just to make sure.

'Oh yes.' I nodded.

'That makes me feel a bit better. If I'm lots like Dad then it's almost as if I know him – or at least part of him. That's better than not being anything like him at all. Can I go out on my bike?'

The abrupt change of subject threw me for a moment. It never ceased to amaze me how Rose could just skip from one subject to the next in the blink of an eye.

'Only up and down this road and only on the pavement and watch out for pedestrians – that means people walking.'

'Yes, Mum. I know.' Rose spun round to get her safety helmet from the cupboard under the stairs. And there stood Meggie in the doorway, listening to every word I'd said about her son.

thirteen. Rose is 8½

Nana Meggie was staring at Mummy and she had a very peculiar look on her face. And Mummy was looking straight back at Nana Meggie with a different kind of peculiar look. It was kind of the way I look when Jinn in my class takes my pencil without asking and then won't give it back.

'What's wrong, Nana Meggie?' I asked.

'Nothing, pet.' Nana Meggie's frowny, stern look sagged into a smile.

'I'm off to ride my bike,' I told her.

'Be careful,' said Nana.

'Yes, I know,' I interrupted. 'Mum's already told me.'

I ran out of the room before Nana Meggie could say all the same things about watching out for cars and people that Mum had already said. Grown-ups like to say the same things over and over. Maybe they all go to a secret grown-up school and get taught to say the same things and act the same way. I ran to get my helmet and then skipped back into the kitchen. Mum was still scrubbing the saucepan, which had to be the cleanest one in the street by now. Nana Meggie had the fridge door open and was searching for something to munch, I guess. I skipped out into the garden. My bike was leaning against the wall underneath the kitchen window. I bent down to check the tyres the way Mum had taught me. I squeezed each tyre like I meant business. They were firm and not squishy like brown bananas. I loved to ride up and down our road. Sometimes I rode so fast, it felt like the wind was jealous and trying to blow me off my bike – but it never did. When Mum took the stabilizers off my bike, she used to run behind me, holding onto the saddle to stop my bike from toppling over. And then sometimes she'd let go and she wouldn't tell me. But I only ever fell off once – and I didn't cry, even though I wanted to 'cause my elbow was really hurting. Mum dusted me off and kissed my forehead and told me I was a brave girl for not crying. So I swallowed down my tears and didn't let a single one escape. Not even one.

'When are you going to tell Callie the truth?' Nana Meggie's voice drifted through the open kitchen window.

'I did,' said Mum.

'My son's death wasn't an accident,' said Nana Meggie.

'No? He was born a Nought in a Cross world. You can't get much more accidental than that.'

'Isn't that just . . . what's the word – sophistry?' There was a pause before Meggie added, 'Don't look so surprised. I might not have had as much schooling as you, but I do read and I'm not stupid.'

'Meggie, I never said you were stupid. And what should I have told Rose?' asked Mum. 'She's too young to hear all the sorry details.'

'You won't let me do it, so when d'you plan to tell her the truth?'

'When she's ready. In the meantime what harm does it do to let her believe her dad lived like a saint and died like a martyr?'

'I think—'

'I already know exactly what you think,' Mum interrupted. 'But you don't want to fight me on this, Meggie. Not this.'

I didn't know what those words meant. What was a 'marter'? And what was 'sofis' . . . 'soap-is' . . . whatever the word was that Nana Meggie said? Why was Nana Meggie so cross with Mum? Maybe she thought Mum shouldn't talk to me about my dad. And Mum's voice was hard like the frost we get on the car windscreen in the winter.

'I'll tell Callie Rose all about her dad when she's old enough to know the *whole* truth,' said Mum.

'You'd better tell her before someone else does,' said Meggie.

'Is that a threat?'

'No, of course not. But don't you think it would be better coming from you?'

'I said, when she's old enough – or are you going to criticize me over that as well?'

'Meaning?' asked Nana Meggie.

'You know what it means,' said Mum. 'You think I don't see the way you watch me when I'm with Rose? You think I don't know what you're thinking?'

I didn't understand what Mum and Nana Meggie were talking about. Why was Nana Meggie watching Mum when she was with me? And what did Mum need to tell me about my dad? What was the 'whole truth'? Had she fibbed when she said that my daddy's death was an accident? But Mum wouldn't lie to me. She just wouldn't.

I was just about to go back indoors to ask Mum about the whole truth when a cream-coloured butterfly, the colour of Mum's music sheets, fluttered in front of me. Holding my breath, I slowly held out my hand. The butterfly settled on my palm, its wings soft and gentle as a blink against my skin. It was so beautiful, so peaceful. Just watching it made me feel smiley inside. Then, with a shake of its wings, it lifted up and fluttered away. I watched it disappear against the sky – it seemed to just melt into the air. And although Mum and Nana Meggie were still talking, I didn't hear any more. I wheeled my bike down the side path and out onto the pavement. Today I'd be . . . a star fighter, flying my spaceship around the universe and fighting evil. Lots of evil.

When Nana Meggie comes back from church each Sunday, I always ask her what happened there. And Nana Meggie always says, 'We discussed evil. Lots of evil.'

I'd like to go to church to see what they all talk about but Mum won't let me. Mum says church is a waste of time. Mum says God is a waste of time. Mum says that in front of Nana Meggie sometimes and then Nana Meggie gets upset. Sometimes I wonder if Mum says it just to wind Nana Meggie up. Sometimes Mum looks at Nana Meggie like she doesn't like her very much. And sometimes Nana Meggie looks at Mum like she's almost afraid of her.

Grown-ups are very strange.

fourteen. Sephy

'I wish he'd hurry up or I won't get to see him,' Rose complained.

The early afternoon sun was making Rose squint but she refused to budge from the living-room window. I glanced down at my watch. Sonny was late arriving and Meggie was late leaving. And the social forecast for today? Frost, as always.

'He's here!' Rose sprinted out of the room. I'd barely made it out of the living room before Rose had the front door wide open.

'Sonny!'

'Hello, pumpkin!'

Rose leaped straight up into his arms, scarcely giving him time to brace himself first.

'Ooof!' Sonny grinned at my daughter as her flying tackle knocked the wind out of him.

'Rose, don't do that,' I admonished. 'You're too big for that sort of thing.'

'Nonsense! My girl will never be too big. Will you, pumpkin?' said Sonny.

He tried to ruffle Rose's hair whilst her head dipped and ducked away from his hand. Sonny treated Rose like . . . like she was his own. Which was the way Rose had always treated Sonny – like one of the family.

But he wasn't.

My heart tipped as I watched them, totally lost in each other's company, oblivious to everything else around them. Including me.

'Come on, Rose. Down you get.'

Rose took her cue from my tone of voice and jumped down from Sonny's grasp.

'Ready to work, Sonny?' I asked.

'Willing and able,' said Sonny. Which was what he always said.

Meggie appeared from the living room, already wearing her coat and carrying Rose's.

'Hello, Mrs McGregor. How are you?'

'Fine, Sonny,' said Meggie without once looking at him.

'You're looking lovely today,' Sonny smiled.

'Maybe you need to get out more,' Meggie said sourly before turning to me. 'We're off to my sister's. We'll be back after dinner.'

'OK,' I said, careful to keep my tone neutral.

Meggie and I did our usual dance; her eyes on me, my eyes on her, an absence of trust, the absolute presence of suspicion. Meggie looked away first.

'Bye,' said Meggie, the front door already open.

'Bye, Mum.' Rose hugged me round my waist, her head against my shoulder. I could still remember when I was able to hold her to me with one hand, when she was about the same length and not an awful lot heavier than a cereal box. And look at her now. I put my hands on her arms. Not to pull her close, but not to push her away either. I kissed the top of her head, breathing in the red rose scent of her baby shampoo.

'Sonny, you won't go before we get back, will you?'

Sonny shook his head. 'You still owe me a game of chess.'

'What's the point? You always win,' said Rose.

'But not for much longer. You're getting so good, one day soon you'll win and I'll lose,' Sonny promised.

Rose beamed at the thought. 'You really think?'

Sonny nodded.

'Come along, Callie Rose,' said Meggie tersely.

'See you later.' Rose waved to Sonny and me as she skipped out.

Sonny and I didn't speak until I'd closed the front door behind Meggie and my daughter.

'D'you wanna try to finish our *Just Ask Me* song?' I asked.

Sonny nodded.

I led the way upstairs to the back bedroom. But some sixth sense kicked in halfway up the stairs and I spun round – to catch Sonny with his gaze firmly fixed on my backside.

'You won't find any musical inspiration there,' I said dryly.

'Oh, I don't know!' Sonny disagreed, his eyes dancing with mischief. 'That sway is poetry in motion!'

'Sonny, behave!' I said, adding pointedly, 'How's Kasha? That is the latest one, isn't it?'

'We've split up.'

'Already?' I asked, aghast then amused.

Kasha had lasted – how long? Two months, if that.

'She wasn't the right one.'

'You say that when you dump all your girlfriends.' I shook my head. 'You wouldn't know the right one from a hole in the ground.'

'Oh yes, I would,' Sonny said immediately.

'Then why don't you just go out with the right one and have done with it?' I asked, exasperated.

Sonny regarded me for the longest moment.

'Look, I'm sorry. It's none of my business,' I said quickly. 'The last thing I want is to antagonize one of my best friends.'

'Is that what I am?'

'Of course.'

'Is that all I am?' asked Sonny.

I frowned. 'What else is there?'

Sonny smiled to himself – a smile with no real amusement in it. 'I could be more – if you'd let me . . .' he said softly.

'I have no intention of joining the masses, thank you very much,' I told him, wryly.

'You wouldn't be one of masses.'

'Oh yeah? What would I be?'

'The one and only.'

'Yeah, right!' I scoffed. Now I knew he wasn't serious.

We carried on up the stairs. I didn't know whether to smile or sigh. Sonny was in one of his silly moods. We'd be lucky if we got one new verse written.

'Why doesn't Meggie like me?' asked Sonny unexpectedly.

I stopped abruptly on the landing, my head whipping round to face him. 'I don't think that's particularly true.'

Meggie just didn't like anyone. It was hard to get to know her, really know her. But then the same could be said about me.

'I've been working with you for over five years and I don't think Meggie's said more than five sentences to me at any one time. You and I have written songs together, songs that sell, I might add; we both make a decent living and yet she still treats me like I'm sponging off you.'

'That's just her way,' I replied, wondering why I was making excuses for her. After all, Meggie and I hadn't had much to say to each other for the longest time.

'You know what I think? She's scared of me,' Sonny said slowly.

'What on earth are you talking about?'

'She's afraid of losing you and her granddaughter,' said Sonny. 'She thinks I'm trying to take Callum's place.'

I stared at Sonny, my lower jaw hanging like a limp piece of wet lettuce.

'But that's just crap,' I said, inelegantly when at last I found my voice.

'Which bit? Her thinking it or my doing it?'

'Sonny, I'm serious,' I said, with impatience.

'What makes you think I'm not?' asked Sonny.

If it wasn't for the amused gleam lighting his eyes, I might've been concerned. I caught myself frowning and had to make a conscious effort to relax the muscles around my mouth. Had Sonny's joking got somewhere close to the truth? Was the cause of Meggie's antipathy towards him the fact that she thought I was looking for Callum's replacement? But that couldn't be right, could it? I mean, why would I wait all this time, almost nine years, if that was what I had in mind? Sonny and me? What a laugh! He didn't even think of me that way any more.

We entered the back bedroom, which had been my workspace since I'd paid for an extension to the back of the house. It wasn't huge and it'd made the small garden even smaller, but at least I had a place to work now and it'd extended the kitchen downstairs. The room had a digital piano in it, two re-upholstered chairs, a tiny self-assembly pine desk, a music stand and some books on the floor. The desk was scattered with music manuscript paper, notepads and pencils. A CD-radio player sat self-consciously towards the back of the desk, plugged in but not turned on. I switched on the keyboard and loaded up the last song Sonny and I had been working on.

I was just about to sit down, but there was something wrong. The room was quiet. Too quiet. I spun round to see Sonny watching me. Lately I'd caught him watching me quite a lot.

'I meant what I said,' Sonny told me. 'You are the one and only. You've always been the one and only.'

And the way he said it . . . so solemn, so sincere. So utterly believable. I was really impressed. No wonder he had so many girlfriends. It took a real master of his game to fake that degree of sincerity.

'Sonny, you have a new girlfriend roughly every three months. You wine 'em, dine 'em, bed 'em and dump 'em – not necessarily in that order.'

'Safety in numbers,' said Sonny. 'I date lots of girls to stop myself brooding about the only one that matters.'

And all the while, his eyes never left mine. And all at once I was drowning in his gaze.

'Sonny, I—'

But I didn't get any further. Sonny took hold of my arms and kissed me. And to the surprise of both of us, I kissed him back. I closed my eyes and let myself get swept away on this fragment of time. Sonny's arms immediately went around me, holding me almost too tight. I clung to him. I was being kissed.

Someone wanted me.

Me.

After all these years.

And all I had to do was keep my eyes closed.

 fifteen. Rose is 9

Hello, Daddy,

How are you, up in heaven? Mr Brewster, my teacher, said we had to write a letter to someone far away. So I immediately thought of writing to you. Nana Meggie said it was a good idea. I don't think Mum thought so though. Mum said I should write to my cousin Taj or make someone up. I don't see the point in writing to Taj when I could just phone him up or send him an email. Besides he's just a little kid, so it's not like I can have a proper conversation with him. And what's the point of writing a letter to a make-believe someone? That's just writing to waste paper. So I chose you. I had to ask Mum about it first. Can you hear what Mum and me say from up in heaven? Well, just in case you can't, I asked her, 'Mummy, where's my dad – exactly?'

'Your dad is in heaven. I've already told you.'

'I mean, where is he buried?'

Mum got that peculiar look on her face that she always gets when I start asking questions she doesn't want to answer. Her gaze always dances away from mine and her hands start to fidget and she lowers her head and shoulders before she speaks. I wonder what that's about?

'Your dad was cremated and his ashes were scattered,' she said at last.

'Scattered where?'

'I can't remember,' Mum said.

'How come you can't remember? If I had to scatter your ashes, I'd remember where I'd put them.'

'It was a long time ago, Rose.'

'Yes, but it's not like losing an umbrella or a glove, is it? Then I could understand if you couldn't remember where you put them. But these were Dad's ashes and—'

'Rose, his ashes were scattered in Nana Jasmine's rose garden,' Mum interrupted.

'But you just said that you couldn't remember where they were.'

Mum sighed. 'Callie Rose, am I going to need a lawyer?'

'Don't be sarky,' I told her. 'So how come you didn't remember and then you did?'

'It slipped my mind – OK? But your incessant nagging brought it back.'

I decided to ignore Mum's snide comment. 'How old was I when Dad died?'

'I've already told you. He died before you were born.'

'Yes, I know. But how old exactly was I?'

'I don't know. I was about four months pregnant. Maybe five. I can't remember.'

'But he knew you were pregnant with me?'

'Of course. I've told you that already.'

'And he was happy about it?'

'Yes, dear. Why all the questions?'

'Just something Tobey said.'

'What did Tobey say?' Mum's tone was suddenly sharp.

'Tobey agreed with me that it was a good idea to write to Dad, that's all. He reckoned I should find out a bit more about him so I can write a letter that doesn't ask obvious questions.'

'Oh, I see.'

That was what Mummy said. So that's how I got the idea to write to you – 'cause heaven is far away, isn't it? I also thought of writing to you because Nana Meggie says we all need someone to tell our troubles to. Nana Meggie tells all her troubles to God. Mum calls her a God-botherer behind her back. But just between you and me, Nana Meggie knows what Mum calls her. Nana Meggie told me that God likes to be bothered. I asked Mummy who she tells her troubles to? Mummy didn't answer. I don't think Mummy tells her troubles to anyone. Maybe she should write to you too. I'm sorry I never got the chance to meet you. I wish we could've met. Mummy told me that you used to work at Nana Jasmine's house as a gardener after you left school.

Mummy told me that Nana Meggie used to work for Nana Jasmine for a while and that's how you and Mum first met. Mummy says you practically grew up together. Did you ever snog Mum? I bet you didn't. Snogging is wet! Nana Meggie has told me loads about you as a child – what you liked to eat, your favourite subjects at school – stuff like that. But every time I ask anything about you and Mum together, Nana Meggie always says, 'Ask your mum.' It's very frustrating.

Which reminds me, I didn't have a very good day at school yesterday. Lucas from the year above me called me a bad name and tried to kick me but I punched him on the nose. I got into trouble for that because I made his nose bleed. The blood fell like a waterfall all down the front of his shirt. It was gross. He started crying and ran and told Mr Brewster. Mr Brewster shouted at me. I hate Lucas Cheshie – he's a poo-head. He tried to hit me first but Mr Brewster didn't believe that because I didn't have any bruises or marks. Is that fair? I don't think so. Nana Jasmine told me when I started school that if anyone called me a bad name that I shouldn't – what's the word? – retaliate. (I hope I've spelled that right.) She said I should tell a teacher or wait and tell my mum or her.

'You should show the peppy-traitor of the abuse that you're better than them and above such things,' Nana Jasmine said.

But Nana Meggie told me, 'If anyone at school calls you horrible names or tries anything worse, give 'em a good smack. Then they won't do it twice!'

And Nana Meggie goes to church! When I asked Mum

a while ago what I should do, she looked at me without blinking and said, 'You come and tell me. Don't lash out or the school will use that as an excuse to give you the boot. Just tell me and I'll sort it out.'

But I didn't tell her what Lucas did. Mum doesn't like it when I get upset or hurt by other people. She gets a funny look on her face, kind of fierce and scary. I think if I did tell her about Lucas, she'd probably go straight round the school or Lucas's house. Maybe she'd stuff Lucas's head down the toilet. That would be fun!

Daddy, did you like snogging? I bet you didn't. I don't understand how anyone could. It's gross. I don't mean kissing – which is bad enough. Nana Meggie gives me a kiss every morning before I leave for school and Nana Jasmine gives me a big kiss every time she sees me. But snogging? Yuk! How can anyone like putting their lips against someone else's? Very unhygienic. Germs galore! Nana Meggie said that you and Mum were best friends and in love for ever. That's really soppy. I asked Mum if she still loves you but she just looked away. She doesn't answer that question any more. Mum doesn't like to talk about you. I think she misses you too much. I'm going to stop writing now. My arm is getting tired. I've written loads. I hope I get a gold star for this letter. D'you think Mr Brewster will give me a gold star? Maybe I should take out the bit about Mr Brewster shouting at me. I think I'll leave it in. After all, it did happen. I'm not making it up. Nana Meggie is helping me with my spellings so hopefully this letter will be one of the best ones in my class. I bet it's the longest. I do hope I get a star. Mummy will be happy if I get a star. Maybe she'll hug me if I get a star. My arm's really aching now.

Bye, Daddy. See you in heaven one day.

Love,

Rose

 ## sixteen. Rose is 9

Hello, Daddy,

I was thinking about you a lot today. I wish I had a photo of you but Mum says she doesn't have any. And Nana Meggie said that she had loads but she put them all in a box and now she can't remember where she put it. I offered to help Nana Meggie search through the house for it but she said it'll turn up one day. I want it to turn up today. I want to see you. Very much. Nana Meggie says you didn't like to have your photo taken anyway. I wish you did. It'd be so cool to see how much I look like you. I want to see how much my eyes or my nose or my lips or my forehead or the shape of my face look like yours. What were you like on the inside? I wonder about that a lot. I don't mean what your blood and your heart and your liver looked like. They probably looked like everyone else's. I mean deep on the inside, the bit that sometimes shows itself and sometimes doesn't. I know you liked the outdoors, you loved trees and flowers and nature and stuff. I guess that's why you became a gardener. And I guess that's why you wanted to call me Rose. Mum says that was your idea. I must admit, I didn't like my name until Mum told me it came from you. I guess that's why she calls me Rose instead of Callie Rose, so that you can almost be with us. You must love being in heaven. I bet it's got lots of fields and flowers and sunshine. Perfect for gardeners. I miss you, Daddy. Very much. Mummy doesn't believe me when I say that.

'You can't miss something you've never had,' she told me. (Have I wrote that right? Mummy said whenever I write down what someone says, I have to put speech marks around the bits that they say and start each person's bit on a new line. I don't suppose you'll mind much if it's wrong.)

Daddy, I do miss you. I'll write again soon. You're not my homework any more but I like writing – especially to you. It makes me feel like we're talking – or at least I'm talking and you're listening. I really feel like you're looking over my shoulder or you're in my head or my heart, listening. Nana Jasmine said I can have one of her tidy boxes, the velvety one. I'm going to keep my letters to you and all my other precious things in it. And no one can see them except you because it's got a key. (Don't worry, I'll keep the key in a safe place.) I'm not going to write every day – only when I feel like it. I hope that's OK – because, like I said, you're not homework any more. But I will keep talking to you because I love you.

Toodles, Daddy.

Love,

Rose

seventeen. Sephy

The night held a silence that only really ocurred in the early hours of the morning. I could hear a police siren somewhere out there in the distance but the sound was easy to block out. I glanced through the window up at the stars, trying to find the familiar ones which Callum had taught me to look out for. I was in Sonny's house, in a downstairs room that had been turned into a mini-studio. Sonny sat at the keyboard across from me as we tried to put the finishing touches on our latest song, *Just Ask Me*.

We'd been commissioned to write this for one of the new and happening Cross girl groups. Usually my heart sank when we were commissioned to write for a new pop group, but these girls had been together since school and had been practising for years before landing a recording contract. Designer groups put together by the music companies for the sole purpose of fulfilling a so-called demand or gap in the market usually had a limited shelf-life of about two years. And when they disappeared, their songs usually disappeared with them. Which meant our songs disappeared. In this business, to make money it's longevity that counts.

In a meeting with Dale Applegate, an executive producer at Sometime-Anytime Music, he told us he wanted a dance track where the words would be easy to remember. Sonny and I had to hide our true feelings from Dale when we heard the brief. I could feel the waves of hostility emanating from Sonny at Dale's words, but luckily the producer was too thick-skinned to feel it. And after all, it wasn't the most inane brief we'd ever been given. Plus Sometime-Anytime Music were excellent, not to mention prompt, payers. We were supposed to deliver the song the following week, so we really had to get it right.

Except that I was fading and Sonny had faded and was fast asleep! I read through what we'd written so far, singing softly so as not to wake up Sleeping Beauty.

A pinch of dedication
A dash of consolation
Sling in some deep frustration
Then add a tear or two

A longing for salvation
Disguise the revelation
In a web of conversation
That's all you have to do

Chorus:
Just ask me
What I need
To make me laugh
To make me sigh

What makes me dance
What makes me cry
Just ask me
What I'd like to own
What turns me on
What brings me home
Just ask me

Strokes of stimulation
Don't believe in simulations
With a little relaxation
I'll do what you want me to

And be swept up by elation
One kiss for my salvation
I will give in to temptation
But the rest is up to you

Chorus:
Just ask me
What I need
To make me laugh
To make me sigh
What makes me dance
What makes me cry
Just ask me
What I'd like to own
What turns me on
What brings me home
Just ask me

I don't mind if we take for ever
I don't mind if it's just one night
I just want the thrill of something new
To make me feel all right

Chorus:
Just ask me
What I need
To make me laugh
To make me cry
Just ask me
What I'd like to own
What turns me on
What brings me home
Just ask me
(Just ask me)
Why don't you
Ask me
(Just ask me)
You'll never know
If you won't
Ask me

I shook my head. It still wasn't quite right. Now I just had to figure out why. Sonny was usually really good at homing in on why a song or lyric wasn't working but he'd been scribbling away for the last half an hour without coming up with a single new idea. Still, we were both tired. Maybe we should give in and just call it a night, then come back to it fresh in the morning.

My eyes were so full of sleep-sand, I had to keep

rubbing them to try and get the stuff out. Sleep-sand . . . One of my mother's sayings from when we were children, fighting against drifting off to sleep. I sighed. Life was very strange. Mother and I were getting on so well at the moment. We had the kind of relationship I could only dream of as a teenager. But with Meggie and me it was a different story. Sometimes I felt like Meggie and I stood on different planets playing tug-of-war with my poor daughter. And as for Sonny . . . His head was turned to one side and resting on his folded arms upon the lid of the keyboard as he slept soundlessly. I sat back in my chair and watched him, surprised at how contented I felt to just watch him sleep. We seemed to be getting on so well at the moment. Better than I could've dared to hope. But there was a part of me that stood apart, watching. Sonny made all the running in our relationship, something he'd pointed out more than once. We'd been going out for over six months now, or at least that's what I called it. According to Sonny, we rarely went out. We watched DVDs, or listened to music and had dinner at his place or at my place on the very rare occasions when both Meggie and Rose were somewhere else. But there wasn't an awful lot of 'going out'. And making love was always at Sonny's instigation. I wasn't unwilling. It wasn't that. Sonny was a kind, considerate lover. And I did care about him – as much as I could care about anyone who wasn't my daughter. It was just . . . it was just that—

My thoughts skidded to an abrupt halt at the sight of the piece of paper almost totally hidden beneath Sonny's arm. I thought at first it was just his notes on the song we'd been trying to write together. Until I saw the beginning of my name at the top of the sheet. The rest was obscured by his forearm, but I was sure the 'Seph' I could see was the beginning of my name.

Was he writing something to me? Something he didn't feel able to say, even though I was sitting directly opposite him? Surely that could only be one thing . . . ? I leaned forward and slowly pulled at the sheet. Grunting his sleepy protest, Sonny lifted his arm a fraction. I used the opportunity to successfully whip out the piece of paper from under him. He turned his head on his folded forearms, but didn't wake up. My heart hiccupping in my chest, I sat back and read. I was right. My name was at the top of the paper, but Sonny was writing about me, not to me.

Sephy Scared

She is so scared
She just lashes out
She's afraid that I'll see
What she's all about
She thinks I don't know
That I cannot feel,
Can't see what is false
And can't tell what is real.

She is so lost
She doesn't want to be found
Wants to lift up and soar
But can't get off the ground
All I want is her heart
To beg, borrow, steal

She can't see what is false
And can't tell what is real.

Oh, she's alone in her heart
She's alone in her head
As her loneliness grows.
Oh, I'm not a part of her life
I'm just the man in her bed
Who loves her more than she knows

She is so . . .

I couldn't bear to read any more.
Sephy Scared . . .

Is that how Sonny saw me? Is that what I was? I put down the sheet of paper which was suddenly burning my fingers. I picked up my bag, stood up and, after one last look at Sonny, walked quietly out of the room.

 # eighteen. Rose is 9

Ella and me were playing. It was the first time Ella had come round to my house after school – and it was great. We've never been particular friends before this term, but she always asks to play with me at lunch time. And when we have games and have to find a partner, she always rushes over to stand by me. So we're good friends now. And she was good fun – not like her brother Lucas, who was a real pain. We played a couple of computer games, but Ella wasn't really into them so then we played hide and seek. Mum made us sausages, chips and beans for dinner and it was lovely. I sort of drowned the chips in too much vinegar when Mum wasn't looking, so they tasted all soggy and sour. I couldn't eat them but I told Mum I wasn't too hungry for chips. I didn't tell her that I could've sucked out at least half a cup of vinegar from each one.

'My compliments to the chef, Mum!' I said as I put down my knife and fork.

She always lets me off eating what's left on my plate when I say that.

'Thank you, kind miss,' smiled Mum. Then she curtsied. Mum and I both laughed whilst Ella looked at Mum like she was a fruit-and-nut bar. Ella and me went out into the garden to play on the swing until we both got bored of that as well. Then I had a brilliant idea.

'D'you want to play with my puppet theatre?' I asked. 'Nana Jasmine gave it to me for my birthday.'

'Yes, please,' said Ella.

We'd only just got it out when the front doorbell went.

'Ohhh!' Both Ella and me groaned. Ella's mum had come round much too soon.

'Rose, could you open the door please?' Mum called from the kitchen.

'I'll stay here and set up the puppets,' said Ella.

'OK. I'll be right back,' I said, hoping hard that Ella's mum would want to stay. 'What's your mum's name?'

'Nichelle.'

'That's pretty.'

I headed downstairs to open the door. I liked Ella's mum. She wore her hair in long, skinny locks that were never tied back – at least, I'd never seen them tied back. Every time I saw her in the playground, she wore lipstick and eye shadow and she wasn't spotty or anything. She always looked like she'd just stepped out of the pages of one of Nana Meggie's fashion magazines. As I opened the door, Ella's mum smiled.

'Hi, Mrs Cheshie,' I said.

'Hello, Rose,' she replied. 'Call me Nichelle.'

Which was very nice of her. Some grown-ups are allergic to being called by their first names by anyone younger than them. Maybe she would let Ella stay for a while . . . ?

But then I saw him – Ella's older brother Lucas. Ella had already warned me about him – as if I needed warning. I still hadn't forgotten the time he got me into trouble with Mr Brewster. I still hadn't forgotten the bad name he'd called me either. He was just over a year older than me and Ella, but he went around like he was years and years above us. He looked a bit like Ella, though his locks were shorter, and he had the longest eyelashes I'd ever seen on a boy. He had eyes the colour of baked conkers, and I guess he was OK-looking, but he was scowling at me so hard, it was a bit tricky to tell. Well, two could do that! I glared at him. His frown faded whilst mine grew stronger. He stepped behind his mum. My mum came down the hall, wiping her hands on a couple of sheets of kitchen towel.

'Can I help you?' Mum said politely from behind me.

'I'm here for Ella.'

'You're Nichelle?'

'That's right.'

'Hi. I'm Persephone. Callie Rose's mum. Call me Sephy. Please come in. Would you like a cup of tea?'

For some reason, Ella's mum looked surprised. Had she never had a cup of tea before?

'I'd love one,' she smiled.

Yes! Fantastic! Because that meant that Ella and me could play together for longer. We could make up a story for the puppets. Mum and Nichelle disappeared into the kitchen for a mums' chat. So I knew they'd be *ages*. Lucas shut the door behind him. I ran back upstairs to my bedroom, leaving him in the hall. Ella had made a sign for my door which said, KEEP OUT, LUCAS! GIRLS ONLY! and stuck it up with sticky-tacky from my craft box. I went into my room and shut the door. A few seconds later, it opened again. And in walked Lucas.

'Can't you read?' asked Ella. 'The sign on the door says keep out, Lucas.'

'No, it doesn't.'

'Yes, it does.'

'Go away, Lucas,' I told him.

'Won't.' Lucas stood in the middle of the room, his legs planted in my carpet like tree roots.

Ella and me glared at him but he wouldn't move. He hadn't changed at all. I thought about pulling him out of my bedroom, but then Mum would shout and Ella's mum would take her home.

'Just ignore him,' said Ella. 'Then he'll soon get the message and scram.'

Looking at Lucas, I wasn't so sure. The scowl was gone from his face and now he was just watching me like I'd sprouted an extra head or something. He had the kind of look on his face that I get when I get lost in a really good book. Lucas didn't look like he'd care much if we ignored him. He was where he wanted to be and anything else would be jam on top. Ella and I kneeled down, deciding which puppets we wanted to play with.

'Can I play?' asked Lucas.

'NO!' Ella snapped.

I looked at Lucas. Maybe he'd go now? The answer to that was no. He stood there watching us. When he saw me looking at him, to my amazement he smiled. Even more amazingly, I smiled back. Lucas had a surprisingly nice smile!

'Rose! Don't encourage him,' Ella told me off.

'Sorry,' I muttered and returned to the puppets.

Ella and me – but mainly Ella – made up a story about a nasty little boy called Lucas who was captured by a dragon. The dragon tried to eat him but Lucas was so tough and gristly that the dragon spat him out, unfortunately without biting him to death first (Ella came up with that bit). Then Lucas's sister and her best friend (we're best friends now!) set off on an epic adventure to rescue him. We acted out the whole thing with our puppets and put on different voices for the different characters. It was so much fun – except for Lucas standing there the entire time, watching us. Now and then, he'd ask if he could join in, but Ella always said no. I would've let him play rather than have him just stand in my room, watching.

At last Ella's mum called her and Lucas downstairs. Lucas ran out of the room immediately – thank goodness.

'Let's pack this stuff away,' said Ella, surprising me. I would've thought she'd want to play some more.

'We can carry on for a little while longer,' I said.

'No, we can't. Mum said that if I didn't come the first time she called me, I couldn't come here again,' Ella whispered.

We put all the puppets back in their boxes and packed away the puppet theatre before leaving my bedroom. I didn't miss the stern look Ella's mum gave her as we headed downstairs.

'Ella was helping me put away my puppet theatre,' I quickly explained. I didn't want Ella to get into trouble.

I glanced at Lucas and didn't miss the way he was looking at me either. He had the same puzzled look on his face that he'd had in my bedroom.

'Mum, what's wrong with Rose?' Lucas whispered loud enough for practically the whole street to hear.

I frowned at him. And what was he talking about? There wasn't anything wrong with me.

'Nothing – as far as I know. What d'you mean?' asked his mum.

'Why didn't Dad want Ella to come here and play with her then?' asked Lucas.

'Nonsense.' Nichelle's voice was sharp as pins. 'Your dad never said that.'

'Yes, he did,' Lucas argued. 'I heard you two talking last night. He said he didn't want Callie Rose setting foot in our house and he didn't want Ella playing with some dirty halfer.'

The whole world stopped. The house stopped. My breath stopped. My heart stopped. My heart froze solid. Just for a moment.

'Lucas, that's quite enough,' his mum hissed like an angry snake.

Lucas looked at her, bewildered.

'Your dad never said that,' Nichelle said, really cross.

'But I heard him . . .' said Lucas, even more puzzled. 'I heard you and Dad talking last night. But Rose isn't dirty. I don't get—'

'Lucas, don't you say another word. D'you hear?'

I thought Nichelle was going to slap him. I turned to look at Ella on the stair beside me, but she looked away from me. She didn't say a word – which said a lot.

'We have to go now. Ella, get down here,' Nichelle ordered.

I stayed put halfway up the stairs. I looked at Lucas; he didn't take his eyes off me. Out of the corner of my eye, I saw Nichelle snatch up Ella's school bag.

'Ella, what d'you say to Rose and her mum?'

'Thank you for having me,' said Ella politely.

'Don't mention it,' Mum replied quietly.

Nichelle opened the door and ushered Ella outside. Lucas was still watching me.

'Lucas, move!' Nichelle ordered.

'Bye, Rose,' said Lucas.

I didn't answer.

'Bye, Rose,' Lucas repeated.

'Bye.'

Making sure he smiled at me first, Lucas left, followed by Ella and Nichelle. Mum shut the door quietly behind them before immediately turning to look at me.

'Mum, what's a halfer?'

'It's an ignorant word said by ignorant people to mean someone whose Mum was a Cross and whose Dad was a Nought or vice versa,' said Mum quietly. But each word came out clipped and precise.

'I thought that was it,' I said.

'You shouldn't've had to hear it now,' Mum said.

'Why doesn't Ella's dad like me?'

'Ella's dad doesn't know you. And some people . . . a lot of people are afraid of things they don't know.'

A grown man scared of me? That didn't make any sense at all. 'What's he afraid of?'

'Change,' Mum replied immediately. 'A lot of people are terrified of changes. They worship the status quo – which means when things stay exactly the same. But that's not what life is about. Life is all about changes – some good, some bad. Some people, like Ella's dad, don't get that.'

I looked at Mum, not sure I totally understood. I started making my way back up the stairs.

'Rose, d'you . . . I mean . . . d'you want to ask me anything?' asked Mum solemnly.

I turned and shook my head. 'I have to tidy up my room.'

'I'm sorry you had to hear that horrible word,' Mum said from behind me.

'Don't worry, Mum. It's not the first time I've heard it and I knew it wasn't a compliment. I just wondered what it meant, that's all.'

'Has someone called you that before?' Mum said sharply. 'You never told me.'

'It doesn't matter.' I shrugged.

'Yes, it does. You listen to me, Callie Rose Hadley, you're not "half" anything. D'you understand me? You're wholly you. Half implies short measures or a fraction of something. You haven't got half a tongue or half a brain. And you're not a zebra with black and white stripes.'

'Yes, I know, Mum.'

'I hope you do,' Mum said, coming up the stairs. 'Because you're lucky. You can take the best of being a Cross and the best of being a Nought and put them together to create the person you want to be. D'you understand?'

'Chill, Mum. It's OK.' Mum was getting all hetted and fretted up. 'I think it's lucky that I've got a Cross mum and a Nought dad.'

'Why?'

''Cause I can't go round liking one and not the other, can I? 'Cause I'm both.'

It took three attempts before Mum finally managed a proper smile.

'What's the matter, Mum?' I had to ask: even though she was still smiling, she looked like she wanted to cry.

'I just . . . sometimes I forget just how sensible you are.'

Mum kissed my forehead. I put my arms round her waist to hug her. I was glad she'd cheered up a bit.

'We shouldn't cuddle on the stairs – it's dangerous,' Mum told me. She unwrapped my arms from round her middle. Again.

I carried on upstairs.

'OK, Rose?' Mum called after me.

I didn't answer.

What was the point?

nineteen. Rose is 9

Hello, Daddy,

It's my birthday tomorrow, but I didn't have a very good day today. I was searching through Mum's wardrobe trying to find my birthday present and guess what I found? A diary. Mum's diary. I opened it and an old piece of folded paper fell out. I looked around but luckily no one was behind me. Mum would get all stressy if she caught me searching for my birthday present. I lifted up one corner of the folded paper, but it was just handwriting – nothing interesting. I put the tatty bit of paper back and flicked through the rest of the diary. My mum's got terrible writing. I could only recognize the odd word. I flicked through it but there were no drawings or anything. Nothing to make it interesting. But then, right at the back of the diary there was a photo. It was a Nought man with his arm around the shoulders of a Cross girl. And they were both grinning away and they looked so happy. I looked closer. And guess what? It was Mum! She looked so young.

And who was the Nought man? Was it . . . maybe it was my dad? I bent even closer to the photograph to get a really good look. He smiled like me, with his mouth and his eyes. Our faces weren't the same shape but our eyes were. Was this really my dad? I took out the photo and put the diary back where I'd found it. Then I headed downstairs.

Mum was in the kitchen, getting herself a glass of orange juice.

'Mum, is this my dad?'

Mum came over to get a closer look at the photo. And when she saw it, her face changed faster than a blink. She turned to me, her expression sharp as broken glass.

'Where did you get that?' Her voice was strangely quiet.

I could've sworn she was going to shout. Looking at her, I think it would've been better if she had shouted.

'Callie Rose Hadley, I asked you a question.'

Mum was using my whole, full name. I was for it now. 'I found it.'

'Found it – where?'

I decided to say nothing now. Mum looked like a kettle about to boil.

'Did you go searching through my wardrobe? ANSWER ME.'

'Yes, Mummy.'

Mum drew back her hand and it came rushing towards my face as she went to slap me. But then her hand froze just a couple of centimetres away from my cheek. I couldn't move. I couldn't breathe. Mum's open hand turned into a fist – I could see it out of the corner of my eye. Then her hand dropped to her side. My face was wet.

I was crying and I hadn't even realized. Mum looked at me. I looked at Mum. Neither of us spoke.

'What're you crying for?' said Mum fiercely. 'I didn't hit you, did I?'

But she was going to. Mum had never hit me before. She'd never even tried. Until now.

'Give me that photo,' Mum demanded.

I handed it over without a word.

'Now go to your room and stay there until I call you,' said Mum.

I ran away. I didn't want to be anywhere near Mum. She was actually going to hit me. And all I'd done was ask about a photograph. If that was the way she was going to be, I'd never ask her anything again. Never, ever.

 twenty. Sephy

God, forgive me.

Callum, forgive me.

I'm so sorry, Callie Rose. I wouldn't've done it. I wouldn't've hit you. I promised . . . I promised anyone who would listen that I'd never hurt you again. Never in a million years.

But I came so close.

Fear drove my hand. Fear of the past. Fear of the future. Fear of questions. Fear of answers.

Look at us, Callum. We were so happy in this photo. I'd almost forgotten I had it. Look at us, ready to take on the world. We had each other so it was a fight we couldn't lose.

But we did.

Seeing the photo after all these years made it all come rushing back. And I almost took it out on my daughter.

I'm so sorry, Callie Rose.

I'm so, so sorry.

twenty-one.
Rose is 10

Nana Meggie and Mum sat at opposite ends of the room, ignoring each other. Maybe ignoring was too strong a word. They weren't exactly uninterested in each other, not the way that married couple are in Nana Meggie's favourite soap on the TV. (The programme really sucks! And Mum agrees! Talk about unbelievable! I mean, how long can one restaurant owner date four brothers all at the same time without any of them finding out? And she still finds the time to run the restaurant, buy and run a night-club and bring up her sister's two children. I mean, get real!) Nana and Mum were doing their 'I'm not talking first' routine. They'd both talk to me but would only answer each other. And since no one wanted to ask anything and be the first to crack the silence, it was left to me to do it all. Again.

I wish I could figure out what's wrong with the two of them.

Sometimes, it gets so cold when they are together that I have to leave the room before my toes drop off from frostbite. In fact, I was just standing up when Tobey ambled into the room.

'Hi, everyone,' Tobey smiled.

'How did you get in?' I frowned.

'The back door was open.'

'Which isn't an open invitation for you to just swan in any time you feel like it,' Nana Meggie snapped.

I wasn't the only one who was surprised. Since when did Nana Meggie mind when Tobey visited?

'He doesn't mean any harm,' Mum said quietly.

'That's not the point. This isn't his house. He could at least knock first,' said Nana.

'Come on, Tobey. Let's go outside,' I suggested.

As we left the room, I turned to frown at Nana Meggie but she didn't see it. She was too busy scowling at Tobey like he'd trodden on her bunions and kicked both her shins.

'What's up with your grandma?' Tobey whispered as I closed the door.

'No idea.' I shrugged. I was heading towards the kitchen when I had an excellent idea (even if I do say so myself!). I pointed to the living-room door. Tobey caught on immediately and we tiptoed back to listen at the door.

'. . . not the sort of thing you of all people should be encouraging,' Nana Meggie said.

'For goodness' sake, she's ten, he's eleven.'

'So? You and Callum were younger.'

'Meggie, just what are you implying?'

'I'm just saying that Callie and Tobey are good friends and they're growing up,' said Nana Meggie. 'I just don't want to see Callie hurt the way . . . the way . . .'

'The way Callum was,' Mum finished for her.

'I was thinking of you as well as my son. Callie has a chance to make something of her life.'

'And you think being friends with Tobey is going to hold her back?'

'Tobey is so laid-back, he's horizontal,' Meggie said testily.

I turned to grin at Tobey, but to my surprise he had a face like a bulldog chewing a wasp.

'Tobey has plenty of time to make up his mind what he's going to do with the rest of his life,' said Mum.

'I just don't want his bad habits rubbing off on Callie Rose . . .'

'What bad habits? He doesn't pick his nose and eat it – at least, not in front of me. He doesn't coat door handles in his ear wax. What bad habits are you on about?'

The room went quiet.

'Meggie, you of all people . . .'

'. . . know what the world is like. This society expects the least and condemns the most when it comes to my son and Tobey and all other nought men.'

'Callum died over ten years ago. Things have got better . . .'

'Better for who?' asked Meggie. 'I used to love swimming at the local baths. I was even considering joining the gym on my doctor's recommendation, just to keep my body active. Well, did you ever wonder why I stopped going? 'Cause all the cleaners and serving staff at the local gym and pool are noughts, but the reception staff are all Crosses and the managers are all Crosses. That's why. Since Callie started school, has she had any nought teachers? I don't think so. And I still can't walk around the local bookshop or jewellery store without some idiot following me around. Where's this "better" that everyone keeps telling me about?'

'I know there's still a long way to go – I'm not denying that. But Tobey has a chance to go to university and do any job he wants to do,' I tried. 'That wasn't the case when Callum was alive.'

'And that's my point. Tobey has so many doors open to him that my son never had. And what does he plan to do? In his words, as little as possible. Tobey has no drive, no ambition.'

'He's *eleven*,' Mum argued. 'He's not even in secondary school yet. Give the boy a chance.'

'I'm just saying that Callie can do better – and I hope she knows it.'

'By better, d'you mean Rose should marry a Cross when she grows up?'

Tobey's expression was now as hard as the granite worktops in Nana Jasmine's kitchen. He straightened up and looked directly at me but he was still listening to what was going on inside the living room. By now, I was kicking myself on both bum cheeks for suggesting that we eavesdrop in the first place.

'I don't want Callie to get hurt,' said Nana Meggie. 'And being with Tobey or any other nought is going to cause problems for her.'

'I didn't realize you had Callie Rose's life mapped out in such detail,' said Mum. 'If you deign to let me know what you have planned for her tomorrow and the day after, I'll try not to deviate from your schedule.'

'There's no need for that. I just want Callie to be happy, that's all. She deserves to be happy.'

Tobey spun round and headed towards the kitchen. I wanted to go into the living room and tell off Nana Meggie for being so mean about him, but Tobey was getting further and further away.

'Tobey, wait,' I called after him.

But he didn't wait.

I ran after him, grabbing his arm to stop him stalking off. But he shrugged me off and carried on moving.

'Tobey, I didn't say it,' I protested.

'Maybe you think the same, that I'm not good enough for you,' said Tobey.

I stared at him. 'You know me better than that. Or you should.'

'I'm going home. Next time I come round, I'll ring the doorbell first.'

'Don't be daft,' I said. 'You've never rung our bell in your life.'

'Maybe I should start.'

'Tell you what,' I said crossly. 'After you've rung our bell and we've let you in, you can kiss each of my toes, then my mum's, then you can kiss Nana Meggie's bunions. Would you like that?'

'Only if I wanted a sure way to lose my lunch,' said Tobey, but the trace of a smile flitted across his face.

'Glad to see you've stopped sulking,' I told him.

Tobey's smile faded.

'Just forget about what Nana Meggie said. I have already.'

Tobey looked at me and said very quietly, 'I never will.'

twenty-two. Jasmine

Maybe I'll decorate this bedroom. I haven't had it redecorated since Kamal and I separated. This pale cream colour is very staid. It's time for me to splash out on something more vibrant, more modern, more alive.

I'm scared to death . . .

This . . . this thing inside me, I'm sure it's nothing. A cyst or a benign growth, that's all. Absolutely nothing to get worked up about, I'll be fine. I feel fine. I *am* fine.

So why can't I sleep? This hard lump in my breast is painful. I should've visited my doctor weeks ago when I first noticed it. But it hasn't gone away. It's not getting any bigger, but it's not getting smaller either.

I do so want to talk to Minerva or Persephone about it. But there's no point in upsetting my daughters over nothing. Minerva and her husband Zuri have their own busy lives to lead and I'm glad. Zuri is a good man, just what Minerva deserves. And their son Taj is a joy. They need to focus on each other, not me. And Sephy has been through so much. Too much. So I won't say anything – at least not yet. It's time for me to put my children first. As far as this lump is concerned, I'll wait until it's something and pray that it's nothing.

Jasmine, don't fall apart now. You've been through worse than this. You'll be fine.

Keep telling yourself you'll be fine.

You'll be OK.

Whatever life throws at you, you'll be OK.

 # twenty-three. Sephy

I was drying the dinner plates when the feel of lips on my nape made me jump like a startled doe.

'Hello, gorgeous!' Sonny said softly.

I glanced round anxiously. 'Sonny, don't do that. Anyone could walk in.'

'So? We're both over twenty-one.' Sonny tried to pull me into his arms. Anxiety morphed into pure panic.

'Sonny, don't.'

'Why not?'

'I'm not that kind of girl.'

'What kind of girl?' Sonny said, puzzled.

'The touchy-feely kind. And I don't appreciate being mauled.'

Sonny's arms dropped to his side. 'Since when is a kiss on the neck even in the same ballpark as "being mauled"?'

'I didn't mean that. I just don't like . . . being man-handled.'

'That's not what you said a couple of nights ago.'

What a low blow!

'That was then and this is now,' I snapped. 'And it's not because I'm *scared* either.'

'Oh, so we're back to that,' Sonny sighed. 'Sephy, that was months ago!'

'You're the one who wrote it about me,' I reminded him.

My head was telling me to drop it. Just let it go. But my mouth kept going anyway. I had been so hurt by what Sonny had written about me that it still felt like yesterday. When I had first read his poem, I hadn't spoken to him for a couple of days in spite of the flowers and apologies he had sent round and delivered in person.

'I've already apologized for that,' said Sonny. 'Which I wouldn't've had to do, if you hadn't read it in the first place. And you keep on bringing it up. Now you seem determined to pick a fight for some reason and I'm not in the mood.'

'I just don't want Callie Rose to come in here and catch us necking.'

'Why not? Two grown-ups openly showing love for each other is not only natural but healthy.'

'Why don't we get the neighbours round, have an orgy on the living-room carpet and invite Rose to watch?' I said sourly.

'That's not what I meant and you know it. But there's nothing wrong with kissing and cuddling in front of her. God knows, she needs to see some kind of love displayed somewhere in this house.'

A silent, deadly earthquake opened up the ground between us and sent my mind careering backwards.

'What does that mean?' I asked quietly.

Sonny stood in front of me but I've never felt so far away from him as I did in that moment.

'It doesn't matter. Forget it,' said Sonny, turning away.

I grabbed his arm and turned him round to face me. 'What did that mean?'

'It's just that you and Meggie . . . sometimes when I walk into this house, I'm almost rocked back on my heels by the atmosphere in this place. And Rose isn't stupid. She knows there's something not right between you two.'

'It has nothing to do with Rose—'

'Wrong,' Sonny interrupted. 'It has everything to do with Rose. You and Meggie don't realize what you're doing to her.'

'Rose is my daughter, not yours.'

'I know that,' said Sonny quietly. 'But that doesn't stop my eyes from working.'

'I want you to leave,' I said.

'Why? Because you can't handle the truth? Because you're happy for Rose to be brought up in this loveless house as long as no one mentions it?'

'Get out.'

'If I go, Sephy, I'm not coming back.'

A silent face-off. 'Go on then,' my expression read.

Sonny turned round and marched out of the kitchen.

I followed him, to make sure he definitely left the house – at least that's what I told myself.

After opening the front door, Sonny turned to face me. 'Bye, Persephone.' He stepped out, slowly pulling the door to.

And as the door was closing, it felt like it was pulling my heart behind it.

'Sonny . . .'

The door's journey halted just before the lock clicked into place. Then it opened again, just as slowly. I stared into Sonny's face, across the hall, across the world from each other but just a heartbeat away. Did I look like that? So unsure, so desperately unhappy? Did I look like him, sharing more than just an expression? Sharing something deeper and far more painful.

'Don't go,' I whispered.

After a long moment, the door closed again. But this time, Sonny was in the hall – with me.

twenty-four.
Rose is 10

Just tell her, I told myself. Open your mouth and tell her.

My best friend Nikki and I had both agreed to talk to our parents tonight at exactly eight o'clock. Ella Cheshie had stopped being my friend after the first and only time she came round my house but I didn't care. I had Nikki and Nikki was much nicer. Even when Ella was my friend, she never opened her mouth unless it was to criticize someone else or say nasty things about them. I glanced down at my watch. It was two minutes past eight.

Dad, I know you're watching over me, so could you please help me persuade Mum. Please.

'Mum?'

'Yes, dear.'

'Nikki's going to Farnby Manor Secondary in September.'

'Is she? That's nice.' The black-and-white film on the TV had ninety-five per cent of Mum's attention.

'Nikki and I have decided we'd like to go to the same school.'

'What? Farnby Manor?'

'Yes, please.'

'I don't think so, Rose.' Mum turned back to the TV.

'But Mum, Nikki and me have agreed.'

'You and Nikki can agree that the moon is made of mashed potato with cod-fillet craters, but you're still not going to Farnby Manor. You're going to Heathcroft High.'

'But that's a boffin school.'

'It's the school both your nanas want you to go to and so do I,' said Mum.

'But it's a private school. We can't afford that.'

'Nana Jasmine is going to pay your fees,' Mum told me.

'But what about Nikki and me?'

'Going to a new school doesn't mean that you stop being friends. You can still see each other.'

'It's not the same,' I protested.

'Callie Rose, you're going to Heathcroft High and that's final. End of discussion.'

'Don't I even get a say in where I go?'

'No,' Mum replied. 'Not when it comes to your education. You'll just have to trust that we're doing the best for you.'

'But Nikki can't afford Heathcroft.'

'I can't help that, Rose,' said Mum.

'You just don't want me to be happy.' I ran from the room, tears choking me from the inside out.

'I want you to be very happy,' Mum called after me as I ran upstairs. 'That's why you're going to Heathcroft.'

Halfway up the stairs, I decided that my room wasn't far enough away. It wasn't fair. Heathcroft High was Mum's choice, not mine. Mum always got her own way and it was my life, not hers. It just wasn't fair.

'Mum, I'm going out on my bike,' I shouted out.

'I beg your pardon?' Mum appeared in the doorway faster than I would've thought possible and she had a face like thunder. Attitude always has that effect on her.

'Can I go out on my bike please?'

'That's what I thought you said,' said Mum stonily. 'Just up and down this road, OK? And you've got half an hour. Then I want you back home and getting ready for bed.'

'But I can't do much in half an hour,' I protested.

'How about fifteen minutes then?' said Mum.

'Half an hour is fine,' I muttered.

'Glad to hear it.'

'Yes, Mum.'

'Rose, I'm not sending you to Heathcroft High out of

spite,' said Mum quietly. 'But I want you to have a good, fulfilled life. And a good life is all about choices. If you want to rule the world, or be a lawyer or a doctor or a zookeeper, that's entirely up to you. You'll be the one making the decisions if you get a decent education. Without that, you'll have no choices at all. D'you understand?'

'Yes, Mum.'

'And I'm sorry about Nikki,' Mum continued. 'I know that you and her are very close, but you can't live your life for other people. You have to do what's best for you, not for Nikki.'

'If I can't live my life for other people, then how come you get to tell me what to do?' I asked.

'Because I'm your mother,' said Mum, using grown-up logic.

'Mum, could you just think about it? Please? Just think about Farnby Manor.'

'Rose, you and Farnby Manor are not going to happen. I'm not going to say that I'll think about it when I already know what my final answer is going to be. Come September you'll be going to Heathcroft. If it was good enough for your dad and me, it's good enough for you.'

'But Mum—'

'Callie Rose, which part of "no" don't you understand? The "n" or the "o"?'

Shaking her head, Mum went back into the living room. I headed back downstairs and out into the back garden to get my bike. Less than a minute later I was cycling along the pavement, as far away from Mum and home as I could get. I'd promised Nikki we'd go to the same school together. And now Mum was going to make me break my promise.

It's not fair.

As soon as I'm older, no one will tell me what to do or where to go or what time to be back. My life will be all my own and no one – not even Mum – will be able to boss me about.

I got to the end of the road but I was still jumping up and down inside. Mum said I was only to ride up and down our road, but I was ten now. I wasn't a baby. So why couldn't I cycle all the way around the block. I often went round the block when Mum or Nana Meggie came with me, and at ten I should be able to do it by myself.

After one last look behind to make sure Mum wasn't watching, I turned the corner on my bike and carried on pedalling. There! See! I told you I could cycle round the block by myself.

'Excuse me?'

A Nought man with light-brown hair and dark-brown, almost black eyes stepped right out in front of me. If I hadn't squeezed hard on my brakes, I would've crashed straight into him. As it was, I had to put my feet quickly down on the ground or me and my bike would've toppled over.

'Sorry! I didn't mean to startle you,' smiled the man. 'I'm looking for a woman called Sephy Hadley. I was told she lives around here somewhere. D'you know where I might find her?'

'She's my—'

I bit off the rest of the words. How many times had Mum and both nanas told me never to talk to strangers? The man started walking towards me. My mouth was suddenly as dry as a cream cracker. I pushed back with the balls of my feet so me and my bike moved backwards. The man stopped moving.

'D'you know her?' the man asked again.

'I'm not supposed to talk to strangers,' I told him.

I had a quick glance around. The road was suddenly empty. There was no one around but the strange, tall man – and me. And I wasn't even on the same road as my house any more.

'I have to go now,' I said, one foot back on the pedal.

'No, wait. I'm not going to harm you, I promise.'

'But if you were, you wouldn't exactly tell me, would you?'

The man smiled. 'No, I guess I wouldn't. But I'm looking for Sephy Hadley because I'm hoping she can tell me about a man called Callum McGregor. I've been away for a while and I need to find out where he is.'

One of my feet was on the ground, but I was ready to cycle away like crazy if I had to.

'Who are you?' I asked, still keeping my distance.

'Well, I asked you first!' the man smiled. 'D'you know where Sephy Hadley lives?'

'Are you a friend of hers?' I asked.

The man sighed and shook his head. 'Not really. You see, Sephy and I had a quarrel a long, long time ago and we haven't spoken since. And now I really want to make it up to her – and Callum. I want, more than anything, to put the past behind me.'

'Oh, I see,' I said. I slowly took my foot off the pedal and put it back on the pavement. 'Well, you can't see Callum. He died before I was born.'

'Callum's dead?'

The man stumbled back as if my words had just knocked him off his feet.

'Are you OK?' I asked.

'Yes . . . no . . . I . . . I can't believe Callum's dead. How did he die?'

'In a car accident,' I told him.

The man looked stunned, then his eyes narrowed briefly.

'Who told you that?' he asked sharply.

'My mum. Callum McGregor was my dad,' I replied.

The man stared at me. 'You're Callie Rose?'

'Yeah . . .' I put my right foot back on the pedal.

'And Callum's dead?'

'That's right.'

'And who told you he died in a car accident?'

'My mum. Why?'

'I just wondered,' said the man.

The way he was looking at me was making me feel uncomfortable. 'Who are you?' I asked.

The man replied, 'My name is Jude.'

twenty-five. Jude

There was no trace of recognition on her face when I told her my name. So not only had Sephy failed to mention me, but my mum hadn't bothered to talk about me either. No matter. I can use that. Three weeks of skulking in shadows and watching my mum's house had finally paid off. And not a moment too soon as I was beginning to despair of ever getting a chance to talk to Sephy's bastard alone. Seems like I used the right ploy. Pretending not to know about Callum's death made her relax slightly. And that nonsense about my brother dying in a car crash . . . They've hidden the truth from this girl. I can use that as well. But don't rush it, Jude. You've got plenty of time. Now that she's old enough, I can start grooming her. Nice and easy does it. This little girl is going to play a big part in my future plans. A very big part.

And no one is going to stand in my way.

I'll make sure of that.

The man held out his hand, but if he thought I was going to take it, he had two screws and a hinge loose in his head. I wasn't that stupid. I watched as his hand dropped to his side.

'How come you know my mum and dad?'

'Callum is . . . was my brother.'

'You're my uncle?' Something like a firework burst inside of me. But I deliberately stopped any more from going off. *Be careful, Rose.* Was this man really my uncle? Jude . . . I remembered now. When I was eight or nine, I asked Nana Meggie if I had any aunts or uncles apart from Aunt Minerva. Nana told me I used to have an aunt called Lynette but that she died very young, before I was even born. That made me start to cry, because Nana had lost both my dad and her daughter and it was so sad. That's when Nana told me about my Uncle Jude. He was Dad's older brother. But Nana said I couldn't see him because he was so far away.

But now he was back – if this really was him . . . I had to be careful.

'Yes,' the man replied with a brief smile. 'I'm your . . . uncle.'

'What's your sister's name?' I asked.

'Lynette,' the man replied at once. 'She died a long time ago.'

'What's Nana Meggie's middle name?'

The man frowned at me, then his expression cleared. 'Oh, I see. Well, my mum doesn't have a middle name. Her name is Margaret McGregor although she hates the name Margaret and never uses it.'

A smile covered my entire face. It *was* my uncle!

Yahoo! Dad, look! It's your brother. My uncle. Does he look like you? Uncle Jude has lovely, dark eyes and a friendly smile. I'm afraid to blink in case he vanishes before I can drink him in. I want to memorize everything around him and about him. Dad, look! It's your brother!

'Hello, Uncle Jude,' I grinned.

'I don't know what to say.' Uncle Jude shook his head. 'I . . . I'm so happy to meet you – but to hear that my brother is dead . . .'

'I'm sorry,' I said, my smile vanishing. How horrible was that? To hear that his brother had died and he hadn't even known it. 'Nana Meggie's not home, but come and see my mum. I'm sure she'd love to meet you again.'

'I . . . I don't think so.' Uncle Jude shook his head. 'Not now I know about my brother.'

'Why not?'

'As I said, Sephy and I had a quarrel a long time ago. I'm sure I'm the last person she wants to see.'

'Oh but—'

'No, Callie. Maybe some other time. I've just found out what happened to my brother . . . I need some time alone.'

Uncle Jude turned to walk away.

'Am I going to see you again?' I asked eagerly.

'Would you like to?'

'Yes, please.' I would *love* that.

'On one condition,' said Jude seriously.

'What?'

'I'd rather you didn't say anything to anyone about my visit yet.'

'Why?'

Uncle Jude looked so sad. 'I need to think of a way to heal this rift between your mum and me. We both said some things . . . Anyway, if I were to turn up now or if she heard that I'd contacted you without her permission, then your mum and I will never make up and be friends.'

'Then I won't tell her. Not until you say I can,' I said.

'D'you promise?'

'I promise.'

'Are you a girl who keeps her promises?' asked Uncle Jude.

'Always.'

Uncle Jude tilted his head to one side to watch me. I didn't look away, I looked him straight in the eyes. I wanted him to know that I meant it. I'd never break my promise to him. Never, ever.

'I might not be in touch for a while, maybe even a few months, but you mustn't tell my mum or your mum or anyone else that you saw me. OK?'

'I won't. Not a word.'

'Good girl. I have a good feeling about you, Callie Rose. I think you can be trusted to keep our very grown-up secret.'

If I nodded any faster, my head would fall off. At last I'd found someone who realized that I was ten years old, not ten months. And I would show Uncle Jude I was the best secret-keeper in the whole wide world.

'Bye, Callie Rose. See you soon.'

'Bye, Uncle Jude.'

Uncle Jude strode away from me. His back straight, but his head bent.

Did you walk like that, Dad? Did you talk like Uncle Jude? I bet you're the one who brought my uncle back into my life. Thank you so much, Dad. You do look out for me.

 ## twenty-seven. Sephy

Rose has been in a very quiet mood over the last couple of weeks. At first I thought she was sulking over not going to the same school as her friend Nikki. But I'm not so sure any more. I think it's something deeper than that. I've asked her what's wrong count-less times but all she says is, 'Nothing!' I am so sick of that word.

Nothing.

Don't tell me it's nothing when I can see that it's something.

Oh well. I'll just have to trust that when Callie Rose is good and ready, she'll tell me what's on her mind.

twenty-eight.
Rose is 10

'Rose, stop bouncing on the bed before you end up bouncing out of the window.'

Whilst my feet were off the bed and up in the air, I drew my knees up even higher towards my chest, the way they'd taught us in my trampoline lessons. I bent my knees as I hit the bed and whoosh, I was back in the air again, even higher than before. Yahoo!!

'Rose, am I speaking Martian?'

'But Mum,' I grinned, 'this is fun!'

'Rose, don't make me have to tell you again.'

I looked at Mum as I sailed up, spinning my arms like a watermill. She looked irritated but not annoyed. I reckoned I had a few more bounces before she started shouting.

Up and down! Up and down! Mum's bed is the best

bed in the whole house for trampolining. I did a straddle jump, then a pike, then a seated drop which was quite good, even if I do say so myself.

'Callie Rose, get down,' Mum insisted.

I had time for one more bounce. This one was going to be the highest ever. So high, I'd touch the ceiling. I bounced forward, ready to hit the ground running the moment Mum started to yell. But then it all went wrong! My foot slipped on one corner of the bed and I slid onto the floor faster than a thought. My back hit the corner of the bed and scraped all the way down it as I landed smack on my bum.

I opened my mouth – and howled.

Mum was at my side in an instant. 'Are you OK?' She squatted down. 'Rose, are you all right?'

My back was on fire. I tried to open my mouth to speak but all I could do was scream. I opened my arms to be picked up. Mum began to open her arms as well, but then she took hold of one of my hands and held it in both of hers.

'Rose, calm down, love. Where does it hurt? Show me.'

The door was flung open and Nana Meggie came running in. 'What the hell was that? It sounded like the whole ceiling was coming down.'

Nana took one look at me sitting on the floor and bawling before sweeping me up and closing her arms around me like the Venus flytrap we saw at the botanical gardens. My face was buried in the folds of her powder-blue dress which smelled of flowery perfume and chicken. Nana had her hands pressed against my back, right where it was hurting the most. And she was hugging me so tight I had to turn my face to the side just so I could breathe.

'Nana, I fell off the bed and hurt my back,' I cried. Nana hugged me tighter, which made me cry harder. 'You're hurting me.'

Moving her hands off my back, Nana Meggie bent over to kiss the top of my head and each of my wet cheeks.

'It's OK, love. Nana's here. Let's have a look-see, shall we?' She lifted up the back of my T-shirt while my face was still buried in her dress.

'Goodness! You've already got some swelling under one of your shoulder blades,' said Nana. 'You're going to have a beaut of a bruise there tomorrow.'

'She needs an ice pack on that to reduce the swelling,' said Mum from behind me.

I pulled away from Nana Meggie and turned to Mum, my arms outstretched. 'Mum, it really hurts.'

Mum took hold of my hands. 'Come on, love. Let's get that bruise sorted out.' And with that, she led the way past Nana Meggie.

'Will you carry me, Mummy?'

Mum looked down at me. 'You're too heavy, Rose. Besides, I might make your back hurt worse. You'd better walk.'

So we walked to the bathroom further along the landing. Mum dampened a face flannel, wrung out the water and, lifting up my T-shirt, put the flannel very carefully on my back. She didn't hurry, she didn't rush, she was very careful. I watched her, the tears drying on my face.

The cool flannel made my back feel a little better, but it still hurt. I was still sniffing, trying to stop myself from crying. Mum didn't like it when I cried.

I held my arms out again. Mum smiled and kissed the top of my head.

'Don't you think you're a bit old to have a cuddle every time you scrape your knee or stub your toe?' said Mum.

I looked at her, my arms dropping to my sides. 'Yes, Mum.'

'Good girl,' said Mum. 'You've scraped your back quite badly and a bit of it is bleeding but it doesn't need a plaster.'

'Yes, Mum.'

'What's the matter?'

'Nothing, Mum.'

I looked down at the ground then. I didn't want Mum to see my face. My back was throbbing now. Mum turned me round so that my back was towards her and stroked over my bruise very gently, so gently that it hardly hurt. Then to my surprise, she kissed my back just where it was hurting.

'There you are, love. Does that feel better?'

I spun around and put my arms around Mum's neck.

'Oh yes, Mummy. Much better.'

'I'm glad.' Mum stroked my arms before pulling them from around her neck. 'You're strangling me, Rose.'

'Sorry.' I let her go.

By now my back was only aching instead of throbbing. But something inside my chest was hurting worse.

Mum kissed my forehead. 'Come and have some ice cream for being so brave,' she said. 'Not many people know this but ice cream is very good for bruised backs.'

So Mum got me some chocolate ice cream and it was yummy.

And after a while the pain in my back faded away until I could hardly feel it any more.

But the pain in my chest took a lot longer.

twenty-nine.
Rose is 10

Tobey was in a funny mood today. And I don't mean funny-haha either. Mum and me visited Nana Jasmine's and as Tobey was round our house yet again, Mum invited him along.

'We're off to see my mum, Tobey,' said Mum. 'Wanna come?'

'Yes, please,' he said straight away. But the moment he said it, he got this very strange look on his face, like his mouth had run away from his brain and now his brain was regretting it. He'd never been to Nana Jasmine's house before, but I'd certainly told him enough about it. Maybe that's why he wanted to see it, but then got nervous thinking about what it must be like and meeting my nana. After we got permission from his mum, we set off. He was really quiet whilst Mum drove us to Nana Jasmine's. I tried to talk to him loads of times, but he just shrugged or said yes or no, so after a while I gave up and chatted to Mum instead.

'Are you OK, Tobey?' Mum asked more than once.

'Yes, thanks, Miss Hadley,' said Tobey. But that was all he said.

'Rose, stay in the house for at least ten minutes before disappearing off with Tobey,' warned Mum as we got out of the car.

'Yes, Mum,' I sighed. We had this conversation about me running off to the garden or down by the beach, every time we visited Nana Jasmine. Mum reckoned it looked bad to greet Nana Jasmine with, 'Hi, Nana. Can I go away and play now?'

We sat down in Nana Jasmine's huge living room. Nana Jasmine called it her drawing room, which made it sound like it should've been more fun than it was. Drawing room sounded like a room you should be able to paint in and draw and make a mess. Just goes to show, doesn't it? Nana Jasmine's two sofas cost more than Mum's car (so Mum said) and I had to be very careful not to touch any of Nana's ornaments or walk on her rug with my shoes. Mum won't let me drink anything more colourful than water in Nana's drawing room even though Nana Jasmine says she really doesn't mind what I eat or drink in there.

'That's not what you used to tell me,' Mum said once. 'You wouldn't let me drink tea or orange juice or anything else in this room.'

'That was a long time ago,' Nana told her. 'Times change. People change.'

'Not that much,' Mum scoffed.

'Sephy, you should have more faith in people,' Nana told her.

'How do I do that?' asked Mum.

'You start by having more faith in yourself,' said Nana.

Then Nana looked down at me as if she'd just remembered I was there.

'Young ears are flapping,' said Nana Jasmine. Like I wouldn't know what that was supposed to mean!

So there I was, perched on the sofa, trying to look like all the little crystal figures Nana Jasmine had in her cabinet were actually interesting. I counted to one hundred before I thought my head would turn inside out if I stayed there one more moment. I turned to nudge Tobey, who was sitting next to me. But he wasn't paying any attention to me. His eyes were here, there and everywhere, taking in everything in Nana's room. What was so fascinating? I looked around, trying to see the room through Tobey's eyes as if I was seeing it for the very first time. The room was big, as big as our kitchen, living room and conservatory at home all rolled into one. But it was still too neat and tidy.

'Nana, can Tobey and me go down to the beach?' I asked, ignoring the frown Mum was sending in my direction.

'Tobey and I,' Nana corrected.

Nana was so fussy. She understood me, didn't she? But I knew from past experience that she wouldn't answer until I used the proper lingo.

'Can Tobey and I go down to the beach?' I asked.

'You could,' said Nana Jasmine. 'But that doesn't mean I'm going to let you!'

Tobey was getting all embarrassed next to me, but for the wrong reason. I sighed and tried again.

'*May* Tobey and I go down to the beach?'

'Yes, but be back in time for lunch.'

'Yes, Nana.' I sprang up, grabbing Tobey's arm before Mum could have a go.

I pulled him out of the room and into the kitchen.

'Fancy a game of beach tennis?' I asked.

'What's that?' said Tobey.

'Tennis on the beach.' Duh!!

'OK.'

I led the way into the conservatory. A medium-sized cupboard held all the garden and beach games like croquet and boules and plastic tennis rackets. I grabbed two and a couple of tennis balls and ran out into the garden.

'This way,' I told Tobey.

We ran all the way across Nana's garden. I stopped for a moment when we got to the rose garden. Nana Jasmine had told me that the whole rose garden used to be under glass, like in a huge greenhouse – but after her divorce she'd had it removed. When I had asked her why, she'd said, 'I wanted the flowers to enjoy the wind and the rain. Flowers should know winter and summer, it makes them stronger. It doesn't do to keep plants too cosseted. Or people for that matter.' And although I'd asked her the question, Nana Jasmine had looked at my mum as she answered.

It was strange to think that my dad used to work in the same spot before I was even born. And his ashes had been scattered here too. I knew they'd be long gone, but it was still kinda lovely to think that Dad could be swirling around me at that very moment – in the fresh air I breathed, in the flowers I saw and could smell, even in the birdsong I could hear. After all, birds ate worms and maybe a worm ate some of Dad's ashes years and years ago and then a bird ate the worm and now it wasn't really a bird singing, but Dad! (How long did birds live anyway?) Every time we visited Nana Jasmine, I'd go out to the rose garden. I know it sounds silly but I really felt closer to Dad there.

'Hi, Dad,' I whispered. I didn't want Tobey to hear me or he might think I was cracking up.

Then we carried on running. Once we hit the beach, we got straight into the game.

'Where's the net?' asked Tobey.

'In our heads.'

So we started playing. But Tobey was in a very funny-strange mood. We played tennis on the beach, but the ball kept bouncing off in all directions. I mean, that was the whole point. But every time the ball flew off, Tobey would huff and puff and scowl as he went to get it. He obviously wasn't enjoying himself, so after about ten minutes I gave up on the tennis idea.

'What's wrong, Tobey?'

'Your grandma's house is huge.'

'So?'

'And she lives there just by herself?'

'Yeah, but she has a full-time secretary called Sarah and a cook.'

'And that's it?'

'Yeah. Why?'

'That's not right – one woman living in a huge big house like that all alone.'

'Well, she and my grandad divorced years ago.'

'That's not what I meant. Her home is big enough to be a hotel and the whole thing is just hers. A quarter of Meadowview could fit in that place. It's not right.'

I'd never thought of it that way before. Tobey had a point. It was a big house for just one person. When I thought of all the homeless people in Meadowview who lived under cardboard boxes . . . But at the same time, if Nana and Grandad had worked for their money and then decided to buy a big house and have people working for them, what was wrong with that?

'Mum says if you get a good education, then anything is possible. That's why she wants me to go to Heathcroft. She says with a good education behind me I could sweep the streets or be Prime Minister one day. But the choice would be mine. She says a good education gives you lots of choices.'

'Except that the choice of a "good education" isn't available to everyone,' said Tobey.

I had to think about that as well. Heathcroft School wasn't free. Nana Jasmine was going to pay my school fees.

'What're you going to do about secondary school?'

'Work my arse off to get a full scholarship,' said Tobey.

He swore! He's not supposed to swear.

'If your mum heard that, you'd get what for,' I told him.

'Mum's the one who told me that I need to work my arse off to get anywhere,' said Tobey.

'And she used those words?'

'Those exact words,' said Tobey.

Maybe one day I would work out grown-ups and their 'do as I say, don't do as I do' escape route. But not today.

Jude versus Jasmine

thirty. Jude

I still can't believe it. Jasmine Mad-Bitch Hadley is in my hotel room. *My* hotel room. How did she know where to find me? I'd fallen down on Jude's law number fourteen: *Stay organized, stay one step ahead, stay alive.* It served me right. I'd been celebrating my final act of revenge on Persephone Hadley and her offspring. A couple of beers from the mini-bar and then I'd thought, Sod it, this calls for more than just beer. This calls for *champagne*. So I'd rung room service and ordered a bottle of the best vintage the hotel had.

'None of your fizzy muck pulled down from the top of a cupboard,' I warned the man at the other end. And then I'd sat back on the bed, watching TV and waiting for my champagne to be brought up. I was too busy revelling in the brilliance of my final move to be on my guard the way I should've been. A knock on the door and the assumption that the room service in this hotel was, for once, actually on the ball were all it took for me to lower my guard.

And now thanks to that one lapse in concentration, this crazy bitch is sitting on my bed, smiling at me. Not that I blame her. In her position I'd be smiling too. Even now

I can't believe I've been quite so stupid. Jasmine Hadley had me where years of countless police undercover operations and the odd traitor or two had failed. How had she found out where I was? Callie couldn't've told her. And the green windcheater Jasmine wore on her scrawny, meagre body – that was Callie's. It was unmistakable. The inside of the windcheater was lined with the pockets I'd instructed Callie to sew into it, and each pocket was filled with explosives. Enough to send this room and the roof above it into orbit. Wearing the windcheater, Jasmine looked like a stick wrapped in a double duvet. She must've had liposuction and nips and tucks up to yazoo to look the way she did. There wasn't a spare bit of fat anywhere on her. Her hair was black with the odd wisp of silver around her temples and her face was very carefully made up, with just the right shade of burgundy lipstick, just the right amount of black mascara on her eyelashes, eyebrows professionally shaped, eyelids coloured with silver and the merest smudge of purple. All very immaculately done. Here was a woman who definitely meant business. I'd have to figure out very carefully what my next move should be because I had no doubt, one false move on my part and Jasmine Hadley would blow us both to kingdom come. I thought about trying to distract her and then charging. But we were a good two metres apart, more than enough time for her to flick the switch. I thought about the knife I had strapped to the inside of one leg and the backup gun I had strapped to the other, both hidden by my trouser legs. There had to be a way to get to my gun and blow her away before she could return the favour. I just had to bide my time and wait for my moment. And life had taught me that opportunities always came, you just had to wait for them and recognize them when they arrived.

'So what happens now?' I asked softly.

Jasmine shrugged. 'We wait.'

'For what?'

Jasmine glanced down at her watch, before looking back at me.

'We wait,' she repeated.

And she didn't take her finger off that switch.

Not once.

thirty-one. Jasmine

I'll say one thing for Jude, he met my gaze without flinching or turning away. I was more nervous than he was. I guess he did this kind of thing every other day. How did someone like Jude spend his days? Dreaming and scheming? And how did he sleep at night? Probably like a log. There'd be no doubts or anxieties to cloud his sky. And no regrets either. Lucky him. There came an unexpected knock at the door behind me.

'Room service,' said a cheery voice.

I turned my head. Big mistake. I sensed rather than saw the moment Jude pounced.

'Come in!' I screamed out, and I leaned back rather than trying to jump up. Half a heartbeat later, I was flat against the bed with Jude's guns digging into my back through my coat and Jude's hands around my throat. The hotel door opened. My heart shrieking inside me, I tried to get my hand on the switch in my pocket. Jude's body was a dead weight on mine as his hands descended to fumble around for my own. He should've gone for my hands straight away. Pouncing like that had knocked the stuffing out of me, but the couple of seconds where he'd gone for my throat had afforded me just enough time to get my thumb back on the switch.

'Boom!' I whispered as his hand closed over mine.

Jude instantly removed his hand.

The waiter emerged from round the corner to see Jude lying on top of me on the bed.

'Oh, excuse me!'

'Get off me,' I hissed at Jude. Jude pushed himself up onto his hands and moved away. I sat up, fighting to get my breath back. Now that the adrenalin had stopped coursing through my body, I felt an ache in my back where the guns had been pressing and a burning pain in my chest. I didn't want to do that again in a hurry. I glanced at the nought waiter, who was redder than a summer sunset.

'S-sorry! I'm so sorry. I did knock.' The waiter looked at the carpet, the wardrobe, back at the bathroom door – anywhere but at me and Jude.

'Sit. You're embarrassing the waiter.' I pointed to Jude's previous chair with my free hand.

Jude reluctantly sat down.

'W-where would you like your champagne?' asked the waiter.

'Next to me on the bed,' I replied, not taking my eyes off Jude for a second.

I felt the bottle slightly depress the bed beside me.

'Who'd like to sign for it?' queried the waiter with diffidence.

'Put the bill on the table in front of my friend and then step back please,' I said pleasantly.

Curious, but too well trained to question my directions, the waiter did as asked, placing a small, cheap plastic pen on top of the narrow bill. Faking nonchalance, he had both hands on his stomach, one on top of the other. But his hands kept twitching and switching places, and he kept stealing glances at Jude and me. Did he think Jude was my toy-boy lover? My bit of nought on the side? How amusing!

'Well, sign it, please – darling,' I told Jude.

Jude leaned forward to do as I asked. I watched him intently to make sure he signed his name and didn't write anything else. He didn't write Jude McGregor. It was some name like Steve Wine or Steven Winter or something like that. It was hard to read upside down. But at least it wasn't a secret message. Then I wondered if the name he'd signed was a message in itself. What better way to arouse suspicion and have the manager up here than by signing a false name?

'Sit back, cupcake. You're making the waiter nervous,' I said easily.

Slowly Jude sat back.

'All yours,' I said to the waiter.

I watched as the waiter picked up the bill and checked the signature. He smiled and didn't seem the least bit perturbed, so I relaxed. It was only natural that Jude would use any name but his own when booking into this hotel.

The waiter looked from me to Jude expectantly.

Sorry, love. No gratuity today.

'Sir. Madam.' His plastered-on, polite smile wavering only slightly, the waiter started to turn round.

'Thank you so much.' I smiled at him as he went to walk past me. 'Could you do me one last favour?'

'Of course.'

'Could you put the DO NOT DISTURB sign on the outside of the door as you leave?'

'Certainly.'

I kept my eyes on Jude as the waiter left the room, shutting the door quietly behind him. I heard him briefly fumble around with the handle as he hung up the sign.

Then silence.

Further along the corridor, a woman laughed – a happy, carefree sound. A TV started up in the room below us and the sound was instantly lowered. Then there was nothing. Just the awareness that comes with utter silence.

'So what name are you using at the moment?' I asked Jude.

'Steven Winner,' Jude replied at last.

'Steven Winner,' I repeated. 'Where did you get that from?'

Jude didn't answer.

'When was the last time you were Jude McGregor?' I couldn't help asking.

I didn't really expect an answer, but I got one.

'When my brother died,' said Jude.

I nodded slowly. I was beginning to feel sick – and it wasn't just the situation I found myself in. I needed one of my painkillers, but they fogged my brain and clouded my judgement and I couldn't afford that. I had to stay sharp to deal with the man before me. A secret smile slashed its way across Jude's face. Inside, I went very still. Jude's eyes narrowed till I could barely see his irises. What was he thinking? What was he up to? Or was this just a mind game, meant to throw me off guard?

Careful, Jasmine.

Be very, very careful.

 ## thirty-two. Jude

Could she do it? Could she really kill both of us by pressing that switch? If she was holding a knife or even a gun, I'd've been at her throat again before she could draw her next breath. Stabbing someone took a great deal of motivation. To feel a knife slip through skin and muscle, to feel hot, gushing blood rush over your hand as you did so, that took a great deal. To look someone in the eye and pull a trigger knowing that you were about to end their life, that still took a great deal even if it wasn't as *intimate* as stabbing. But flicking a switch, that was different. Detached. Remote. Like turning out a light. What had Mad-Bitch Hadley told herself before she'd entered this room? That she wasn't really killing me? That the bomb was going to kill her and if I happened to be in the room, then it was just so much collateral damage? The ultimate in sanitary killing. Flick the switch and then nothing. No mess, no fuss – not for either of us at any rate. For those left behind to pick up our pieces afterwards, it'd be a different story. But that wouldn't be her problem and no doubt she was counting on it not being mine either.

But would she do it? It was hard to tell. She was practised at keeping her expression mask-like. So what to do, Jude? What to do? Talk her down? Reason with her? Get her to talk to me, make a connection, make her see me as a person so that when the crucial moment comes . . .

But what should I say? Hell, this woman and me have nothing in common. I don't know her. I don't want to know her. But I've got so much that I still have to do. So much to organize. More dreams and schemes to put into operation. I can't let this woman stop all that. So talk to her, Jude. Say something.

'How's your daughter Minerva?'

'The one you shot all those years ago?'

I almost flinched at her words. I'd forgotten all about that. I'd allowed Minerva to fly beneath my radar years ago. Minerva didn't interest me. Only her sister, Sephy.

'Minerva's fine,' Jasmine continued.

'Still a journalist?'

'News subeditor now,' said Jasmine.

'Is she married?'

'For five years. She has a boy called Taj and she's expecting her second child.'

That, I pounced on. 'I bet you can't wait.'

Jasmine didn't answer.

'You must be so excited,' I said, trying unsubtly to get her to think about all the things she'd miss out on if she flicked that switch. 'Will it be a boy or a girl? D'you know?'

'A boy – so Minerva tells me.'

'Another boy,' I nodded. 'Another grandchild for you to love.'

'What would you know about love, Jude?' asked Jasmine quietly. 'Have you ever loved anyone in your entire life?'

My heartbeat slowed at the question, but regained its regular rhythm almost immediately.

'Has anyone ever touched you? Moved you? Made you forget who and what you are for long enough to make you happy?' Jasmine persisted. 'Have you ever even liked anyone – including yourself? Especially yourself?'

'What difference could it possibly make to you?' I asked.

'None, I guess,' Jasmine agreed. 'I'm just curious.'

I didn't reply. We sat in silence for a while. Jasmine began to rock on the bed, backwards and forwards, very slowly. Her eyes were clouding over, her expression pinching in on itself. I frowned inwardly, careful to keep it off my face. If I didn't know any better, I'd say she was in pain. But she couldn't be – unless I'd managed to hurt her more than I'd thought when I was trying to get her hand away from the switch in her pocket. I should've snapped her twig-like arm when I had the chance, rather than going for her scrawny neck. That'd been a big mistake on my part. I wouldn't make another. What to say? What should I ask her? I was trained for this. There were many gambits open to me – but I chose a risky one.

'Why haven't you detonated your bomb yet?'

'It's not time.' Jasmine glanced at her watch again.

'What're we waiting for?' I said.

'Company.'

Sephy versus
Callie Rose

thirty-three. Sephy

Callie Rose was ricocheting off the cellar door like a squash ball being hit incessantly off a wall. Rattling the handle and screaming for my mum for the last hour hadn't worked so now she was trying something more drastic. She was also giving me a headache. I sat down on the stone floor, my back against the cool, plastered wall. The wine cellar was on the chilly side of comfortable and the two sixty-watt bulbs which provided the only dim yellowy light didn't exactly add to the ambience. Hell, could I sound any more like my mother!

'Callie, please sit down. That won't do any good,' I told her.

She ignored me and carried on bounce, bounce, bouncing off the solid, wooden door. It would take a bulldozer to get through that door, anyone with half an eye could see that – but then my daughter never was one to admit defeat.

I looked around the cellar. Well, we wouldn't die of thirst at any rate. Cirrhosis of the liver maybe, but not thirst. How like my mother to keep a full cellar for her guests, even though she herself, as an ex-alcoholic, could never touch a drop. Just another example of her iron self-control. There were no windows and the only door to the cellar had been locked from the outside. I glanced at my watch. It was early afternoon, although it certainly didn't feel like it. It felt like the middle of the night. With no windows to indicate the time of day, the quality of time had subtly changed.

'Isn't your shoulder hurting yet?' I asked.

Ignoring me, Callie walked – well, more like stalked – angrily across the room and ran towards the door at full throttle. She hit it with her shoulder and, in the time it took to yowl with pain, she was flat on her backside, her legs an ungainly mess on the stone floor as she tried to figure out which part of her body hurt most.

My patience ran out. 'That's enough, Callie Rose. More than enough. If you break your fool neck, there's not much I can do for you in here.'

'You put Nana Jasmine up to this, didn't you?' Callie spun round to blaze at me.

I sighed. I had been waiting for that. We'd been in here for a couple of hours now and Callie hadn't said a single word to me. She'd strode up and down the cellar in between chucking herself at the door at irregular intervals and calling for my mum, but I was totally ignored. But I knew that sooner or later the accusations and recriminations would start. I watched as my daughter rubbed her arm, which had to be sore as hell by now. She'd have a whole assortment of bruises there in a few hours, not to mention one or two stunners in other places where she'd hit the stone floor as she fell backwards. She was just lucky that she hadn't dislocated her shoulder – not that I was stupid enough to say that out loud. Callie kneeled up, then stood up, still rubbing her shoulder and arm. I watched as she marched across the wine cellar to the furthest point away from me that she could get. She sat down so that we were directly opposite each other and at least six metres apart.

'Did you tell Nana Jasmine to lock this door?' Callie demanded.

'Now why would I do that?' I replied.

'How did she know what I was going to do? Did you tell her?'

'How could I tell her? Did you tell me anything?'

'Then how did she find out?'

'Find out what?'

'Don't act any dumber than you already are,' Callie hissed at me.

'Don't take that tone with me, Callie Rose. I'm still your mother.'

'In name only.'

And though I'd heard it before, it still hurt. It always hurt. I turned away.

'Believe me, I don't like this any more than you do.'

Callie snorted her disbelief. I sat still, watching her as she drew up her feet and put her arms around her knees. Even after all these years, I still found it hard to keep my eyes off her. She was so incredibly beautiful. The most beautiful thing I've seen in this world. From the day she was born, sixteen years ago today, I thought she was the most incredibly beautiful thing I'd ever seen. Callie turned to face me. I immediately looked away.

'So what happens now?' asked Callie with venom.

I shrugged. 'We wait for your nan to come to her senses and open the door, I guess.'

'This isn't on,' cried Callie. 'I've got to get out of here.'

'Are you really in such a hurry to complete your mission?' It slipped out before I could stop myself.

Callie's expression turned truly glacial as she regarded me.

'So much for not knowing what I was up to.'

For once I didn't look away immediately. I forced myself to meet her contemptuous gaze. I allowed myself to be swept away by it, to drown in it – the way I'd done so many times before. The way I would willingly do again. Because at least she was here to hate me. At least I had that. I watched my daughter conjure up the filthiest look in her vast arsenal before she turned away with complete disdain. I didn't mind that so much. It meant I could watch her, drink her in without her protest.

Look at our daughter, Callum. Isn't she beautiful, so very beautiful? She laughs like me, but when she smiles . . . Oh, Callum, when she smiles, it's picnics in Celebration Park and sunsets on our beach and our very first kiss all over again. When Callie Rose smiles at me, she lights up my life.

When Callie Rose smiles at me.

thirty-four.
Callie Rose

If Mum thinks I'm going to even look at her, let alone speak to her, then she's got another think coming. I'll just sit this out. I can do that. And eventually Nana Jasmine will tire of playing silly buggers and open the cellar door. Besides, I know Mum did this. Nana Jasmine might've locked us in here but I bet Mum put her up to it. And after bashing into the door like they do in films in an effort to break it down, all I had to show for it was an arm that felt like it'd been used as a punch bag by the world heavyweight champion.

'Callie Rose, I promise I didn't tell your nan to lock us in here,' said Mum.

'I don't believe you,' I shot back.

'Why would I lie, love?'

'Don't call me that,' I said, stung. 'Don't ever call me that.'

'Why does it bother you so much?' Mum asked quietly.

'Because you don't mean it,' I snapped back. 'So why bother saying it? It's just more lies.'

Mum sat silently watching me for moment after long moment. I wondered what she was thinking. It was so hard to read her expression, to read her moods and her face – not like Nana Jasmine and Nana Meggie. I knew where I was with them.

'Callie, d'you remember when you were about seven and we were having breakfast together one day and I told you what you could do if we were in a plane crash together?'

Vaguely. I frowned at Mum. 'Why?'

'What d'you remember of our conversation?' asked Mum.

My frown deepened. Why was she bringing that up now? Why bring up something that happened nine years ago? But I remembered more and more about that morning as the seconds slunk by. That morning began to play in my head like a film.

Mum kept looking at me in an odd way. A very odd way. I sat at the table, eating bran flakes with warm milk and a sprinkle of demerara on the top and Mum sat opposite me, eating purple grapes. One individual grape after another, not handfuls at once the way I liked to eat them. Anyway, I looked up from my bran flakes 'cause I sensed I was being watched. And I was right.

'Yes, Mum?'

'Rosie, if we're in a plane and it crashes onto a snow-covered mountain and everyone stops looking for us 'cause they think we're already dead, well if I'm dead and you're alive, you have my permission to eat me to keep yourself alive,' said Mum. 'I'd recommend the muscles in my thighs and my arms first. They're not too fatty.'

Tears sprang up from nowhere, watering my eyes before escaping down my cheeks.

'What's wrong with you?' Mum asked, surprised.

'Don't talk about plane crashes. I don't like it.'

'I was just saying,' said Mum. 'Talking about it doesn't mean it's going to happen.'

'Stop talking about it.' I raised my voice.

'OK, OK. I didn't mean to upset you.'

'Well, you did,' I said, wiping my eyes. 'I don't want to talk about you in a plane crash any more.'

Mum pulled another purple grape off the stem before her. 'I was just saying,' she shrugged, before popping the grape into her mouth.

I picked up my dessertspoon and shoved it down into my bran flakes. Then I rammed the full spoon into my mouth.

'Rose, love, there's no need to bite the bowl off the spoon. I said I was sorry,' said Mum. 'And change your expression. You've got a face like a smacked bum at the moment.'

I carried on chewing, although I did slow down a bit. But I was still upset. What a thing to say to me. Mum picked up her grapes and went into the kitchen. I watched her walk away from me, wondering why on earth she'd started talking about planes crashing. I couldn't figure it out.

Even now I didn't know what that was all about. At seven I had just thought she was being very weird. But then, to my mind, she always had been. I've lost count of the number of times we'd be watching TV or I'd be lying on the living-room floor, reading, and I'd look up to find Mum watching me. And always with the same, strange look on her face. And sometimes I caught Mum watching me and Nana Meggie watching Mum.

That was our house, everyone watching everyone else.

'What d'you think Nana Jasmine will do?' I asked reluctantly, admitting, 'I'm worried.'

I risked a glance at Mum without moving my head.

'Your nan will be fine,' Mum dismissed.

'Not if she messes about with the carrier bag I brought with me,' I said.

'Why? What's in it?'

I didn't want to tell her but what could I do? I had to get out of here. If Nana Jasmine took my windcheater out of the bag and fiddled around with the switch . . . With the stone walls and the thickness of the door, we'd probably be safe from the blast here in the cellar, but Nana Jasmine . . . It didn't bear thinking about.

'What's in it, Callie Rose?'

'Something . . . dangerous if you don't know what you're doing. And Nana Jasmine doesn't.'

'I see.'

I doubted it.

'It's a bomb, isn't it?' said Mum quietly.

I stared at her.

'Answer me, Callie Rose.'

I nodded, then cursed myself for doing so. Mum's tone had momentarily cast me back at least ten years. I was a little girl again, cowering in her angry wake. Mum pushed herself up onto her feet and headed for the locked door. She banged on the door as hard as she could. I saw her wince as her fists made impact with the door but she only stopped banging on the door for long enough to shout, 'Mother? Can you hear me? Mother?'

Silence.

My mum tried again. 'Mother, open the door. Mother?'

Still nothing. Mum turned to look at me, her eyes like lasers, searing into mine. But she blinked and blinked again, and behind her anger, I could see something else: wide-eyed anxiety.

'What will Nana Jasmine do with my carrier bag?' I whispered.

'Is the bomb hidden?'

I lowered my head. 'Not particularly. I packed my windcheater full of explosives and the switch is in the windcheater pocket.'

'Does Mother know what's in your carrier bag?'

'I . . . don't know,' I admitted. 'I think she suspects . . . something. What will she do?'

Mum shook her head. 'I don't know. I hope that when she sees what's in it, she'll put the windcheater some-where safe and away from here, then phone the police and tell them where to find it.'

'Then she'll come back here and give me a long lecture about the way my life is going,' I said with disdain.

'If you're lucky,' Mum shot back. 'Who was the bomb for? Or didn't you care?'

I didn't answer.

Mum banged on the door one more time, her frustra-tion evident, before she turned back to me. She took a step, only to stop abruptly. I watched myriad discernible expressions pass over Mum's face as she looked at me, glared at me, stared at me. 'You . . . you were really will-ing to maim and kill innocent people? You were prepared to do that?'

I said nothing.

'Do you really have so much rage inside that you're ready to kill yourself and others?'

Not rage, Mum. Something else. But not rage.

Mum walked slowly back to her previous place away from me and sat down.

'Callie Rose, what the hell are you doing? Does your life mean so little to you?'

'My life is my own,' I told Mum, adding pointedly, 'No thanks to you.'

We regarded each other.

'I see,' Mum said at last, nodding slowly. 'I see.'

And I knew she did.

thirty-five. Sephy

No thanks to you . . .

Who told her? Mother? No, it had to be Meggie. Who else? How long had she known? I suddenly felt very sick. I pulled my thick-knit cardigan more tightly around me. It was one of my favourites, purple with white flowers embroidered onto it. The cardigan had been a present from Mother, who had impeccable taste. Although I was wearing a long skirt and a light-knit lilac jumper under my cardigan, I could still feel that the cellar had moved from distinctly chilly and graduated to downright cold. I risked a glance at Callie Rose. Her black short-sleeved T-shirt and thin, black fashion jacket couldn't have been doing much to keep out the chill.

'Would you like my cardigan?' I asked.

'No. I don't want anything from you,' snapped Callie.

Talk about cutting off your nose to spite your entire face. I could see my daughter shivering from across the cellar but she'd rather turn into an icicle than take anything from me. I stood up and walked over to her. She watched my approach with a malignant frown. I pulled off my cardigan and held it out.

'Take it, Callie Rose,' I told her.

'I just said—'

'I don't care what you said,' I interrupted. 'Take the cardigan. Then you'll have the pleasure of watching me freeze.'

Common sense battled rebellious defiance on Callie's face. I could read every advance and retreat each side made. Finally common sense won out and Callie raised a reluctant hand to take the cardigan. Careful to keep my expression neutral, I handed it over and headed back to my corner of the room.

Now that my cardigan was gone, the cold was even more oppressive. When did Mother plan to let us out? Our plan, such as it was, didn't seem to be working. And to make things worse, Meggie had told my daughter what'd happened when she was a baby. I'd suspected as much for a while but suspicions weren't the same as direct confirmation. What exactly had Meggie told her?

And when?

And why?

Or was I being totally naïve? The why was only too obvious. And as far as Meggie was concerned it was mission accomplished. I watched Callie, making no attempt now to hide what I was doing. She wore my cardigan over her jacket. Her arms were wrapped around her bent legs with her head resting on her knees. Her long braids draped like a curtain across her face as she looked to one side.

Do something, Sephy. You might not get another chance. Do something.

But what? A wave of hopelessness washed over me. Suppose nothing I said or did at this point made the slightest bit of difference? Well, if that was the case, what did I have to lose?

'D'you want to see a photo of your dad?'

Callie's head snapped up. Shocked, she stared at me.

'You've got a picture?'

I nodded. 'D'you want to see it?'

'Which photo is it?'

'The only one I've got of me and your dad together.'

Callie was on her feet and halfway towards me before she even realized what she was doing.

'It was taken just before I went to Chivers boarding school,' I told her as I got to my feet. 'I was around fifteen and your dad was sixteen or seventeen. I think that's right. Maybe I was fourteen. It's hard to remember exactly.'

Callie stood before me. She stretched out her hand. I dug the photograph out of my left skirt pocket and handed it over. Callie looked down at it for the longest time. When she looked at me I was taken aback by the fury on her face.

'Callie . . . ?'

'This is the photograph I found hidden in your wardrobe all those years ago, isn't it? The one you nearly hit me for looking at?'

'I didn't—'

Callie Rose tore my photograph in two. Then tore it again and again.

'Noooo.' I tried to snatch the photo away from her but she stepped back and carried on ripping. I tried to catch the pieces as they fluttered to the ground but their erratic, irregular dance eluded me and I caught only a couple of fragments. I fell to my knees, scooping up the pieces as best I could, but the scraps were slippery and slid under my fingers. It was futile. The last – the *only* – photograph I had of Callum and me was gone. I looked down at the pieces, each fragment evoking a memory. The years since the photo had been taken rolled back in an instant.

I was a girl again, screaming with laughter as I ran from Callum as he chased me on the beach. Callum and I doing schoolwork together, sharing answers and smiles. Our picnics in Celebration Park, followed by the inevitable food fights. Exchanging Crossmas presents on the beach. The look on Callum's face when I gave him the best astronomy book I could afford for his thirteenth birthday. I was young again, still a teenager and watching Callum die, wishing I'd done as my father told me to save my love's life. If I could've found my dad in the crowd as they placed the hood over Callum's head, I would've got down on my knees and begged for Callum's life. I would've promised Dad anything he wanted.

I looked up at Callie Rose, tears tumbling down my cheeks.

'How could you?' I whispered, my voice cracking. 'How could you be so cruel?'

'Easy,' Callie Rose replied. 'You taught me.'

thirty-six.
Callie Rose

She's stopped crying now. The tears didn't last very long. I hate this. She's radiating defeat and it's like X-rays passing straight through me. I never meant to make her cry. But that photograph . . .

Mum and Dad together.

Proof positive that they were an item. And Dad was smiling and he looked so happy. That's why I tore it up. I couldn't bear it. Him and Mum looking so happy. What about me? He had no right to be happy after all the things he did, all the things I've read and heard about. He had no right.

But he was still my dad.

I've followed in his footsteps, 'cause I'm my father's daughter. But I hate him so much. He left me with no path but his. And following it has left me so tired. My head is all over the place. My throat has swollen to twice its normal size so that I can't swallow and I can hardly breathe. I grit my teeth and stretch out my fingers until my joints ache. I make a fist so fierce and strong, it's watertight. The floor starts to swim and blur beneath me.

Mum wipes her eyes. I wanted her to hurt like me, a way-down-inside, deep-rooted kind of hurt. So deep inside it can't be separated from anything else.

But I didn't mean to make her cry.

thirty-seven. Sephy

Callum, if you're up there, somewhere, I need your help. Our daughter hates you and me and the whole world. And I did that. Because I wore my fear like a dress of nettles. Because I lied to her. And when I was ready to tell the truth, it was too late. Oh, Callum, what should I do? I have to do something or all this will be for nothing. You and I will have been for nothing.

Mother said the only way Callie Rose and I were ever going to resolve our differences was if we sat down and talked together, really talked. But it's hard to talk when the other person doesn't want to listen. Not that I blame her. If my life were a canvas, I'd paint over it and start again from scratch. I left my canvas semi-blank for years, terrified of messing it up. A little daub here, a smear of paint there and I convinced myself I was doing great work. I was just deluding myself.

Callum, please open her heart to hear me.

Please, God, give me another chance.

What a joke! Except the joke's on me. I'm praying to a God I told myself I didn't believe in any more. When Callum died, I stopped believing.

But, God, if you are up there, somewhere, then please help us.

It was Mother's idea to put us both in here.

'She'll have no choice but to listen to you and you'll have to listen to her,' Mother argued.

'But she'll just walk out,' I said. 'Callie Rose can't even bear to be in the same house as me, never mind the same room.'

'We'll just see about that,' said Mother. 'I'll get her into the cellar, then the rest is up to you.'

But now I'm sitting here, worrying about Mum handling Callie's carrier bag. And Callie Rose and I are as far apart as ever.

I don't wish for impossible things. I don't expect Callie Rose to love me or respect me. But I want her to find peace. I want her to stop hating the world. I need her to believe that people are worth fighting for, that life is worth not just living, but celebrating. But how can she ever learn that? Certainly not from my example. I buried myself in the past for years, until it was almost too late for me and definitely too late for my daughter. I wasn't there, but Jude was. And now she's walking down Jude's road.

And I know only too well where it ends.

Please, God, I don't want that for my daughter.

Am I being naïve in thinking that hating and dying for a cause is the easy way out? Surely it's far harder to live and love and fight and survive? I remember a lifetime ago when I was locked in a dirty room and held for ransom. I remember when there was just me and Callum.

I tried to tell him the same thing, but he wouldn't listen. He didn't believe me any more than his daughter does now.

'Was that really the only photo you had of you and my dad?' Callie's voice made me jump.

'Yes,' I replied, not looking at her.

Silence.

'I bet you hate me even more now,' Callie said at last.

I turned shocked eyes towards her. 'Never. I could never hate you, Callie Rose. And there's nothing you could do that would ever make me hate you.'

'Yeah, right,' Callie scoffed.

'That's the truth.'

'Don't pretend, Mum. You've hated me from the day I was born,' she flung at me.

'I could never hate you.' I would repeat it and repeat it until she heard me. I'd repeat it until my dying day if I had to.

'You don't hate me, Mum?' Callie said with scorn. 'Then why did you try to kill me?'

Sonny came round to childsit today. (Not babysit. I'm not a baby any more – thank you very much!) I like Sonny. He makes me laugh. We went to the park for a walk and to feed the ducks on the kidney-shaped lake, which was his idea, not mine. After that we had lunch outside the local café even though the wind was sharp enough to make me shiver once or twice. We both had a couple of buttery baguettes stuffed with sausages, fried onions and enough dripping tomato ketchup on mine to make my hand look like a crime scene. And I enjoyed it all the more because I knew Nana Jasmine would be horrified to see me eating on the street, and eating something so messy. Ha! After that we ambled home and sat together on the sofa watching cartoons on the TV.

'Rose, I need to ask you something,' said Sonny.

I turned to face him. Sonny pressed the button on the remote control to turn off the TV – which was a shame 'cause it was right in the middle of one of my most favourite bits. But Sonny looked very serious so I didn't argue.

'Rose, what d'you think of the idea of your mum and me getting together?'

'To do what?' I asked. 'Sing some more?'

'No, love. What I mean is, I want your mum and me to live together. What d'you think of that idea?'

'Where would I go?'

'You'd live with us too, silly head,' said Sonny ruffling my hair – which I hate.

'Why d'you want Mum and me to live with you?' I frowned.

'Because I love you both very much, silly head,' said Sonny. He tried to ruffle my hair again, but I was too fast for him. I ducked out of the way in time. Ha! And then I realized with a start what he'd just said.

'Do you really love me?' I asked Sonny.

'Of course I do,' said Sonny. 'What's not to love?'

No one had ever told me that before.

'Wait till I tell Mum . . .'

'No, don't do that,' said Sonny quickly. 'I want to tell your mum myself. These things have to be done just right.'

'Oh, OK,' I said, feeling like a balloon with all the air let out of it. Then I thought of something else. 'Would you be my dad then?'

Sonny didn't answer at once. Then he said, 'I wouldn't try to take the place of your real dad, but I'd be happy to call you my daughter. I'd legally adopt you – if you were willing. And in the future if you ever wanted to, I'd be proud to have you call me your dad.'

Which meant a lot to me – and the words hadn't even sunk in fully yet. He was saying that I could call him Dad if I wanted to – which was so, so wonderful. To have a real, live dad. Not a substitute, but kind of like an addition.

'So when are you going to ask Mum about living together?' I asked.

'As soon as she gets home,' smiled Sonny.

As if she knew we were talking about her, Mum chose just that moment to step through the front door. I sprang up from the sofa and ran into the hall to meet her, skidding a bit on the wooden floor as I was still in my socks. Mum put down the four bulging carrier bags she was carrying before turning to shut the door.

'Mum, guess what? Sonny wants to—'

'Rose, let me tell your mum myself,' Sonny interrupted from behind me.

I clapped both hands over my mouth. I'd forgotten that I wasn't supposed to say anything.

Sonny picked up Mum's shopping and carried it into the kitchen, winking at me as he walked past. Mum and me followed him.

Mum smiled suspiciously. 'What're you two up to?'

'Sonny has something to ask you.' I nodded at Mum. I knew something she didn't. Ha!

'I'm listening,' Mum said directly to Sonny.

'Actually, I was hoping we could discuss it over dinner later,' said Sonny.

'Sounds serious,' said Mum, her smile slowly falling off her face.

'It's nothing bad,' said Sonny. 'Meggie has agreed to babysit, so I thought we could have a few hours to ourselves. I've booked us a table at your favourite restaurant.'

From the look on Mum's face, I thought she was going to insist that Sonny spill the beans immediately, but she said, 'OK then. Pick me up at seven-thirty?'

'That's fine. I'll see you later, Sephy. Bye, Rosie.' Sonny walked past me, ruffling my hair again. When I gave him my very best stern look, he grinned at me, which didn't help. He and Mum had a kiss (yuk!) which would've grown up into a snog but Mum pulled away first. Sonny smiled at Mum then headed out the door.

'What was that all about?' Mum asked me when the front door was shut.

'I promised I wouldn't say,' I said in my most grown-up voice. 'It's a surprise.'

'I don't like surprises.'

'You'll like this one.'

Mum shrugged and started unpacking the groceries.

'Want some help? No? OK!' I said quickly before scooting back into the living room.

'Callie Rose, get your lazy bum back in here please,' said Mum.

Charming!

I headed back to the kitchen.

'Nice try, love,' Mum said wryly. 'Grab a bag.'

'I just need to run away faster,' I replied.

I looked at Mum and started smiling – and then I couldn't stop.

'What's the matter with you?' asked Mum.

'Nothing. I'm just happy,' I told her.

The look Mum gave me was almost . . . worried. But then she smiled and I shook my head, telling myself not to imagine things. Mum and Sonny were going to live together, maybe even get married. How cool was that!

thirty-nine. Sephy

Specimens was a strange name for a restaurant, but I loved it there. It was classy and understated and they served the best monkfish in lemon sauce I'd ever eaten. I looked around, soaking up the mellow atmosphere. Sonny and I got the occasional look but on the whole, nothing too hostile. Mostly just curious. Well, let them look. Let the whole world look.

'Sephy, can I ask you something?'

'You don't need my permission, Sonny,' I smiled. Why did he always ask that before every question? It drove me mad!

'I want you to count to at least ten before answering,' said Sonny. He rubbed at his right eyebrow, the way he always did when he was nervous.

'I'm all agog!' I teased.

And still he didn't spit it out. I took a sip of my white wine, waiting for Sonny to get to the point. He took hold of my free hand, which up until that point had been resting on the restaurant table minding its own business.

And it still didn't click. I took another sip of my wine. I never had more than one glass a day, under any circumstances. I was good at making a glass of wine last all evening. Sonny raised my hand to his lips and kissed it.

'I love you, Sephy – you know that. So . . . will you marry me?'

My mouthful of white wine decided to make a break for it. Some shot out of my mouth and most shot out of my nose. I was mortified. I grabbed my napkin and tried to dab up the last of my shattered composure. I coughed and spluttered into the napkin, trying and failing to not draw attention to myself.

'Is that a yes or a no?' said Sonny wryly.

'Are you serious?'

Sonny's smile faded. 'Yes, of course.'

'Oh, Sonny . . .'

Sonny raised a hand to stop me in mid-flight. 'You promised me ten seconds before you answered.'

Ten seconds or ten years – my answer would still be the same.

'Sonny, why can't we just carry on as we are?' I asked.

'Because I love you and what we have isn't enough any more. I want to be a permanent part of your life. I want you to be a permanent part of mine,' said Sonny seriously.

'Isn't that what we have now?' I tried desperately.

'You know it isn't,' said Sonny.

I tried to find some way to answer him, but my mind had emptied, all rational thoughts vanishing in a puff of panic. Sonny took the napkin off his lap and threw it down on the table before he sat back and studied me.

'Sometimes I think it wouldn't bother you if you never saw me again.'

'That's not true.'

'Isn't it?' Sonny crossed his arms.

His body language was speaking volumes.

'If that's what you really believe then why marry me?' I asked.

'I'm an optimist,' Sonny shot back. 'I'm hoping you'll let yourself love me – one day.'

'Sonny, I don't want to marry you or anyone else,' I said unhappily.

'Why not? I know I'm not Callum but—'

'He has nothing to do with this,' I said more harshly than I'd intended.

'No? Then why do I always feel like a minor player in a *ménage à trois* whenever we're together?'

'What're you talking about?'

'Callum surrounds every part of your life, but in bed with you is where I feel his presence most strongly.'

'That's not . . .' I lowered my voice, aware that we were beginning to attract a great deal of unwelcome attention. 'That's not true. If I felt that way about him, you wouldn't've made it past my bedroom door.'

'So how d'you feel about him?' Sonny challenged. 'You've never said.'

'That's because you've never asked.'

'I'm asking now.'

Sonny was making a poor job of masking his disappointment, although I knew I was doing him a disservice to call it that. His feelings went far deeper, ran far hotter.

'Callum is . . . was the past. I let go of the past a long time ago.'

'You've never let it go, Sephy. The past rules your life, it dictates your actions and clouds your judgement.'

'What're you talking about?'

'You judge everyone you meet by what happened to you and Callum. You don't let anyone get close to you because you immediately judge the whole world to be your enemy. You expect everyone to be against you so you never let your guard down.'

'That's not true.'

'Isn't it? If you'd really let go of the past like you claim, then you'd love me the way I love you.'

My heart doubled in size and weight inside my chest and told me – as if I didn't already know – just how unwelcome were Sonny's words. My gaze danced away from his as I struggled to find the right thing to say.

'I want us to get married, Sephy,' Sonny continued.

Had I imagined the trace of desperation in his voice? Unfortunately I didn't think so.

'Sonny, we're happy the way we are, aren't we? I don't want to lose that.'

'Marrying me will give us both more. That's what I want. More,' Sonny immediately replied.

But there was no more.

Sonny sat back, never taking his eyes off me. 'Do you love me?'

I couldn't lie. Even my silence couldn't lie.

Sonny nodded to himself, acknowledging his own private thoughts. I wondered what he was thinking but I was too afraid to ask. I so desperately didn't want to lose him.

'I guess if you don't love me by now, you never will,' said Sonny. The finality of his tone was soft and sad and brought unbidden tears to my eyes.

'Sonny, I—'

'No.' Sonny raised a hand to stave off my words. 'I lost you when Jaxon threw you out of the band just after Callie was born and I did nothing to stop him.'

'Sonny, that was many moons ago. When you came back into my life, I was glad to see you. You know I was.'

Sonny came knocking on my door less than a year after I came out of hospital, when Callie was a toddler. I still remember how happy I was to see him. It'd been instant hugs and smiles — and a certain amount of relief on Sonny's part. I think he half expected me to slam the door in his face. And a few months after that, we'd started working together.

'But I didn't stand up for you, did I?' said Sonny. 'Jaxon bounced you out of our band and I never argued. That's when I lost your respect and you'd never love someone you couldn't respect.'

'Sonny, that's nonsense. I forgave you years ago.'

'But you haven't forgotten, have you?'

How to answer that? I couldn't lie.

'I . . . I don't . . . forget . . .' I murmured unhappily. How many times over the years had I wished I could do exactly that? How many times had I longed for even my dreams to be free from memories? 'But that doesn't mean anything. Sonny, what happened before, that's not why I don't want to get married. It's not that I don't want to marry you. I just don't want to marry anyone.'

'You just haven't found the right man yet,' Sonny surmised.

'Even the right man couldn't convince me to marry him,' I dismissed carelessly.

'Thanks, Persephone,' said Sonny quietly.

Oh hell! 'I didn't mean it like that,' I tried.

Sonny didn't reply. I didn't know what to say to make things better. He regarded me with such resigned sadness that tears pricked my eyes again. God knows, the last thing I wanted to do was hurt him.

'I need to get out of here.' Sonny started to stand up.

I grabbed his arm. 'Sonny, please . . .'

'What?'

'Don't go.'

'Why?'

What to do? What to say? 'Thousands of reasons.'

Sonny looked at me before he said at last, 'Just one would've done.'

We regarded each other, the same quality of sadness on both our faces. And where we'd been swimming together before, I could now feel the current tearing us apart and pulling us in opposite directions.

'D'you hate me?' I whispered.

Sonny looked at me, his eyes shimmering with tears he didn't even try to hide. 'I couldn't hate you – even if I wanted to. But I don't think we should see each other any more.'

And I thought about how much Callie Rose was going to miss him.

And I thought about how much he'd done for Meggie over the years, without any sign of welcome or appreciation or gratitude from her.

And I thought about how lost I was going to be without his warmth and friendship.

But I couldn't speak.

I watched as Sonny pulled some notes out of his wallet. He dropped them on the table, more than generous in his estimate of the cost of our meal.

'Shall we go?' he asked, standing up.

I followed his lead and stood up. We walked out of the restaurant, neither of us saying a word.

forty. Rose is 11

'Nana Meggie, d'you think Sonny will ask Mum to marry him?'

'I don't know, Callie Rose. And keep still. Every time you move your head this plait comes undone.'

'I hope he does. But even if he doesn't, he still wants me and Mum to live with him. He told me so. Isn't that great?'

Nana Meggie's hands stilled in my hair, even though I hadn't been moving my head. I turned, just in time to catch the strangest look on her face.

'What's wrong, Nana?'

'Nothing, dear,' said Nana Meggie with a smile. 'D'you . . . d'you think your mum cares for Sonny?'

''Course she does,' I said. 'He's cool.'

'So you like him too?'

'Yep. Don't you?'

'I guess,' said Nana Meggie, her fingers weaving in and out of my hair.

'It'd be so wonderful to have a home of our own,' I sighed. 'I'd miss you though, Nana Meggie.'

'Not as much as I'd miss you.' Nana Meggie kissed the top of my head. Her lips were soft on the parting in my hair and I could feel her warm breath tickling my scalp.

'We'd still be able to visit you, wouldn't we?' I turned to ask.

'Keep your head still. Of course you would, if you wanted to.'

'And you'd come and visit us?'

'I guess.'

'That's all right then,' I relaxed.

I like changes, but only when everything stays the same.

forty-one. Meggie

My chocolate-brown curtains were drawn. My bedroom door was closed and one bedside lamp provided the only light I needed. I sat at the edge of my bed, seeing more clearly than I had in a long while. Different futures rolled out before me like rugs, each with its own distinct pattern.

One pattern had Sephy and Sonny married and moving

far away with my darling Callie Rose. In that scenario, Sephy tells my granddaughter about a foolish threat made many moons ago. Something I said to Sephy which I almost instantly regretted and that neither of us have ever forgotten. Something that opened up a chasm between us that neither of us have ever been able to overcome.

Or perhaps another pattern where Sephy makes enough money to move out of my house into a place of her own with my granddaughter. Maybe she's made enough money already but stays because of the threat I made.

Or she could just tell Callie Rose the truth about why they still live with me. Then Callie Rose would despise me almost as much as I despise myself.

I couldn't bear that.

It was a mistake, a simple, desperate mistake that happened when Callie Rose was still only a toddler and Sephy had just come out of hospital after the . . . incident.

Sephy wasn't the same.

Neither was I.

During the weeks that Sephy had been away, I'd fed Callie Rose, changed her nappies, stayed up with her when she couldn't sleep, cleared up her little puddles of vomit – and relished each moment. I'd also hugged her and kissed her and loved her as my own. I watched as she became more aware of me. I thrilled as she calmed down when I picked her up. My heart soared when I blew raspberries on her tummy and she laughed joyously. It was like having Lynny and Callum back, like they'd both been reborn to me. I had someone who relied on me again. Someone I could be there for, day in, day out. And someone who *needed* me. Being with Callie Rose every day convinced me that there was something, someone worth carrying on for.

And then Sephy came home.

And each time Callie Rose cried harder when Sephy picked her up, I was secretly glad.

And every time Sephy got something wrong, I was there to shoo her out of the way and take over.

Sephy grew more and more tense as I watched her and never let her out of my sight. I knew what I was doing, but I couldn't stop. So the inevitable moment came when Sephy confronted me.

I came home one afternoon from shopping and wandered unsuspectingly into the living room to find Sephy waiting for me. She stood in the middle of the room with a large suitcase at her feet and a crying Callie Rose in her arms.

'What's going on?' I asked, my heart beating faster than a hummingbird's wings.

'Meggie, I've decided that Rose and I are going to move in with my mother. Not for ever, just for a while until I get my bearings again,' Sephy told me.

The bottom fell out of my world and I started free-falling with panic spiralling relentlessly round me.

'You can't do that,' I told Sephy.

'Yes, I can, Meggie. It's for the best. I'm just waiting for my taxi to arrive and I promise I'll phone you when I get to Mother's house,' said Sephy.

'I won't let you leave.'

'You can't stop me. Meggie, this isn't working and if I'm ever to have any kind of life with my daughter we need some time alone.' Sephy was ready to leave the room, leave my house, leave my life.

'You set foot out of this house and I'll be on to the Social Services before the front door is closed,' I warned her.

Sephy spun round. 'What did you say?'

'D'you really think the Social Services will allow Callie Rose to live with a drunk and a mental case?' My tongue began to dig feverishly at the gap opening between us. 'D'you think I'd let you take my grand-daughter away from me so you can have a second chance at killing her—'

'SHUT UP! JUST SHUT UP!' Sephy screamed at me. 'I never tried to kill her. I'd never hurt my baby. Never.'

Callie Rose started crying even louder and harder when she saw Sephy shouting at me. My granddaughter reached out her arms towards me. I stepped forward to take her, but Sephy backed away. She tried to hold Callie Rose to her but Callie wriggled harder to get out of her mum's grasp, holding out her arms to me again.

And I was *glad*.

'If you want to go to Jasmine's, you go right ahead, but you're going alone.'

'If I want to leave and take my daughter, there's not a damned thing you can do to stop me,' Sephy told me, a look on her face I'd never seen before.

'Maybe I can't, but I'll take you to court and sue for custody – and what's more, I'll win. Your dad doesn't want anything to do with you or Callie Rose and neither you nor your mum is exactly competent. You're not taking my granddaughter away from me.'

'You know my mum doesn't drink any more. And I'm better,' said Sephy.

'Let's see what the courts think, shall we? Let's see you

hold Callie Rose in court without her screaming for me. See how much of an impression that makes on the judge.'

'And you'd do that?' Sephy asked quietly.

I could only just hear the words over Callie Rose's crying. I took a look at Callie Rose and Sephy, a good look. And it was only then that I realized just what I'd been saying. My words had flown out like bullets, but now they were ricocheting around the room, and Sephy wasn't the only one they were hitting and hurting.

No, I wouldn't do that, I wanted to shout. No, I'd never do that. You're Callie's mum, you're Callum's love. I love you as my own. But please don't take my Callie Rose away. I'll die if you take Callie Rose from me . . .

Those words I wanted to say were in my eyes and in my heart.

But all Sephy had to hold onto were my desperate threats. And hold onto them she did.

That was the last true conversation we had. I took Callie Rose from Sephy's unresisting arms and watched as she picked up her suitcase and took it back upstairs.

That day I won.

That day I lost.

And now the inevitable has happened. Sephy is going to marry Sonny. I knew from the minute Sonny turned up at our doorstep all those years ago that this moment would come, but that doesn't make it any easier to take. Poor Sonny. All those years of curt animosity on my part and he could never figure out why. But now I knew what I must do. I had to show Sephy what I'd been too ashamed to say all these years.

And the only way to do that was to let her and Callie Rose go.

forty-two. Sephy

I heard Sonny's new song on the radio today. I'd heard a lot *about* it but this was the first time I'd actually heard it for myself. After only one week on release, it was already number nine in the charts with a bullet. Michaela in our local music shop reckoned it was a dead cert to get to number one. But every time it came on the radio, I deliberately ignored it – turned off the radio or switched stations.

Until today.

Today I decided to stop being quite so cowardly and just listen to it. Funny how Sonny and I had worked together for years and the couple of songs we'd sung and released together had never achieved the kind of success that Sonny had almost instantly found on his own. As a song-writing team, writing for others, we did fine. As a duet, we just didn't seem to click.

Maybe some things were just not meant to be.

Now that we were no longer together, I missed Sonny more than I ever imagined possible. How many times had I picked up the phone, ready to call him and say anything he wanted to hear? Then I'd always put it down, telling myself in no uncertain terms that I was better off without Sonny or any other man clouding my life.

But I was having more and more trouble believing that. The moments spent trying to convince myself that I'd done the right thing were getting fewer and farther between.

Had I made the biggest blunder of my life? Sonny was my dam to stop the memories overwhelming me. At least he was at the beginning of our relationship. And what did he get out of it? Not much. Only me. But that was evidently not enough. Not content with my body, he wanted my love as well.

And God knows I'd tried, but I didn't love him. I'd tried to make myself feel for him some of what I'd felt for Callum, but it just wasn't there. I wanted the same burning, yearning, tidal wave of insane passion I'd felt for Callum. But even when Sonny and I were making love, part of me held back, watching and waiting and wondering. So that couldn't be love.

Could it . . . ?

How I wished I could make myself feel. I was fond of Sonny but that seemed to be as far as I could get. And I'd had no idea how much it was eating at him – until I heard his song. It had a gentle melody, hauntingly beautiful. Just a guitar to begin with, then soft background drums and a piano. There was a solo guitar riff in the middle and I had to admit the song was one of his best. I guess it worked because it'd come from his heart.

'And now, for my song of the week,' announced the DJ, talking over the musical intro. '*Ménage à trois* by Sonny.'

I've never dipped in kinky
That ride just ain't for me

Don't need no writhing masses
To set my genie free
I don't want five, four's a crowd
Hell! More than two is one too far
I just need a single touch
Don't need a ménage à trois

And all I ever wanted
Each wish on every star
Was you, your love
All to myself
And no ménage à trois

See, when we lie together
Just me – and him and you
Every time your lips meet mine
He's kissing your lips too

And every time I touch you
He's been there before me
Don't try to reassure me
How can you even see me
When he's standing in the way?
Should I just call it a day? Yes
I guess it's time to walk away

And all I ever wanted
Each wish on every star
Was you, your love

All to myself
And no ménage à trois

I wish I'd never touched you
But my love has roots too deep
So if I want to keep you
I've no choice but to treat you
Like the couple that you are
I'm never going to win this
It's a waste of time to try
We make love, you fall asleep
I lie awake and cry

I'm throwing in the towel
It's time for me to fold
You both live on the inside
I'm out here in the cold

And all I ever wanted
Each wish on every star
Was you and your love
All to myself
And no ménage à trois

Oh, Sonny . . .

The rain finally stopped spitting on my hood. I shook my head and then pulled my hood down. The sun was already out, shining gleefully through the remaining grey-white clouds. But I was soaked. My socks felt damp and my back felt unpleasantly warm and clammy but I wasn't sure if the rain had found its way past my hood and down my back or if it was just perspiration. I unzipped my coat, welcoming the fresh breeze blowing round me. The pavement glistened from the downpour and rain raced along the gutter into the open mouth of the drain at the side of the road.

School was over for another day. In a few more weeks, junior school would be over for good. Soon I'd be starting at senior school and I was actually looking forward to it. I really couldn't wait. Neither could Mum. She was almost as excited as I was.

'Hi, Rose. Wait.'

I turned to see Tobey chugging up behind me. My heart sank like a fossilized poo. What on earth did he want? The last time we'd been together, we'd ended up having a big argument. And the time before that. And the time before that. Tobey and I did nothing but clash like angry cymbals these days. Tobey fell into step next to me. He was wearing jeans, a T-shirt with 'Whatever' written all over it in graffiti-style writing and a denim jacket.

'How did you do at your Heathcroft High interview?' asked Tobey.

I shrugged and carried on walking. 'OK, I guess. They offered me a place.'

'Same here,' Tobey told me. 'They offered me a full scholarship.'

'Congratulations. Is Heathcroft High your first choice?'

'Of course. Why? Isn't it yours?'

'It wasn't, but it is now,' I admitted. 'Mum's keen for me to go there. She says the headmistress Mrs Paxton is fantastic.'

'How does she know?'

'Mrs Paxton was a teacher at the school when Mum was there,' I told him.

Tobey was stunned. 'Mrs Paxton must be ancient.'

'Oi! My mum isn't that old,' I replied. Although I must admit, I'd thought exactly the same thing when Mum told me about the headmistress.

'It'd be fantastic if we were in the same class,' said Tobey.

'Yeah,' I said dryly. 'Because we really don't see enough of each other as it is.'

The look on Tobey's face made me instantly regret what I'd just said.

'Are you trying to tell me something?' Tobey asked quietly.

'No, Tobey. It was a joke. You do remember those, don't you?'

Tobey forced a smile. 'Even if we are in the same class, that doesn't necessarily mean that we'll be sitting next to each other.'

'Tobey, read my lips – it was a joke.'

'Maybe it'll be a joke when it grows up,' Tobey suggested.

'Pook off!'

'Charming! You'd better not let your Nana Jasmine hear you use language like that.'

'Pook doesn't mean anything,' I replied.

'Tell that to your nana when she hears it. Besides, it's the context that counts,' Tobey informed me loftily.

Sometimes he was so ruddy smart, he was almost unbearable. Tobey had spent years telling me tale after tall tale just to prove how ruddy smart he was. And I can't even remember all the times I'd got into trouble for believing him.

But not any more.

I'm eleven now. Not some kid who believes everything she's told. And certainly not from Tobey Durbridge, thank you very much. If Tobey told me blood was red, I'd deliberately cut my finger to check first.

'I hear Ella was being her usual self today,' said Tobey.

I shrugged. I didn't want to talk about Ella Cheshie. It was bad enough having to put up with her during school without talking about her after school as well. It's funny–sad about Ella and me. She was my good friend for a while – until the first time she came round my house to play. After that she didn't talk to me for ages and was always partners with someone else when we did games or dance at school. I tried my hardest to be friends with her but she'd barely even speak to me. And once she found new friends she started being nasty to me. She'd do things like come up behind me and mess about with my hair and call me a spaghetti head or string hair just because my hair just hangs and is really limp. But when it's just me and her and no one else is around, she calls it blanker hair. That really made me mad the first time she said it. I pushed her against the wall and she tripped over. Then she ran over to Miss Gardener and told on me. Tell-tale, snitching poo-head! I guess snitching runs in their family. Miss Gardener sent a letter home and Mum had to come to the school. Mum hardly said a word in the head teacher's room and she was silent in the car all the way home. I thought when we got back, Mum would scream at me. But all she said was, 'I'm very disappointed in you, Rose.' She shook her head and looked at me with that look she sometimes gets that makes me feel like a maggoty piece of rotting meat. Then she went out and I didn't see her for the rest of the evening.

Ella still calls me spaghetti head but only when she's got her friends around her. She's too scared to do it when we're alone. I still get angry when she calls me things like that, but I don't want another letter going home. And that's not all. Whenever I answer a question in class, she pulls stupid faces and she doesn't particularly mind whether or not I see her. Silly cow! And she's going to Heathcroft too – worst luck.

The strange thing was that as Ella got nastier, her brother Lucas got nicer. Mum and I sometimes saw them at the shopping centre. Mum and Nichelle would nod politely to each other without saying a word and Ella just ignored me or looked right through me. But not Lucas. He was different. Every time he saw me – which I must admit wasn't very often – he'd say hi or smile or wave or something. They were the strangest family. It was really hard to know where I was with any of them. They were what Nana Meggie called 'too now and then'. I knew that Lucas was already at Heathcroft but he was in the year above me.

'Is it true Ella made you cry?'

'No way,' I flared up. 'Ella couldn't make me cry in a million years.'

'You make it sound like no one could,' smiled Tobey.

I thought about it. 'No one could,' I decided.

'What a load of crap. Anyone you care about can make you cry.'

'No, they can't.'

'Yes, they can,' Tobey argued. 'Even I could make you cry.'

'I thought you said only those people I care about could do that,' I said.

Tobey glared at me, then marched off. I opened my mouth to call him back but then decided against it.

After all, he started it.

forty-four. Sephy

I carefully applied my burgundy lipstick. I could hear the crowd in Specimens, laughing and loud, even through my closed dressing-room door. Here I was, back in a restaurant-bar, but not as a customer. I was about to do the one thing I'd promised myself I'd never do again. How I hated singing in public. The memories of my short stint as a singer with Jaxon, Sonny and Rhino were still raw and sore. And now I didn't even have the luxury of a band to back me up and stem the feeling of isolation singing in public gave me.

But money talked.

And it hadn't spoken to me in a long while 'cause I was almost stony broke. Even though my mum is paying Callie Rose's school fees, I'd insisted on paying for everything else myself. But the uniform and the school meals and the books and stationery on top of my normal bills had eaten large chunks out of my savings. And now that Sonny and I were no longer working together, money was too tight to even mention. I spent most of my pregnancy without two pennies to rub together. I wasn't about to go through that again.

Nathaniel Ealing, the Cross owner of Specimens, had

advertised for a singer for Thursdays, Fridays and Saturdays in his restaurant. Someone to play the piano mostly, but sing old favourites occasionally and definitely when requested. Just the sort of thing I loathed.

But thou shalt pay the bills!

The dressing room wasn't too bad, a little bigger than our bathroom at home. And there was a plug-in heater in one corner which actually worked. The walls were an uninspiring pale green colour. A single light bulb hung from the ceiling but at least there were decent lights around the mirror. I surveyed my face critically. My lipstick needed some gloss on top of it. And another layer of mascara ought to finish the job. I was just giving my hair a final pat when the door opened. Nathan, the owner, popped his head round the door. He was a tall man, taller than me by at least a head, and he wore his designer suit with casual style, like it was no big deal. He was extremely good looking and what's more, he knew it, but it didn't rule his life. He wore his hair very short and had pure honey-brown eyes, framed under strong, straight eyebrows and full lips which curved easily into a smile. I'd watched him as he greeted his guests, flirting with the women and making the men feel like he was one of them and not just the owner of one of the most successful scenes in town. Nathan knew every aspect of his club, from how many bottles of ginger ale he had in stock out the back, to when the electricity bill was due, but for all that he wasn't afraid to delegate. I guess that's why his manager, Ron, told me that Nathan was a great boss to work for. Nathan gave one hundred per cent and he expected – and got no less – from his employees.

'We've got a good crowd tonight,' Nathan smiled. 'Ready, Sephy?'

'As I'll ever be,' I told him, adding, 'And you wouldn't like to knock before you open that door, would you?'

'Sorry!' Nathan grinned at me and shut the door on his way out. I stood up and checked out the dress I was wearing. It was a slinky black and silver creation with a slit up one side and not really my style but, as Nathan had pointed out, a venue like his needed its singer to stand out, not fade into the furniture.

I headed out the door and down the narrow, badly lit corridor to the bar. The Specimens entrance opened straight onto the bar, but all the customers had to do was veer to the left to get to the restaurant. The restaurant where I was to work occupied its own discrete area. Each table in the restaurant was adorned with a crisp, white tablecloth. On the tables, the crystal wine glasses shone and the wall lights around the restaurant were so ornate in their workmanship that they wouldn't've been out of place in my mother's house. Even the bar wasn't the 'spit and sawdust' type of effort that was typical around this area. Although the bar itself was made of granite, the rest of the place was all glass and chrome. The bar and restaurant were separated by a semi-frosted glass wall and door. And somehow the whole thing worked. And I wasn't the only one to think so, judging by the crowds in the bar and the restaurant, which was already three-quarters full.

Because of the location of the dressing room, I had to duck and weave around the bar customers to get to the restaurant. I finally sat down at the piano, but my thoughts weren't on my new job. They were with Sonny. As always. What was he doing now? Proving that he didn't need me as much as I needed him? Professionally speaking, of course. Personally speaking, I didn't need anyone.

So why was there such a hollow feeling inside me? A raging emptiness that was eating me up from the inside out. And whose fault was that? As I played the intro to my first song, that one phrase kept playing through my head.

Whose fault was that?

I hadn't seen Sonny in months and I missed him so much. More than missed him. And he wasn't the only one I missed. Callie Rose was eleven, nearly twelve. And what did I really know about her? Not as much as I should. Some mother I was. Scared to feel, scared to touch, scared to give. Scared, scared, scared. The first chance I got, I'd tell Rose the truth. No more running. I stopped playing the intro to *Loving State of Mind*.

Sing something else, Sephy.

Sing from the heart, sing how you feel. Or are you too afraid to do even that?

'Persephone, is something wrong?' Nathan appeared from nowhere to ask.

His voice made me jump. I'd forgotten where I was. I took a quick look around. Nathan wasn't the only one who was giving me strange looks.

'I'm fine, Nathan,' I said. 'Sorry.'

'Can I get you a drink, or anything else?'

'No, I'm fine. Honestly.'

I began to play the intro to *What I Haven't Got* – a song I really wished I'd written. Even so, this was a song I could sing with everything I was. No hiding, no evasion.

I woke up this morning
The way I went to sleep
I know that what we did last night was
My way of counting sheep

I'm scared when we're together
Afraid to be alone
Your love is such a wonder
And in your arms I'm home

But your love will never hold me
Why can't you understand?
What I haven't got is
The nerve to love one man

I know there's something missing
But I just can't track it down
So I wear my 'I don't care'
Like a smile upon a clown

I laugh when we're together
Nothing ever seems quite real
'Cept when the night surrounds me
And fear is all I feel

Your love will never hold me
Why can't you understand?
What I haven't got is
The nerve to love one man

What I haven't got is
The nerve to love
(The nerve to love)
The nerve to love
Just one man

I finished on an improvised instrumental ending, hitting the final chord as I hummed into the microphone. The applause wasn't rapturous but I didn't get booed off either. I started playing the second song. I could've sung but I decided to leave this one as an instrumental. I hadn't done this in a long time and I didn't want to exhaust my voice. I had to pace myself.

My mind went back to Sonny. I'd got him and me all wrong. I'd expected the way I felt about him to be exactly the way I felt about Callum. I hadn't allowed for the fact that I'd grown up in the meantime. And it'd taken a lot of painful thinking to realize that I did love Sonny in a way that was equal but different to the way I loved Callum. Maybe part of me thought I'd be betraying Callum by allowing myself to love someone else so I'd convinced myself that I was incapable of loving anyone except my daughter.

Maybe it wasn't too late. I just had to pick myself up, take a deep breath and revive myself. All the parts of me that stopped me functioning, just let them go. Drop them, leave them behind and keep moving. I'd spent long enough standing still. First thing tomorrow, I'd phone Sonny. Not to give false hope but with the promise that he'd get *me* this time, all of me. I smiled, actually feeling hopeful inside. A weird and wonderfully warm wave I hadn't felt in so very long. Still smiling, I looked around the room.

Sonny was looking straight at me.

My heart bounced. I almost stopped playing. Where had he sprung from? It felt like I'd conjured him out of thin but welcome air, just by thinking about him. I beamed at him as I carried on playing, so happy to see him. I tried to tell him with my expression and smile what I'd never been able to say to him before.

Hello, Sonny. Yes, it's me. And I'm here for both of us, if you still want me. I've spent so long mourning the past that I almost missed my present. But not any more. So here I—

Sonny wasn't alone. A beautiful Nought woman with jet-black hair leaned across to whisper something in his ear. I didn't miss the way her hand rested possessively on his arm as it lay on the table. I didn't miss the way she glanced at me before turning her full attention to Sonny as she whispered. I turned back to my piano.

Just keep playing, Sephy.

Whatever happens, just keep playing.

I worked for the next half an hour, singing a couple of songs but just playing the piano for all the others. And I made sure to sing into my microphone and not look around at anything or anyone. When at last it was time for my break, I announced I'd be back in fifteen minutes and headed straight for my dressing room.

Didn't quite make it though.

Sonny was waiting for me in the staff corridor.

'Hello, Sonny,' I said, slowing down when I caught sight of him.

'Hello, Persephone.'

God, he looked good. He was wearing a navy shirt and matching trousers. He'd had his hair professionally cut by the look of it instead of popping to the barber round the corner from where he lived the way he usually did. In fact, it wasn't just the haircut that was working. He'd had his eyebrows trimmed and his hair highlighted, I think. Funny what a little tender, loving care and a top ten hit song could do for you. Sonny had moved from 'OK, with an onion and salt', gone straight past fit and was now in the super-fit category.

I smiled with embarrassment. Goodness! I sounded like my daughter!

'I hate to be a jobsworth about this, but customers aren't allowed back here and I have to change for my next set,' I said, in what I hoped was a light tone. 'Besides your . . . your girlfriend will be missing you.'

The word stuck in my throat like a wedge of dry, crumpled printer paper.

'I told her I wanted to have a word with you,' said Sonny.

'Oh yes? What about?'

'How are you?'

'Fine.' I shrugged and tried to move past him but Sonny stepped in front of me, barring my way. And the corridor was so narrow and he was so broad that there was no way I could get past, short of flying over him.

'How long have you been singing here?'

'Tonight's my first night.' I painted on the happiest, most cheerful smile I could dredge up.

Sonny looked down at me. I looked up at him and for the life of me I couldn't think of another thing to say.

'D'you and your girlfriend come here often?' Rats! I couldn't believe what I'd just said. 'Scratch that. It's none of my business.'

'Sherona's never been here and it's her birthday so . . .' Sonny shrugged away the rest of his sentence.

'Is she enjoying herself?'

'I think so. She says you're a good singer but you don't have much presence.'

I raised my eyebrows. 'D'you agree with her?'

'Well, you're coming across as if you're not really enjoying yourself,' said Sonny.

'Hence the reason you came back here?' I realized. 'Well, I'm fine. And tell your girlfriend that I'll try to do better when I go out again. Excuse me.'

I scooted past Sonny before he could realize what I was about to do. I headed into my dressing room, shutting the door behind me. It opened again almost immediately.

'Did you forget something, Sonny?'

I watched as he shut the door before leaning against it. And he didn't once take his eyes off me. He was making me nervous.

'How's Callie Rose?'

After a moment's pause, I decided to be truthful. 'She's missing you.'

'And what about you? Are you missing me too?'

No way was I going to answer that one. Not when he had a girlfriend in tow.

'How come you never phoned me?' asked Sonny.

'You didn't phone me either,' I pointed out. 'Mind you, after seeing Sherona and her pneumatic boobs, I can understand why.'

'You're the one who dumped me, remember?'

'I didn't dump you, I just didn't want to get married.'

'And I didn't want to spend the rest of our lives together going absolutely nowhere. Staying still wasn't good enough for me. It shouldn't've been good enough for you either.'

'Well, you got over me PDQ.' I smiled sweetly. 'Off with the old, on with the new.'

'PDQ?'

'Pretty damned quick.'

'Are you jealous?' asked Sonny.

''Course not,' I lied. 'Besides which, Sonny, it really isn't any of my business. Not any more. Now, if you'll excuse me.' I put my hands behind my head and pulled at the zip of my dress but my dramatic attempt at dismissal backfired when it got stuck after only a few centimetres. I tugged and twisted but the damned thing wouldn't work loose.

'I'll do it,' said Sonny. He stepped forward, pulled my hands down to my sides and pulled the zip down before I could draw breath to tell him not to bother.

I spun away from him. 'Thanks. I can take it from here. Could you shut the door on your way out?'

I turned my head to watch him leave. Leave the room. Leave my life. But when Sonny did move, it wasn't towards the door. I was in his arms and we were kissing like our lives depended on it. Sonny's arms were wrapped round me and his hands moved up and down my bare back, burning into my skin.

'I've missed you so much,' Sonny breathed against my cheek.

'I'm so sorry for how I treated you, Sonny. You don't know how many times I've picked up the phone . . .'

And then we were kissing again like the last two people on earth. I poured all the longing and loneliness and love I had in me into that kiss. He had me burning and fizzing like a firework.

But then the door opened and in walked Nathan, closely followed by Sherona. I pulled away from Sonny, but not before our uninvited guests saw us. And my ridiculous fantasy of Sonny and me was blasted away like spring snow in a furnace.

 forty-five. Rose is 11

'Rose, can I talk to you for a moment?' asked Mum.

I looked up from my homework. 'Yes, Mum?'

'I need to talk to you about something.'

'What?'

Mum chewed on her bottom lip. 'It's about . . . your dad.'

I put down my pen. Mum now had my full attention. 'Yes, Mum?'

'Your dad . . .' Mum sighed. 'Your dad loved you very much.'

Was that all? 'Yes, I know, Mum. You've already told me.'

'I just didn't want you to forget, that's all,' said Mum. 'Back to your homework.'

I didn't need to be told twice. All that build-up to tell me something I already knew. Honestly!

forty-six. Jude

Here she comes. Look at her! She's actually pleased to see me. Got her brains from her mother's side of the family obviously. And meeting up like this at the cinema was a stroke of genius, even if I do say so myself. The brat has been blathering on about this film for the last month and how her mum won't let her see it because of its fifteen certificate. So naturally I said I'd take her.

Our secret, of course.

If the film was some nonsense love story then I wouldn't've bothered, but this film has violence rather than sex as its main ingredient. Perfect. I'm going to start taking her to a number of these, to show her what the world is really like. Good old Uncle Jude, who'll let Callie do all the things her mum won't allow. And a few others her mother never even thought of. How old is the brat now? Twelve? Thirteen? Plenty old enough to learn a few facts of life. Anyone for a game of corruption? I hate to brag, but I'm a grand master.

Standing in this queue is fraying my nerves though. Morgan has arranged backup at a discreet distance further down the line, but even so I'm not keen on standing out in the open like this. Not in my line of work. And my profile hasn't exactly diminished in any way. I'm working my way up the government's most wanted hit parade, not down.

'Hi, Uncle.'

'Hello, Callie Rose. How're you?'

'Fine,' Callie smiled. 'Thanks for doing this. I really appreciate it.'

'You can show your appreciation by not telling anyone what we're doing.'

'I won't.' Callie Rose worried the corner of her bottom lip. I'd seen that gesture too many times before not to know what was coming. 'When are we going to tell Mum about you?'

I made up a deep sigh. 'You know how tricky it is, Callie Rose. And you only know a fraction of the things that happened in the past.'

'Well, why don't you tell me the rest then, Uncle?'

'It's for your mother to tell you, not me.'

'But you—'

'I know,' I interrupted. 'I've told you not to ask her, but you've got to see it from my point of view. I'm in an invidious position, Callie. Anything I say about the past could make things considerably worse.'

'You're talking like a cryptic crossword,' Callie sighed. 'Again!'

'I'm a grown-up, that's my job.'

'Uncle Jude! You made a joke! That's not like you!' Callie said incredulously.

I almost laughed. Almost. But I caught myself in time. I wouldn't let this girl get under my skin. I let a Cross get under my skin once before, just once, and it almost cost me everything I was and everything I knew.

That'd never happen again.

'Don't you like my mum, Uncle Jude?'

'It's not that . . . It's just that I think I'd respect her more if she told you the truth,' I said, selecting my words with overt care.

'The truth about what?'

'I've said too much.' I shook my head.

'Oh, Uncle. I wish you wouldn't do that,' said Callie. 'It's really frustrating.'

'You just have to trust that when the time is right, you'll know all there is to know,' I said. 'Now let's go in and see the film. D'you want to have something to eat with me afterwards?'

'I'd better not. I told Nana Meggie I was popping round to Nikki's house and I'd be back before dinner,' said Callie. 'If I'm late she'll get very cross with me.'

'You mean she'll clear her throat *twice*!' I said wryly.

'She's a lot more strict than that,' Callie laughed.

'Not with you. Not from what you've told me over the last year,' I said. 'Besides, my mum . . .'

'What?'

'My mum will do whatever she can to protect you, even if it means shielding you from the truth.'

'Is the truth bad?'

'No, Callie. The truth will set you free – when you're old enough to handle it.'

A little seed here. A dash of water there. Just enough to keep suspicion and doubt alive and modestly thriving until they could be nurtured into something far more spectacular.

'Callie Rose,' I said in all seriousness, 'I want you to know that I'll never lie to you. If you ask me something I don't want to answer, then I won't. But I won't lie. You can trust me. OK?'

'OK, Uncle.'

A little seed here. A splash of water there.

We went into the cinema.

forty-seven.
Callie Rose is 11

'Excuse me . . .'

The older girls barged past me, spinning me around as they went. I turned and tried to ask two passing boys where SC12 was. They completely ignored me. My second day at Heathcroft High was shaping up to be worse than the first. The school was huge and busy and I felt like I was drowning in this unknown sea of faces.

'Hiya, Rose.'

'Oh hello, Lucas.' Lucas Cheshie and two of his mates stood in front of me. And I've never been so happy to see anyone in my life.

'You look lost,' said Lucas.

Was it so pathetically obvious?

'I was trying to find Room SC12.'

'That's in the science block. The quickest way is to cut across the quad and head for that grey and green building over there,' said Lucas, pointing through the window beside us. 'SC12 is on the first floor of that building. Didn't you get your school map?'

I wasn't about to tell him that Ella, his cow of a sister, had seen me looking at it on our first day at school and had snatched it from me and torn it up right in front of my nose.

'I must've mislaid it.' I shrugged.

'Hang on,' said Lucas.

I watched as he slid his rucksack off his back and started rummaging through it.

'Lucas, we're going to be late,' one of his friends protested.

The boy on the other side of him frowned as he looked from Lucas to me and back again. Ignoring him, Lucas drew a crumpled and disgusting-looking piece of paper out of his bag.

'There you go,' he said. 'You can have mine.'

'Thanks,' I said, taking the map carefully between my thumb and index finger. 'That's very kind of you.'

'*That's very kind of you,*' Lucas's friend mimicked.

My face started to burn.

'Shut up,' Lucas hissed at his friend. Then he turned to me and smiled. 'Hope the map helps.'

And with that, he walked off. I was left watching him, wondering why he'd bothered to help me.

forty-eight. Meggie

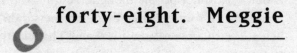

'Can I get you a drink?'

I smiled at the nought waiter before giving the menu one last glance. Even though I was ready to order, I didn't say so.

'Yes, er . . . can I have a cup of tea please.'

'Peppermint, camomile, jasmine green or breakfast?' asked the waiter.

'Er . . . breakfast please.'

'Certainly.'

'Thank you so much.'

I looked down at the menu again, even though I knew what I wanted. Eating out wasn't a comfortable experience for me. I still remembered when we noughts weren't allowed in places like this. It wasn't too many years ago when we weren't welcome in any Cross restaurants. So it was a case of get a take-away meal or pack up a load of food from home, especially if we were visiting relatives who lived more than a couple of hours' drive away. There was no such thing as stopping off at a restaurant or café for a meal along the way. And now here I was in The Garden

Experience, one of the best restaurants in the Dundale Shopping Centre in town, but I was finding it hard to look at my surroundings or catch anyone's eye. I guess I was too apprehensive about meeting stares of disapproval. My husband Ryan always used to say I cared too much about what other people thought. And he was right.

So what if some of the other customers didn't like me being in the same restaurant as them? That was their problem, not mine. I took a deep breath and forced myself to look around quickly. No one was looking at me. At least, I don't think anyone was. My quick glance around hadn't rested in any one place long enough for me to be sure. How foolish was that?

Let go of the past, Meggie. That was then and this is now.

But letting go of the past was easier said than done when it stuck to my head and my heart like superglue. I was better now than I used to be though. Some people didn't give me enough credit for that. Some people couldn't see how hard I was trying to move forward. The place was filled with late-night shoppers or those who'd just come out of, or who were about to go into, the multiplex cinema. I was quite hungry but I decided a light dinner would be best. That way, I wouldn't have to stay too long.

'Hello.'

I looked up at the man who'd just spoken. His appearance made me start. I stared, trying to take in the changes. His hair colour had changed from the last time I saw him. He was almost blond now and he'd dyed his eyebrows to match. He wore glasses, which was also different. He was still very muscular, almost thick-set. No doubt he was still boxing and working out.

'Hello, son,' I said quietly.

Jude sat down, his eyes darting around restlessly. He reminded me of a hunted animal.

'Did you—?'

'Yes. I took two buses and a taxi,' I interrupted. 'I wasn't followed.'

We had this same conversation every time we met. Why did I bother to do this? Jude and I met irregularly, about three or four times a year, sometimes more, often less. Jude was still a wanted man. And every time I met up with him, he broke my heart.

'How are you?'

I shrugged. 'I'm fine.'

'Still living with the enemy?'

'Don't start, Jude,' I sighed.

'Is she never going to move out of your house?'

'I don't want her to go. I'd miss her and my granddaughter too much.'

'Granddaughter?'

'Yes, your niece. The daughter of your brother—'

'Let's change the subject,' Jude said abruptly.

'What d'you want to talk about?'

'D'you need anything? Money?'

'No, I'm fine.'

'Living off that woman's money,' said Jude bitterly.

'I work, Jude. Sephy helps out with some of the bills but I don't expect her to do it all.'

'If you got rid of her, I'd pay your bills for you.'

'I don't want you to,' I said bluntly.

'So you're happy to take her money, but not mine.'

'Hers isn't covered in blood.'

'I work in admin, I told you,' said Jude.

'But you work for the L.M.'

Jude sat back in his chair, regarding me steadily. I was aware of my own heartbeat, pounding ever faster as my son sat and watched me. Jude opened his mouth to speak, just as the waiter appeared with my tea.

'Ready to order?' asked the waiter cheerfully.

'Yes, thank you. I'll have the chicken salad.'

'Anything to start?'

'No, thank you.'

The waiter turned to Jude. 'Anything for you, sir?'

'No, thank you.'

'Can I get you a drink?'

'Don't your ears work? I said no.'

'Jude,' I admonished.

'Very good, sir,' said the waiter, his smile wavering.

As he walked off, I said to my son, 'There was no need to be so rude.'

'Don't use my name in public, Mum,' Jude said softly. 'I've told you before.'

'So what should I call you?' I asked. 'Jude is your name. Your dad picked it out especially.'

'Are you so anxious to see me hang?' asked Jude.

Ah, there they were. Words to squeeze my heart. And it had taken no time at all for them to be uttered. Less than five minutes.

'You think seeing one son hanged wasn't enough?'

Jude had the grace to look away, however briefly.

'Sorry, Mum.'

My heart still felt like it was being pinched. Jude slid a padded envelope towards me.

'Please take it. I want to help,' he said.

So I picked it up and put it in my handbag — the way I always did. And the envelope would find its way, unopened, onto the church collection plate — the way it always did.

'You look tired,' said Jude after a long moment's silence.

'I am tired,' I agreed. 'If you hadn't phoned me to arrange this meeting, I would've stayed in bed today.'

'You should've said.'

'You're my son, Jude, and I love you. I'm not going to pass up the chance to see you,' I told him.

Jude looked away, almost embarrassed. At least, that's what it looked like to me. He was so uncomfortable with any word or sign of affection from me.

'D'you have anyone, Jude?'

'That again.' Jude sighed with impatience.

'It's a simple question.'

'No, Mum. There's no one. I'm too busy.'

'Too busy to share your life with someone? Too busy to have someone care about you? And I would love more grandchildren.'

Jude didn't answer.

'You're too busy doing what?'

Jude looked me straight in the eyes, his lips a thin line. I had my answer. Jude's life was entwined with his one and only love — the Liberation Militia. No one else could even compete.

'Callie Rose is at secondary school now, isn't she?' asked Jude.

'Yes,' I smiled. 'She's been there two terms now. It took her a while to settle in but now she's . . .'

Jude leaned forward, intent on my every word. The restaurant suddenly became very hot. When did it get this hot? Why on earth didn't they turn the heating down?

Wary, I licked my lips. 'Why the sudden interest?'

'Like you said, Mum, she is my niece,' said Jude.

Very carefully, I rested my hands on my lap, right hand on top of my left. And there was no sound in the restaurant except my breathing. I looked around. I could see other people, chatting, laughing; one Cross woman was even leaning across the table to kiss the man opposite. But no sound. I watched them all. In slow motion the Cross woman turned to smile. She caught me watching and smiled happily at me. Then all the noise and bustle of the place descended like a rain of bricks over me. It made my head ache.

'Jude, stay away from Callie Rose. OK?'

'I was only—'

'I don't want to hear it. I'm warning you, leave my granddaughter alone or else.'

'Or else what?'

I stood up. 'You can pay for my meal. I've lost my appetite.'

I walked out of the restaurant, my neck muscles aching, the light hurting my eyes, my stomach turning over. I groaned inwardly as my headache flowered into a migraine. I turned round to take another look at my son.

He wasn't watching me but even from across the restaurant I could see his cold, cold smile.

forty-nine. Sephy

Rose pushed her hair back from her face with an impatient hand.

'Why don't you tie it back if it's getting on your nerves?' I suggested.

Rose looked up at me. 'It's OK.'

She pronged one of the sausages on her plate and bit into it. Her mind wasn't on her dinner though, that much was obvious.

'How was school today, Rose?'

'Mum, could you call me Callie Rose, please? I have asked you before.'

'I know, but I've spent years calling you Rose,' I pointed out. 'I'll try to remember. Anyway, why the sudden urge to change?'

'I just prefer Callie Rose. I think it's prettier and less weedy and it reminds me of my dad.'

'Rose isn't a weedy name – by definition.'

'You know what I mean,' said Rose impatiently. She dug her fork into her mashed potato and stuffed that into her mouth as well.

'Rose, I mean Callie Rose, your food isn't about to run

off your plate so there's no need to stuff so much into your mouth at once.'

'Yes, Mum,' said Rose, her mouth more than half full.

I was about to nag her about that as well, when I decided against it. I didn't want our entire conversation around the table to be me nagging and Rose arguing. What I wanted to do was open my arms and tell her . . .

'Where's Nana Meggie?' Rose asked.

'She went into town to have dinner with a friend,' I replied.

'She did?' Rose couldn't've been any more astonished. And I couldn't blame her. Meggie had gone out for dinner. We'd have blue snow falling by morning.

'Who's the friend?' asked Rose.

I shrugged. 'No idea. I don't pry into Meggie's business.'

'So you didn't ask her?'

'No.'

Rose studied me, that thoughtful expression on her face that I've come to know so well and dread so much. She was about to ask me one of her impossible-to-answer questions.

'How come you pry into my business but not Nana Meggie's?'

'Callie Rose, I don't *pry*, but you're my daughter so I'm interested in everything you do. More than interested. I . . . I care about you,' I tried to explain.

Just say the words. Why d'you find them so difficult to say? Lack of practice? Yes, lack of practice. Then tell your daughter how you feel. The more you say it, the easier it becomes. Just say it . . .

'Don't you care about Meggie then?'

I frowned.

'Is that why you two never really talk to each other?' Rose continued.

'We do talk.'

'No.' Rose shook her head. 'She asks you a question and you answer or vice versa. She tells you something or you pass on information, but you and Nana don't sit and talk like you and Nana Jasmine do.'

'Well, your Nana Jasmine is my mother . . .'

'And Nana Meggie is my dad's mum,' said Rose. 'Don't you like her?'

'Of course I . . . I do. It's just that . . .'

Rose looked at me expectantly, waiting for me to continue.

'Meggie and I . . . we have a lot of history to deal with.'

'What kind of history?'

I sighed deeply. Why on earth hadn't I just said that Meggie was the best thing since grated cheese and left it at that?

'Rose, a lot of the things you now take for granted weren't the same in my day,' I began.

In my day . . . ! How old did that sound?

'Like what?'

'Like Noughts and Crosses going to the same schools for one. When I was your age, Noughts weren't allowed to go to public schools past the age of fourteen.'

'But that was decades ago when people didn't like Noughts and Crosses mixing,' said Rose.

'It wasn't "decades" ago,' I said dryly. 'I'm not that old. The law was only changed a few years before you were born.'

'I thought you said Dad and you went to the same school,' said Rose.

'Only because the law was changed in the year your dad started at Heathcroft. Callum was one of the first Noughts to go to a Cross school.'

'I still don't understand. What has that to do with you and Nana Meggie?'

'Meggie lost a lot, Rose, because of those times. She watched her family disintegrate around her. Disintegrate means—'

'I know what it means,' Rose interrupted.

'There's no need to snap my head off.'

'Don't change the subject.'

She'd noticed.

'It's not your fault that Aunt Lynette was knocked down or that my dad died. They were just accidents. Does Nana Meggie blame you for all the horrible things that happened to her?' asked Rose.

Accidents? Tell Callie Rose the truth, Sephy. Here's your chance. Tell your daughter how Callum really died. And why. Tell Rose about her Grandad Ryan's trial and what happened to him in prison. Tell her. Don't wimp out again. Just do it.

But I couldn't. The timing wasn't right. I ignored the voice inside asking if the timing would ever be right?

'No, I don't think she blames me . . .' I began. 'But she grew up in a time when it was hard for Noughts and Crosses to be true friends.'

'So doesn't she like you?'

'It's not that simple, Rose.' I sighed again. I felt like a fly in a spider's web and the more I tried to extricate myself, the worse I was making things. 'When you were born I was ill for a while and Meggie had to sort things out. After I stopped being ill, Meggie and I—'

'Hello, Nana Meggie,' smiled Rose.

I turned quickly. How long had Meggie been standing there, listening?

'Hi, sweetie.' Meggie smiled at Rose. 'You'd better hurry up and eat your dinner before it gets cold. Hello, Sephy.'

'Hello, Meggie.'

'How was your dinner, Nana?' asked Rose.

'Not very good,' said Meggie. 'That's why I ducked out early.'

'D'you want some dinner with us?' I asked. 'There's plenty.'

'No, thanks,' said Meggie. 'I'm not hungry. Actually, I've got a bit of a headache so I'm going to have a lie down for a while.'

After directing another warm smile at Rose, Meggie headed out of the room.

'Mum, you—'

The doorbell rang. Thank God! I practically sprinted from the room. I couldn't cope with any more questions about the past. I really couldn't. I opened the door and my heart bounced like a tennis ball.

'Hello, Sephy.'

'Sonny! Hi. I . . . er . . . d'you want to come in?' I was all confusion.

I stood to one side as Sonny stepped past me.

'Mum, who is it? Sonny!'

Rose launched herself forward into Sonny's open arms. The smile on her face could've lit the whole street.

'I've missed you, Sonny. How come you haven't been around for ages?'

'I've missed you too, pumpkin,' Sonny grinned. 'Very, very much.'

'Are you back now?'

Sonny put Rose to her feet. 'I need to speak to your mum, pumpkin.'

Rose stood there, smiling at him.

'In private, Callie Rose,' Sonny said ruefully.

'Oh. I'll go and finish my dinner then,' said Rose. She looked at me, fierce suspicion on her face, before turning back to Sonny. 'You're not going to leave without saying goodbye, are you?'

'I'd never do that,' said Sonny.

'That's all right then,' said Rose, satisfied.

She trotted back into the kitchen. Now that we were alone, I felt my face begin to burn. I couldn't help remembering the last humiliating time Sonny and I had been together. And what'd happened when his girlfriend caught us kissing.

'Let's go into the living room,' I suggested. 'Can I get you a drink? Tea? Coffee?'

'No thanks. I'm fine.'

I waited for Sonny to choose a seat so I could sit opposite, but he waited for me to do the same. I finally sat down in the armchair. I moved the cushion from behind me and hugged it to my stomach.

'How are you?' I asked.

'Fine.'

'How's Sherona?'

I had no doubt that Sherona was more than fine. A

pit bull had nothing on that woman. When she had caught me and Sonny together, I had thought she was going to rip my throat out. Not that I blamed her. There I'd stood in the dressing room with the zip of my dress undone and my dress half off and Sonny's arms wrapped round me. In Sherona's shoes I would've put two and two together and made plenty as well. Mind you, in Sherona's shoes I would've probably just walked away, closing the door behind me. Part of me admired her for wanting to tear my head off. She was a girl who fought for what she wanted. Me? I rolled over and played dead. I never used to be like that, when I was a teenager. But after Callie Rose was born, all the spark had seemed to desert me.

Until recently.

'Sherona's fine.'

'I'm glad you two didn't break up because of me,' I said.

'Are you?' asked Sonny pointedly.

'Sonny, what d'you want me to say?' I asked.

'Tell me why you took up with me in the first place? Propinquity? Expediency?'

'You really believe I'm that shallow?'

'I don't know,' Sonny admitted. 'After all these years, I still don't know you.'

'How could you get to know me when I didn't know myself?'

'What does that mean?'

'It doesn't matter. I was just a bit lost for a while. A long while.'

'And what happened?'

'You did,' I said truthfully. 'For a long time I felt like I

didn't deserve to be loved or to love anyone. I thought . . .
I thought our relationship was mostly propinquity – oh,
not from my point of view, but yours.'

'Thanks a lot,' Sonny said bitterly.

'I'm just being honest,' I said.

'If that's all you thought it was, why did you let me in
your bed?'

'I was fond of you and grateful that . . . that you wanted
me. I didn't realize how desperate I was for someone to
want me.'

'So you put up with me touching you out of gratitude
and you thought all I wanted was sex?' Sonny spoke as if
the words were hot ashes in his mouth.

'No. Of course not,' I sighed. 'I'm not explaining this
very well. It was more than just sex. You could've had
sex with anyone, but you wanted me. You wanted to
be with *me*. Not Kamal Hadley's daughter, not Callum
McGregor's lover, not Callie Rose's mother. Me. I started
to see myself the way you saw me, as someone worth
holding onto instead of someone dead inside.'

'And then I asked you to marry me.'

I looked down at the cushion on my lap, worrying the
corner of it with restless fingers.

'And then you asked me to marry you,' I repeated.

I forced myself to look at Sonny. I wanted to say so
much, but I could tell from the look on his face that I
didn't have to.

'And where are you now?' asked Sonny.

'I'm beginning to remember who and what I am and
what I want,' I said. 'It's like waking up inside. Does that
make sense?'

Sonny didn't answer.

'I'm sorry for the way I treated you, Sonny. You deserved better.'

'And now?' asked Sonny.

'And now you have Sherona.' I forced a smile. 'And I wish you only good things.'

'I see,' said Sonny.

He stood up. I did the same, dropping the cushion back in the chair.

'D'you . . . still want to work together? I'd like to . . .'

'I don't think that's a very good idea,' Sonny said quietly.

Who would've thought that words could weigh so much? They sat on my chest, crushing my heart.

'OK.' I nodded. 'You're probably right. And your girl-friend would never trust the two of us together now.'

'Sherona isn't . . .'

'Isn't what?'

'Isn't very forgiving. So I think it'd be better if we didn't see each other any more – just for a little while.'

'I understand. Don't forget to say goodbye to Rose.'

'I won't.'

We went out into the hallway just as Rose emerged from the kitchen.

'Are you staying for dinner?' she asked.

'No, Callie Rose. I have to go now,' said Sonny.

'When are you coming back?'

'I'm not sure,' said Sonny. 'I have to do a lot of travelling in the next few months. I'm not sure when I'll be round this way again.'

'Oh,' said Rose, her face wilting. 'Don't you like me any more?'

'Callie Rose, I love you,' said Sonny, getting down on one knee. 'Don't you ever think anything else.'

'Then why're you going away?'

'I have to, Callie Rose. I wouldn't leave unless I had no other choice.'

'Will you come and see me when you get back?'

'I promise. Just as soon as I can,' said Sonny.

I watched as Sonny and Rose hugged each other, her arms around his neck, his arms around her waist. I had to force myself not to look away. Sonny stood up.

'Bye, Callie Rose. Be good.'

Rose sniffed but didn't answer.

'Goodbye, Sephy,' said Sonny.

'Bye, Sonny.'

I watched him open the door and leave, shutting the door carefully behind him.

'What did you do?' Rose rounded on me immediately.

'Pardon?' It took me a couple of seconds to tear my gaze away from the closed door.

'You sent him away, didn't you?' Rose exploded. 'You ruin everything. You hate everyone and everything and you drove him away.'

'Rose,' I said, stunned. 'I didn't send him away.'

'I don't believe you. You just want everyone to be as miserable as you are,' Rose shouted. 'Well, I am. Are you happy now?'

Rose sprinted upstairs, leaving me drowning in her wake.

fifty. Jasmine

Go away!

When would the person on the phone get the hint and ring off? I didn't want to talk to anyone. I wasn't in a sociable state of mind. Besides, my chest was hurting again. I really would have to go and get it checked out. But I hate doctors and all things medical. Doctors are like the police, they only deal in bad news. Maybe I'd ask Sephy to go with me this time. She'd be more than willing to do it. I just wish . . . My poor Sephy.

In another lifetime, months had turned into years when all I had cared about was my next drink and being the perfect wife. I'd been too coiled around the nearest wine bottle to pay attention to my children, far less worry about them. But I was making up for that now with a vengeance. Minerva was settled, though we didn't speak very often. A fortnightly phone call to exchange platitudes. A visit every two or three months to show my face. Minerva and her family very rarely come to me, but I don't mind that. This house holds bad memories for Minerva. She spent years cleaning up my vomit and washing me off and putting me to bed when I was too drunk to do it for myself. Things that no child should have to do. And she managed to hide what she was doing for me from Sephy for so long. So long. I robbed Minerva of a normal childhood, I know that.

But Sephy . . . Sephy had her dad and Minerva and me all looking out for her, but it didn't help. It's as if when she became a teenager, she left all her happiness behind in her childhood. I don't blame Callum for that any more. I don't blame anyone really. Maybe myself, maybe the fates. But Sephy deserves some happiness now. After all these years that's not too much to ask. I thought she'd get that with Sonny but they've broken up. Sephy tells me that it's for good but I can't believe that. Maybe I just don't want to believe that. And Meggie and Sephy are still wary around each other. And Sephy and Callie Rose are arguing more and more these days.

Go away! The phone was still ringing!

'Oh, for heaven's sake!' I snatched it up off the occasional table and barked into it, 'Hello?'

'Mother? It's me, Sephy.'

'Sephy? Is everything OK?'

'No . . . we've been burgled.'

I stared down at the ground. 'You're joking . . .'

'It's not something I'd joke about,' Sephy told me.

'Did they take much?'

'The TV, the DVD player, the music centre, a couple of cameras, stuff like that.'

'Are you insured?'

'Yes, but—'

Silence.

I moved forward to sit at the edge of my seat. 'What is it, love? What're you not telling me?'

'Mother, they took Callum's last letter to me.' I could hear the tears in Sephy's voice.

I counted to ten before I spoke. I'd been about to launch in with 'Good riddance' but thank goodness my brain kicked in before my mouth. That was the last thing Sephy wanted to hear, I could tell that much from her voice.

'Persephone, why did you hold onto that letter? I never saw it, but from what you told me it was pure poison.'

'I know, but I . . . I didn't know how to let it go. I should've torn it up or burned it years ago but every time I tried, I couldn't bring myself to do it,' Sephy told me. 'I had it hidden where I thought no one would find it.'

'Where?'

'You know the shoe boxes stacked up at the back of my wardrobe? I kept the letter in the bottom box, inside one of the shoes.'

'And the burglars found it there?' I asked, aghast.

'I know,' said Sephy. 'That's what's worrying me. I had my jewellery box in front of the shoe boxes and they didn't touch that.'

'They left all your jewellery to rummage through your shoe boxes?' My frown deepened considerably.

'See! You think it's just as strange as I do.'

'It's probably nothing,' I said, trying to soothe my daughter.

'But suppose it's *something*, Mother? Suppose they sell the letter to the newspapers and the whole thing gets dragged into the public arena again? I can just see some hack journalist reading out the juiciest phrases – *Sephy, I don't love you. I never did. You were just an assignment to me.*

A way for all of us in our cell of the Liberation Militia to get money — a lot of money — from your dad. Or suppose some-one shows the letter to Rose? I couldn't bear that.'

'Sephy, calm down. You're getting a bit ahead of your-self here. The thieves probably thought it was something valuable and were interrupted before they could see that it wasn't. So they probably just took it with them and now it's lying in some dustbin somewhere.'

'D'you really think so?'

'Of course,' I smiled. 'Since when are burglars inter-ested in personal letters?'

'I guess you're right.'

'I know I am. So stop worrying about it,' I told Sephy. 'In fact, if anything, the filching beggars have done you a favour. They got rid of that thing for you.'

'I suppose so,' said Sephy, not entirely convinced.

'D'you want me to come over?' I asked.

'No, 'course not. There's nothing you can do,' Sephy dismissed. 'I was just a bit worried, that's all.'

'You've got nothing to worry about, love.'

'OK. Thanks, Mother.'

'You're welcome. Just phone me if you need money or anything else.'

'I will. Bye.'

I put down the phone slowly, my smile fading rap-idly. Why would burglars take a personal letter? In spite of what I'd said to Sephy, I was concerned. If that letter made its way into the wrong hands . . . Or if, God forbid, my Callie Rose should see it . . .

I shook my head. Just how many more lives was that letter going to destroy?

fifty-one.
Callie Rose is 12

I got to school late – again. I took a deep breath and opened the door. I don't know what I was hoping for. Maybe if I strode to my seat with dignity and purpose, Mr March wouldn't have a go at me. And to mutilate a line from the play we were currently doing in English: 'Is this a flying pig I see before me?'

'Callie Rose Hadley, what time is it on the planet you live on? Do you even occupy the same space-time continuum as the rest of us?' asked Mr March in his usual convoluted way.

'Pardon, sir?' I pretended ignorance.

'Why can everyone in this class get to school on time except you?'

'Sorry, sir,' I mumbled. I kept my head down and headed for my desk.

'Sorry doesn't cut it,' said Mr March.

I could tell from his voice that he wasn't going to give me a break. He'd be on my case all day now. I stopped short about a metre from my desk. A Cross boy sat in what had been the free seat next to me. He had collar-length, jet-black locks and the biggest, darkest eyes I've ever seen. He was a bit plump, although it looked like he was trying to hide it by slouching in his chair. He was quite good looking actually – as boys go. I frowned at him. He looked at me, then turned to face the front. I sat down. When had this new boy arrived then?

'Callie Rose, see me after class,' said Mr March.

'Yes, sir.' I sighed inwardly. I'd probably get a letter home now – as if Mum needed another reason to be disappointed in me. Mr March turned back to the whiteboard to continue the lesson. I turned to the new boy.

'I didn't catch your name,' I whispered.

He looked at me. 'That's 'cause I didn't throw it,' he replied. And he turned to face the front again.

Be like that then, I thought, eyebrows raised.

And we didn't exchange another word for the rest of the lesson. But I found out his name when Mr March asked him a question.

Amyas.

fifty-two. Sephy

I was very pleased with the way my new song was coming along. This one almost wrote itself. I'd recorded the guitar and bass guitar tracks. Now I just needed to use my keyboard to lay down the piano and drum fillers. But I couldn't make up my mind whether or not to start with a saxophone intro or strings. After giving it some more thought, I decided to try each in turn and see which one sounded better. I hadn't sold my last two songs but I was hopeful that this one would do better. I could certainly use the money.

A tap on my shoulder brought me out of my reverie. I saw Callie Rose mouth my name. I took off my headphones.

'Yes, dear?'

'Mum, I . . . I went to the toilet and I . . . I think I've started my period . . .'

'You have?' A grin burst across my face. 'My baby! Come here!'

I was about to give Callie a hug, but I caught myself in time. I gave her a pat on the head and a kiss on the forehead instead.

'Mum, I'm not a dog who just retrieved a bone, thank you very much,' Callie complained. 'And it's nothing to grin about either. It's yuk and messy. And how come boys don't have to go through this? It's not fair.'

'I know, dear. But you've got the next forty-odd years to get used to it,' I smiled. 'Besides, now you're in tune with nature. You have a season, a rhythm, like the moon and the tides. You're linked to the cosmos—'

'What a load of crap!' said Callie.

'I beg your pardon!' I admonished, trying not to laugh. 'Language, Callie! Though I must admit, I thought the same when my sister Minerva told me that when I had my first period.'

'Aunt Minerva?' Callie said surprised. 'How come you told Aunt Minerva and not Nana Jasmine?'

I could feel my face begin to get warm. 'I can't remember. Maybe Mother was out somewhere.'

Yeah, out like a light.

'Callie, come with me.'

I took Callie into my bedroom and fished out the assortment of sanitary protection I'd been hoarding over the last few months. When I caught Callie scowling at me, I quickly wiped the smile off my face, even though I felt so . . . so proud inside. I took Callie through the use of each one, telling her the pros and cons of each product. When Callie made her selection, I watched her leave my bedroom, still grumbling about how unfair it was that boys had it so much easier than girls.

Look at our baby, Callum. She's growing up.

I just had to tell someone! I phoned my sister, Minerva.

'Hi, Minnie, it's me. You OK?'

'I'm fine,' Minerva said, surprised. I didn't phone her very often.

'Guess what? Callie Rose has started her period!'

'Already?' said Minerva. 'She's a bit young, isn't she?'

'She's twelve, nearly thirteen,' I pointed out.

'That makes me feel ancient,' Minerva complained. 'I still think of my niece as being five or six.'

'Hardly. In fact—'

'Why did you phone Aunt Minerva just to tell her that?' Callie shouted from my bedroom door. 'My period is my private business. Why don't you just put an ad in Aunt Minerva's newspaper and tell the whole world!'

And she marched off in a real huff.

'Minerva, I'm going to have to call you back,' I sighed.

'I heard,' Minerva laughed. 'She's so like you, isn't she?'

That made me pause. 'What d'you mean?'

'She speaks her mind, that one. No messing about.'

'I guess,' I said. 'Talk to you soon.'

'Good luck,' said Minerva, still laughing. And she hung up.

Now to find my daughter and apologize profusely!

fifty-three.
Callie Rose is 12

'The new boy is soooo cool!'

Was I the only one in our group who hadn't totally lost her mind? 'You're not *still* talking about Amyas, are you?' I asked.

'Even his name is way cool!' said Sammi.

I mean – *please!* Amyas was about as cool as an erupting zit.

'What's so cool about him?' I asked, sourly. 'I must've blinked and missed it.'

'Callie, don't your eyes work?' said Rafiya.

'My eyes work just fine, thank you?'

'Look! There he is!' Sammi drooled. 'Yummy!'

I shook my head. If Rafiya and Sammi were going to dribble on about Amyas all lunch time then I was off. I had far better things to do than talk about that rude fart.

'He's looking this way! He's looking this way!' Rafiya cried out.

For the last ten minutes they'd been looking out for Amyas, just dying for him to notice them. And the moment he did, Sammi and Rafiya immediately looked away. What was the point? I glared at Amyas, still remembering what he'd said to me in our first lesson together. Unfriendly twerp!

'Is he still looking? Callie, is he still looking?'

'Yes, he is,' I replied. I stood up. Enough was enough. Reading horoscopes in the library would be better than this and horoscopes were the *dregs*. 'And I'm off. You'll have to dribble over him by yourselves.'

'Callie Rose, you are so immature,' Sammi told me loftily.

'Girls should check out the boys. What's the point of being a teenager otherwise?' said Rafiya.

'I'm not a teenager yet,' I pointed out. 'I'm only twelve. And if turning thirteen means that I salivate over a moron like Amyas then I'll just skip ahead to twenty.'

'So childish!' Rafiya called after me as I marched off.

I spun around. 'Boys go to Jupiter, to get more stupider! Girls go to college to get more knowledge!'

I was very pleased with myself. Huh! Me? Childish?

Rafiya raised an eyebrow. 'Actually, boys go to Venus, to play with their—'

'Rafiya!' Sammi interrupted in a fit of giggles.

Sammi and Rafiya had become too silly for words. I flounced off. At least I didn't sit on the bench in the school courtyard making a fool of myself over some *boy*.

And what's more, that was never, ever going to happen.

fifty-four. Jasmine

Please, God, let me be mistaken. Please.

Take a deep breath, Jasmine, and calm down. It's probably your mind just playing tricks on you. That's all it is. Use your fingertips the way the doctor showed you at your last check-up and work your way around the . . . area. And even if it's something, it's probably nothing. Why should it be something? The last time, the lump disappeared all on its own. The last time it was probably just hormones or a bruise maybe or something that your body could sort out for itself. The last time, it was nothing.

So why should it be any different now? You've been in good health for years now. It's probably just stress or nerves or your imagination. So calm down.

But I hardly have to press to feel it. It's hard like a marble, irregular in shape, not spherical, bigger than before and more painful.

The lump in my breast is back.

fifty-five. Sephy

I looked around Specimens with interest. It was so still and quiet. Although it was open every evening till late, we only opened for lunch on Thursdays, Fridays and Saturdays. It was always so totally different when it was closed. Empty, it was sad as a wind-up toy just waiting for people to come along and play with it. Empty, it looked like it was trying too hard. And the glass wall separating the bar from the restaurant looked exclusive in the worse sense of the word. It was a teaser, mocking each space with its 'look, but don't touch' window on the other world. Different types of people came to each. The bar was more of a first-date, out-with-friends or have-a-laugh kind of place. The restaurant was more subdued, more intimate and was becoming very much an 'in' place. A venue in which to see and be seen.

Nathan had poured a great deal of time and money as well as himself into the place. Specimens felt like my second home. I'd grown comfortable here. Playing the piano and singing in the restaurant wasn't too taxing, although I had to be careful to rest my voice on my days off, and Nathan had even put a sign outside the place saying, 'Specimens – featuring Sephy'. No full names, no last names. I'd never be *that* comfortable.

'Sorry I'm late.' Nathan walked in from the street. He shook his head and immediately pulled off his dripping coat. He looked like he'd just had a bucket of water tipped over him.

'Hi, Nathan. Still raining, is it?'

It'd been raining since early morning and at one in the afternoon it was only just beginning to show signs of letting up.

'Your powers of deduction are astounding,' said Nathan, locking and bolting the door behind him. 'What happened to the sunshine we were promised for today?'

I smiled. Nathan had a dry, almost sarcastic manner which hid a heart as soft as yoghurt. After my first mortifying evening when he and Sherona had walked into my dressing room to find me in Sonny's arms, I had thought I'd get fired for sure. But all he had said once Sherona and Sonny were gone was, 'If you'd rather take the rest of the evening off, that's fine.'

I'd remained silent, wondering if this had been his subtle way of telling me to leave and not come back, but then he'd said, 'So I'll see you tomorrow?'

I hadn't left. I'd stayed. No more running away. And that had been Nathan's last word on the subject.

After that first day, he always knocked on my dressing-room door before entering and in all the time I'd worked for him he'd never once made me feel cheap – which was precisely what I'd been feeling after the debacle with Sonny and his new girlfriend. It still made me wince to remember all the names Sherona had flung at me because, bad as they were, I deserved every one.

Nathan had proved himself to be one of my true friends

and after keeping myself deliberately isolated for so long, I didn't have too many of those.

'You look lovely,' said Nathan.

I glanced down at my attire. Yes, I had remembered correctly! I had on an old pair of jeans and a yellow T-shirt. Hardly *haute couture*!

'Thanks, Nathan. But maybe you need to get out more? Frequent more places than your home and this bar?'

'I hear they're starting classes at the local adult education centre,' said Nathan.

'Classes in what?' I asked, wondering at the change of subject.

'Classes in learning to take a compliment.'

Laborious point taken!

'Thank you. Now that's out of the way, any ideas on the type of songs you want me to perform tonight?' I asked as Nathan hung up his coat.

Most of the time he left it to me but I always checked just in case.

'We've got two birthday parties coming in later so nothing too thoughtful.'

'Light and fluffy. Got it,' I replied.

I began to sort through my music on the table before me, dividing the sheets into the two required groups. Nathan was halfway across the floor when someone started pounding on the door. Through the frosted glass in the door, I could just make out the silhouettes of two men. With a frown, Nathan turned to look, only to turn back to me almost at once. And there was no mistaking the look on his face.

'Sephy, disappear. NOW!' Nathan's eyes were hard, his lips set.

If he had butterflies in his stomach, they were obviously infectious because now my stomach was jittering too. I didn't need to be told twice.

'Head out the back,' Nathan ordered in a whisper.

I headed through the door which led past my dressing room and to the back door beyond, but halfway down the hallway I changed my mind. I had no idea what was going on but suppose Nathan needed my help? I tiptoed back the way I came, catching the door which opened into the bar just before it shut completely. I peered past it, watching as Nathan steeled himself before unbolting and unlocking the main entrance. He barely had time to step out of the way before the door was flung open. Two Nought men in power suits strode inside, uninvited. Then a Nought man wearing clothes that would've cost me at least half a year's salary sauntered into the bar, smiling serenely. There were no bumps in the road of his life. His smile became even more pleasant when he caught sight of Nathan.

'Nathaniel, I'm pleased, if a little surprised, to see you here. That I am.'

'Why wouldn't I be in my own place, Mr Carson?' Nathan asked coldly.

'Your place, is it? Your place as long as you pay me to keep it,' said Mr Carson silkily.

Nathan said nothing.

'Now you didn't pay me last weekend and I let you be because anyone can forget or have a bad week. But I can't let it slide for another week. Miss one week and that's bad luck. Miss two weeks and that's bad habits. So I'll just be taking my money and going,' said Mr Carson.

My heart was thundering like an express train through a tunnel by now. I should've just left when Nathan told me to. Now what? I couldn't sneak away, they might hear me. If I revealed myself I might suffer whatever fate was in store for Nathan. Or worse.

I recognized the thug threatening Nathan now. Not by his face but by his name. He had to be Jordy Carson. I think Jordy was short for Jordache. He was known as Mr Teflon because the police had never managed to charge him with anything and make it stick. Jordy was supposed to have his evil little fingers in a number of pies: extortion, gambling, prostitution; he was even rumoured to have funded umpteen Liberation Militia operations. The buzz said that he financed L.M. bank robberies and jewel heists and the like for a generous percentage of the takings. And weapons technology was also supposed to be shared between his mob and the L.M. He was one of the untouchables. And here he was in Specimens, trying to intimidate my boss and there wasn't a thing I could do about it. Why would a man like him even bother with a relatively small-time operation like Specimens? It didn't make any sense. Unless smaller concerns like Specimens financed his larger operations. And one rebel like Nathan could give a lot of other people ideas.

What should I do?

Inside, panic began to rise like flood waters, sweeping away all my attempts to think rationally.

'I don't have anything for you,' said Nathan, drawing himself up, his back ramrod straight.

'Now I don't believe that, Nathaniel,' said Jordy, making himself comfortable on a bar stool. 'I'll just sit here and wait for you to come to your senses and give me my money.'

'I'm not paying you or anyone else another penny,' said Nathan quietly. 'Between you and the Audley family, you're bleeding me dry.'

'Not giving me what you owe me is bad for business – and hazardous to your health,' said Jordy.

'I'm not paying you a penny,' Nathan repeated.

'I'll have to see if I can change your mind,' said Jordy evenly.

He nodded at his two muscle-bound, muscle-brained goons, who smiled at each other before they started for Nathan.

'I'm going to enjoy this,' said the biggest thug.

I gasped involuntarily, then bit my lip. The goons carried on advancing on Nathan, but Jordy Carson looked around, the smile fading from his face for the first time since he'd arrived.

'Wait,' he ordered. 'There's someone else here.'

I didn't wait to hear any more. I turned and ran.

fifty-six.
Callie Rose is 12

I looked up from my book and glanced around. No
Tobey. The playing field wasn't too busy as the grass
was still soggy from the earlier rain, plus there was a late
lunch-time basketball match between the sixth-form
senior teams. Most of my friends had gone to watch that,
but as far as I was concerned, watching basketball was like
watching grass grow. The sun was out and hot on my
legs and face. Almost uncomfortably so. I scanned around
again. Definitely no Tobey. We'd fallen out – again – the
morning before. Some silly argument that I couldn't even
remember. And even though we'd only not been speaking
for one day, I missed him. I knocked for him after school
yesterday but he said he couldn't come round 'cause he
had to finish his homework. When I suggested we worked
together, he made an excuse about that as well. And he
left for school this morning without knocking for me first.
I guess he's still mad at me. But I'm hoping it won't last.
Tobey will always be my friend – at least, I hope so. I can't
imagine not being friends with him and I have a pretty
good imagination. I returned to my book, but after a couple
of minutes I still didn't know what it said on the page.

'Hi, Callie Rose.' Lucas sat down next to me.

I immediately shut my book.

'Hi, Lucas.'

Lucas returned my smile. I waited for him to speak. He waited for me. Lucas was so lovely. He always stopped to chat whenever he saw me. I hadn't quite figured out why but it was very sweet of him.

'So what're you reading?' he asked at last. 'A romance?'

'Are you kidding?' I said, deeply offended. 'It's a history book about world conflicts over the last century. Nana Meggie got it for me.'

'Why on earth are you reading that?'

'The past is often the key to the future,' I said grandly, admitting, 'At least that's what Nana Meggie says.'

'D'you believe her?'

'I don't know,' I admitted. 'That's why I'm reading this book, I suppose. Nana Meggie says I should know more about the history of both Noughts and Crosses and she reckons the school will only teach me Cross history.'

'There's Nought history week every October,' Lucas pointed out.

'That's what I told her,' I admitted. 'But Nana says Nought history shouldn't be confined to just one week of every year and only when the schools can be bothered. She says the history of Crosses and Noughts is intertwined and should be taught that way.'

'D'you and your nan talk about stuff like that a lot?'

I nodded. 'Well, Nana does most of the talking! Mum and Nana Meggie have always talked to me about current events but most of the time I just switch off. I must admit, I'm not really into politics and all that stuff. Do you talk about history and politics and stuff with your mum and dad?'

'Are you nuts?' Lucas scoffed. 'Dad's too busy to talk to any of us. And Mum's not interested in anything that doesn't have a price tag attached. She shops, she goes to the gym, she shops some more. End of story.'

'Oh, I see. Well, you can read this book after me if you'd like,' I offered.

'Is it any good?'

'Not bad. I thought I'd get some more info about the bits that interest me after I've finished reading it though.'

'Why?'

'I'm not going to believe just one book,' I told him.

'You're a girl who likes to make up her own mind, eh?'

'I guess.'

'If you like history, you should go and see that new film, *Black Sails*.'

'I'm hoping to see it this weekend actually.'

'I want to see it too,' said Lucas. 'Fancy going with me? Not on a date or anything but as friends. Or maybe we could arrange for a group of us to go and see it.'

But before I could answer – 'Hi, Loo–cassss!' Bliss from my class plonked herself right in front of Lucas, completely ignoring me. And the way she said his name – *please!* Talk about making a meal out of each and every syllable.

'How are you?' Bliss continued.

'Fine,' Lucas smiled.

And I still didn't exist. There wasn't even a contemptuous, dismissive flick of her eyelashes. Nothing.

'Are you still coming to my party on Saturday?' Bliss wheedled. 'Everyone will be there.'

I won't, I thought with a wry smile.

'I said I was coming, didn't I?' said Lucas tetchily. 'I haven't changed my mind since this morning.'

'I'm so glad,' fawned Bliss.

I mean, really! Why didn't she just fall to her knees and kiss his sweaty feet?

'What time are you going, Callie Rose?' Lucas turned to ask me. 'I can call for you if you'd like. We could share a cab?'

'I'm not going to Bliss's party,' I replied.

'How come?' said Lucas.

'I wasn't invited.'

'Oh, I see. Well, would you rather go to the cinema instead? We could go to a late screening rather than an early one.'

I glanced at Bliss. If looks could kill, Bliss would've been banged up for life with no possibility of parole.

'Callie Rose, of course you're invited to my party,' said Bliss, insincerity positively dripping from every pore. 'Your invitation must've got lost in the post.'

Of course it did, along with my invitation to lunch with the Prime Minister.

'So what d'you think?' smiled Lucas. 'The cinema or Bliss's party?'

'What would you rather do?' I asked.

'I really don't mind. It's entirely up to you.'

I looked at Bliss, enjoying the look of pure panic on her face. Serve her right – stuck-up snob.

'Can I think about it, Lucas?' I asked.

'That's fine.' Lucas shrugged and stood up. 'Let me know what you decide.'

'I will,' I called after him as he walked off. Bliss and I watched him leave, but at least I looked away first. I decided it was time for me to make myself scarce as well, but no sooner had I stood up than Bliss stepped in front of me, blocking my way. Alexia and Rachel, two of Bliss's fashion-victim friends, appeared from nowhere to stand on either side of her. They all looked like clones, dressed alike in school skirts hitched up to exactly the same length and royal-blue shirts with the same top three buttons undone, ties around their necks instead of their shirt collars. There wasn't a spark of originality or individuality between them. And they each wore the same expression, revealing the same hostility.

'You don't want to miss my party,' Bliss told me.

'Well, I haven't made up my mind yet—'

'You *really* don't want to miss my party,' Bliss repeated.

'I'm flattered that my presence means that much to you.'

'I don't want you there,' said Bliss bluntly. 'But if Lucas doesn't turn up, I'm going to hold you personally responsible.'

'I don't tell Lucas what to do,' I protested.

Bliss leaned forward so that she was right in my face. 'If I find out that Lucas went to the cinema with you instead of to my party, I'll make sure you're really sorry.'

'Oh yeah? How're you going to do that?'

'You wouldn't want to find out.'

'I don't doubt it,' I replied.

Bliss gave me a quick shove for good luck and marched off with her entourage. For a minute or two it was fun thinking of the look on her face on Saturday if Lucas didn't show up for her party because he was with me. But I knew it wouldn't happen. Part of me, pathetic as I knew it was, wanted to go to Bliss's party. I'd heard her house was something else, with an indoor swimming pool no less. And most of the girls in my class had spoken of nothing else for the past week.

So I decided to go.

'Just so she won't be disappointed and miss me too much!' I told myself. 'I'll go for Bliss's sake, rather than my own.'

And if I said it enough times, maybe I'd start to believe it.

fifty-seven. Sephy

I heard all kinds of shouting and crashing and swearing behind me but I didn't look back and I certainly didn't stop. A terrifying feeling of *déjà vu* bit savagely at me. The past and present combined to play tricks in my head. A hallway, a beach . . . the smell of the sea, the smell of my sweat dripping past my eyes, the feel of perspiration prickling the skin beneath my nose, tiny rocks and stones pricking the soles of my feet, the sound of the sea crash-ing on the shore . . . Only it wasn't the sound of the sea, it was the sound of my blood racing through me. Being chased by Callum, being chased by Noughts, being chased . . .

Run, Sephy. Run.

I flung myself at the back door, pushing down on the bar handle that ran across the width of the door to open it. A blast of traffic noise hit me. The restaurant bins had been put out, ready to be emptied, and although the rain had now stopped, huge drops of water dripped off them, audibly hitting the pavement. Should I stop and push one in front of the exit? No time. Just run, Sephy. Lose yourself in the afternoon crowd.

Don't let them catch you.

Not again.

I weaved in and out of those around me, who all seemed to be walking towards rather than away from me so that I was moving against the flow. Some still had their umbrellas up, unaware that the rain had now stopped. Maybe that would work in my favour?

'Ow!'

'Watch it!'

Sharp comments and dirty looks followed in my wake, but I didn't stop running. Had I been followed? Were Jordy's henchmen still after me? I didn't even know. I hadn't turned my head once to find out. I ducked into a fairly crowded boutique and ran straight up to the Nought woman serving behind the counter. I was going to ask for her help but then I saw the phone on the counter.

'May I use your phone please?'

'I'm sorry, but our phones are not for customer use—' The woman began an obviously well-rehearsed line.

'Please. It's urgent. A matter of life and death,' I said.

The woman eyed me with suspicion. I knew what I must look like, some down-and-out hiding out of the rain and trying her luck. My T-shirt was clinging like a second skin and my jeans felt horribly cool and clammy, but they were the least of my problems.

'I'm not joking. Please,' I pleaded. 'I need to use a phone.'

'Go on then,' she said, still eyeing me, not bothering to hide her chary expression. 'But you'll have to pay for the call.'

'Fine. Whatever,' I said, grabbing at the phone.

I had a quick scan around but I couldn't see Jordy or the others. Were they back at Specimens? And what were they doing to Nathan?

Without wasting any more time, I dialled the police.

fifty-eight. Jude

'Hello, Callie Rose.'

'Uncle! What're you doing here?' Callie's face broke into an instant smile.

I looked around as others swarmed out of the hallowed gates of Heathcroft High. There were more luxury cars and top-down convertibles and SUVs coming out of the school driveway than in the biggest car dealership in town. The early autumn sunshine shone down on the favoured like the earlier rain was just an illusion. Lots of Cross mums and a few Cross dads ensuring that their little Cross darlings mixed with the right sort. After all, you were never too young to start networking. Friends made now became the business contacts of tomorrow. There were some halfers, Callie included, but very few Noughts – which was probably one of the top five reasons why a number of these Crosses wanted their bastard kids to go to Heathcroft in the first place.

'I've got a surprise for you,' I said, turning my attention back to my quarry.

'Oh yeah? What's that?' Callie asked eagerly.

'Do you have to go straight home or can I borrow you for an hour or two?' I said so that only Callie would hear me. 'The rain has finally stopped so what I have in mind will be fun.'

Callie worried the corner of her lip. 'I suppose I could tell Nana that I'm going round to Sammi's to do some homework again. Can I use your mobile to phone home?'

'Of course you can,' I smiled.

It really shouldn't be this easy.

'I don't like lying to Nana and Mum though,' said Callie.

'It's only a little Cross lie, not an evil Nought lie,' I said deliberately.

'I don't like that saying.' Callie scowled at me. 'Lies aren't people.'

I almost had to bite my lip to stop myself from answering that one, however tempting. Callie was incredibly book smart and very real-world ignorant. That's what came from too much cosseting.

'It's a little lie which isn't going to harm anyone and I'll get you home in time to do your homework,' I promised.

'OK then. Where's your car?'

I led the way through the throng of home-goers. No one was paying too much attention to us, which was just the way I wanted it. This was going to be dangerous enough. I couldn't risk using backup this time. Where I was going made it too dangerous and I couldn't risk the lives of any of my associates in that way. I hadn't even told Morgan. I used my key to open the car doors and we both got in, with Callie sitting in the passenger seat next to me.

'Seat belt,' I said with patience. I always had to remind Callie to put on her seat belt. There was no way I wanted her flying through my windscreen, at least not until I'd finished using her.

As Callie buckled up, she asked, 'So where are we going?'

'You'll see,' I told her.

'You're being very mysterious,' Callie complained.

'Years of training and practice,' I told her.

'Why does an insurance salesman need to practise being mysterious?' asked Callie.

'How else would I sell something as boring as insurance otherwise? I do magic tricks and play all kinds of sleight-of-hand games with this hand.' I waved my right hand at her. 'And with *this* hand, I get people to sign up for whatever I want.'

'Are you good?'

'I'm the best,' I told her.

And we set off.

★

'Here we are,' I announced.

'At last,' said Callie. She looked out of her car window. 'Where are we?'

'Your grandfather's house,' I told her.

'Grandad Kamal?' Callie turned eyes as big as saucers to me.

'That's right.'

'Which one is Grandad's house?' Callie asked urgently.

'You see that road? He lives just round the corner, in the last house on the right. You can't miss it. It's one of only two houses in the entire street.'

I'd seen photos of Kamal Hadley's house and its neighbour. They faced each other like gloating sentinels, surrounded by immaculate lawns and an abundance of shrubs and flowers. It was tempting to drive round the corner and take a look for myself, but I couldn't risk getting any closer than this. Kamal's house had two guards on permanent duty patrolling its perimeter at all times. We in the Liberation Militia knew the addresses and details of all Members of Parliament, plus the habits and security arrangements of the major players in both the government and the Opposition.

'Is Grandad Kamal in?' asked Callie.

'I have it on good authority that he is.'

'Can I go and see him?' Callie was almost bouncing in her seat.

'Have you met him before?'

'No. I've only seen him on TV or in newspapers. Mum says he does a lot of travelling up and down the country and abroad,' said Callie, adding thoughtfully, 'Lots of people travel a lot but they still make time for their families.

I must admit, I wondered if maybe Grandad and my mum had a big quarrel and he didn't want to see me.'

'I'm sure that's not true. Maybe it was your mum who didn't want you to see your grandad?' I said lightly.

I was gratified to see Callie considering this.

'Can we get closer?'

'I can't.' I shook my head. 'But you can.'

'Why can't you?' asked Callie, surprised.

'A major part of the reason your mum and I . . . fell out, was because of your grandad.'

'What did he do?'

'Maybe we'll discuss it when you're older.'

Callie huffed. 'Why do all adults say that? How old do I have to be before my family start telling me the truth?'

'Only you can decide that.' I smiled inwardly. She thought her family were lying to her. Excellent. 'Off you go. You've got about half an hour before I have to get you back.'

'OK, Uncle. Well, the sun is shining, so that's a good sign.' Callie started to get out of the car.

'Oh, Callie Rose, don't tell anyone that I brought you here. If anyone asks, you took the train and a bus. OK?'

Callie nodded.

I watched her as she walked up the wide road and round the corner towards Kamal Hadley's house. In a detached, careless kind of way, I almost felt sorry for her. The outcome of this event was almost mundane in its predictability.

fifty-nine. Sephy

At first, Nathan didn't want to go to hospital but the paramedics weren't the only ones to insist. One eye was completely swollen shut and he had a puffy cheek and cuts and bruises all over his face. The paramedic I spoke to suspected by the way Nathan was holding his side that he might be nursing one or more cracked ribs. But the police refused to let us go until we'd answered what they called 'a few' questions first.

The Cross woman in charge was Detective Inspector Muswell. She questioned Nathan first, then turned her attention to me.

'So two men pushed their way in here when you opened the door?' DI Muswell asked.

'I didn't open the door, Nathan did,' I replied, resisting the temptation to look at Nathan for confirmation that I was saying the right thing.

'Can you describe them please?' An eager Nought policeman stood next to DI Muswell, a small spiral-bound notebook in one hand, a pencil poised in the other.

'Two Nought men.' I shrugged. 'One about six feet, the other taller.'

'Were either of them carrying weapons?'

'Not that I saw, but I didn't see much. I was in my dressing room most of the time.'

'But you did see the attackers?'

I nodded. The DI looked at me expectantly but I decided to shut up. It was best to keep my answers short and simple.

'What colour hair did they both have?'

'Lightish brown. Dark blond. Not too dark.'

'What else?'

'What d'you mean?'

'You watched two men beat up your employer and you can't remember more than their hair colour?' DI Muswell asked, not bothering to hide her scepticism.

'They came in the front, I was in the back. When they started threatening Nathan, I sneaked a peek, saw it was serious and then ran out the back to get help,' I explained.

'Well, is there anything else you can tell me about either one of the assailants?'

I opened my mouth to tell her what they were wearing but I sensed rather than saw Nathan's frown. So I shook my head instead.

'I wasn't paying much attention and, as I said, when the aggro started, I ran for help.'

The detective inspector didn't like it but she must've known she wouldn't get much more information out of me.

'And you, Mr Ealing, do you have anything more to add to your previous statement?'

'. . . hard to see faces when eyes pummelled shut,' Nathan said haltingly, trying not to wince. His bottom lip was cut and swollen.

DI Muswell looked from Nathan to me and back again. 'Mr Ealing, do you know a man called Jordache Carson?'

Nathan tried to shake his head, but grimaced as his neck muscles protested. 'No. Why?'

'Because I smell his hands all over this,' said the DI. 'Mr Ealing, I promise you that if you testify against him, we'll protect you. You too, Miss Hadley.'

Nathan gave what sounded suspiciously like a snort.

'We can put you in our witness protection programme,' DI Muswell said sincerely.

'Protect from whom? Carson, or busloads police in . . . back pocket?' stammered Nathan.

'Mr Ealing, listen—' DI Muswell began, but she didn't get very far. The paramedics were now insisting on taking Nathan to hospital, so the DI had no choice but to let us go. And not a moment too soon. My legs were turning boneless under me.

Once the phone was dusted for prints, the crime scene officer gave me permission to use it. I phoned Ron, Nathan's manager, to come and sort the place out. Then I insisted on travelling in the back of the ambulance with Nathan.

'How're you feeling?' I asked softly once the ambulance was under way.

'Under weather,' said Nathan.

I had to smile, even though the sight of Nathan's battered face brought tears to my eyes.

'Specimens stays open,' said Nathan, touching a tentative hand to his bottom lip. 'Tell Ron.'

'I'll tell him.'

There was plenty I wanted to say but the paramedic

riding in the back of the ambulance with us was inhibiting to say the least.

'OK, till I'm back,' said Nathan awkwardly.

It took me a moment to figure out what he was trying to say. 'Me or the restaurant?'

'Both.'

'I'll be fine,' I assured him. 'I've been through worse. And Ron and I will take care of the place.'

'Nothing till come back,' said Nathan, his voice trailing off.

'He's going into shock,' said the paramedic, pushing me to one side.

I watched Nathan through anxious eyes. I understood what he was saying. He reckoned nothing would happen to Specimens or us until he got out of the hospital and back to work.

But what then?

And in the meantime, would Jordache Carson be back to try and find out who'd witnessed that evening's events? One way or another my life had suddenly become very complicated.

'Just where d'you think you're going?'

A Cross man, the size of a haystack and with the personality of a rabid Dobermann, stopped me several metres away from Grandad Kamal's house. I felt so strange. I was actually going to meet my grandfather. I couldn't wait.

'I asked you a question.' The Cross man frowned.

'I've come to see my grandad, Kamal Hadley. I'm Callie Rose Hadley.' I held out my hand but the Dobermann ignored it.

He looked me up and down and then got out a mobile phone. Two key presses later and he turned slightly away from me. His eyes were still on me but his attention was on the phone and his conversation.

'I've got a girl out here claiming to be Mr Hadley's granddaughter. She says her name is Sally Hadley.'

'Callie Hadley,' I corrected. 'Callie Rose Hadley.'

Look, Dad. I'm going to meet my grandad. My heart is skipping. This is one of the best days of my life. Look, Dad . . .

The man turned even further away from me.

'Yes . . . yes, that's right.' The man looked up and down the exclusive street. 'No, there's no one else with her.'

'How did you get here?' the man asked me.

'A train and a bus and then I walked.'

'Did anyone come with you?'

'No.'

The man repeated our conversation into the phone.

'Do you have some ID?'

I had to think about that one. 'I've got my school library card – and my bus pass.'

The man listened to someone at the other end of the phone for quite a few seconds. Then he flipped his phone shut and glared down at me.

'Come with me,' he said.

And if I'd wanted to argue with him, his tone would've discouraged me. We walked along the driveway, paved with precision tessellations. Mr Carlos, my maths teacher, would've been proud. The front door was already open. A tall Cross woman stood in the doorway. She wore a cream dress with purple flowers printed on it and matching cream shoes with a purple trim. Her clothes were stylish and expensive, I think, just like Nana Jasmine's. In fact she reminded me a lot of Nana Jasmine, except this woman was a younger version. Her braided hair was swept up in a careless bun and tied up with a cream ribbon.

'Can I help you?' the woman asked when I reached her door.

'I've come to see my grandad. I'm Callie Rose Hadley,' I told her. I wondered how many people I'd have to repeat that to before I got to see my grandad. The woman looked me up and down.

'How is your mum?'

'She's fine,' I smiled.

'Wait there,' said the woman and she lightly stepped across the vast marble hallway to one of the rooms beyond.

My heartbeat was loud and heavy, like a grandfather clock chiming the hour. I glanced up at the security guard, who was still eyeing me. Why was he looking at me with so much suspicion? Maybe he didn't believe I was who I said. The woman reappeared, her head down as if she didn't want to look me in the eye.

'I'm afraid my husband can't see you,' said the woman. Her tone didn't hold an apology but her eyes did.

'Why not?'

Before the woman could answer, a man past middle age appeared from one of the downstairs rooms. He marched over to the woman, his expression set.

'Are you my grandfather?' I asked.

I drank him in, sure it was him. He was taller and his hair was darker than I'd expected. I thought he'd have streaks of grey all over his head but his hair was jet-black. Maybe he dyed it? Nana Jasmine has streaks of silver all over her head and if this was my grandad, he was a lot older than Nana. He was still quite good looking, though his face was a bit stern. He wore sweat pants and a old T-shirt but he wasn't perspiring or anything so I reckoned he was probably about to go for a run.

The man looked me in the eyes and said, 'You need to go home before your family wonder where you are.'

'You don't understand,' I tried to explain. 'Are you Kamal Hadley?'

The man didn't reply, but he didn't have to. I'd seen him on the TV news more than once. Mind you, I used to just watch him, I never bothered to listen very closely. He was always talking about boring political stuff.

'I'm Callie Rose, your granddaughter,' I grinned. 'I've come to see you. I'm so happy to finally meet you.'

The man looked me up and down, but there wasn't a trace of a smile on his face. Not even a hint. As he looked at my face, his eyes narrowed into a frown.

'I don't have a granddaughter called Callie Rose,' he said coldly. 'Go home.'

'But—' Now I was the one who didn't understand. 'I'm Sephy's daughter.'

'You've made a mistake coming here. I don't have a daughter called Sephy,' said Grandad. 'Max, could you escort this girl off the premises.'

'Kamal, I really think—' began the woman next to him.

'I don't want to hear it, Grace,' Grandad snapped at her. He turned back to me. 'And as for you, don't come here again.'

And very slowly but firmly he closed the black gloss-painted door in my face. I stood stock-still, trying to sort out my frantic thoughts. Maybe Grandad didn't understand what I was telling him? He obviously didn't realize that I was his granddaughter. But how could he not understand? I'd said it as plain as I could.

'Come on,' said Max gently. 'You need to go home now. D'you want me to organize a lift home, or phone for someone to come and pick you up?'

I slowly turned away from the closed front door and

stared at Max. He looked so sorry for me that in that moment, I knew I wasn't dreaming. Grandad didn't want me. He didn't want to know me.

But to close the door in my face . . .

'Do you want—?' Max began again.

I shook my head. 'No, thank you.'

'I'm sorry,' said Max.

I took one last look at Grandad's house and went back the way I came. But halfway along the road, I had to stop because I couldn't see where I was going. I wiped the tears from my eyes and carried on down the road and round the corner to Uncle Jude.

 ## sixty-one. Sephy

There it was again, that strange, muffled noise coming from Callie Rose's bedroom. I knocked on the door and entered immediately.

'Callie,' I whispered. 'Are you OK?'

No answer. But the light from the landing was enough for me to see that Callie wasn't asleep. Her body was held too rigidly under the covers for that. I walked softly towards her bed.

'Callie?'

I could just see the top of her head peeking out from

beneath the duvet. Her head was tilted away from mine slightly but as I watched, a tear ran across the bridge of her nose and down towards the pillow.

'Callie, what's wrong?' I asked.

The pretence over, Callie turned her face towards me. And even in the half-light of the bedroom I could see that she'd been crying for quite some time. I sat down, feeling my way so that I didn't sit on her.

'What's wrong, angel?'

'I . . . I went to see Grandad today . . .' Callie Rose whispered.

No . . . Please, no.

I stared at her. 'Why did you do that?'

'He hates me,' said Callie.

I shook my head. 'He doesn't.'

'Mum, he hates me. He told me not to come back and slammed the door in my face.'

My blood began to bubble inside me, hot and hotter. My teeth were clamped together so hard they instantly began to hurt. I was shaking, actually shaking. I took a deep breath, then another to stop myself from trembling with a rage I hadn't felt since I was a teenager.

'He slammed the door in your face?'

Callie nodded, her tears running faster. She struggled to sit up.

'Why does he hate me? What've I done?'

'Nothing, Callie Rose. Your grandad is angry with me and he's taking it out on you.'

'Why is he angry with you?'

I shook my head. No way did I want to go into that now. I wanted to tuck Callie into bed and watch over her until she fell asleep and then jump in my car and go and see my dad – and rip his heart out. God knows that was what he was doing to mine. How dare he treat my daughter like that? *How dare he?*

'Callie, your grandad and I quarrelled a long time ago and we haven't spoken since.'

'What did you quarrel about? Was it about you and Dad?'

'Yes, dear.'

'Didn't he want you to be with my dad?'

I shook my head.

'Because Dad worked as a gardener at Grandad's house?'

Sephy, tell her the truth. Now's your chance to share your past, to share something real with your daughter. Tell her . . .

'Yes, love. Because your dad was a gardener at Nana Jasmine's house.'

'Did Grandad like Dad when you were both at Heathcroft High?' said Callie.

'My dad didn't really know Callum. And Callum didn't stay at school for very long. And after that he . . . he . . .'

Tell her the truth . . .

'He became a gardener,' I finished, despising my own weakness.

'What's wrong with that?' asked Callie.

I sighed. 'Your grandad is a politician. He didn't like the idea of me and Callum together partly because he thought it wouldn't look good for him in government.'

'Because Dad was a Nought?'

'Yes, dear.'

'That's what Unc—'

'Pardon?'

'It doesn't matter. You know the way Grandad felt

about you and my dad, is that like Nana Meggie not wanting me to hang around with Tobey?'

I couldn't answer that.

'Is Grandad upset because you didn't marry my dad?' asked Callie.

'No. Marrying Callum wouldn't've made any difference to your grandad.'

'So he's just a snob.'

Amongst other things.

'Is Nana Meggie a snob too?' Callie asked.

'Your Nana Meggie wants what's best for you.' I had to pick through the words before presenting them to my daughter. 'Your grandad was only interested in what was best for himself.'

'Well, I hate him,' said Callie vehemently.

'Callie Rose—'

'I do, Mum. I hate him. And I'll never forget the way he treated me. Never, ever.'

'Darling, don't let him poison—'

'Goodnight, Mum.' Callie slid down in her bed and turned her back on me.

What should I do now? It wasn't too late to tell her some of the truth. Maybe not all of it but some of it. But with each second, the opportunity slipped further away from me. I stood up and bent to kiss Callie's cheek.

'Goodnight, love.'

'Goodnight, Mum,' said Callie.

The tears had stopped but that was no comfort. Callie was staring wide-eyed at the wall.

'Callie . . .'

'Goodnight, Mum,' Callie repeated.

With a sigh, I took the hint and left her in peace. But I wasn't going to leave it there. Shutting Callie's door quietly behind me, I leaned against it. I needed to make a couple of phone calls. The first one would be to my sister, Minerva, to get my dad's address and phone number.

No way was he going to get away with this one. No way.

sixty-two. Jude

I hated winter. Dark and damp and too damned cold. And the rain was pitching down outside, which didn't help. I watched as Callie picked at her chocolate ice cream. For the last few months, we had met up at least every six weeks after school. And I usually brought her here to the Cuckoo's Egg café in the Dundale Centre for a quick meal or an ice cream. It had become our ritual, a place where I could drip-feed Callie the realities of life. And the Cuckoo's Egg café was ironically appropriate.

'What's wrong, Callie?' I asked.

I knew damn well what was going on in Callie's head. I can read her like a picture book. Kamal Hadley had slammed the door in Callie's face almost half a year ago, but she still felt it as keenly as if it were a mere half an hour before. Sometimes she'd be talking or laughing or joking and then the memory would come slashing back.

And then her ready smile would die and she'd get a hurt, haunted look on her face that was easy to recognize because I used to see it on my own face so many times as a child. But that was before I took the power the Crosses had to hurt me away from them and back into my own hands. I told myself, Why should you care what any of them think? The Crosses mean nothing to you. After that I was free.

'What is it about me, Uncle Jude?' said Callie, her voice soft with sadness. 'Why can't I get anyone to . . . to like me?'

'Is that true?' I asked.

'My grandad hates me and Mum can't bear to be around me.'

Take it slow, Jude. Don't blow it.

'I don't know about your mum, but I remember Kamal Hadley as being a very rigid, blinkered man. He's a man who's not prepared to tolerate any other view but his own. He doesn't like Noughts and with you being half-Nought . . .' I shrugged, leaving the rest deliberately unsaid. 'But Callie, remember this, he only has the power to hurt you if you give him that power.'

'But I can't help being half-Nought. Any more than I can help being half-Cross,' said Callie. 'Isn't anyone ever going to like me just for *me*? Even Nana Meggie never—'

'Hello, Jude.'

My head snapped up. Mum stood beside our table, her expression rigid.

'Hello, Mum.'

'Nana Meggie!' said Callie. 'What're you doing here?'

'Meeting a friend for coffee and finding you, Callie,' said my mum.

And although she was talking to Callie, she was looking straight at me. So it'd come at last. I suppose it was inevitable. But Mum was too late on one score at least. Callie Rose trusted me to tell her what no one else would.

'Callie, go and wait for me outside.'

'But Nana—'

'Callie Rose, outside. NOW!'

Mum shouting like that made Callie jump. It was obviously something which just didn't happen, from Callie's stunned response. And we were attracting attention, the very last thing I could afford.

'Go on, Callie. It's OK.' I smiled.

Callie stood up reluctantly. 'I'll phone you, Uncle. OK?'

'You do that,' I agreed.

My mum and I both watched Callie leave the café. Mum ensured Callie was out of earshot before she sat down, though poised for flight, on the chair Callie had just vacated.

'How long have you been meeting up with my granddaughter?'

A lie? The truth? 'A few months . . .'

Mum inhaled sharply. 'Jude, what've you been doing?'

'Nothing, Mum. I've just been getting to know Callum's child. That's what you've wanted all these years, isn't it?'

'Don't play games with me, Jude,' Mum said quietly.

I smiled. 'What're you panicking about? I knew you and . . . Sephy would have . . . reservations about my meeting my niece and I wanted to get to know her. That's why I had to go behind your backs.'

'So it's our fault?'

'That's not what I said.'

'And what have you been telling Callie in all the months you've been seeing her?'

'I didn't keep a diary, Mum.'

'Jude, I want a straight answer. What've you been up to all this time?'

'Mum, what d'you think I've been doing?' I asked, exasperated. 'What's going on in that suspicious mind of yours? Maybe you've been living with a Cross too long if it makes you suspicious of your own flesh and blood.'

'So it's like that,' said Mum quietly.

'It's like what, Mum?' I said, not even trying to hide my irritation.

'If you're not up to anything, why the big secret?'

'Because I knew this was exactly how you'd react. I can't go blabbing about my whereabouts to everyone, you know that. And I just wanted to get to know my niece a little better.'

'So you encouraged her to lie to her mum and me about meeting you?'

'I didn't tell her to lie. I just told her not to volunteer the information.' This conversation was getting on my nerves. 'What's the big deal, Mum? After all, d'you tell Sephy about all your meetings with me?'

Mum's face flushed red. My point was made.

'So what's the harm if Callie does the same. You can keep a secret? Well, so can she.'

Mum shook her head. 'Jude, I know you—'

'You don't know a damned thing about me,' I flared up. 'And you stopped caring when your granddaughter was born.'

'That's not true. And you still haven't answered my question,' said Mum.

'I haven't said, done or shown anything to Callie that she wouldn't've found out for herself eventually,' I said.

Mum regarded me. 'Jude, why are you doing this? I can't believe all this is just—?' She broke off abruptly to stare at me, realization radiating from her. 'It was you . . . *You're* the one who took Callie to see Kamal.'

'I was just trying to help. I thought it was time for Callie to meet her grandfather.'

'How could you?' Mum breathed, appalled.

'Did I know the bastard would slam the door in her face? Did I know that would happen?'

'You knew exactly what would happen,' said Mum stonily. 'In fact, I bet that's what you were counting on.'

'Mum, you're giving me way too much credit.'

Careful, Jude. Careful. She's your mum. She knows things about you, she can guess things about you. You can't let her know for sure . . .

Mum shook her head and stood up. 'Jude, you're to stay away from Callie. D'you hear me?'

'Don't you trust me, Mum?'

Mum's eyes narrowed, almost in pain. 'Stay away from her, Jude. I'm not going to tell you again.'

And she walked away from me without a backwards glance. The weird thing was that deep down inside, I felt . . . nothing. No pain, no sorrow, no elation, no satisfaction. Nothing. Just a hollow, echoing emptiness where no emotions would ever take root again. And there was nothing inside me to even feel glad about it.

Jude versus Jasmine

sixty-three. Jasmine

This hotel room was beginning to feel oppressive. It almost felt like Jude and I had been swallowed whole and could do nothing but watch each other and wait to see who dissolved first. So here we both sat, bathed in a silence so stony it was bruising my nerves. And I was hurting. I had to concentrate on not moving a muscle each time the next wave of pain crested inside my body. To move would be to cry out, to scream out against this invader, devouring me from the inside out.

So I did nothing but blink. One blink for each wave of pain.

Blink. Blink.

Focus on Jude.

Don't say a word.

Don't move a muscle.

Except to blink.

I watched without interest as Jude scratched at his calf. The man had tied his shoelaces twice and scratched and rubbed his calf at least three times. What was his problem? He was watching me watching him. I had no intention of taking my eyes off him for a single second. He really was too creepy for words.

'What the hell are we waiting for?' Jude suddenly leaped to his feet to shout at me.

I admit it, he made me jump. I started to my feet, only to change my mind. The less I moved the better. I was hurting too much.

'Sit down, Jude.'

'You know what, I've had enough of this.'

'I said, sit down,' I ordered.

'Suppose I told you to do your worst?' Jude challenged. 'Suppose I don't think you'll really press that switch?'

I regarded him. 'Suppose you don't try your luck, then who knows, you might just make it out of here alive.'

'I thought the outcome of this . . . this farce was a foregone conclusion,' said Jude, through narrowed eyes.

'In my experience, there's no such thing,' I told him.

He flopped down in his chair and sat back, frustration at not having the upper hand gnawing away at him like a ravenous rat.

'When is this company you were talking about going to arrive?'

'Soon,' I replied.

With perfect timing, there came a sharp rap at the door. In the silence of the room, it resounded like machine-gun fire. I almost turned my head to look in the direction of the door.

Almost.

Three sharp taps, followed by two, then one. The pre-arranged signal. I struggled to my feet, my finger never leaving the switch.

'Jude, could you get that please?'

Eyeing me carefully, Jude got to his feet. I kept half an

eye on his face and one and a half eyes on what his hands were doing.

'Put your hands on your head please until you reach the door.' I was most polite – which was more than this creature deserved.

Jude complied. He walked before me, his hands on his head. With his back towards me, I slipped my free hand into my left jacket pocket and fished out a couple of the morphine sulphate painkillers I'd emptied into my pocket earlier. I wasn't due to take one for at least another hour, but what the hell! As he reached the door, I said, 'Keep one hand on your head and use the other to open the door. When the door is open, put your free hand back on your head. And no funny business. I'm really not in the mood.'

Jude did as I asked but his free hand slowed and stilled on its way back to the top of his head when he saw who was at the door.

'Hello, son,' said Meggie.

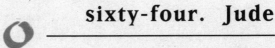

sixty-four. Jude

'Mum?'

What was she doing here? Very rarely did she turn up at my hotel room unannounced. What a moment to break the habit of a lifetime.

'Hello, Meggie,' Jasmine said from behind me. 'Jude, could you move back to your previous seat please?'

But I hardly heard her. Mum was standing in the doorway. And though I hadn't seen her in a while, she'd hardly changed. A few more lines around her eyes, a few more white hairs perhaps.

'Jude, could you return to your chair please?' said Jasmine.

'Let me in, Jude,' said Mum.

My hands still on the top of my head, I returned to my seat. Now what? What was Mum doing here? Whatever the reason, she was more than welcome. No way would Mum let mad-cow Jasmine harm me. No way. Mum was a McGregor. And when it came to the McGregors against the Hadleys, there were no grey areas, no blurred lines. Mum knew that. She might dote on Callie Rose, but Callie Rose wasn't here – and I was.

Now I just had to wait for the right opportunity to present itself. I'd strike and Mum would be right behind me. Letting Mum in was the first mistake Jasmine had made. It might very well prove to be her last.

sixty-five.
Callie Rose is 13

The noise in the food hall was cacophonous. And I loved it. I loved the sound of busy and bustling. I let it wash through me as I picked at my soggy cabbage and overcooked potatoes. I loved loud. At home, when I was doing my homework, I played my music just as loud as I could get away with. Loud enough to drown out any unwelcome thoughts that might try to swim to the surface. And there were a lot of those at the moment.

'The article in the *Science Today* journal said that the military tried to develop a chemical agent they could spray into the air which would cause Noughts to have nose bleeds but nothing would happen to Crosses . . .' Tobey was droning on and on about the latest edition of his monthly science magazine.

I sighed inwardly. I was beginning to dread the arrival of Tobey's ruddy magazine. He'd spend a day reading it, followed by a week of discussing each and every article with me like I gave a monkey's fart what the thing said. I looked around. Amyas was at the front of the food queue. He was so tall now. I couldn't believe how much he'd shot up in the summer holidays. His face was leaner and longer and it suited him, and the rest of his body wasn't too bad either. He was certainly tastier than the washed-out cabbage I was pushing round my plate.

'Rose, are you listening to me?' said Tobey.

'Don't you think Amyas is lush?' I asked Tobey, my eyes still on the food queue.

'Can't see it myself,' Tobey said sourly.

'That's 'cause you're not looking,' I told him, still studying his lushness.

'How many fingers am I holding up, Rose?' asked Tobey. For the first time since I'd spotted Amyas, I looked at Tobey, only to instantly regret it. He was using his fingers to be his usual charming self.

'What's your problem?' I asked.

'Oh, for God's sake!' Tobey snapped. 'If you could tear your eyes away from Mr Bumface for two seconds you might discover what time of day it is.'

I glanced down at my watch. 'It's one forty or thirteen forty hours.'

'What's happened to you?' asked Tobey. 'You never used to be all "girlie"!'

'It's called growing up, Tobey. It's called *hormones*,' I told him loftily.

It's called needing something, someone, anyone to dream about.

'Stuff this!' Tobey sprang up. 'If you think I'm going to sit here and watch you bat your eyelashes at that cretin, then you've got another think coming.'

Tobey picked up his tray and strode away from me in a right strop. What was up with him? What was up with *us* come to that? The older we got, the less I understood him. Was this something to do with getting older or were we just drifting apart?

'Hi, Rose. Lost your shadow then?'

'Huh?' I stared stupidly at Lucas, who'd appeared from nowhere to stand in front of me with some of his friends, Axel and Jack – and Amyas. Inside I groaned. His Chronic Lushness was standing before me and all I could say was – huh!

'Tobey Durbrain. He *is* your shadow, isn't he?'

'They're in love!' said Axel. What an idiot!

'Don't be ridiculous. As if I'd ever have Tobey as my boyfriend. We're just friends, that's all – and barely that at the moment.' The words were more dismissive than I'd meant them to be, but I didn't want Amyas to get the wrong idea. Then Lucas, Amyas and the others started laughing, but it wasn't directed at me. My antennae started to quiver. I turned sharply, just in time to see Tobey turn away. And though I only caught his face in profile, I saw enough.

'Tobey, wait.'

With the laughter of Lucas and the others pushing me forward, I ran after Tobey.

'Tobey, I didn't mean that the way it sounded,' I said.

'Thanks for sticking up for me, Callie Rose. I really appreciate it,' Tobey said, with quiet bitterness.

At that moment, I felt I'd have to stretch up to scratch an amoeba's kneecaps.

'I just meant we're always arguing these days,' I tried to explain. 'That's all I meant.'

'And you think that's why I'm upset?'

'Well, yes. What else have you got to be upset about?'

'You really don't know, do you?' said Tobey.

'What have I done?'

'Nothing,' said Tobey. 'You haven't done anything or said anything. And I didn't expect anything else.'

'I don't understand.'

'I know you don't,' said Tobey. 'That's the problem.'

And this time when he walked away from me, I let him go. Because I was wrong about the tone of his voice and the look on his face. It wasn't bitterness he was directing at me. It was something far stronger and much deeper.

sixty-six. Sephy

'You do realize that Jordy Carson is never going to leave you alone,' I said, sweeping up the last of the glass. 'I know his type. He's got the scent of blood in his nostrils and he's not going to stop.'

'Now tell me something I don't know,' said Nathan with understandable tetchiness.

'So what're you going to do about it?'

Nathan emptied his dustpan full of broken glass into the large cardboard box, liberally lined with crumpled newspapers. I looked around Specimens. Jordy's cronies had done a better than average demolition job on the place. The last time they'd done this, we were up and running again in a couple of days. This time it would take longer. And Jordy's tactics were beginning to work. This was the third time there'd been a 'break in' at Specimens where nothing had been stolen but the place had been trashed. It was getting almost impossible for Nathan to get insurance on the place any more. And his staff turnover rate had to be eligible for entry in *The World Book of Records*. Jordy Carson had been very clever. This way he got the best of both worlds. Nathan was going broke rapidly, losing days having to fix up the place, some of our regular clients were staying away and the staff were leaving anyway. And it was so frustrating to sit at my piano, sing cover versions and watch it all happen.

I slowly became aware of Nathan watching me.

'Sephy, I'm sorry but I'm going to have to let you go.'

'What? Why?'

'Look at the place,' Nathan indicated. 'It's not safe. And I don't want you in the middle of this.'

'I'm a big girl now,' I told him. 'I can take care of myself.'

'Not against the likes of Carson and his lot. They don't play by any rules you've ever heard of.'

'I'm not leaving, Nathan.'

'Then you're fired.'

'Then I'll sing just inside the restaurant door or sing from the toilets as a patron if I have to. You can't stop me doing that.'

'I could have you thrown out as a nut job!'

'If you throw me out, I'll come straight back in.'

Nathan stared at me. 'Are you serious?'

'What d'you think?'

'God, you're stubborn.'

I grinned at him. 'I know.'

'Persephone, listen. Bless you for wanting to stick by me but this place is just bricks and mortar—'

'And years of your life and sweat and tears,' I interrupted.

'But there's nothing here that I couldn't walk away from if I had to. I'll just move to another town and open up a new bar and restaurant. Everything here is replaceable. You're not,' said Nathan.

Surprised, I regarded Nathan. The last thing I wanted was for him to capitulate to a low-life, pond-slime weasel like Jordy Carson because of me.

'You're worrying too much—'

'It's not just you. All my staff are irreplaceable and I'm not going to take any more chances. Sooner rather than later, Jordy Carson is going to move on from breaking the furniture and start breaking bones,' said Nathan. 'If I don't let Jordy have what he wants, someone is going to end up on a slab.'

'But you can't just let him win,' I urged. 'You can't just let him have it all without a fight.'

'Don't worry, Sephy. I still have a trick or two up my sleeve.'

'As long as your tricks don't—' My mobile phone started to ring.

Impatiently, I flicked it open. Minerva was phoning me. It had to be serious then. My sister never phoned just to chat. I pressed the button to answer the call.

'Hang on, Nathan. It's my sister,' I told him before talking into the phone. 'Hi, Minerva. What's up?'

Our conversation lasted less than five minutes. But they had to be amongst the worst five minutes of my life.

'Sephy? What is it? What's happened?' asked Nathan. 'Your face has gone ashen.'

'I have to go, Nathan,' I said. I propped my broom against the bar in a daze.

'Has something happened to Callie Rose?' Nathan took hold of my arm and turned me round to face him.

I shook my head. My head felt so strange, like I had sleepwalked my way into a new world and I couldn't understand anything that was going on.

'I have to go . . . ' I said.

'I'll take you,' said Nathan.

'No, I—'

'You're in no fit state to drive,' Nathan insisted. 'Has your sister had an accident?'

I shook my head again. 'It's not Minerva, it's Mother. She's in hospital.'

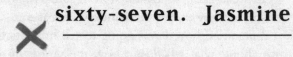

sixty-seven. Jasmine

'Mother, why didn't you tell us? You should've told us.'

'What would you have done, Minerva?' I asked.

'We could've been here for you. You wouldn't've had to go through all this alone,' my daughter said angrily.

Children! Honestly! They thought all they had to do was rage against something to get what they wanted.

They thought all they had to do was shout, 'I DON'T WANT THIS!' and whatever it was would disappear. The optimism of youth. But at least I'd told them now. I had to tell them some time, but this was even worse than I'd imagined. Minerva couldn't stop shouting at me. Sephy stood by the window, staring out of it, her arms folded; her profile could've been cast in bronze. And she hadn't said a word since she'd entered my hospital room.

'Why on earth didn't you go to the doctor as soon as you felt a lump in your breast?' Minerva was the picture of angry bewilderment, eyes blazing, words spoken through tight lips and gritted teeth. She thought of me as an ornament in her life, old and getting older, definitely out of fashion but something that would be around for ever – with a little dusting now and again! 'Why did you put it off and put it off?'

Minerva looked at me expectantly. She really believed that was a question I could answer.

'How bad is it?' Sephy asked from across the room. She was still looking out of the window, not at me.

I'd practised how I was going to tell my daughters the truth about what I had, but now the words in my head seemed blunt and stark. And there was no other way to say it.

'I have stage one breast cancer. As the tumour is still relatively small and there are no lymph nodes involved, I'm to have a lumpectomy and then start a course of radiotherapy. As long as there are clear margins when they remove the tumour I should be fine after the radiation therapy.'

'Clear margins? What does that mean?' Minerva asked sharply.

'As long as there are no cancer cells in the tissue surrounding the tumour,' I explained.

'And if the margins aren't clear?' asked Minerva.

'Let's cross that bridge if and when we get to it,' I told her.

'How long did you wait before going to see a doctor?' asked Sephy quietly.

Ah! Sephy knew me better than I thought. And it was a question to which she probably already knew the sorry answer. She was still looking out of the window. How I wished she'd look at me. But she was bristling with anger and trying to keep it from me.

'I went to my GP as soon as I realized the lump wasn't going away,' I said.

I wasn't about to add that worry had turned days into weeks, before the fear of not knowing had overtaken the fear of what it might be.

'Why didn't you go straight away as soon as the lump appeared?' asked Sephy.

I shrugged. 'It could've been nothing. Besides, I . . . I find it awkward discussing these things. You girls know that.'

Sephy turned to face me for the first time. 'If something happens to you, Mother, I know just what we should write on your gravestone,' she said. '*Here lies Jasmine Hadley. She died of embarrassment.*'

'Sephy!' Minerva admonished.

Sephy turned away to stare out of the window again. But not before I saw the tears streaming down her face.

Oh, dear.

sixty-eight.
Callie Rose is 13

Double science was fantastic today – 'cause I got to sit next to *him*. Of course, when Mrs Mayne split us into pairs and said we had to work together, he moaned like the north wind down a chimney about having to be my partner. But then he had to do that – otherwise his friends would've teased him about sitting next to me and working with me. But I bet he was just as *thrilled* as I was.

I got to sit next to Amyas. Yippee!!

I know I didn't like him much when he joined the school, but since then he's got really buff and become knock-down yummy on a stick. And I've grown up in a year. Grown up a lot. I can appreciate boys now – well, some boys. Well, one boy.

'I'm in charge of this experiment and I'm going to do all the mixing. You can write up everything,' Amyas told me.

'OK. Whatever you think best.' I smiled. Not too many teeth, smile with the mouth *and* the eyes – I read that in *Ms Young Thing* magazine two weeks ago (*How to Win His Heart With a Winning Smile – Part 1*). Smirking, I glanced around to make a note of all the girls who were jealous of me. And the first person I saw looking at me was Tobey. Looking straight at me, with that knowing, mocking smile of his. His expression immediately made me feel self-conscious, not to mention put my back up. What was his problem? Maybe I was drooling a bit around Amyas, but he was soooo lush. Cool? He was red hot!

Amyas and I worked together for the whole double lesson. He did all the best, most interesting bits, but I really didn't mind. I enjoyed working with him. He was so clever without even having to try at it. I made a couple of suggestions for our experiments, both of which he shot down with flaming arrows of sarcasm. But I didn't even mind that, although I didn't suggest anything else.

Once the second buzzer had sounded, Amyas was one of the first out of the room. I ambled out, only to find myself walking next to Tobey, who started up immediately.

'If you could see how ridiculous you look when you're around Amyas, you'd run a mile from him,' he said. 'Everyone's laughing at you.'

'What're you on about?'

'Rose, why don't you wake up and smell the toast burning?' Tobey said blisteringly. 'If you really believe Amyas would go out with someone like you, then you need to get back to the same postcode as reality.'

'What does that mean – someone like me?' I asked through narrowed eyes.

'You're half-Nought,' Tobey shot back.

My body blazed hot, then burned icy-cold. 'So?'

'So Amyas would never go out with a Nought or a halfer. He's said so.'

'I don't believe you. And I'm not half anything,' I said with contempt. 'Where's the line running down my body to separate the Nought bit from the Cross bit?'

'Amyas doesn't see it that way.'

'That's not true. You're just sorry that I don't fancy you instead of Amyas,' I challenged.

Tobey inhaled sharply, his cheeks blooming like red roses. 'D'you really think I'd want a loser like you dripping all over me. The whole class is laughing at the way you carry on around Amyas and you're too stupid to realize. It's embarrassing.'

'You're jealous! How funny!'

I didn't for one second believe that Tobey really was jealous of me and Amyas. After all, Tobey and I had been good friends for ever. And if Tobey hadn't launched in with all that spiteful poison, I might've taken it back and apologized, but Tobey was scowling at me like I'd accused him of fancying his mum's best friend or something. The last couple of stragglers in the class trooped past us, leaving only Tobey and me in the science lab.

'Jealous of Amyas? You must be joking.' A strange, icy look swept up and over Tobey's face. A look I'd never seen before.

'You *are* jealous.' I began to sing tunelessly at him, '"*Cause you want to kiss me and have a smoochie, because you lurve me, you're green with envy, because you lurve me . . . !*'

'Your dad was in the Liberation Militia. He killed loads of people. Amyas could have his pick of any girl in our year, so why on earth would he choose *you* – the daughter of Callum McGregor, a bastard Nought terrorist they hanged 'cause he was so evil!'

The ground beneath my feet suddenly vanished. I was like a character in a cartoon, standing stock-still on nothing at all for what felt like an eternity. My mind started free-falling, spinning out of control. I didn't move, didn't even blink. The slightest gesture would've had me crashing like bad software. The hard, scathing look on Tobey's face softened almost as soon as the words were out of his mouth. Softened and shifted into regret and something even more contrite. But I was outside myself and looking through my shell, watching him apologize with everything he was, every part of his body, but without a single word being spoken.

'What did you say?' I whispered inanely. As if Tobey saying it again would somehow cancel out the first time he'd said it. 'I don't believe you. What did you say?'

'Oh my God!' Tobey breathed. 'You ... you didn't know?'

I pushed him back just as hard as I could. 'YOU'RE A LIAR!' I shouted.

Tobey didn't speak.

'Tell me you were lying.' Each word was a plea. It was all lies. My dad ... my dad was a gardener. It was just a mistake ... mistaken identity ...

'Callie Rose, I didn't mean it,' said Tobey. There was no mistaking the desperation in his voice. 'I was just being ... I didn't mean it. It's not true.'

His voice was a long way off, but like a sonic boom each syllable had me cracking, crumbling, tumbling inside. I couldn't stop it. This was pure hell. My mind couldn't stop replaying Tobey's words. It was like being constantly put back together just so I could feel the pain of being demolished all over again. What was it that convinced me Tobey had been speaking the truth? The anger which flushed out his words in the first place or the sorrow on his face because his words had sprouted wings and taken on a life and flight of their own? Not that any of that mattered now.

I whispered, 'My dad was a terrorist?'

'No. Listen, it wasn't your dad. It was someone else.' Tobey took hold of my arm. 'It wasn't your dad – honest.'

But my dad was Callum McGregor . . .

'Rose, listen to me. It's not true,' Tobey persisted. 'He wasn't a terrorist. I just made that up . . .'

I pulled away from his grasp. 'We may not be friends but let's have honesty between us if nothing else.'

Tobey's hand dropped to his side.

'When and where did you hear about . . . about my dad?'

Tobey didn't speak. He just looked at me.

'Answer me. How did you find out about my dad?'

'I heard my mum and dad talking about it when I was younger,' Tobey admitted.

My mind was dive-bombing, kamikaze style. Thoughts like desperate arms scrambled to find something real, something true to hold onto.

My dad was a gardener.

My dad was a terrorist.

My dad loved my mum and me.

My dad was a terrorist.

My dad was evil.

My dad was a terrorist.

My dad didn't kill anyone. My dad killed – what was Tobey's phrase? – 'loads of people'.

My dad my dad my dad my dad my dad my dad my dad my dad my dad mydadmydadmydad . . . Spinning around me. Laughing at me. Mocking me. I should've found out the truth for myself. But how could I find what I hadn't been looking for?

'Mum said my dad died in an accident . . .' I whispered.

A lie. Tobey was a liar. My mum was a liar.

Someone help me, please.

I closed my eyes briefly. Was it true? Did all our neighbours know? How many people knew the truth about my dad? If it was the truth. If there was any such thing.

'And you've told everyone here at school?'

'No, I haven't,' Tobey denied. 'I've never said a word to anyone.'

'But everyone knows?'

'Not from me. And there's no reason why they should. It happened years and years ago and most people can't even remember what happened last month. Your surname is Hadley, not McGregor. And not many people have figured out who your mum really is. Everyone expects Kamal Hadley's daughter to be living in luxury and rolling in pots of money, not living with a Nought woman in Meadowview.'

'A Nought called McGregor,' I pointed out.

'Yes, but apart from church, your nan keeps herself pretty much to herself and so does your mum.'

Tobey knew all about me. Every sordid little detail. He knew more than I knew myself.

'Everyone knows.' I closed my eyes against the sick humiliation I felt.

'Everyone doesn't know, Callie. And most of the Noughts who do know don't care. My mum admires your mum for going against your grandad and fighting for one of us.'

'And what about the Crosses who know?'

'They're either your friends or they aren't,' said Tobey.

Thousands of butterflies fluttered against my stomach lining. I was going to be sick.

'All this time you knew the truth and you never told me?'

'You never said anything either—'

''Cause I didn't *know* – not about how my dad really died.'

But I remembered so many things now – TV channels being turned over when I entered the room, quiet asides to teachers at the beginning of each academic year, history books being read by my mum first before they were given to me . . . And I'd never clicked. I was too happy living in my bubble of fantasy to question what I'd been told. But I had trusted my family to tell me the truth. I'd never make that mistake again.

'Rose, I'm so sorry. I honestly thought you already knew. I'd've cut my own tongue out before saying anything otherwise.'

'All this time, that's how you've thought of me – as the terrorist's daughter? The daughter of a bastard?'

'That's not true. I don't think of you that way at all—'

'But that's what you just said.'

'Please, Rose, I didn't mean it. Didn't you ever say or do something that you instantly regretted?'

'Yeah,' I replied. 'I believed in you and my mum and everyone else around me and you've all been lying to me.'

'Rose—'

I pushed past him and walked then ran away. And all the while, Tobey kept calling out my name.

'Wait! Rose, wait.'

But I didn't recognize that name. The person who was Rose and whose dad was a gardener didn't exist. A bomb had exploded within me and every bit of happiness had been blown out of me and scattered to the four winds.

sixty-nine.
Callie Rose is 13

I slammed the front door shut so forcefully the glass in it rattled in protest.

'Mum, where are you?'

'In the kitchen, love.'

I strode into the kitchen, my expression kiln-baked. Mum was just popping a home-made white chocolate cheesecake in the fridge. She straightened up and turned to smile at me. Her smile retreated when she saw the look on my face. If fury was fire, I'd've reduced her to ash in a nanosecond.

'What is it? What's wrong?' Mum started towards me.

She stopped abruptly. 'You've heard then? Who told you? Did Nana Jasmine phone you directly?'

'Is it true?' My question came out in a bitter hiss. 'About my dad – is it true?'

Mum gasped, then stared at me. I could see her tongue working in her mouth like she was trying to swallow but couldn't. I realized in that instant that Mum knew what I was asking her. Three words, 'Is it true?' and she knew exactly what I was talking about. My anger heated up several more degrees. I walked towards her until we were only centimetres apart, face to face, eye to eye.

'Was my dad a terrorist who was hanged for murder?'

Stall? Laugh? Lie? Deny it? Stay silent? What would she do?

'Answer me,' I ordered.

'I can see from your face that you already think you know the answer,' said Mum.

Which was no answer at all – and we both knew it.

'Rose, let me explain—'

'WAS DAD HANGED FOR BEING A TERRORIST?'

Silence. Then Mum nodded.

'Rose, listen—' Mum tried to take me into her arms, to hold me tight against her. I pushed her back, hard. Then before either of us knew what was happening, I slapped her face. The sound ricocheted around the kitchen. Mum's hand flew up to cover her cheek. My hand was stinging. It was hard to say which one of us was more shocked.

I'd hit my mum.

I'd never, ever done anything like that before. Never

come close. Never even thought about it. My whole body crumpled into misery before I turned and fled. I raced up the stairs and into my room, hating my hand, hating myself.

But loathing Mum most of all.

Callum McGregor was my dad. A terrorist, a murderer and God only knew what else. Tobey had been right. I sat down in the chair at my window and stared out over the back garden and beyond. Why wasn't I crying? I should be crying. I should be howling.

Callum McGregor was my dad. A murderer and a terrorist was my dad.

'Callie Rose, can I come in?'

I didn't answer. I was never going to answer her again. The door handle turned and Mum came in, uninvited.

'Rose, we need to talk,' Mum began.

'I have nothing to say to you.' I didn't even bother to look at her.

'Rose, I'm sorry. I should've told you long before this but I . . . I was waiting for the right moment.'

I didn't speak.

'The trouble is, the right moment never came,' said Mum.

'D'you know how I found out?' I asked. 'Tobey threw it at me. D'you know what that felt like?'

'I'm sorry, Rosie.'

'Why did you lie? All these years you told me Dad was a gardener and he died in a car accident.'

'I'm sorry, Rosie. I didn't want you to be hurt.'

'Then you failed. I've just learned I'm a murderer's daughter, Mum. How do I handle that?'

'Rose, let's just talk about this. There's a lot I need to explain—'

I spun round on my chair. 'You're too late, Mum. I know now.'

'You don't know everything. Rose, let me—'

'Mum, I need to be by myself. Please.'

Mum wanted to argue, but I turned away from her to stare out of the window again. I heard her start towards the door. And then something else clicked into horrifying place.

'That's why Grandad Kamal hates me, isn't it? Because of who my dad was.' It all made sense now. If Dad was a terrorist when he and Mum were together, that would explain why my grandad didn't want anything more to do with her – or me.

'Callie, your grandad hates everyone in this world who doesn't look, think and act exactly the same as him. If you're not his clone, then you're his enemy – at least, that's how he sees it.'

But I hardly heard Mum. I understood so much. 'Does Grandad hate me because my dad was a terrorist or does he hate me because he hates Noughts and I'm half-Nought?' I asked.

Mum didn't reply. She didn't have to. I could read the answer on her face.

'Uncle Jude tried to tell me—'

'What?' Mum was back at my side faster than I could blink. 'What d'you mean? You've seen Jude?'

'Yes. I met him a couple of years ago.'

'A couple of—' Mum said, aghast. 'And you didn't tell me?'

I shrugged. 'Meggie knew.'

Mum's mouth fell open, but she quickly regained her composure. 'When was the last time you saw him? Answer me, Callie Rose.'

I shrugged again.

'You're not to see him again,' Mum ordered. 'D'you hear me? He's a very dangerous man, Callie. Stay away from him.'

'But at least he tells the truth,' I told her.

We regarded each other, both of us very still, very quiet.

'Callie Rose, I forbid you to see him again. Do I make myself clear?'

'Yes, Mum. Can I be alone now please?'

'Rose, I'm not leaving here until you know the truth. And that's not what Jude would've told you.'

I got up as Mum was speaking and headed over to my portable music centre, an eleventh birthday present. Pressing the button to switch it on, I turned the volume right up, loud enough to drown out all of Mum's words.

Mum marched over to the music player and switched it off. I immediately switched it back on. Mum pulled the plug out of the socket. I went back to my armchair.

'Rose, listen to me. I know you're angry but you need to listen. Your dad and me . . .'

I started singing, quietly at first, but each syllable got louder.

I turned away from Mum to look out of my window again.

'Callie Rose, please . . .' Mum tried to shout over me.

I carried on singing.

Mum wanted to say more, a lot more – I could tell. But I carried on looking out of the window and the singing didn't stop so finally Mum had no choice but to leave.

'Uncle Jude, it's me. It's Callie Rose.'

I sat down in my armchair, using my shoulder to keep the phone against my ear as I opened a can of lager.

'Hi, Callie. Are you OK? You sound a bit strange.'

'Uncle Jude, did you know my dad was hanged for being a terrorist?'

I put down my can on the carpet. Callie now had my full attention. The moment I'd been waiting so impatiently for had finally arrived.

'Uncle Jude, are you there?'

'How did you find out?' I asked her.

'If you knew, why didn't you tell me?' Callie shouted down the phone.

'I wanted to tell you so many times but I couldn't. When I learned that Callum had died, I did some digging and found out the truth. But it was your mum's place to tell you the facts, not mine,' I replied. 'When did she finally pluck up the courage to do it?'

'She didn't,' Callie said harshly. 'Someone else told me. I've just spent the day in the library reading everything I could find about Callum McGregor. Did you know he kidnapped my mum? And he . . . and he . . . D'you know what he *did* to her?'

'Look, Callie, this isn't a conversation to have over the phone. Where are you?'

'I'm in the park, Uncle. I can't go home. Not yet. But I don't want any company.'

'Callie, I want to see you,' I began.

But I was talking to the dialling tone. As I put down the phone, a slow, unfamiliar smile burned its way across my face.

'Yes!' I punched the air with satisfaction.

Yes! Yes! Yes!

Jude's law number thirteen was the one I'd had to hold onto in my dealings with Callie Rose over the last couple of years: *Staying focused requires more than keen eyesight.*

I stood up, grabbing my car keys off the arm of the chair I'd just been sitting in. At long last, I had her. Callie Rose Hadley was all mine.

seventy-one.
Callie Rose is 13

The rich, heavy scent of the roses all around me was making me feel nauseous. The roses were all vivid colours, blood-orange, blood-red, blood-pink. Their sweet, pungent, almost overpowering smell vied with their vibrant colours. The breeze dancing around them released yet more of their bonbon smell. I sat alone on the park bench, longing for their presence to overload my senses, driving all else out of my mind.

But it didn't work.

I sat on the park bench staring into nothing, staring into my father, the flowers fading from consciousness. My dad was Callum McGregor. Hanged for political terrorism. Hanged for being a rapist and a murderer. Hanged for being a son of a bitch.

So what did that make me?

Where did that leave me?

More memories slipped and clicked into place. All those funny little looks passing between Mum and Nana Meggie. All those quiet little asides between Mum and Nana Jasmine. The reluctance to tell me anything about my dad.

The lies . . .

No wonder Mum couldn't bear to be around me. Every time she looked at me I was a reminder of someone she was desperate to forget. Why did she even have me in the first place. To punish herself? Me? Nana Meggie? All those times she told me I was like my father . . . Was that true? Did I look like him? Act like him? Was I evil on the inside like him? Is that what Mum meant? And all those times she told me how much Dad loved me . . . And how much she and my dad had been in love . . . All lies. I knew how I'd been conceived. Every time I thought of it, I wanted to die. And I thought about it all the time. My life which I'd thought was safe and ordinary was twisted and tainted. Tobey's words had picked me up, spun me higher and higher, then dropped me from such a great height that every part of my body was irrevocably shattered.

Are you watching me now, Dad? Are you down in hell, roaring with vicious laughter at all the letters, all the hopes and dreams I shared with you – like you'd ever give a damn? Are you congratulating yourself on the number of lives you've managed to ruin? How I wish you were in front of me right now, so I could tell you just how much I despise you. I want to scream it from the highest place I can find. No matter how much Mum hates me, it doesn't come close to how I feel about you. If you were in front of me now and I had a knife or a gun, I wouldn't hesitate to use it.

Or maybe I would . . .

Not because I wouldn't be able to start. But because once I'd started hurting you, I wouldn't be able to stop.

I hate you, Dad.

Thinking about you is making something deep inside me set hard like cement.

I hate you so much.

'Is anyone sitting here?'

Uncle Jude's voice made me start. How had he got here so fast? Why had he come here at all? I watched as he sat down at the opposite end of the park bench to me.

'We don't have to speak until you're good and ready,' said Uncle Jude.

I turned away from him to stare straight ahead. I had told him not to come. I wasn't going to say a word. So we sat and sat, neither of us breaking the silence. And I was grateful for that. And I was so glad that he hadn't sat next to me or tried to put his arm around me or anything like that. Otherwise, my whole body would've turned into teardrops and fallen to the ground, never to stand up again.

We sat for a long while in silence. I glanced at Uncle Jude once or twice, but he just looked ahead or looked around. At last, I felt I could trust myself to speak.

'Are you going to lie to me too, Uncle Jude?'

'Never,' Uncle replied. 'Callie Rose, d'you . . . hate me because of what my brother did? I'd understand if you did . . .'

Shocked, I turned to him. 'No, Uncle, of course I don't hate you.' That hadn't even occurred to me.

I waited another few minutes for the swelling in my throat to subside.

'What . . . what was my dad like?'

'Where to start?' sighed Uncle Jude. 'What has your mum told you about Callum?'

'Only lies. She said he was a junior gardener who used to work at Nana Jasmine's house,' I replied.

'I see,' said Uncle Jude. And some wary note in his voice sent a frisson of fear snaking down my spine.

'What's the matter?' I asked.

'Callie Rose, d'you really want to know the truth about your dad?'

'Of course.'

'The whole truth, not the stuff you've been told so far. Not lies and not the truth diluted. Are you strong enough to handle it?'

I pressed the pause button in my head so that my mind couldn't work any more, couldn't read between the lines of my uncle's words. Think about what he's asking you, Callie Rose. Are you strong enough . . . ?

'Uncle, I want to know,' I replied at last.

'I want you to know, Callie Rose, that I'll never lie to you. Your mum – and even my mum – may bend the truth around you until it fits, but I won't. So please don't ask me to be honest if that's not what you really want.'

'What was my dad like?' I asked again.

Uncle Jude nodded slowly. 'OK. Well, for a start, your dad wasn't a gardener. He wouldn't've known one end of a rake from the other.'

'What was he then?' I frowned. 'Before . . . before he was a . . . terrorist.'

'Callum was . . . he was a dreamer. But then he woke up.'

'I don't understand.'

'Did you know that my mum used to work for Jasmine Hadley?'

'Nana Jasmine – yes, I know.'

'That's how our two families met. That's how Callum and Persephone met. They grew up together.'

'So that part was true?'

'That part was true.' Uncle Jude nodded. 'Callum went to Sephy's school for a while, but it didn't work. They kicked him out.'

'Why?'

'There was a bombing at the Dundale Centre . . .'

'I read about that,' I began.

'Well, even though our dad had nothing to do with it, he was arrested and charged and found guilty of being a terrorist. Heathcroft High knew our dad was innocent but as far as that school was concerned, Callum was guilty by association. And Heathcroft decided they didn't want the son of an alleged terrorist walking their hallowed halls. So Callum was out.'

'What did my dad do then?'

'There wasn't an awful lot he could do. He was out. No other school would take him. He tried to do other things, but once prospective employers found out who he was, he could never get a job. The Liberation Militia have been fighting for decades for equality between Noughts and Crosses, so Callum joined them.'

'But the L.M. are terrorists.' I frowned.

'No, they're not,' Uncle Jude said, adding deliberately, 'No, *we're* not. We're fighting for equality for all.'

'You're in the L.M. too?' I hadn't expected that.

'But only on the strategic side, like Callum. Your dad refused to get involved in anything . . . destructive. He wrote articles and letters and talked at L.M. rallies – that sort of thing.'

'But I looked it up. He was hanged for political terrorism. The newspaper said he kidnapped and . . . raped my mum. The newspaper said—'

'Callum only did all that when our dad died in prison,' said Uncle Jude. 'I think a part of Callum died too when he heard about our dad. He wanted to get back at all Crosses everywhere – and then he was ordered by the head of the L.M. to kidnap your mum. It was supposed to force your grandad Kamal into handing over lots of money for the L.M. cause.'

'And even though he and Mum had grown up together, Dad did it,' I said, my throat beginning to swell up again.

'Well, they used to be lovers before the kidnapping.' I saw Uncle Jude choosing his words so carefully. I said nothing, waiting for him to continue. 'I think Callum hated himself for that too and maybe . . . maybe what he did to Sephy was his way of trying to punish both of them.'

Punish both of them? Or punish Mum by making her pregnant with me? I wasn't sure how much more 'truth' I could take.

'You know, I can't help blaming myself,' sighed Uncle Jude. 'If only I'd known what he was ordered to do, but I was working with another L.M. cell across the country. I had no idea about the kidnapping or any of it until Callum was captured.'

'It's not your fault, Uncle Jude,' I said.

Uncle Jude sighed again. 'I had no idea Callum was so filled with . . . rage against your mother and all Crosses. I should've taken him under my wing. I should've insisted that he worked with me for the betterment of everyone in our society. I had no idea—'

Uncle Jude's voice broke off, distressed. We both sat in silence for a while. I watched a runner across the park jog on the spot as he talked to another runner who'd approached from the opposite direction. I wondered what they were talking about. Noughts and Crosses? Men and women? Truth and lies? Or their latest trainers? Did any of it matter? It was all so trivial, so pointless.

'Callie, I was given a letter that your dad wrote to your mum just before he died,' Uncle Jude said reluctantly. 'I'm not sure if you should see it . . .'

I turned to Uncle Jude. 'What does it say?'

'It doesn't say nice things . . . but it does tell the truth.'

Uncle was holding a piece of paper in his hand. It was a browny-yellow colour, folded, and looked like it might crumble into dust at any moment. But as Uncle said, it held the truth – and that's what I craved right now. Good or bad, I didn't want anything else.

'D'you want to read it?' asked Uncle. 'I think you're old enough to handle it, but just say if you're not . . .'

I held out my hand. Uncle Jude reluctantly passed me the letter. I swallowed hard, then opened it carefully – and read:

Sephy,

I'm writing this to you because I want you to know the way things really are. I don't want you to spend the rest of your life believing a lie.

I don't love you. I never did. You were just an assignment to me. A way for all of us in my cell of the Liberation Militia to get money – a lot of money from your dad. And as for the sex – well, you were available and I had nothing better to do.

You should've seen yourself, lapping up every word of that nonsense I spouted about loving you and living for only you and being too scared to say it before. I don't know how I stopped myself from laughing out loud as you bought all that rubbish. As if I could love someone like you – a Cross, and worse than that, the daughter of one of our worst enemies. Having sex with you was just my way of getting back at your dad for being a bastard and your mum for looking down her nose at me all those years. And now you're pregnant.

Well, I'm ecstatic. Now the whole world will know you're having my child, the child of a blanker. That if nothing else is worth dying for. Whether you come to my hanging or not, I'm going to announce to the world that you're having <u>my</u> child. MINE. Even if you do get rid of our child, everyone will still know.

But no one will know how much I despise you. I loathe the very thought of you and now when I think about all the things we did when we were alone in the cabin, I feel physically sick. To think I actually kissed you, licked you, touched you, joined my body with yours. I had to think of my other lovers the entire time to stop myself from pulling away from you in disgust. God knows, I'm disgusted with myself but the object of the exercise was your total humiliation – and at least I can console myself with the knowledge that that's what I've achieved. Did you really in your wildest dreams believe that I could love someone like you? . . .

I carried on reading until the end of the letter. And when I'd finished, the poison in each sentence had turned my body so deathly cold, the swelling in my throat had gone down and my eyes were no longer stinging. I re-read it one more time – the whole thing from top to bottom. And then I stared at the words on the piece of paper, stared without blinking.

My dad . . .

'You can keep it if you like,' said Uncle Jude.

I thought about it, then decided I had to. It was my legacy from my dad. But I couldn't bear to hold it any more with those awful words jutting out like shards of broken glass. I folded it up and placed it deep inside my trouser pocket. I didn't need to keep it open to remember what was in it. I'd remember every word until the day I died.

'I just thought it would be better for you to know the truth,' said Uncle sadly. 'Was I wrong?'

I shook my head.

'I don't think you should tell anyone about the letter.

It'd be better if you didn't mention it at all,' said Uncle Jude. He added reluctantly, 'And I found out something else. When Callum was arrested and sentenced to hang, your grandad Kamal told your mum that he'd spare Callum's life if she had an abortion – but she didn't. She had to choose between you and Callum and she chose you. I guess that's why your grandad slammed the door in your face.'

'But why did she have me? Why didn't she . . . just do what Grandad wanted?'

'I don't know. Maybe it was her way of getting back at Kamal?' Uncle Jude suggested. 'Or maybe she just hated Callum so much by then that she wanted to see him hang?'

I nodded. I couldn't speak. I understood so much now. Dad hated Mum and all Crosses, Mum hated me for reminding her of Dad. My grandad hated me and Mum. Mum and Meggie hated each other. Everyone hated everyone.

And now so did I. It was frighteningly easy.

And I was just a beginner.

But I'd get better with practice. Uncle Jude slid along the park bench until he was sitting next to me.

'Callie Rose, we could use someone like you in the L.M.,' he said softly, putting his arm around me. 'Someone like you could really make a difference.'

I turned to look up at my uncle. Once, I would've asked questions. A difference to what? Working where? Doing what? Why?

But now I didn't care.

'OK, Uncle.' I shrugged. 'I'll do whatever you say.'

seventy-two.
Callie Rose is 13

I placed my head on my folded arms, resting on the table. The library was quieter than usual. I was one of only about five people in it. Everyone else was outside enjoying the warmer than usual spring sunshine. But I didn't want to go out. The weather didn't match my mood. I spent most of my lunch breaks in the library now. My friends were getting really fed up with me. Rafiya, Audra and Sammi, my best friends, said I was turning into a real misery. I wasn't into the same things as them any more. I didn't read teenage magazines about make-up and boys. I didn't believe soppy love stories where the woman met Mr Right, had an orgasm, got married and lived happily ever after. What a load of crap! I read up on all kinds of things I hadn't been particularly interested in before except maybe in an abstract way: civil rights, the Liberation Militia, all the people hanged in the past for political terrorism – of which ninety-nine point nine per cent were Noughts. It wasn't just someone else's history any more, it was my history – my past, my present.

It felt like until now I hadn't known anything about

anything. Not real stuff. Not important stuff. Who cared which king married which queen from across the sea over five hundred years ago? I couldn't care less about kings and queens and dukes and earls. They didn't make history. Ordinary people did. Kings and queens and the privileged few had a vested interest in keeping the status quo. The only reason we'd moved forward at all was because ordinary people had fought for every step. I hadn't known anything. But I was definitely learning.

'Hello, Callie.'

I didn't even notice him until he plonked himself down at my table. I sat up, then sat back. I closed the books before me on the table and started stuffing them back into my school bag. There were plenty of empty tables in the library. I'd just find another one, that was all.

'Callie, can't . . . can't we be friends again?'

'You really want to be my friend, Tobey?'

Tobey nodded.

'Go back to the day you told me about my dad and this time keep your mouth shut. Or get into my head and rub out all memory of what my dad really was and what he did and the way I found out. Then we'll be friends again. Can you do that?'

Tobey bowed his head.

'Didn't think so.' I went off to find another table.

seventy-three.
Meggie

I'd been in Jude's favourite room in the Isis Hotel a number of times, but now I found myself noticing things that had never registered before. The sealant on the right side of the window behind Jude had a blue stain on it, like ink. But just on the one side – at child height. And the carpet beneath the table Jude sat at was particularly worn, almost frayed. Is that why they'd put the table over it? From the bathroom, there came the steady 'plink' of water droplets where a tap hadn't been quite turned off properly.

Jasmine sat on the bed looking at Jude. Jude looked from her to me. But I was a mere spectator. I spared Jasmine no more than a glance. I could just see her hand at home in her pocket. I knew what was in there and I didn't doubt for a second that unless I could convince her otherwise she'd press the switch to get my son. What to say? What to even think? I just stood there, staring at my son throughout the seasons of his life. A season of colic and sleepless nights. A season of laughter and hugs. Of all my children, Jude had been the most affectionate, the most openly loving.

But as he grew older, awareness caught up with him.

Awareness and idealism were such a dangerous combination in my oldest son.

Awareness of the misguided attitudes and false perceptions and cruel condescension of others. And the love was still there, but the laughter wasn't as free and easy. And then Jude was ten or eleven. And my goodness, how he loved to read. And write. And study. He'd run to me with every new word he learned, eager to share its sound and meaning, happy to put it in a sentence to show me how it worked in context. Most of the fancy words I know came from Jude. The written word was his best friend and he was so desperate to learn more, to stay on at school and devour the words out of every book he studied.

But I lost my job and that was the end of that. We couldn't afford it.

I still remember Jude's face when his dad and I told him that. I don't even have to close my eyes to see his grief set hard into icy anger.

'Why can't I stay on at school?' he pleaded. 'Why can't I?'

'We don't have the money, son,' Ryan tried to explain.

'But you could get it,' Jude insisted. 'Work for it.'

'We've always worked, Jude. And you know I can't get another job right now.' My words came out as a snap – which I didn't mean. I really didn't.

'So why can't I stay on at school?'

'Jude, noughts aren't allowed to go to school past fourteen anyway.'

'Why not?'

'Because that's the way it is,' said Ryan.

'But most of my friends are staying at school,' Jude protested.

'Most of your friends are Crosses,' I pointed out.

'Mike is a nought and he's staying on at school.'

I wondered when we'd get to Mike.

'He can stay at school because his family have got pots of money and he's going to one of the two schools in the country which take noughts – if they can pay.'

'How come Mike's family have money and we don't?'

'Because Mike's mum invented the spray-on tan for noughts,' I snapped. 'With so many noughts trying to look like Crosses, it's no wonder Mike's family are so rich.'

'Well, can't we ask them to help . . . ?'

'Never.' Not whilst I had breath in my body.

'Why can't we just pay the school fees then?'

Jude just didn't get it.

'Are you deaf?' I shouted. 'We don't have that kind of money to waste on your education. Get your head out of the clouds and come back to reality.'

'Meggie . . .' Ryan warned.

I really hadn't meant to be so bloody, but what Jude felt went way beyond disappointment and I was going through every moment of it with him.

And hating it.

And hating myself because I couldn't do any better.

And resenting Ryan – because he couldn't do any better either.

I had to watch helplessly as all the open-mindedness and love Jude had inside him curled up and slowly but surely withered away after that.

And now just the shell of my son sits over there, watching me.

'Mum,' said Jude quietly. 'What're you doing here?'

'Jasmine phoned me from the foyer before she came up.'

Jude started with surprise. He turned narrowed eyes towards Jasmine. 'Your quarrel is with me, not my mum. She has nothing to do with this. Let her go.'

Jasmine raised one eyebrow. 'Finer feelings, Jude? Meggie is free to leave whenever she wants.'

I could hardly see Jude's irises after that, his eyelids were so close together. And I could feel his uncertainty as he looked from me to Jasmine and back again. I moved further into the room to sit across the table from my son.

'What's going on? Why're you here, Mum?'

I glanced at Jasmine, my gaze sliding back to my son. 'I'm trying to save you.'

'I see.'

'D'you see, Jude? D'you really?' I asked. ''Cause I think you can't see for looking. That's always been your trouble.'

'I'm still waiting for the punch line.' Jude's tone was growing icier. And then he clicked. 'You! *You* told this woman where I was, what room I was in . . .'

Not a question, not a statement, but somewhere in between the two.

'I had to,' I tried to explain.

'Why?' Jude still couldn't believe it.

'Because she needed my help,' I replied.

Jude shook his head slowly. He got the what, but not the why. But then, how could he?

'Jude, do you . . . is there anyone special in your life?'

'Why d'you always ask me that?' Jude said with hostility. 'Like who?'

'I don't know. A special woman?' Hell, at this point, I'd even settle for a special man!

Jude didn't answer, but he couldn't stop the sweep of puzzlement that brushed over his face. He still hadn't figured out why I was there in the room.

'No, Mum. There's no one.' He frowned.

I could read his face so easily. And he was right, it was a strange place to discuss his love life. But it was now or never. And if not here, then where?

'When was the last time you were in love, Jude?'

Did I imagine that flicker of pain across his face? Whatever it was, it came and went as quickly as a flash of summer lightning. I waited for his answer but Jude kept silent. He began to fidget in his chair, shifting restlessly whilst still seated. His right hand rubbed at his calf, then his shin, before returning to the arm of the chair.

'Have you ever been in love, Jude?' I asked.

'What's the point of all this, Mum? That murderous' – Jude bit back the word he was about to use – 'woman has enough explosives on her to blow us into permanent orbit and you're asking about *girlfriends*?'

'Was Cara Imega your girlfriend?'

The fidgeting stopped abruptly. 'I told you before, I had nothing to do with her death,' said Jude harshly.

'That's not what I asked you,' I pointed out. 'Was Cara Imega your girlfriend?'

Jude frowned. 'Yes. For a while.'

But that wasn't what Jude had said before. It was obviously so long ago that he couldn't even remember what he'd told me. But I could remember every word.

'I knew her . . . She was a good friend . . .'

He announced that on the TV when he was protesting

his innocence, when he was telling the world that the real killer was some man called Andrew Dorn.

When had she gone beyond a good friend and become his girlfriend?

'Jude, tell me the truth. Did you kill her?'

'Mum, I didn't kill anyone . . .'

That's what he said to me all those years ago when I asked him the same question. A statement and a promise.

'Mum, I didn't kill anyone . . .'

'What possible difference could it make now?'

Not the answer I was looking for, but maybe the one I should've expected. Jude was angry with me. How ironic!

'No, I didn't kill her,' Jude said, exasperated.

I took one last look at Jude as the boy he used to be. I closed my eyes and counted to three − one number for each of my children − then re-opened them. I forced myself to see Jude for the man he was.

If only he'd let himself love someone, anyone. If only he'd allowed himself to be loved. Then maybe that love would've drowned out the cacophonous, clamouring hatred that filled his heart. But then again, maybe it wouldn't've. If only I could turn back time like the hands on a clock. If only I could go back to when Jude . . .

I allowed myself a tiny smile.

Those two words would be my epitaph − *if only* . . . Jude's life was Jude's choice, I had to start believing that. But it was so hard.

He was still my son. And no matter what he did, that would never change. And he was the only child I had left. And now his fate, the fate of everyone in this room, rested in my hands.

Sephy versus
Callie Rose

seventy-four.
Callie Rose

The cold of the cellar just highlighted the chill between Mum and me. My last question still echoed between us.

'You really think I tried to kill you?' said Mum sombrely. 'What did Meggie say to you?'

Mum was looking directly at me now. No more sideways glances. We watched each other, only blinking when we absolutely had to. Well, if she really wanted to know, then I would tell her.

'Nana Meggie said that when I was a baby, you were ill and no one realized how bad it was,' I said.

'I had post-natal depression. Puerperal psychosis, to be precise.'

That stunned me. Nana Meggie never told me that. 'So what's puer-whatsit psychosis?'

'It's like a severe form of post-natal depression. You can feel fine for a few hours or days but then the depression comes back. It took a bit longer to manifest itself in me apparently. Usually it's detectable within a few weeks. Mine wasn't apparent until a few months had gone by.'

'Why not?'

'No one was paying much attention,' said Mum.

'To you?' I surmised.

Mum nodded. 'Everyone was focused on you, including me. I couldn't figure out what I was thinking or feeling half the time. And I felt so guilty because I wasn't coping. I was failing miserably and was so desperate not to fail that I got it into my head that you'd be better off without me, without all of us.'

The ground beneath my feet was shifting, like sand on a cloud. I didn't realize Mum's illness had been real.

'Nana Meggie said you . . . you tried to hurt me.'

'I see.'

'She said I almost died, my heart stopped, and after that you went and got some help,' I rushed on.

'I didn't try to hurt you, Callie Rose. Even if you never believe another word I say, it's important that you believe that.'

'So what did happen?' I asked.

'Didn't Meggie tell you all the details?' Mum asked, the bitterness she'd struggled to keep out of her voice now evident.

'No.' I shook my head. 'She only told me what I just told you and she made me promise never to repeat it to anyone, least of all to you.'

'And that way I can't defend myself,' said Mum.

'That's not why she said it,' I said vehemently.

Mum didn't answer.

'Nana Meggie didn't mean it like that,' I persisted.

'If you say so.' Mum shrugged, like she was ambivalent about believing me.

'So are you going to tell me what happened or not?' Inside my head, the words were an entreaty. That's not how they came out though. They came out spiky as barbed wire. At first I thought Mum wasn't going to answer. And to be honest, I wouldn't've blamed her.

'I held you too tight,' Mum said at last. 'That's what it was. I held you too tight.'

'But you weren't trying to hurt me?'

'Never. I'd die first,' said Mum quietly.

If she'd shouted it, I probably wouldn't've believed her. But her tone carried a resolute conviction of its own.

'Callie, all I wanted was to keep you safe and with me. Always and for ever. No one was going to hurt you the way I'd been hurt. No one was going to get to you. So I held on much too tight . . . and you stopped breathing.'

Silence was a third presence in the room, mocking both of us, I think.

'What happened then?' I eventually dared to ask.

'When I realized you'd stopped breathing, I collapsed. Your nan managed to revive you, then she called an ambulance for both of us. I don't remember much after that. Just images like snapshots or bits and pieces of a film playing but never the whole picture.'

'Why? What happened to you?'

'I had a breakdown. I didn't speak for over a month and I was away from you for almost five months.'

'Five months!' I had no idea about that either.

'Your Nana Jasmine paid for my treatment in a special hospital, a clinic, and then she looked after me. I don't know what I would've done if it hadn't been for her. Mother saved my sanity – such as it is.'

I swallowed that down but had problems digesting it. Mum and Nana Jasmine were always sniping at each other. More than five minutes in each other's company and they rubbed together like fingernails on a cheese grater. Or so I'd thought.

'So did Nana Jasmine look after me whilst you were in hospital?' I asked.

Mum shook her head. 'No. Meggie did that.'

And I didn't imagine the strange note in Mum's voice. Silence stood before me now, bearing down, suffocating me. No more questions, I told myself. Not if you don't already know the answers. No more questions.

Well, just one more.

'Did I get to see you when you were in hospital?'

Mum's lips tightened. If she didn't want to answer then that was OK. That'd be answer enough. I wouldn't push.

'No,' said Mum. 'Not once.'

'Why not?'

One more question.

'It was a long time ago, Callie Rose.' Mum shrugged.

'That's not an answer.'

Mum smiled. 'You noticed!'

'How come I didn't get to see you?' I persisted.

'D'you really want to know?'

A merest pause, then I nodded. I knew that question from Mum well enough to realize I wouldn't like the answer.

'Nana Meggie decided it wouldn't be . . . wise.'

'Didn't you want to see me?' I asked, surprised and more than a little dismayed at the hurt I felt. I thought I'd taken away Mum's power to hurt me a long time ago.

'Oh, Callie, I wanted you every day. I asked for you every hour. I missed you every second. I remember that if nothing else.'

'So I didn't see you for a whole five months?'

Mum shook her head. 'Just remember, Callie, that when you weren't seeing me, I wasn't seeing you either.'

'Meaning?'

'Meaning I missed you very much.'

I looked at Mum and caught that look in her eyes I'd seen so many times before when she looked at me. A look of loss. And for the last couple of years I'd thought she was looking at me and remembering my dad. But this had nothing to do with Dad. This was just Mum and me.

I regarded Mum. 'And when you came out of hospital?'

'I was better,' said Mum.

That wasn't what I meant. I sat perfectly still, waiting for my mind to slow down enough to match the sedentary pace of my body. But it didn't seem to be happening. If anything, my mind was whirling faster.

'Why . . . ?' But I couldn't finish my question. Just saying the words would be like driving a stake through my own heart.

'Why what?' Mum prompted softly.

I opened my mouth but the words I longed to say still wouldn't come. So I asked something else instead. So much for one more question.

'Why did Nana Meggie stop us from being together when you were in the hospital? Didn't she know you wanted to see me?'

'She knew. Your Nana Jasmine told her, more than once.'

'So why didn't she take me to the hospital to see you?'

Mum didn't reply.

'Callie, it was such a long time ago.'

'Don't start with that excuse again, please,' I pleaded. 'Why didn't Nana Meggie take me to see you? Mum, what're you not telling me?'

seventy-five.
Callie Rose is 13

I'm scared . . .

I knew I should go home but I couldn't face it. Not yet. Mum had already phoned me to ask where I was. I lied and told her I was at Sammi's house. She told me she was going to Specimens as she had to sort something out with Nathan. Why bother telling me at all? She'd never done that in the past. 'I'm off to work. Be good!' was the extent of her monologues about Specimens before. Even now I wondered why I hadn't just told her the truth.

'Mum, I'm wandering the streets because I don't want to see you. I can't cope with looking at you, knowing how and why I was born.'

The evening sky had moved beyond blue and was now purple, with a bright half-moon and the odd star shining through. It was cold, but at least it was dry. I stopped walking to look at the sky properly. All those stars . . .

Tobey told me once that stars were souls, waiting to be reborn. Tobey told me a lot of things.

How could I not have known?

My own dad and I didn't know who he really was. I didn't understand how I could have reached thirteen and not have known the truth. But no one could know the whole truth without seeing Dad's letter to Mum. I never volunteered information about my dad to any of my friends. If they asked, I always said he was a gardener who died in a car accident. I don't think I even told them his name. But I can't believe that, of all my friends, Tobey is the only one who knows that Dad was a terrorist. Maybe Ella and Lucas know. Maybe that's why Ella's dad didn't want her coming round my house to play when we were in junior school. Has Ella told anyone? There's no reason why she shouldn't have; after all, we're not even friends any more. Do others at school know? I'll die if they do. I could've been stronger, more prepared if Mum had told me the truth sooner. I'm sure Nana Meggie would've told me the whole truth − if Mum had let her. But Mum's obviously ashamed of Dad and even more ashamed of me. Maybe that's why she and Sonny broke up, because he found out about my dad? Something else to hate my dad for. If Mum and Sonny had got married, things could've been so different. Someone would've cared about *me*. Sonny told me he loved me, which is more than my mum ever did. And Sonny wasn't too ashamed to hug me − until he found out about my dad. Yet another part of my life that my dad has ruined. He's like a long, bleak shadow reaching out from hell and devouring every dream I've ever had. And with every second that passes, my hatred for him doubles.

This is driving me crazy.

I'll wait till I'm certain Mum has left for work and then I'll go home. I don't want to see Mum. Not yet. I'm afraid of what I'll say, what I'll do if I see her.

I'm scared.

Scared by how much Mum must hate me.

Scared by how much I hate her, not just for the lies, but for having me in the first place.

 ## seventy-six. Sephy

Nathan's office at Specimens was too crowded. Detective Inspector Muswell was fiddling with a microphone and receiver, making sure that they worked.

'Nathan, please don't do this,' I begged him. 'It's too dangerous.'

'Sephy, we've been through this before. I have to,' said Nathan.

I watched Nathan, forcing myself not to even blink unless absolutely necessary. I could keep him safe if I didn't take my eyes off him for a second. Callie Rose, Mother, Meggie, Sonny and now Nathan. I detested my own selfishness, but all I could think about was what I'd do if something happened to Nathan. Inside, I was being worn away and there wasn't a thing I could do about it.

'If Jordy Carson finds out, he'll kill you,' I whispered.

'Then I'll just have to make sure that he doesn't find out.' Nathan shrugged.

'But—'

'Sephy, there comes a time when a man has to either stand up for himself and say enough is enough or spend the rest of his life letting others knock him down,' said Nathan.

'Spare me the cowboy bull crap, please,' I said.

'Does your mum know about your potty mouth?' Nathan teased.

'She suspects!' I told him tersely.

Nathan grinned at me. He'd met my mother once, when she came to Specimens to see me in action. It's just as well she didn't tell me she was coming beforehand or I would've been a nervous wreck. I looked up from my piano in the middle of my set, and there was Mother smiling at me. During my break, I introduced Mother to Nathan and she'd scrutinized him openly, not even attempting to hide what she was doing.

'He's quite good looking,' Mother told me in front of him, her eyes twinkling. 'If I were ten years younger, I'd fight you for him.'

'Mother!' I admonished, cheeks flaming. 'Nathan isn't used to your peculiar sense of humour.'

Mother turned a lighthouse smile on Nathan. 'My daughter thinks sex was invented by her generation.'

'Mother!'

'Tell me, Nathan,' Mother said, ignoring me. 'What're your intentions towards my daughter?'

'Strictly honourable, Mrs Hadley,' Nathan rushed to

assure her. 'I'm her employer, she's my employee. Strictly professional, nothing more to it.'

'Ah!' Mother sighed. 'What a shame!'

Nathan burst out laughing, whilst I shook my head and gave up trying to get her to behave. After that he and Mother became good friends. But all that had happened many months ago. I wondered what she'd say to Nathan if she were here now. No doubt she'd tell him straight what a fool he was being. And she'd be able to tell him so that he'd listen. I just wasn't getting through to him.

Detective Inspector Muswell used one more piece of body tape to secure the rest of the microphone lead to Nathan's stomach. The microphone was taped to his chest, the transmitter to his back. The thin black plastic covered the wire that ran between the two. Nathan winked at me. He was doing his best to pass this off as nothing at all, but he wasn't convincing anyone. Not me, not himself.

'Nathan, if you go through with this, you'll end up with a tag around your toe.'

'Either way, I'll get Jordache Carson off my back,' said Nathan.

I swallowed hard two or three times but the tears in my throat refused to budge.

'Sephy, I'm sorry. I didn't mean to snap at you, but d'you think if there was another way to get that bastard I'd be doing this?' sighed Nathan. 'Jordy's a maniac. I have to do something.'

'Why does it have to be you?'

'Would you rather I hid away for the rest of my life?' asked Nathan. 'Jordy believes his own publicity. He believes nothing and no one can touch him. That's why this will work.'

'Miss Hadley, we all want the same thing,' Detective Inspector Muswell said, exasperated. 'This is the only way to put Carson away for keeps.'

I glared at her. She was afraid I'd talk Nathan out of the best chance the police had of getting Jordy Carson. I eyed Nathan critically as he shrugged his black shirt back on and started to do up the buttons.

'Jordy Carson isn't a fool, Nathan,' I said. 'You phoned him to tell him you wanted to see him. Of course he's going to suspect a trap and the first thing he's going to do is have you frisked for a mic.'

Nathan's hands slowed on his buttons.

'Then what would you suggest?' DI Muswell snapped.

'I don't know, but not a body tap for goodness' sake,' I argued. 'It's too obvious.'

'Sephy has a point,' said Nathan. 'I don't want to wind up dead within ten seconds of meeting the guy.'

'If you are going to wire him for sound, you need to put the mic somewhere where they won't find it. Somewhere Jordy and his men wouldn't even think of looking,' I said.

Nathan raised an eyebrow. 'And where might that be?'

I looked him up and down, as did DI Muswell.

'If you ladies could stop undressing me with your eyes,' said Nathan. 'I'm beginning to get chilly!'

'Your head!' I exclaimed.

'What about it?' frowned DI Muswell.

'How about a cap?' I said. 'If you could fit the microphone and transmitter into a cap somehow, then maybe that would work. The microphone could be hidden under the fabric in the peak and the transmitter could be sewn into the cap band on the crown. Even if they do search him, they're unlikely to search a cap that thoroughly.'

DI Muswell looked sceptical.

'It's more likely to work than the body tap,' I argued.

DI Muswell only needed a moment more to think about it. She turned to her colleague, Sergeant Hall. 'Get me a cap. Now,' she barked.

He didn't need to be told twice.

Half an hour later, Nathan was all set. The microphone wouldn't fit unobtrusively onto the peak so it had to be placed at the front of the crown of the cap. DI Muswell got Nathan to talk with the cap tilted back and then placed well forward before she was satisfied it would work from any angle. An unmarked police car was going to follow him to Jordy's penthouse flat, where they were supposed to meet, and Nathan's entire conversation was going to be taped. I wanted to go with the police but DI Muswell put her foot down.

'No way. It's too dangerous.'

'I can look after myself,' I told her. 'Nathan, tell her.'

'I agree with her, Sephy. I don't want you there,' he told me, serious for the first time that evening.

'But why?' I said.

'For two reasons.'

'Which are?'

'It might all go wrong,' said Nathan.

I inhaled sharply. 'And the second reason?'

'It might all go wrong,' said Nathan again.

'I'm scared, Nathan,' I admitted.

Nathan smiled at me and said, 'So am I. How about a kiss for luck?'

I stepped forward to give him a quick kiss on the lips. But then he had his arms around me and I had my arms around him and the rest of the world was forgotten. DI Muswell had to cough several times to get our attention.

Nathan stroked a finger down my cheek. 'Now I'll definitely come back in one piece.'

'One alive piece please,' I whispered.

'If you insist. Lock up when we leave. OK?'

Nathan left the restaurant through the front door. The officers left via the back just in case Jordy was already having Nathan watched. Sooner or later it had had to come to this. Jordy had made no secret of the fact that he was fed up with Nathan not toeing the line. And when the police approached Nathan to tell him that Jordy had put a contract out on his life, then Nathan had no choice but to 'go down fighting', as he had put it.

A single tear escaped down my cheek. I brushed it away impatiently. That wouldn't help Nathan now. There was nothing I could do but sit in this empty restaurant and count the seconds. And pray.

seventy-seven.
Meggie

Should I say something? I should do something. But what? It's not really any of my business. Except that if I don't say something, the situation between Callie Rose and Sephy will go from bad to worse. But I'm loath to intrude. Sephy already hates me for what I did to her when Callie Rose was born. If she knew I'd been seeing Jude or, worse still, that I knew Callie had been seeing Jude . . . So I can't interfere. Because Callie Rose might end up hating me too. I couldn't bear that.

But I have to do something.

Please God, don't let all this be because of Jude.

What's happening with Callie Rose? It's like she's stumbled over a cliff and is hanging on for dear life. But I can't do anything. I'm not even sure if her mum can. We can only help Callie if she wants to be rescued. But the closer we get, the more she screams at us to leave her alone. What would've happened if I'd told Callie the truth about her dad years ago? Where would we all be now? One thing's for sure, we couldn't've been any worse off than we are now. This life is dissolving all our hopes and dreams – every one. If something doesn't happen to fix this, and soon, we'll never make it, any of us.

God, if you're listening . . .

Callum, if you're listening . . .

I don't want to find out Jude is behind all this. But every time I think about him, I get an icy, hollow feeling in the pit of my stomach. And if his hand is in this somewhere – what then? He's my son. My only remaining son. Not matter what he does, I can't turn my back on him. He's my own flesh and blood.

But so is Callie Rose.

If Jude has anything at all to do with this, it will force me to make a choice – my son or my granddaughter.

A choice sent from hell.

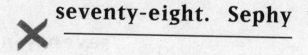

seventy-eight. Sephy

It's been over three hours. Something must've gone wrong. The police were supposed to be taping the conversation between Nathan and Jordy, but suppose something went wrong? Suppose Jordy decided to shoot Nathan or stab him or hit him over the head? The police would never get up to Jordy's penthouse in time. Nathan had to know that. So why had he agreed to this foolhardy scheme?

Because it was him or Jordy. There was no middle ground.

But the waiting was driving me crazy. If anything should happen ... Moving in slow motion, I decided to turn off the lights and head over to the police station. Oh God! Something must've gone wrong. There came a knock at the restaurant door. I spun round. Nathan stood outside grinning at me through the glass. The front door was open and I was in his arms less than a couple of seconds later.

'You!' I almost screamed at him. 'I've been worried sick. What happened? Are you hurt? Are you all right?'

'Don't cry, Sephy. I'm fine,' said Nathan.

'I'm not crying,' I sobbed. 'I'm ... I'm—'

Nathan held me tight. And just like that I didn't need an explanation or the details. They could wait. As long as Nathan was safe that was enough.

seventy-nine.
Callie is 14

'I hate you! You make me sick!'

'Callie Rose, don't talk to me like that,' Mum shot back.

'I can talk to you any way I want to and you can't stop me. You make me sick!'

'You know what? The feeling is mutual.'

I glared at her. I'd said it first, but that still gave her no right to say it back to me. No right at all. It hurt. And I hated her even more for that.

'I wish you'd go away. I wish you'd disappear. I wish you'd *die*!' I screamed.

'Do you?'

'Yeah, and then you'd go to hell.'

'I'm already there.'

'I mean *real* hell. Then you and my murdering bastard dad could be together.'

'That's what I'm counting on,' Mum told me.

And those words were all it took to steal the breath from my body, like all the air inside me had escaped in a mad rush and all at once.

'I don't know why you even had me.' I'd finished shouting now. I turned away from Mum so she wouldn't see me swallow my tears. No more crying for me.

No one would ever make me cry again.

'Callie, I'm not going into all this again. I'm tired. I'm going to bed,' Mum sighed from behind me. I forced myself not to turn round as I listened to her footsteps retreat behind me. Mum wasn't the only one who was tired. I wanted to stop burning up inside and lashing out but I didn't know how. I wanted to stop being so furiously angry all the time. Something inside me was shrinking, drawing in on itself, the part of me that had seen good in everything and everyone around me. All the trust I'd had in other people was withering and dying and there was nothing I could do about it. I had a constant feeling of wanting to take things and break things so that everything around me looked the way I felt on the inside.

Uncle Jude says I should hold onto that feeling. He says it's a feeling the Liberation Militia can use.

But it scares me.

eighty. Sephy

My body felt twice as heavy and twice as old as I trudged up the stairs. Why was it so impossible for all the wheels of my life to move in sync? Nathan and I had become really close after what'd happened with Jordy. Nathan had taped Jordy Carson boasting about what he'd done to Nathan in the past and what he was going to personally do to him in the future. I'd been right about Jordy getting his men to search Nathan. They'd had Nathan strip down to his underpants to make sure he wasn't wearing a wire, but they hadn't bothered to tell him to take off his cap, nor had they searched it – thank goodness. Nathan managed to get Jordy to admit to a number of his despicable activities; in fact Jordy had positively revelled in them. After all, as Jordy had put it, 'it wasn't as if Nathan was going to leave the penthouse in a fit state to tell anyone'. The police had waited till they had enough to hang Jordy before charging in to arrest him. And from what Nathan said, they'd only just got there in time. Jordy had a gun in his hand and the barrel was pointing straight at Nathan's head when the police smashed their way in.

After that night, Nathan and I started seeing each other, though I insisted on taking it real slow. I didn't want to ruin this the way I had with Sonny. But the relationship between myself and Nathan was getting ever closer. He was my island in shark-infested waters.

Because my relationship with my daughter was falling apart.

We couldn't say a word to each other now unless it drew blood. I was desperate to sit her down and talk to her, just talk, but she wouldn't let me. I entered a room, she left it within minutes. All my lies, all my bad decisions had kicked their way into the light at the same time. Callie looked at me and I could see exactly what she was thinking. She didn't know who I was. She thought I didn't know her. And our last exchange had ripped chunks out of my heart. I had to keep blinking my now smarting eyes and my chin was so low it was against my chest, so I didn't see Meggie at the top of the stairs until I was three-quarters of the way up. I looked straight at her. She'd obviously been listening to every razor-sharp barb Callie Rose had tossed at me.

'Happy now?' I asked quietly. 'You and your son have both got exactly what you've always wanted. Congratulations.'

'Callum wouldn't've wanted—'

'I'm not talking about Callum,' I interrupted. 'I'm talking about Jude.'

Meggie lowered her gaze. 'Sephy, I didn't—'

I waved away her useless words. 'Spare me your

insincere protestations please. My daughter was seeing Jude and you knew and you never told me. You know what he's like, how much he hates me – and you never told me. I bet you're loving every minute of this. My mum has cancer and my daughter hates my guts. Your cup is full, Meggie.'

I had to get past her before I broke down completely. There was a time when I thought I'd used up a lifetime's supply of tears. I had actually believed that nothing could make me cry again. But I'd done more crying about Callie in the last two months than in the ten years before that.

I was losing my daughter and I didn't know what to do to make things right between us.

I was losing my daughter.

I had lost my daughter.

eighty-one.
Callie is 14

I eyed myself critically in the mirror one last time. I didn't look too bad, even if I did say so myself. My mascara made my already long lashes seem twice as long, and I'd plucked my eyebrows without giving myself that permanently surprised look I'd managed the last time I tried plucking them. The lipstick was working too. The shade of red suited the colour of my skin. I'd washed my hair myself and let it dry naturally. It was wavy rather than curly, and thick, falling well past my shoulders. It'd never be Cross hair but it was *my* hair. And if Ella or Bliss or anyone else for that matter had anything to say about it, I was ready for them. I wore a black T-shirt with 'READY?' written on it in silver glittery writing and torn jeans. This was the third outfit combination I'd tried and the one I'd finally settled on. It looked partyish without trying too hard. Snatching up my denim jacket, I headed downstairs on tiptoe. I'd reached the bottom stair when Mum came out of the living room. So much for trying to sneak out then.

'Where're you going, Callie Rose?'

'Out.'

'Out where?'

'Bliss is having a party and I was invited,' I told Mum.

'I see. Why didn't you tell me about it before?'

'I didn't think you'd be interested in what your halfer daughter was doing,' I snapped.

Mum looked like I'd hit her again. Score one for me. When at last she did speak, she said quietly, 'I'll drive you there.'

She reached for her car keys off the telephone table.

'No, thanks. It's not raining. I'll take the bus and walk.'

'I don't mind driving you,' said Mum.

'But I don't want to be around you,' I told her. 'See you later.'

'What time will you be back?'

'When I feel like it.'

'Not in this house, you won't. You'll come back when

I say,' said Mum. 'I want you back home by half ten at the latest.'

'Whatever you say, Mother,' I said. I hoped my tone told her that I had no intention of leaving Bliss's party so early. For goodness' sake, it was only eight o'clock now.

Mum sighed. 'When're you going to stop punishing me, Callie Rose?'

'I'll see you later, Mum.'

I didn't have to stay and listen to this. I had better things to do. I headed out into the darkening night.

Bliss had invited me to one of her parties once before, under duress admittedly, but it was still an invitation. And I'd had every intention of going. But Bliss's birthday do had been only a day or two after my disastrous trip to see Grandad Kamal. That visit had left me too bruised to even think about partying. For days afterwards, all I'd wanted was to be left alone. I didn't want to see anyone, I didn't want to be with anyone. I remember I spent that entire weekend in my bedroom, staring at myself in the mirror. I analysed every part of my face, my hair, my body, desperately trying to find the reason why Grandad had slammed the door on me.

But that was then.

This time I'd actually made it to Bliss's party and I was determined to enjoy myself. Bliss wasn't my favourite person, but she sure lived in a fabulous house. At my junior school, I'd been invited to loads of parties and most of my friends there lived in houses that were nothing to sing and dance about, just like mine. But then, my junior school wasn't a private, fee-paying school. Not everyone at

Heathcroft was wealthy, but there was no getting around the fact that an awful lot were.

Bliss's huge living room had been cleared of all furniture except for the music centre with surround speakers. Apparently she had one of those systems where you could load up a whole bunch of CDs, copy the track or tracks you wanted to hear and you could then set up any number of playlists to suit your mood.

'I set up a party playlist this morning,' Bliss announced to anyone who'd listen. 'And it's eight hours long! That should keep us going!'

She'd switched on the surround and ceiling speakers in the living room and the ceiling speakers in the kitchen and the music rang out like we were all in some kind of club or something. The wall lights shone with dim blue light bulbs. They were bright enough to see the person you were chatting to, but not bright enough to spoil the party mood. It was a lovely place, not as imposing as my Nana Jasmine's but still impressive. The music was great, the food was good and most of our school year seemed to be present. A few brave souls were already dancing.

I was in the kitchen, helping myself to a few crisps and snacks from the army of bowls set out when the back of my neck started to tingle.

'Hello, Callie.'

I turned my head. 'Hello, Tobey.'

No wonder the hairs on my nape were standing up. It had to be some kind of allergic reaction to Tobey.

'You OK?' asked Tobey.

'Fine. Just fine. Excuse me.' I walked off, with one hand full of salt and vinegar crisps. I was halfway to the living room when I realized that Tobey was only a step behind me. I turned to frown at him. The last thing I needed or wanted was Tobey following me.

'D'you want to dance?' Tobey asked as we entered the living room.

I shook my head and pointed to my full hand. And if my hand wasn't full I would've used some other excuse, like an in-growing hangnail or a bad hair hour to avoid him. Like I'd ever dance with him again.

'Callie, if our positions were reversed and you were the one who said all that stuff to me, I would've forgiven you,' said Tobey. 'I would've forgiven you long ago.'

'Which is easy for you to say because our positions aren't reversed, are they?' I pointed out, walking further into the room. 'And I'm not the one looking down on you and thinking you're the scum of the earth just because of your dad.'

'That's not true. Look, can we talk in private please? I've got something to tell you. It's important,' said Tobey, raising his voice to be heard over the music.

'Not now, Tobey,' I said. And if he couldn't hear the words, my expression must've made my answer clear enough. Tobey looked like he was about to insist, but he was interrupted.

'Hi, Callie Rose. I was hoping you'd be here.' Amyas appeared from nowhere to stand beside me. He had to practically shout to make himself heard over the noise of the music and laughing and talking and dancing.

'It's Callie,' I shouted back.

'What?'

'Just Callie. Not Callie Rose. Not any more.'

'Oh, OK,' smiled Amyas.

I turned to see Tobey walking out of the room and back to the kitchen. I felt something strange in my stomach – if I didn't know any better, I'd say it was a guilty pang. But what did I have to feel guilty about? Nothing, that's what.

'Enjoying yourself?' asked Amyas.

I shrugged. 'Yeah. I like this song that's playing. He's a good singer.'

'I agree. D'you . . . would you like to go out some time?'

'What? On a date?' I asked.

Amyas nodded. I was stunned. I used to drool over him and he'd scarcely given me the time of day. So that crush had rushed in and eventually ebbed out. But now Amyas wanted to go out with *me*. I should've been thrilled. Why wasn't I thrilled? I could barely make it to pleased.

'Yeah, OK,' I said. Luckily for me, it was still noisy around us or Amyas might've been hurt by my lack of enthusiasm. As it was he grinned at me with relief.

'That's great. Want a drink?'

'Yeah, OK. I'll have a lemonade please.'

'Is that all?'

'Yes, please. I'm pacing myself,' I lied. I was allowed half a glass of champagne at Crossmas, that was it. I didn't want any alcohol. I wasn't sure I could handle it and I didn't want to make a fool of myself.

'I'll be right back,' Amyas told me. He had to practically press his lips to my ear so that I could hear him. His warm breath tickled. 'By the way, you smell nice.'

I blushed. 'Thanks. I used some of my mum's perfume.'

'It suits you.' Amyas smiled.

He went off to the kitchen to get my drink.

'Hello, you!'

'Hi, Lucas,' I smiled. 'You OK?'

'I'm fine. You here with anyone?'

I considered. 'Amyas is getting me a drink,' I told him.

'Looooo-cassssss!' Bliss was at Lucas's side before he could say another word. He gave me a rueful smile as Bliss put her arm through his, almost spilling his drink. The pitiful girl was still trying, even though it was obvious to everyone in our year that Lucas wasn't interested. Besides, no one in his year would ever go out with anyone younger than them. Everyone knew that.

'See you later, Callie,' said Lucas as Bliss practically dragged him away from me.

Poor Lucas! I almost felt sorry for him. Amyas came back with my drink.

'Can I talk to you?' he asked.

'What's the matter?'

'Can we talk somewhere private?' Amyas shouted in my ear. 'Follow me.'

Why was everyone so keen on private conversations all of a sudden? Amyas led the way upstairs. He opened the first door he came to. It was a bedroom, the bed strewn with jackets and coats. Amyas closed the door behind him. Immediately the music became a throbbing hum from beneath us. I looked around. This was obviously supposed to be one of the lesser bedrooms but it was as big as Nana Meggie's at home.

Amyas pushed the coats back and sat down on the edge of the bed. He patted the space next to him. I sat down, wondering what was so urgent that he had to drag me away from the party. I looked at him, waiting for him to tell me.

'Callie,' Amyas smiled. 'I just wanted to say . . . well, I like you very much.'

'I like you too, Amyas.' I frowned. This wasn't going where I thought it was going, was it?

'You're one of the few girls in our year that I can have a decent conversation with,' said Amyas.

When was the last time we'd had a decent conversation? When was the first time? Amyas and I didn't exactly hang around together.

'I really like you.'

He'd already said that.

'I'm glad,' I said, edging away from him.

But not fast enough. The next thing I knew, he'd pounced and was pressing his lips against mine – hard. I certainly wouldn't call it kissing.

'Amyas, get off,' I managed to gasp out as I turned my head.

'Oh, come on. You like me, I know you do. Sammi told me. And I like you. We can just have a bit of fun before we go back downstairs.'

'No. Besides, if my mum knew what I was doing, she'd skin me alive,' I said, pushing at Amyas's forehead.

But it was like trying to move a planet.

'Just one kiss,' said Amyas, before his lips were back on mine.

I couldn't move. I couldn't breathe. I was being smothered. Amyas had his arms locked round me and his mouth open as he did his anaconda impersonation and tried to swallow me whole. I pushed against his shoulders but he wouldn't move. If anything, he started kissing me harder. I bit down on the inside of my bottom lip to stop him sticking his rotten tongue in my mouth. I was unbearably hot and my T-shirt and the coats under us were twisting around me like sheets on an unmade bed and my heart sounded like thunderclaps inside my body. Enough was enough. I balled up my fist and punched Amyas as hard as I could on the side of his head. He fell off me and off the bed and landed with a terrific thump on the floor. Immediately, there came a bang at the door. 'Enjoying yourselves in there!!'

'Just what the hell do you think you're doing?' I asked, jumping up and trying to straighten my clothing.

'I was just trying to kiss you,' Amyas wheedled. 'I like you.'

I went to the door and opened it – wide. 'Just so you don't get any more funny ideas,' I frowned.

'It was only kissing, Callie. Haven't you kissed a boy before?'

I wasn't about to admit that I hadn't.

'I like you too, but there's kissing – and then there's being pawed!' I said. 'Have some bloody class.'

Amyas sat down on the bed. I sat down on the chair. And we regarded each other for silent moments. Outside, others were wandering back and forth, trying to find a free bedroom for snogging sessions, I guess.

'Audra let me kiss her – and more. And she didn't complain once,' Amyas told me.

It'd taken him nearly half a minute to try and win me round and that was the best he could come up with?

'I'm not Audra,' I told him.

'No, you're not,' Amyas said, his eyes narrowing.

'D'you want me to go?' I asked, standing up again.

'No.' Amyas leaped up. 'I want you to want to be with me.'

'I do, but not if you're going to behave like an arse just because I won't let you grope me.'

'But why not?' Amyas couldn't sound any more puzzled. He really believed that not only should I let him feel me up, but I should beg him to do it beforehand and thank him for it during and afterwards.

'I don't want to, Amyas. And if you push it, I really will go back downstairs.'

'Go then. Who wants you?'

'Amyas, don't be like that. I'm just not ready.' I didn't want us to fight. I'd had enough of that recently to last me a lifetime. 'Besides, if my mum found out—'

'If you don't want to be with me, just say,' said Amyas. 'But stop using your mum as an excuse.'

'I'm not. But my mum—' I didn't get any further before Amyas interrupted.

'Who're you trying to kid? Everyone knows what your mum's like,' said Amyas.

Outside the room I was vaguely aware that others were beginning to stop and gather. But the music, the party, the whole world zoomed as far out as it could get until it was less than the size of a full stop. There was just me and Amyas and an all too familiar cocktail being mixed and stirred inside me, making it harder and harder to breathe. 'What does everyone know?' I asked.

'Oh, come off it. It's common knowledge that she was sleeping with her nought boyfriend from the time he started at the same school as her. That was what? When she was thirteen, fourteen? Why do you think I brought you up here? Everyone knows noughts are easy . . .'

I couldn't've said a word then if my life had depended on it. How could I ever have thought I fancied this . . . toad!

'Not exactly like mother like daughter, is it?' Amyas continued. There was a moment's silence before he added, 'Or maybe that's the problem. Maybe you two are more alike than I thought.'

My heart was thumping again. But not like before, not with pain or panic. This time it was leaping with something far more deadly.

'I'm not listening to any more,' I told him. I had to get out of there before I did something I'd regret. I turned to find most of the party outside the open bedroom door. And at the front of all of them stood Tobey, with Lucas just behind him. I regarded Tobey, too angry to even scowl at him. He wore the same stupid, apologetic expression he always had on his face whenever he saw me.

'Maybe if I was a blanker and a terrorist, you'd be more interested in me,' Amyas called after me.

That did it. I spun round and started back to him. But someone pushed past me to get there first. The next thing I knew, Amyas was rolling back and forth on the floor holding his nose, which was pouring with blood. Lucas was shaking his now unclenched hand and trying not to wince from the pain.

'The carpet!' Bliss rushed into the room as well. 'Amyas, don't bleed on the carpet. Mum'll kill me!'

Amyas tried to sit up.

'You'll stay down there if you know what's good for you,' Lucas warned him.

Amyas collapsed back down, still cupping his bleeding nose.

Bliss yelled at me, 'What the hell d'you think you're doing? You're *ruining* my party.'

'Don't worry. I'm leaving,' I told her.

I grabbed my jacket off the bed and headed out of the door. The crowd of people just outside parted to let me through without me having to say a word. After directing a final, icy stare at Tobey, I headed downstairs and out of the front door. And I was proud of myself. My eyes were dry. A year ago, it would've been a different story.

'Callie, wait!'

Someone was calling me. I turned to see Lucas running up behind me.

'What're you doing here?' I asked.

'It's late. I'll take you home.'

'You don't have to do that.'

'I want to.'

'Bliss won't like it,' I said dryly.

'Bliss doesn't own me. She'll just have to put up with it,' said Lucas, shrugging on his jacket.

We carried on walking.

'You didn't have to do that, you know,' I told him sourly. 'I can fight my own battles.'

'I know,' Lucas agreed. 'But I probably did him less damage than you would've.'

'Too right. I was going to thump him but I wasn't going to aim for his face.'

'Ouch! Then I did Amyas a favour,' Lucas grinned.

I looked at him then, really looked at him, and couldn't help but remember the boy standing in my hallway, questioning his mum about the things his dad had said.

'Why did you do it?'

'Well, he had it coming,' said Lucas as if it were obvious.

Not quite what I meant, but never mind.

'Want to go and get a coffee before you go home?' asked Lucas.

I looked at him. 'What about your mum and dad?'

'They're not coming,' Lucas frowned.

'No, I meant, won't they mind if you're out with me?'

'I couldn't care less if they do,' Lucas shot back at me. 'You know, I wondered if you still remembered what I said as a child when Ella came round to your house?'

'It's kind of hard to forget,' I admitted.

'Callie, I didn't know any better then. But I do now. My dad's views aren't mine.'

'Fair enough.'

'I mean it. I like you – very much.'

Did he really like me? Or was he lying? Everyone lies. What was he up to? What was he after?

'So how about that coffee?' asked Lucas.

Well, he might try to use me, but he couldn't. I wouldn't let him. Not if I knew what he was doing. Not if I used him first.

So I said, 'Yeah, all right then,' adding with a grin, 'but only if you're paying.'

eighty-two. Sephy

I walked out into Mother's garden, breathing in the sweet mixture of fresh-cut grass and lavender on the borders of the path. I spotted Mother straight away, in the rose garden. Early October and she still had roses in bloom. I walked over to her, enjoying the peace of her garden.

'Mother, how're you feeling today?'

'I've been better, I've been worse,' she smiled.

Which meant nothing at all. She dug into the soil beneath a rose bush, where the fading, wilting roses were past their best, to remove a particularly stubborn weed.

'D'you want some help?' I asked.

'No, thanks. I've got it. No Callie Rose today?'

'She . . . she had homework to finish,' I replied.

I looked down at Mother's back, as she dug and pulled and dug some more.

'When did you take up gardening?' I asked. 'I thought you hated to get your hands dirty.'

'Everyone should get their hands dirty once in a while.' Mother shrugged. 'Besides I like planting things and watching them grow. It makes me feel like I'm part of something.'

She was already part of something. She was an essential part of my life. I didn't know where I'd be now if it wasn't for her. It didn't bear thinking about.

'What did the doctors say about . . . about your cancer? Do you need more radiotherapy?'

'Just one more session. It seems my cancer is in complete remission, thank goodness. I was told yesterday,' said Mother, her tone matter-of-fact.

One more pull at the weed and it finally gave up and came out of the ground.

'Stubborn bugger!' Mother told it with uncharacteristic vulgarity.

I bit back a smile. After what my mother had been through in the last few months, she was entitled. But as I watched her, my smile faded.

'Mother, is . . . is anything wrong?'

'No, love. Why?'

'You've just been given the all-clear, but you don't seem terribly happy about it.'

'Don't be silly.' Mother struggled to stand up. I placed a hand under her arm and helped her to her feet. 'Of course, I'm thrilled. I feel like my head was in a noose and now I've— Oh my God! I'm so sorry, Sephy.'

The feeling of being kicked in the stomach by Mother's words had obviously shown on my face.

'It's OK,' I breathed, turning away slightly so Mother couldn't see my eyes.

'Persephone, I'm so sorry. I didn't think.'

'Don't worry about it, Mother.' I tried for a shrug but failed halfway.

Then, turning back to her, I caught the whiff of something I hadn't smelled on Mother in a long, long time. I stared at her, shocked.

'Mother, have you been drinking?'

'Don't be silly, dear.' Mother immediately backed away from me.

'Mother, don't lie to me.'

Silence. My stare turned into a glare.

'OK, I had one.' At the appalled look on my face, Mother added, 'One celebratory glass of wine doesn't mean I've fallen off the wagon.'

I regarded her, my heart too bruised to speak.

'Don't look at me like that, Sephy. It was just one glass,' Mother said, exasperated. 'Doctor Rider phoned me to let me know the good news and I wanted to commemorate the occasion.'

'You said she told you yesterday. I can still smell wine on you. How big was this one glass?'

'Now, Sephy, you're overreacting. I had a glass when she told me and I had another just before you arrived. That's all.'

'You should've commemorated the occasion with a glass of orange juice or fizzy water,' I told her harshly.

'Sephy, you worry too much,' Mother dismissed.

'Mother, don't start up again, please,' I begged. 'You were doing so well. After all this time, why start drinking again?'

'I had one glass today . . .' Mother said, impatiently. 'I don't intend to have any more.'

'Mother, please don't. I couldn't bear it,' I implored, close to tears.

'*You* couldn't bear it? For heaven's sake. This isn't about you,' Mother snapped. 'I've been sleepwalking through the last few months, too terrified to wake up. I just needed something to . . . to . . .'

'To smooth out the rough edges? Where've I heard that before?' I almost shouted. 'You've got Minerva and her family and me and Callie Rose and all your friends to smooth out any rough edges. You said you weren't going to drink any more. You were so *sure*. So strong. You keep all that wine down in your cellar but never even lapsed once. So why *now*?'

'It was just one drink,' said Mother. 'Just one . . .'

Embarrassed, awkward tears slid unexpectedly down her cheeks. As soon as she wiped them away, more took their place. I couldn't bear to see my mother cry and I couldn't stay angry in the face of her tears. I opened my arms and hugged her, realizing that it was the first time I'd ever done so. When I was a child Mother used to hug me. But then she started drinking and I started to grow up and the hugs stopped. Except from Callum on our beach. Except from Callum.

'Mother, why did you do it?' I whispered. 'All those years of hard work, all those Alcoholics Anonymous meetings and women's support groups and now you'll have to start again from scratch.'

I wasn't even sure that I expected an answer. But I got one.

'Sephy, I was so frightened . . .' Mother sobbed. 'I still am. I've never felt so alone. Suppose . . . suppose the cancer comes back.'

'Then you'll fight it again. And I'll be right by your side and so will Minerva.'

'You will?'

'Of course we will. You're not alone, Mother. Didn't you know that?'

Sammi plonked herself down next to me. Her tie was pulled down and the top two buttons of her shirt were undone, as were mine. That's how we wore our uniform, boys and girls alike, even though the teachers were always ranting at us to do up our shirt buttons and wear our ties properly. Sammi pulled her beaded hair back into a pony-tail and secured it with a rubber band.

'You shouldn't do that, you know. The rubber band will make your hair break,' I told her.

Sammi shrugged. 'This classroom is too hot. How're you doing, Callie? I hardly ever see you these days.'

'I've just had a lot on my plate recently.'

'We are still friends, aren't we?' asked Sammi.

'Yeah, of course,' I frowned. What a peculiar question.

'And friends share things?'

I nodded. Where was all this coming from?

'Then how come you didn't tell me that you and Amyas were an item?'

I stared at her. 'We're nothing of the kind.'

'Come off it. It's all over the school how the two of you were an item but you broke up at Bliss's party because he caught you doing it with Lucas.'

My jaw hit the floor. 'He caught me *what*?'

'I do think you could've told me what you were up to. I mean, I am your best friend,' sniffed Sammi.

'Sammi, I haven't been bonking Amyas, Lucas or anyone else. And Amyas was never my boyfriend. Well, maybe for about a minute, but that's it. He tried it on at the party and Lucas took him out,' I explained furiously.

'Really?'

'Really,' I insisted. 'And thanks so much for believing all that junk about me without even asking first.'

'I did come and ask you,' said Sammi.

'No, you wanted to know why I hadn't told you any of it. There's a big difference.'

Sammi had the grace to look ashamed of herself. 'Sorry, Callie. I didn't think.'

'I'm not putting up with this. Who's been spreading all those lies about me?' I said, leaping up.

'Shush!' Sammi had a quick look around the rapidly filling classroom. We were beginning to attract attention.

'Samantha, who's been—?'

'I heard you,' said Sammi, pulling me down onto my seat again. 'Listen. They may be lies but Amyas is the one spreading them. That's why I thought it was true.'

'Amyas! I should've kneed him in the goolies when I had the chance,' I fumed. 'And to think I used to fancy him!'

'Well, don't do anything stupid, will you?' Sammi looked worried. 'If you attack his tenders, Mrs Paxton will throw you of out the school.'

'It'd almost be worth it,' I argued.

'Callie . . .'

'OK! OK! But he's not getting away with it,' I said.

'Well, you can't go round telling everyone it's not true because then they'll believe it is,' Sammi pointed out. 'And if you confront Amyas, he'll just tell everyone that you're angry because you were busted.'

I glared at Sammi, because every word she'd said was true. That's exactly what would happen.

'So what do I do?'

'Just ignore it?' Sammi suggested.

'Can't do that.'

'Didn't think so. Promise me you won't do anything stupid,' said Sammi.

I shook my head. 'I can't do that either.'

Sammi sighed. 'Didn't think so.'

'Amyas is using me to salve his battered nose and his bruised ego,' I seethed. 'He's just like everyone else – a liar and a user.'

'That's not true,' Sammi protested.

'Of course it is,' I scoffed. 'No one does anything for anyone unless there's something in it for them first.'

'Callie! Don't be so cynical. Tell her, Tobey!' said Sammi.

I turned my head to see Tobey sitting behind me, his history books out for the next lesson. I hadn't even noticed him come into the class. Too busy ranting at Sammi, I guess. How much of our conversation had he heard? Not that I cared if he'd heard the whole lot.

'Go on then, Tobey. Tell me I'm wrong,' I challenged.

'You are wrong,' Tobey said quietly. 'Once you start believing that no one does anything kind or good unless there's a selfish ulterior motive, then what's the point of even getting out of bed in the morning? What's the point of anything?'

'My point exactly,' I told him.

I turned to face the front as the teacher came in. I wasn't wrong about people. They were all the same. Hadn't I seen the proof of that for myself?

eighty-four. Sephy

I watched as he planted a sincere, earnest smile on his face before answering the question put to him.

'Our party is the party of democracy and freedom. We are the party who brought in the reforms which led to not just a better life, but a better world for all our citizens. We are the party who brought in educational reforms allowing noughts to be educated on an equal footing with their Cross counterparts. We are the party which has this current government on the run.'

'And yet, Minister, you're now talking about more than halving immigration quotas and pulling out of the Pangaean Accord, which states that every country has to take a certain number of asylum seekers per year.'

'We are just responding to the concerns of our nation. We are not a country with limitless space and resources. The majority of our citizens feel enough is enough and, unlike this current government, we're listening. This country has all the noughts it can handle.'

'All the *Noughts*, Minister?'

'I misspoke,' Kamal Hadley said quickly. 'I didn't of course mean noughts per se. I was referring to the immigrant population of this country as a whole.'

'Surely your new immigration policies have more to do with the fact that your party is becoming a bit of a non-entity as far as politics in this country is concerned? Isn't this just your cheap, manipulative ploy to get yourself back on the political map?'

'Am I really meant to dignify that with an answer?' asked Dad.

'Noughts in this country make up less than ten per cent of the total population and their contribution to our society in cultural and monetary terms is incalculable. Are we really meant to vote for a party who believe – and I quote – "this country has all the noughts it can handle"?'

'I told you before, I misspoke,' Dad snapped. 'We're not just talking about noughts here, we're talking about immigrants from a host of other nations as well.'

I watched Dad wriggle like a worm on a hook as the interviewer pounced on his slip of the tongue. A humourless smile played briefly over my lips. Dad was getting old. His hair might still be artificially jet-black, but the wrinkles and bags under his eyes multiplied every time I saw him on the TV – even though his forehead was suspiciously wrinkle-free. And his eyes were old. Very old, but not very wise. A sad combination. Dad was behaving like a tyro at politics. He was allowing himself to get wound up and I was glad. My dad . . . the bigoted hypocrite. Like Janus, he had two faces, showing one face to the public and another to Mother and me. I'd bet his treatment of the two of us and his granddaughter Callie Rose didn't cause him to lose a single second of sleep. I'd bet we didn't even impinge on his subconscious, never mind his conscience. Minerva and her family were still in favour. I would never be.

And I'd had over a decade to come to terms with that. Dad was just the man who'd been present when I'd been conceived, that was all. Just a face on the TV screen, a face I could regard with curious detachment. But when it came to my daughter, that was a different story. I'd never forgive him for the way he'd treated her when she went to see him. What a shame the country couldn't've seen him at that moment. So much for all his talk about getting back to basics and family values.

'Minister, d'you really believe that a quota system for the asylum seekers we in this country are prepared to aid is fair – never mind the legality of it?'

'We cannot keep taking in any person who comes knocking at our shores for entry,' said Dad.

'So if, for example, a major civil war caused a number of people to be dispossessed, you'd be happy to tell them that they will be accepted on a first come, first served basis and after our quota is met, the rest would have to go back to where they came from to face oblivion?' asked the interviewer.

'I think the specific details will need to be thrashed out with the PEC—' Dad began.

'But your proposal is to pull us out of the Pangaean Accord as ratified by the Pangaean Economic Community,' said the interviewer. 'Wouldn't that leave us in a rather invidious position as far as discussing anything with the PEC is concerned?'

'The PEC has placed an unfair burden on this country

in terms of the number of immigrants we're supposed to allow into our country,' said Dad. 'I believe . . .'

I wasn't going to watch any more of that man. He wasn't worth my time. He wasn't worth my tears. But my mother definitely was. I needed to go and see her to make sure the drinking had well and truly stopped. She was scaring me to death, in more ways than one. Meggie entered the room, just as I was standing up.

'Sephy, can I talk to you?' she said as I walked past her.

It was as if she'd had to pluck up the courage to even ask me. I turned round. 'Yes, Meggie?'

'Is there any chance of you and Sonny getting back together?' Meggie surprised me by asking.

Frowning, I shook my head. Sonny was long ago and far away. I hadn't even seen him in close to a year.

'I hope . . . I hope it wasn't me . . . I mean . . . if you want to live with him or anyone else, I wouldn't stand in your way,' said Meggie.

I kept my mouth shut. Where was this going?

'I'd miss you . . . and Callie, but I'd wish you well and I wouldn't try to stop you,' said Meggie, her cheeks getting more and more red. She was looking anywhere but at me. 'I just wanted you to know.'

'It's a shame you didn't let me know years ago when it might've made a difference,' I told her icily. 'It's easy to say now, when my daughter and I are always at each other's throats. Thanks for nothing, Meggie.'

'I intended to say something the night you . . . you and Sonny split up. But it seemed academic then as you weren't together any more.'

Oh, Callum, look at your mum and me. So apart, that

she's still considering Sonny, when I'm now going out with Nathan.

'Sephy, I . . . I'm so sorry for what I said and did when you came out of hospital.'

At my bewildered expression, she said, 'When . . . when Callie was a toddler. When you were very ill . . .'

My expression had nothing to do with trying to figure out what she was talking about. I just couldn't believe what I was hearing, that's all.

'I think I must've gone a little crazy.' Meggie shook her head. 'I've regretted it so much ever since . . .'

'Are you serious? And it's taken you over fourteen years to apologize?'

'Sephy, please. We need to talk—'

'Talk to your son,' I sneered. 'Get him to tell you the truth about Cara Imega and the countless others he's slaughtered. Get him to stay away from my daughter.'

'This isn't about Jude or even Callum. This is about you and me—' said Meggie.

'You made sure that any relationship I entered into after Callum was doomed to failure from the start. You blackmailed me into staying in your house. And you think sorry is going to cut it now?'

'Sephy, please. I just want—'

But I'd had enough. I couldn't bear to hear another inane word. Yes, I was being unfair. I knew Meggie's threats all those years ago had little to do with what happened to Sonny and me, but I didn't want her to think her coercion had made no difference to my life.

Because it had.

Callum's letters

eighty-five. Sephy

I stared at the label on the bottle of claret next to me. How long had we been in this cellar now? How long had the bottle been in this cellar?

'I'm going to keep asking until you tell me,' said my daughter, interrupting my meandering thoughts. 'Why didn't Nana Meggie take me to see you when you were ill?'

I'd promised myself that there'd be no more lies between Callie Rose and me. But how could I tell her the truth? How do I tell my daughter about what Meggie did to me? Some things are just better left unsaid, left dead and buried in the past. Callie loves her nan. I can't take that away from her. Not on top of everything else – no matter what Meggie did. Because if I told Callie, she'd hate her nan but hate me too for making her despise someone she's loved for ever. And I can't do that to her. And I won't do that to myself. I love my daughter too much for that. I've got so much wrong. About Callum. About my family – my mother, and Minerva and Callie. I can't afford to get anything else wrong.

'Are you going to tell me or not?' said Callie.

I sighed, then said with a great deal of care, 'Your nana

acted with the best of intentions. She did what she thought was right at the time.'

'Mum, I want to propose something?' said Callie, unexpectedly.

'I'm listening.'

'Until Nana Jasmine lets us out, I want to ask you some questions and I want you to promise that you'll only tell me the truth, the whole truth and nothing but.'

I considered. 'I promise to tell you the truth or say nothing at all,' I said at last. I raised my hand to ward off Callie's protest. 'That's the best I can do.'

'Uncle Jude once said the same thing to me,' Callie Rose remembered.

'Yes, but unlike him, I'm not lying,' I replied.

Jude . . . If I had that man in front of me, I'd more than happily swing for him – in every sense.

I didn't look away from my daughter. I wanted her to believe me. To trust me again. Did she? I was so desperate for her to trust me. At least she wasn't shouting at me any more, but we still had such a long way to go. I couldn't help but wonder if we'd make it. I watched as Callie chose her next words very carefully.

'Why . . . why didn't you tell me any of this before?'

I took a deep breath to marshal my thoughts. I had to get this right. This was my chance to let Callie Rose know the true story and I couldn't afford to blow it.

If this didn't work then Callie Rose and I would be nowhere. We'd have nothing. Then everything Callum and I had been through would be for nothing. I had to let her know the truth.

And I'd never been so scared of failing in my life.

Mum bent her head briefly before looking straight at me. What was she doing? Preparing more lies? Or balking at the unfamiliar taste of the truth in her mouth?

'Callie Rose, I've wanted to tell you about the past for so long now, but as usual, my timing was off,' said Mum. 'I wanted to sit down with you and say . . . say all kinds of things.'

'Like what?' I asked, trying hard to keep the desperate edge out of my voice.

'Like no matter what other people might tell you, your dad loved us both very much.'

What a load of crap! 'I thought you promised not to lie to me.'

'I'm not lying, Callie.'

'Uncle Jude said—'

'Jude isn't your uncle, Callie. He just happens to be Callum's brother.'

'Then he's my uncle,' I frowned, confused.

'Callie, "uncle" implies a relationship. It implies more than just an accident of birth.'

'But Uncle Jude was the one who told me the truth

about my dad when you and my nanas wouldn't. Uncle Jude told me about Dad joining the Liberation Militia and how he was . . . he was hanged for what he did to you. Dad hated you and me and every Cross. D'you know what it's like to know how I was conceived?' I looked away so Mum couldn't see the tears gleam in my eyes. 'So I understand . . . I don't blame you for hating me so much.'

'That's not true!' Mum leaped to her feet and came straight over to me. She kneeled down before me. 'Listen to me, Callie Rose, not a word Jude told you is true. Not one single word.'

She tried to pull me to her but I pushed her away.

'Don't lie, Mum. Stop lying. I . . . I've got Dad's letter.'

'What?' Mum sat back on her heels and stared at me, shocked.

'The letter Dad wrote to you. The letter that made you hate me when I was a baby. I've got it. I read it.'

I dug into my trouser pocket and pulled the thing out. I'd wanted to carry it with me on my first and last L.M. assignment. The paper was beginning to fall apart from all the times I'd read it in spite of myself. The tears on my face were a poor imitation of what was going on inside me.

'I read it,' I cried.

And then I lost it and broke down completely.

'Callie, darling. Listen to me . . .' said Mum. She tried to take me in her arms again, but I pulled out of her grasp. I bent my head, mortified by the tears that wouldn't stop, ashamed of the sobs I couldn't control.

I was bigger than this.

I was older than this.

I was harder than this.

But I wasn't . . .

'Callie, where did you get that letter from?' Mum asked earnestly, her eyes boring into mine.

'I . . . Does it matter?' I hiccupped.

'Callie, love, listen.' Mum's hand stroked my hair. 'You couldn't've seen the real letter your dad wrote because only I've seen that.'

I sat back, uncomfortable with the unfamiliar feel of Mum's hand. It was almost irritating, just like the way she kept denying that I'd seen Dad's letter.

'Mum, Uncle Jude gave me Dad's letter. It was just after I found out who Dad really was – when I was thirteen.'

'Jude again. I should've guessed . . .' Mum said through gritted teeth. Her eyes began to flash with quiet rage. 'Callie, the only reason that man got in touch with you was to use you for his own ends. What he feels for me goes beyond reason and far beyond hatred. Stop thinking he's your friend. He couldn't care less about you. He's just using you to get back at me.'

'No. He told me the truth.'

'His warped, hate-filled version of it,' Mum dismissed. 'Give me that thing.'

I looked down at Dad's letter, still clutched in my hand. My dad wrote every hate-filled word, yet I held onto it like it was a priceless jewel. It was my standard. I was determined to be my father's daughter and every time I felt my resolve wavering, I took it out and read it. Every time I wondered who I was, I took it out and read it. It was the only thing I had of his. I told myself it was the only thing I needed. If Dad could be single-minded in his ambitions, then so could I. Dad let nothing get in the way of what he wanted, and neither would I.

'Give it to me,' Mum ordered, her tone not encouraging argument.

The moment I handed it over, Mum took the letter and ripped it into tiny pieces, her gaze never leaving my face. I stared at her as she did it. I know it wasn't a photograph, but it was still from my dad.

'I should've done that the first time I read the wretched thing,' said Mum, more to herself than me.

She flung the shreds away from her without a glance. I watched them flutter and fall, and then they were still.

'D'you remember when we were burgled all those years ago?' asked Mum. 'They took our TV and some other bits and pieces.'

I nodded, wondering at the sudden change of subject.

'Well, the thief or thieves also took that letter. In fact, I'm convinced the letter was what the thief was really after. Taking all the other stuff was just a smokescreen.'

'What makes you think that?'

'Why would thieves want a private letter? The only reason anyone would take it was for personal gain or personal use. I'm not rich enough to blackmail. I'm not famous enough for the newspapers to want to publish it and embarrass me. And it'd only be a mild annoyance to your grandad – a five-minute wonder, if that. So that leaves personal use. I had that letter hidden away where no one should've been able to find it. Meggie must've told Jude about its existence and he got a couple of his L.M. buddies to do the honours.'

'But it's still the letter Dad wrote just before he was hanged—' I began.

'It's a fake,' Mum said.

I stared at Mum. Something deep inside me started to unfurl. Something too fragile to even begin to acknowledge, let alone analyse. 'Dad didn't write the letter I read?'

'Oh, he wrote it all right,' said Mum. 'But it was filled with lies. It wasn't the first letter he wrote to me. I've got the first letter Callum wrote. And the first one is filled with the truth.'

'I don't understand,' I whispered.

Mum dug down into her jeans pocket and took out a folded, yellowing piece of paper.

'I brought this to show you,' she said.

'What is it?'

'Callum's first letter. The one he decided he didn't want me to see. The one filled with the truth. The letter you saw was the second one he wrote, the one full of lies. This is the real one.' Mum held it out for me. 'D'you want to read it?'

I slid backwards even though my back was already against the wall. I had to get away from Mum's outstretched hand. 'No. No more of Dad's letters. Please. I couldn't bear it.'

'Hi, Callie Rose.'

I glanced up. 'Oh hi, Lucas.'

Lucas faked a shiver. 'Brrrr! That greeting came with an Arctic wind!'

'Should I jump up and down and clap my hands with glee instead? Or how about I call you Looooo–cassssss!' I asked, affecting Bliss's pathetic girlie tone.

'Please don't,' Lucas said seriously.

I looked around. Already we were the focus of an awful lot of attention. This whole situation was getting beyond a joke. Sammi believed my story about what happened at Bliss's party, but I'm not sure Rafiya and Audra did. The sly or snide comments and hushed asides around me were too many to ignore.

'I've never been so popular,' said Lucas dryly.

'I'm glad one of us is enjoying this,' I said, annoyed.

'I didn't mean it that way,' said Lucas. 'I told all my friends the truth about what really happened but even the ones who were at the party reckon there must've been more to it than what they saw.'

'If you can't believe your own eyes, don't believe your own eyes. And if you don't like the story you're told, make one up,' I said with disgust.

'Something like that,' Lucas agreed. 'I keep telling everyone that we're just good friends but everyone wants a love story.'

'You mean a sex story,' I corrected.

Lucas nodded. I looked at him, slightly puzzled. Just good friends . . . When did that happen? Not that I was about to argue. I liked Lucas and it was kind of cool having him like me. That didn't happen too often.

'What?' Lucas asked.

'I was just thinking about the meal we had after Bliss's party that night,' I said.

'What about it?'

'It was kind of you to bother.'

'No bother. I enjoyed it,' said Lucas. 'And to be honest, I was glad to get away. Bliss calling my name every five seconds was giving me a headache. I hope your boyfriend didn't give you too much grief for having a meal with me.'

'What boyfriend would that be?' I asked, surprised.

'Isn't Tobey your boyfriend?'

'Are you kidding me? Of course not.'

'Oh, I thought he was.'

'I don't have a boyfriend,' I denied.

A smile lit a path across Lucas's face. 'Wanna go out with me then?'

'What? And let everyone think they're right about the two of us?' I asked.

'They're going to think that anyway. Besides, you didn't strike me as the type who cared what other people thought,' said Lucas.

'I don't.'

'Prove it then,' Lucas challenged.

'Yeah, OK,' I replied. 'I'd love to.'

'This weekend? Cinema and a meal?'

Lucas obviously wasn't one to hang about.

'Fine.'

'I'll see what's on and phone you,' said Lucas.

I watched him run off to join his mates further down the corridor. Sammi and Audra came running up to me from nowhere.

'We were watching,' said Audra breathlessly. 'What was that all about?'

'Lucas asked me out on a date,' I said.

'And you're going?' asked Sammi.

'Yeah. Why not?'

Sammi and Audra exchanged a significant glance.

'What?' I asked.

'Nothing,' they both replied at once.

I was about to ask them what that swapped look meant, but decided against it. After all, like Lucas said, I didn't particularly care what anyone thought. Much.

eighty-eight.
Jasmine

I thought, I *hoped* I'd seen the last of this hospital room. But here I am again and the prognosis isn't promising. I offered to let them do a full mastectomy this time, not just the lumpectomy I'd insisted on before. But apparently that ship has not only sailed but is now on the other side of the world. So I'm to have regular chemotherapy sessions and I have to take a whole pharmacy of pills. What was it Sephy said would be my epitaph?

Here lies Jasmine Hadley,
She died of embarrassment.

And two years ago, she would've been right. When I look back at that time, I can't believe how foolishly I behaved. How ridiculous to be afraid to go to my doctor and ask for help on something personal. Almost ridiculously fatal. But my epitaph now would be far worse. Because apart from my daughters there's not a single thing I've done in my life in which I can take pride. I've never really helped anyone. I've never considered anyone besides myself and my girls. I've never done anything useful, made anyone's life better, brought joy to anyone. A pointless, worthless existence. If it weren't for my daughters I might just as well have never been born for all the good I've done in this world.

Here lies Jasmine Hadley,
She died of vanity.
She died a failure.

I hate the sound of that. I don't want to leave this world having contributed nothing. I couldn't bear that.

I know what the doctors won't tell me.

My cancer is back with a vengeance now. I think I'm dying.

And now that it's a definite prospect, all I can think about is living. Funny how dying concentrates the mind. Too little, too late. I've been such a fool. I lived in my huge house and used it to hide away from the rest of the world for so many years that by the time I was ready to emerge, I didn't know how. I was too afraid.

I don't want to die a failure. That thought haunts me more than any other. I've got to try and help Sephy and Callie Rose find each other again. If I could do that then I'd die a happy woman. But how?

How?

eighty-nine.
Callie is 15

'EQUAL RIGHTS FOR BLACKS AND WHITES! EQUAL RIGHTS FOR BLACKS AND WHITES!'

We were marching towards the Houses of Parliament. Alex Luther, the Nought leader of the Coalition for Rights and Equality, had given an inspirational speech at the beginning of our march and now he was leading the huge crowd of Noughts and Crosses, united in one common chant. Alex's mantra was peaceful disobedience and though he was getting on in years, he was still so vibrant, so motivating.

'EQUAL RIGHTS FOR BLACKS AND WHITES!'

There were entire families on the march. Brothers and sisters, mums and dad, friends and neighbours, even kids being pushed along in buggies. And even though I was by myself, I wasn't alone. The middle-aged Nought couple marching next to me had taken me under their wing. In between chants, we'd been laughing and joking together for the last hour. They were Lara and Paul Butler, both retired, both in their late fifties. Before Lara retired, she had been a teacher in an inner-city Nought school. Paul had worked in the steel industry – when the country still had one. And they'd been fighting for the rights of Noughts since before I was born. They weren't afraid of anything.

'You've both been doing this for so long,' I said over the noise of those around me. 'Don't you ever want to just give up?'

'Never,' said Paul.

'*Give up?* What do those words mean?' Lara added, laughing.

'But after all these years you're still having to march to make yourselves heard,' I pointed out.

'Which is how we know we will be heard,' said Paul. 'The authorities would like nothing better than for all of us to stay at home and whine about the way things are and how they'll never change. But that's never going to happen. 'Cause we don't believe that. Only those with no faith and no guts think like that.'

'Or maybe those who can see the world for what it really is?' I suggested.

'You don't really believe that or you wouldn't be taking part in this march. And you're too young to be so pessimistic.' Lara waved a finger at me. 'When friends and family have gone, when all your money and possessions have gone, when even the light has gone, d'you know the one thing that will keep you going?'

I shook my head.

'Hope,' said Lara.

Hope? I wasn't even sure if I knew what the word meant any more. It wasn't something I could touch or hold onto. It felt like something I'd lost quite a while ago.

But maybe I could get it back.

Paul and Lara made me feel that anything was possible.

So we marched in an almost carnival atmosphere, banners flying and us marchers waving at everyone, whether they cheered us or jeered us. It didn't matter. We walked in the road, blocking the traffic so that we couldn't be ignored. I'd never done anything like this before. It was amazing. Of course, I hadn't told Mum or Nana Meggie where I was going or what I was going to do. They'd only have turned the whole thing into an unnecessary drama. So I'd told them I was going out shopping with Sammi and instead Uncle Jude had driven me all the way to the capital so I could be part of the march. As Uncle said, it was my chance to make a difference, the sort of thing the L.M. encouraged. I was part of a protest rally that meant something. And it was the most thrilling experience of my life.

Until the hordes of police arrived. And then the whole thing turned into a nightmare. They came on horseback and on foot, in military formation, and charged at us with truncheons and batons and pepper spray and Taser guns. They charged at us for no reason. They were the mob and we marchers just scattered and ran for our lives. We were screaming and crying and trying to ask them why, but none of them would listen. They laid into us like we were nothing, which in their eyes was exactly what we were.

I tried to duck down out of sight behind some bins. I thought I was safe until some instinct had me spinning round, just in time to see a copper charging at me, a Taser in his hand. I tried to run but the huge bins and the copper were blocking my only escape routes. I put my hand up to surrender but it didn't make any difference. The copper wasn't taking any prisoners. He lunged at me with his Taser gun and an electric shock like nothing I'd ever felt before violently shook my body before I dropped like a stone to the ground. Still shaking violently, I involuntarily wet myself. I couldn't help it. My body was still quaking and I had no control over any of it, not my muscles, not my organs, not even my breathing. I really thought I was going to die. Two of the marchers came running up behind the copper, who was trying to drag me along the ground, and they all started fighting. I could see their feet scuffling around, almost dancing. Terrified one or more of them would step on me, I tried to roll out the way, but I still had no control over my body. I tried to curl into a ball, but the links between my brain and the rest of me had been severed. I could feel that the violent spasms racking my body were beginning to lessen, which was just as well because there wasn't a bone in my body which didn't feel like it was about to snap in half.

The copper suddenly hit the floor and was jerking around like a demented puppet in front of me.

'Let's see how you like it,' the Nought protester shouted at him. I could now turn my head enough to see the Nought protester Taser the copper again with his own weapon. The other demonstrator, a young Cross man with locks, helped me to my feet.

'You need to go home,' said the Cross man. 'Things around here are getting really ugly.'

I nodded, not trusting myself to speak. With the aid of the Cross man I managed to limp painfully to the end of the road.

'There's a tube station just down there,' my rescuer said, pointing towards the river. 'Will you be able to make it?'

I nodded.

'Go home,' he ordered.

I nodded again. 'Thank you.'

The protester smiled briefly before heading back the way he came. The copper was still twitching on the ground. The man with the Taser was long gone. I could hear shouts and screams and sirens and the sounds of glass shattering behind me. My helper was heading back into all that. My trousers were wet and I felt sick and mostly I just wanted to go home. Part of me wanted to head back and help the others in the march, especially Paul and Lara, but I was too afraid.

I pulled off my jacket and tied it round my waist to hide the tell-tale stains on my trousers. Heading towards the tube station, I felt the tears streaming down my face at my lack of courage. I didn't have the nerve to stay. Paul and Lara, old as they were, had more guts than me.

I was a coward, wimping out at the first sign of trouble – and that was the bitter, unwelcome truth.

The march was a glorious, chaotic fiasco. A delicious shambles. A riot. It all worked perfectly. We in the L.M. called in an anonymous warning to say a number of our operatives had infiltrated the group of marchers and had deadly weapons and a couple of explosive devices ready to go off at the appropriate moment. And the police had gone for it. They didn't try to covertly survey the crowd for known L.M. members. They didn't try to separate the marchers into groups that could be scanned and searched. They had tried that the last time there'd been an anti-discrimination march and we'd really been present that time and had made them pay. So this time they panicked. How they panicked. It made worldwide news.

And Callie Rose was in the middle of it all.

I was so proud when I caught sight of her on the TV. She looked afraid and, more importantly, angry in the brief glimpse I caught of her. Very angry. And the next time we get together, I'll let her know just who's responsible for the police charging in like that. Not just this current government, but the man who gave the police such authority when he was in power. The man who wanted to give the police carte blanche to do what they wanted to 'immigrants' and 'undesirables'.

The one, the only, Kamal Hadley.

ninety-one.
Callie is 15

On the news they announced that two people had died in the earlier riots. One of them was a retired steelworker called Paul Butler who apparently died of a heart attack after being Tasered. The newsreader made it sound like he was announcing the arrival of the next train. Paul didn't deserve what happened to him. No one deserved to be treated like that. I didn't know the other guy but he was someone's husband, someone's son. We didn't do anything wrong. All we did was stop a little traffic. Was that worth the deaths of two people? The police had no right to behave as they did. The government had no right. We didn't do anything wrong.

I watched the news, feeling my heart get harder, my soul grow colder.

They had no right.

Is this how my dad felt when his dad was arrested for the Dundale Shopping Centre bombing, for something he didn't do? Is this how it burned inside when Dad was booted out of school through no fault of his own? Is this what he experienced when he realized that no matter what he did, he'd never be good enough, smart enough – *Cross* enough? For the first time since I learned who my dad really was, I felt I understood him – just a little better. I still loathed him, but I was beginning to understand him, something I never expected in a million years.

How ironic.

 ## ninety-two.   Sephy

The silver hatchback had been tailing me from the time I turned into my road. At least, that's when I became aware of it. Who was it this time? Some half-arsed government official trailing me and Meggie in the wake of the riots a fortnight ago? Did they really believe either of us had had anything to do with it? I thought all that trailing and surveillance nonsense had finished years ago. They should know by now that neither Meggie nor I have anything whatsoever to do with the L.M. I walked slowly, the bag of shopping in each hand threatening to cut my fingers off. What should I do? Keep walking? Stop and let the driver know that I knew I was being followed? If only I'd been in my car. Then I could've driven off and lost them in the town traffic. But I was walking and the shopping bags were getting heavier with each step.

If I went home, I'd lead the person following me straight to my front door. But they already knew where I lived if they were waiting for me in my street.

What to do?

I'd go home. It had to be safer there than out on the street. I had to force myself to carry on walking at the same pace so as not to raise any suspicions.

Walk normally, Sephy. Everything's fine, I told myself.

As I approached my front door, I transferred the bag in my right hand to my left and fished into my cavernous coat pocket for my keys. I touched each, feeling for the one that would open the front door. I kept my hand in my pocket until the last possible moment. My hand was shaking as I inserted the key, but luckily I didn't drop it. The next instant, I was in the house like a rat up a drain-pipe, slamming the door shut behind me. The shopping hit the floor a fraction of a moment later as I dashed into the living room. Peering through the net curtains, I saw I wasn't being paranoid. The silver car that'd been follow-ing me pulled up in front of my house. A Cross woman sat behind the wheel. As she turned to scrutinize the house, I sprang back from the window.

Had she seen me?

What was I thinking of? Of course she'd seen me. She'd been following me for goodness' sake.

Don't panic, Persephone.

The days of people following you home to hurl abuse at you are all but over. There was still the occasional word or two, the more frequent stare, but nothing on the scale of the abuse I'd suffered when Callie Rose was younger. At least, not in this part of the country.

The woman in the car sat staring up at the house. How much longer was she going to watch me? Hell, if she'd come to vilify me, she'd find I could give as good as I got – and then some more. Enough was already too much. Flinging open the front door, I marched down the garden path. The woman inside the car looked nervous but she didn't drive away as I'd expected her to. I tapped smartly on the window. The woman pressed a button and the window purred its way downwards.

'Can I help you?' I asked with belligerence.

'You're Persephone Hadley?' asked the woman.

'Who wants to know?' I asked, peering in through the open car window.

'My name is Celine Labinjah.'

The name meant nothing to me and it probably showed in my expression. I stepped back as the woman switched off her engine. She got out of her car and came around to stand before me, a brown envelope in her hand.

'My dad was Jack Labinjah.'

She said it like that would clear up the whole mystery. It didn't.

'My dad was a prison officer at Hewmett Prison. Callum McGregor gave my dad a letter to pass on to you before he died,' said Celine.

My body turned hollow and my heart dropped down to my heels. Jack Labinjah. I remembered him now. I remembered everything about him – his deep voice, his trim moustache, his sad, brown eyes as he handed me Callum's hateful, hurtful letter. The letter that had exploded every naïve, fairy-tale notion I'd held about love. Until I learned how hard it was to love someone else if you couldn't love yourself.

Suspicion turned to unease as I regarded Celine. 'What d'you want?'

'My father died five months ago,' said Celine. 'Before he died he made me promise to find you and give you something.'

All words of sympathy or condolences for the death of her father were swept from my head. 'Give me what?'

'This envelope with your name on it,' said Celine.

'No thank you,' I said, already turning away. The last time Jack Labinjah had delivered something to my door, he'd devastated my life. I wanted nothing else from him. As I made my way back inside, Celine came running up behind me. I hoped to make it inside my house before she reached me but it didn't happen.

'Look, I don't like this any more than you do,' Celine said. She tried to shove the envelope in her hand towards me. I childishly placed my hands behind my back.

'I'm not leaving here until you take it. I promised my dad,' she said again.

'What is it?'

'I don't know much about it,' Celine said with impatience. 'Dad told me that some guy called Callum McGregor wrote a letter to his girlfriend. You?'

I didn't answer.

'Anyway, Dad said that the guy, Callum, scrunched up his first letter, threw it away and then rewrote it. He asked Dad to deliver his second one, but after Callum died, Dad retrieved his first letter and kept it.'

'Why?'

'Dad promised to deliver the second letter but he knew the first one was the real one.'

'I don't understand. How did he know that?'

'This guy Callum told him so. Apparently, Callum said the first letter he wrote to you was . . . selfish? He made Dad promise to deliver the second letter he wrote.'

'So why bother delivering this first letter at all?' I asked bitterly. 'I don't want it and obviously . . . Callum didn't want me to have it either.'

'Dad said he wouldn't rest in peace until you got it. And he made me promise to deliver it. That's all I know.'

When I didn't move, Celine used her free hand to take my right hand and thrust the envelope into it.

'It's going straight in the bin,' I told her.

'That's your prerogative. I've done what Dad asked me to do,' said Celine.

I watched her get back into her car and drive away. I re-entered the house, the envelope making the palm of my hand sweat. I walked into the kitchen, ready to put the damn thing in the bin.

But I couldn't.

I just couldn't.

My heart leaped forward like a skimmed stone as I stared down at the envelope. My stomach began to churn and turn and burn inside. I tore open the envelope and fished out the contents – despising myself for my weakness. I should burn the thing, tear it up unread. Why put myself through more pain from that man?

I remembered a time, just after Sonny left for good but before Nathan, when I sat in my bedroom late one night and forced myself to remember Callum and me. I revisited every memory – good or bad. Some made me laugh out loud, a few made me cry, most made me smile. But with each memory, I became more and more convinced that Callum cared about me the way I cared about him. Each memory made the pain of Callum's letter shrink just that bit more. And when that hateful letter was stolen, yes, I was terrified that it might turn up, raking up the past along with it, but deep down I was glad it was gone. When the days turned to weeks and weeks slipped into months, I relaxed in the knowledge that the letter had almost certainly gone for good. And with the letter no longer in the way to cloud my judgement, it was easier to see the truth.

Callum loved me.

I was as sure of that now as I was when I was a teenager, watching him die before my eyes. I didn't need or want another letter from Callum telling me that what I considered true memories were nothing more than the wistful, wishful imaginings of a teenage girl trapped in a woman's body.

I held two sheets of once-crumpled but now semi-smooth paper, yellow with age. The paper felt almost like a relief map beneath my fingers, full of subtle ridges and defined lines. My heart lurched painfully as I recognized the bold, defiant upright strokes that were Callum's handwriting. I'd already played this scene and it wasn't so great the first time that I wanted to repeat the experience. But Callum's words took me by the hand and led me on, however reluctantly. I told myself I had nothing to fear. This letter couldn't possibly hurt me any more than Callum's first one.

Couldn't possibly.

So why was fear, heavy as a paperweight, sitting in the pit of my stomach?

Calling myself all kinds of a bloody fool, I half sat, half slumped down onto a kitchen chair and began to read.

I sat statue still. Had Celine Labinjah, the guard's daughter, left a minute ago? An hour? A day? Every thought and feeling I possessed had been torn out of me. I sat, waiting to feel something, almost desperate for the pain to start. But there was nothing. Why had he done it? Why hadn't Callum just sent me the letter I had in my hand? Why the other one, dripping with poison from each and every word?

Why, Callum? Why?

Did you really believe that a letter full of hatred would help me move on? Is that it? Did you really think that telling me you hated me would help me get on with my life? Did you? Then you didn't know me at all. But then how could you? We were children together and teen-agers trying and failing to stay together. The world only had two colours for us – black and white. There were no shades of grey. There were no shades. We had romance and drama and dreams and wishful thinking. What we never had was time – time to grow up and grow old together.

All those things you called out to me as you stood on the scaffold, that terrible black hood covering your face . . .

'I love you too, Sephy . . .'

And I believed you.

And then I didn't. Your deadly letter saw to that. All the years spent wondering whether your final words were supposed to negate that letter or vice versa? Or was it just when that last moment came, you needed to tell me the truth?

'I love you too, Sephy . . .'

I stopped believing. I convinced myself I'd heard what my heart wanted me to hear. Another lie. That evil letter . . . How could you profess to love me and still have written something like that? Was it your attempt at one last honourable deed? To atone? To feel better about yourself, about us? How could you have got me so wrong? When I got that toxic letter, it was as if you had ripped out my soul before turning your back on me like everyone else.

The rest of the world I could've coped with. I didn't care about the rest of the world. But you? I cared about you. I *loved* you. And when I thought you loved me, no one could touch me. I had your love and our daughter – and that's all I wanted or needed. Until I received your letter.

When I thought I'd lost you, had never had you, I lost myself. I closed down and hid away from everything, even my own daughter. She had to almost die to bring me crashing back to life. And it was all for nothing. For a letter you didn't mean. Your misguided attempt to be noble. You loved me, Callum. You really loved me and yet you couldn't tell me so.

You were in the L.M. for too long, Callum. Did you really believe that your hatred rather than your love would set me free? Did you really believe I could have any kind of life hating your memory instead of loving all thoughts of the brief time we had together?

You got me so wrong, Callum. But I did the same. I should've believed in what my heart said, not what my eyes read. I tried. God knows I tried. But for far too long my memories were like trying to pin down fog. And your letter was real. I could feel it, the smooth, cool texture of the paper beneath my fingers, the tingle of the creases beneath my fingertips where the letter had been folded. I could see it, black ink on white paper, your bold, upright handwriting. I could smell it, the merest hint of you, as long as I smelled with my imagination. I could hear your thoughts as you wrote it, or at least, I thought I could. I thought I could hear the laughter and scorn inside you as you wrote. I should've had more faith. But faith is so easy to hold onto when you don't need it. And so hard to find when you do. I failed in that as I failed in so many things.

Where do I go from here?

Oh, Callum, you fool. I loved you so very much, just as you loved me. But look at the mess we both made of our lives.

Oh, Callum . . .

Sephy versus
Callie Rose

ninety-three.
Callie Rose

Mum held out the letter again, towards me. Scared, I backed away, knocking into a rack of wine on my left. The bottles clinked in protest.

'Mum, please. Don't make me read it. I don't want to.'

And just like that, I wasn't sixteen any more. I was a little girl, terrified of being hurt all over again.

Mum smiled sadly. 'That's exactly how I felt before I read it. But Callie Rose, you have to decide if you want to live the rest of your life believing a lie. Or are you prepared to take a chance on the truth?'

I looked into Mum's eyes. She smiled at me. Just smiled. And what I saw in that smile . . . I turned away, in case what I could see wasn't real, but mere wishful thinking on my part. Eyeing the piece of paper in Mum's hand, I was tempted to ask her to put it back in her pocket. Or maybe she could read it to me? But that was what a child would do – and I was no longer a child.

I took the folded piece of paper from Mum. It was cool and dry under my fingers. It was frightening that a piece of paper and a few words held so much power.

'Is it . . . is it as awful as the other one?' I whispered.

'Read it.'

I unfolded the paper and had to wait for the words to stop swimming before I could read.

ninety-four. Callum

Darling Sephy,

This is the hardest thing I've ever had to write. I want to say so much to you, but I don't know where to start or how to say it. I'm going to die. I know that as well as I know my own name. I'm going to die and there's nothing I can do about it.

And I've reconciled myself to the idea of dying – if not the fact. I'm not blameless, Sephy. I've done things, terrible things, that I'm not proud of. I've hurt and maimed and killed – and I am so sorry. I'm not a saint. And I want to tell you something else. I wasn't a virgin when you and I made love, my darling, but you were, are, and always will be, the only one I've ever loved. I love you more than my freedom, my family, my life. Making love with you was like touching heaven for the one and only time in my life. All the other crap in my life was worth it just for that one night with you. Being with you, next to you, inside you, was like something I hadn't even dared to dream. A wild, tortuous fantasy I never expected to come true. I hope and pray that you never regret it, Sephy. Even if I were tortured from here to hell and back before they kill me, I wouldn't regret a second.

And I don't want you to blame yourself. My death has nothing to do with you. I made my own choices. Don't waste your life swimming in guilt about something you had no control over. But I know you and I'm so scared that you'll let what's going to happen to me close you down and ruin your life. If you do that, then your dad and all the others who've tried to build a wall between us will have won. Don't let them win, Sephy.

If I'm honest, I do have one regret. Just one. I should've followed you to Chivers boarding school. Watching your car drive away from me was one of the worst moments of my life. I was ready to take a train or a coach or even walk to Chivers, just to be with you. But I began to think it was a sign that we just weren't meant to be. Everything in my life had fallen apart up until then. I didn't want you and me to go the same way. If we'd come together and it hadn't worked – I couldn't've lived with that. I hope you have more courage in your life than I did, Sephy. When a chance for real happiness comes by, grab it with both hands and devour it. If it lasts five minutes or five lifetimes, it's still worth it. There're going to be times when others will trash me to your face. Don't try to defend me. I probably deserve every jibe spoken against me. But remember this if nothing else: I love you more than there are words or stars. I love you more than there are thoughts or feelings. I love you more than there are seconds or moments gone or to come. I love you. I don't know whether we'll have a boy or a girl. I don't even know if you'll go through with the pregnancy, but I hope so. Thanks to you, Sephy, I have hope again. If you do decide to go through with it, all you need tell our child is that I love him or her very much. I love the thought and the fact that we'll have a child together – a child conceived in

*the eye of a storm. My last thought on this Earth will be of you
and our child. Make sure he or she knows how much I love them.*

*Sephy, there's just one last thing I want you to do for me.
One last small favour. And I need your promise you'll do it,
even though I can't hear you say the words in person. But I have
to believe that you'll do this one thing for me.*

*Don't tell our child about the things I've done since I joined
the L.M. And don't tell him or her how I died.*

*I don't want our child to hate me. I need you to do just this
one thing for me. I'm trusting you. All I've ever done in my life
is bring bad luck to those who care about me. I don't want that
to happen to our child. He or she will have a hard enough time
being half-Nought, half-Cross without the additional burden of
having a hanged Nought for a dad.*

*And so my love, don't cry for me. I love you. I'm living and
dying for the time we can be together again − for always and for
ever.*

Yours till the day I die and beyond,
Callum

ninety-five.
Callie Rose

I wasn't in the cold cellar any more. I was in a uncomfortably warm prison cell with my dad, watching as he wrote the letter I now held in my hand. Watching as he poured his heart and soul out through his pen and onto the paper. Watching as he crumpled up the letter and threw it away before writing another version – but this time fictitious and deadly.

It was only on my second reading of the letter that its meaning began to sink in. A bit. A very little bit.

'Why didn't he let you have this one?'

''Cause he was being dramatic. 'Cause he thought it was the only way I'd move on with my life. 'Cause he wanted to make up for how you were conceived. 'Cause we were both so young. Because he thought he was being honourable. Pick a reason.'

'Why d'you think he did it?' I asked.

Mum smiled. 'All of the above. And because he loved me – and it probably seemed like a good idea to him at the time.'

Mum's tone was light, flippant almost – but now that I was looking, I could see past it. I could see beyond to where the pain started. Or maybe it had just never stopped. Now that I was looking, I could see through the smoke-and-mirrors façade Mum presented to everyone – including me. Especially me. Now that I was looking, it was as if the woman before me was someone new, someone I'd have to get to know. That made me sad.

Now that I was looking.

'How much did Dad's poisonous letter hurt you?'

Mum's smile vanished. She regarded me, her face frozen. And then her gaze was looking past me, through me.

'The first letter I got from Callum destroyed my hope,' said Mum at last.

'Your hope for what?'

Her gaze snapped back from long ago and far away to right back with me.

'Callum's letter destroyed my hope,' she repeated.

I struggled to comprehend. I felt I understood so much, and still so very little.

'When did your hope return?' I asked. 'When you got Dad's real letter?'

Mum shook her head.

'When then?' I persisted. Maybe I was deluding myself. Maybe Mum didn't believe that things would ever get better.

'You were three and a half, maybe four,' Mum began. 'I was reading you a bedtime story and at the end of it, you sat up and hugged me and said, "I love you, Mummy." '

Silence.

'So?' I prompted.

'So . . . in that moment I knew I had something to live for. You were my hope.'

'It's all right, Mum. You don't have to spare my feelings.' I had to swallow hard or I would've burst into tears. 'I can stand the truth. I'm a big girl now.'

'That is the truth, love,' said Mum.

'You never loved me, Mum. You couldn't even bear to . . . to touch me and it took me years to realize it, and then more wasted years to get over it.'

'I was too afraid,' Mum admitted.

My whole body went still then. I hadn't expected Mum to say that. I'd replayed this conversation again and again in my head over the years. I'd gone through all the things I'd say . . . if I had the courage. All the things I wanted to say and all Mum's possible responses. But I hadn't expected this one.

'Afraid of what?'

'When you were a baby, I tried to block out the world and keep you safe – and you almost died. When I came out of hospital, I was so scared of it happening again. So I made a deal with a God I didn't believe in but was still scared of. I promised that if He kept you safe, I'd never hurt you again. I'd never put myself in the position where I could hurt you.'

Unbidden, unwelcome tears trickled down my cheeks. 'A promise you kept,' I whispered. 'My bruised knees were dusted off, my trapped fingers were placed under icy water, my tangled hair was brushed and combed. And not one single hug accompanied any of them.'

My arms were held, my forehead kissed, my cheeks stroked – but no cuddles. Mum dealt with my edges, the perimeter of who and what I was. I was never enveloped by her or her love, never made to feel that it was truly mine, never made to feel *secure*.

'I kept you safe,' said Mum.

'And I hated you for it,' I told her.

'I know.' Mum nodded sadly. 'I know.'

'And Dad's letter doesn't . . . solve anything.'

'I know that too,' said Mum.

ninety-six.
Callie is 15

'Nana Meggie?' I called out.

Silence. The afternoon sunlight streamed through the glass in the front door, lighting up the laminated wood floor in our hall. It was almost pretty. I strained to hear any other sounds. Was Mum in? It didn't appear so. The house was quiet as an empty church. I'd only just closed the front door behind me when the doorbell rang. Even though Uncle Jude had just dropped me back home, it couldn't've been him. He would never ring our front doorbell. If he wanted something, or had forgotten something, he'd phone me on the mobile he'd bought me and arrange to meet away from my home. Frowning, I opened the door. I really wasn't in the mood for strangers.

It was the biggest stranger of them all.

Tobey.

'Callie, can I come in?' he asked.

I was about to slam the door in his face but Tobey put out his hand to hold the door open.

'Make it fast,' I said, making my tone as brusque as possible. There was no way he'd fail to get the message from that.

Tobey stepped into the hallway, closing the door behind him. He stood in front of it, blocking out the sunlight, making the hall gloomy and depressing. I headed into the living room. Tobey followed me.

'What is it?' I asked with impatience.

'Who was the man who just dropped you off?' Tobey asked.

'His name is Mr None-of-your-business,' I frowned, dropping my rucksack at my feet.

'If he's Jude McGregor, then you're in trouble,' Tobey informed me. 'He's wanted by the police for murder and political terrorism. They reckon he's one of the top four or five in the Liberation Militia.'

'And what cereal box did you read that off?' I asked.

'I looked him up on the Internet,' Tobey informed me. 'I . . . I took a digital photo of him the last time he dropped you off at your house and scanned it into my computer.'

Shocked, I glared at Tobey.

'Wow! You have been busy,' I said, slow-clapping Tobey's efforts. 'Is your life so empty that you have to stick your nose into mine?'

Tobey didn't answer, not that I expected him to.

'What is it with you, Tobey?' I asked. 'Why're you

always hanging around me? I just have to turn my head at school and you're there, in the background but always in view. Are you stalking me or something? Is that how you get your jollies?'

And he still didn't say anything.

'That's it, isn't it? D'you turn off your lights at night and watch me from your bedroom window?' I was being totally bloody but I didn't know how to stop. If he'd shouted at me or walked out or told me where to go, then I might've stopped. But he just stood there, taking everything I was dishing out. 'Tell me what time you go to bed and I'll stand by my window and put on a show for you, you sad git.'

'What happened to you, Callie?'

'I grew up,' I told him.

'No, you grew bitter and twisted,' Tobey told me quietly. 'Did I do that?'

'Just go away, Tobey. You're boring.'

Tobey headed for the living-room door. I watched him, defiantly.

'I really . . . care about you, Callie Rose,' said Tobey. 'More than anyone else in the world. But you don't make it easy.'

I waited till I heard the sound of the front door being closed before allowing my guard to drop. My face sagged into confusion. What did Tobey mean by that? Since when did he care about me? Or was it just his guilt talking? Or was I just so far gone that I couldn't see what was real and what was make-believe any more?

ninety-seven. Sephy

I watched Mother drift in and out of a fitful sleep. Her eyes finally opened long enough for her to register my presence. She tilted her head towards me and tried to smile. I tried to do the same, failing miserably.

'Hi, Mother. How're you feeling?'

'Tired.'

Understatement of the year. For the first time, Mother looked every year of her age.

'Your hair looks good,' I tried.

'Best wig money can buy,' said Mum, patting it.

'Oh, Mother...' I did the one thing I'd promised myself I wouldn't do. I started to choke up.

'Does this mean you don't want to hear about my mouth sores or my constant diarrhoea or how everything I eat tastes like rusty nails?' Mother smiled.

I forced myself to smile back. 'I'm glad you've kept your sense of humour.'

'With all my other bits being gobbled up by this cancer, it's one of the few things I can hold onto,' said Mother.

'Is there anything I can get you?' I sat down very carefully on the edge of her bed.

'A new body?'

'I'm fresh out. Sorry.'

'In which case, I'll settle for a hug,' said Mother.

'Are you sure it's OK?' I said, doubtfully.

Mother regarded me. 'I read once that children deprived of hugs and cuddles fail to thrive and don't grow physical or mentally as quickly as children who are held frequently with love,' said Mum. 'Isn't that interesting?'

'You're hardly a child,' I pointed out.

'We're all children,' said Mother. 'From the youngest to the oldest of us.' She was watching me expectantly. What did she want from me? 'Sephy, what happened when Callie Rose was a baby was an accident. Nothing more, nothing less and certainly nothing else. When're you going to forgive yourself?'

'Mother, you're worrying about nothing. Besides, I didn't come here to discuss me,' I said clumsily. 'I want to know how you're doing.'

'If you don't open up to Callie Rose soon, you're going to lose her for good,' said Mum.

Lose her . . . I'd tried talking, apologizing, begging her to just give me five minutes of her time. I'd tried – and failed. My daughter wasn't about to forgive or forget any time soon. And I really couldn't blame her. Lose her? That had already happened.

I tried to shrug off the hand in my chest squeezing relentlessly at my heart. I tried to smile away the pin-prick tears making my eyes sting. But I wasn't fooling anyone. 'Mother, I . . . I think I'm too late. Callie Rose won't even speak to me. She can hardly stand to be in the same room as me. I've messed up big time – which I probably would've done anyway, even without Jude's help.'

'Jude?' Mother said sharply. 'What's he got to do with this?'

'He's been seeing Callie Rose.'

'He's what?' Mother winced with pain as she struggled to sit up. 'What's going on?'

I told her everything I knew, which wasn't much. But it was enough if the look on her face when I'd finished was anything to go by.

'Sephy, I want you to do me a favour,' said Mother.

'Anything. Just name it,' I said.

'I want you to ask Meggie to come and visit me.'

'Now, Mother, that won't do any good. Jude is Meggie's one remaining child and she won't hear anything said against him,' I said.

'I just want to chat with her, for old times' sake. Ask Meggie to come and see me please. I'll handle the rest.'

ninety-eight.
Callie is 15

I'm so tired I can hardly stand up. The muscles in my limbs feel like they've been clamped in a vice for hours, which isn't that far from the truth. I was at an L.M. training camp again today. We had field training first as always, which meant we all had to run around and complete an obstacle course. This time, I was over halfway around when I was ready to collapse – so that was progress. The first couple of times, I'd barely made it to the fifth or sixth obstacle. We had to swing over muddy water, wade through muddy water, crawl under cargo nets through muddy water. By the time we'd finished, every atom in my body ached. I also learned how to strip down an assault rifle and put it back together again. Those assault rifles are bloody heavy. And because I kept getting it wrong, I had to do it three times. By the third time, I could hardly lift the thing, never mind shoot straight with it. All in all, I was pretty useless, but Uncle Jude said he was too when he first started. I found that hard to believe but it was sweet of him to say it to make me feel better. And that wasn't all. We learned about making other devices for self-defence like pipe bombs and nail bombs and altering someone's mobile phone so you can listen in to all their calls.

It was so strange sitting in a classroom and learning about bomb-making and weapons instead of algebra or physics. I pinched myself once or twice throughout the lesson to make sure I was really there and not having one of the weirdest dreams of my life. I wasn't even sure what I was doing there. Will I ever be able to pick up a gun and shoot someone? I know Uncle Jude says that we're only learning this stuff so that we can protect ourselves, but the thought of shooting a hole through someone . . . the thought of taking someone's life in cold blood . . .

I'm just not sure I could do it, that's all.

And not because I'm afraid I'd feel too much.

But because I'm terrified I wouldn't feel anything at all.

Uncle Jude stood at the front of the classroom watching me and everyone else. And the way our teacher and all the other adults in the training camp deferred to him made me realize that he was someone very respected in the Liberation Militia. Someone very high up. So Tobey was right about that, after all.

I caught Uncle Jude frowning at me once or twice, but then his expression always relaxed into a smile when he caught me returning his look. It was my third visit to the training camp and I think today was the first time that reality truly set in. The first time I went, it was exciting, an adventure. I didn't even mind when Uncle Jude took me to one side and told me that I shouldn't call him 'Uncle' but 'sir' at the training camp. I was proud to call him 'sir'. I was proud to hear others call him 'sir'. It was all part of the game I was playing. I didn't even mind being one of only a handful of 'dual heritage trainees', as the instructor put it.

But the second time, it wasn't quite so exciting. It was more like hard work. And the instructor started talking about all the things that would be expected of us in 'the field'. We went through basic self-defence training and I hit the mat so many times I'm sure my hips increased at least two dress sizes. But I told myself it was still an adventure. I was like the heroine of an old film, learning the necessary skills to avenge the great wrongs done to her in the past. But at the end of the second training session we were shown an information film.

It was horrific. Relentless images of Noughts being beaten up by Cross police, the battered, misshapen face of the Nought who was beaten to death for being in a 'Cross area', the limp and twisted dead body of the

Nought who was tied up and dragged behind a car by two hate-filled Crosses, a Cross police officer stating quite seriously that the reason Noughts needed to be restrained with so much excessive force was the fact that they loved violence, as any Cross who'd watched them after a football match or coming out of a pub at night had seen for themselves. The Cross officer then went on to say that Noughts also had thicker, tougher necks so more pressure had to be applied to subdue them. That was why so many of them died when being arrested. And all the incidents we were shown had taken place within the last five years. Some of the stories, most of them, had been on the news. But a reporter with a microphone saying what had happened was very different to seeing the images for yourself.

I watched with revulsion as horror after inhumane horror was catalogued and reported in the information film. My eyes were burning, my throat was burning, my heart was burning. Each image fuelled the rage inside me until by the time the film had finished, I was filled with a loathing which blazed out in all directions indiscriminately.

That's when it stopped being a game.

And when the instructor started talking this morning about the best places to stab a person to kill them instantly and silently, that's when the fear started. Maybe Uncle Jude knew how I felt because he said very little as he drove me back home. A phrase of Nana Meggie's keeps playing in my head: 'Never stick your head where your bum can't follow.' But that's exactly what I've done.

And I'm stuck.

And I'm so tired. Tired of it all.

I think I would sell my soul for a way out.

ninety-nine. Meggie

Callie came in from her weekend away and dived straight into the bathroom.

No, she didn't want a cup of tea.

And no, she didn't want anything to eat.

And yes, she was all right.

And yes, she was tired.

And for heaven's sake! Couldn't we leave her alone?

I gave up after that. When Sephy asked Callie through the locked bathroom door where she'd been all weekend, Callie didn't even bother to answer. Sephy pleaded with Callie to open the door and talk to her. I watched as Sephy wearily leaned her head against the door frame when the only response she received was silence. At least Callie Rose had deigned to answer me, even if her replies had been terse. Sephy gave me a look which found me somewhere beneath contempt and then walked away without a backwards glance. I watched from the top of the stairs as she put on her coat.

'Meggie, Mother would like to see you – if it's not too much trouble. If anything happens, I'll be at Nathan's,' Sephy told me before heading out of the house.

Sephy comes home, Callie leaves. Callie comes home,

Sephy needs to go out. It's like a game of musical chairs, where the chairs are rooms in this house and the music is hatred and it's a game no one's enjoying, but none of us can stop playing.

Sephy and Callie are part of my family, just as much as my son Jude. But Jude's on one side of me and Sephy and Callie Rose are on the other and I'm stuck in the middle. And as far as Sephy is concerned, I've already chosen a side.

But I haven't. Have I . . . ?

I don't know anything any more, except that we can't all go on like this.

Each of us is heading for a confrontation, a showdown. I can feel it. And it's going to be bloody and it's going to be brutal. And I'm not sure how – or even if – any of us will survive.

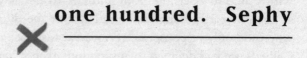

one hundred. Sephy

'So what did you think?' asked Nathan. 'Be honest.'

'Nathan, I've already told you! It was lovely,' I smiled. 'If your chef ever gets ill, you can step into his shoes, no bother!'

'Not in this lifetime!' said Nathan.

I watched as Nathan cleared our dessert bowls away,

trying to concentrate on him and not on my problems at home.

'Are you sure you don't want some help?' I called out.

'No, you just relax on the sofa,' Nathan called back.

The kitchen, lounge and dining room in Nathan's apartment were one big open-plan space. The kitchen was sectioned off by a waist-high breakfast bar but otherwise there were no partitions or walls. His flat was lovely – a definite bachelor pad, but tidy and tastefully if rather neutrally furnished. The floors throughout most of the apartment were covered with hardwood maple. The walls were a light cream colour, decorated with post-Impressionist artwork and a few original, contemporary paintings. It was almost like a bachelor show home – except in the master bedroom's en-suite bathroom. The walls in that were black marble, as was the floor, with a walk-in shower cubicle at one end of the room and at the other one of the largest white bathtubs I'd ever seen. The bath was big enough to easily fit at least three people into it. The fittings and mirrors above the two sinks were all gold or gold-plated. It was sumptuously decadent and quite unexpected after seeing how austerely the rest of the apartment was decorated. But Nathan said that's why he'd had it done that way.

I moved from the dining table, sat down on Nathan's white sofa and leaned back, a glass of medium-dry white wine in my hand. The warmth of the fire filled the whole room and after an excellent meal and a glass of good wine, I should've been more relaxed, more content than I was. My mind should've been on Nathan and our relationship. But half my mind and most of my heart were focused elsewhere – on my daughter.

The shouting and the verbal abuse between us was getting worse. And so were the echoing silences in between. Silences so intense, they scared me. I couldn't remember the last time I'd seen Callie smile. Where had my sunny little girl gone? The one who smiled up at the sky and spoke to her dad like he was skipping along beside her. The Callie Rose who inhabits our house is the shell of the girl I remember. There had to be a way to get through to her, to bring the real Callie Rose back to life.

But how?

'Still worrying about Callie?' Nathan said gently, sitting down beside me.

'Sorry,' I sighed. 'I don't know why you bother with me. I haven't been very good company lately.'

'Is there anything I can do to help?' asked Nathan.

I shook my head and sighed again. 'This is something Callie and I have to sort out ourselves.'

'D'you think a change of environment might help?' asked Nathan.

'Like what?'

'Well,' said Nathan, taking the glass out of my unresisting fingers, 'I was thinking that if you and I got married and the three of us moved into a new house together, that might help to move things forward between the two of you.'

All my senses cranked up a gear. I could hear the coffee-maker in the kitchen bubbling. I could smell Nathan's subtle lemon-musk aftershave and the aroma of the coffee brewing behind us. The white wine lingering on my tongue held a faint sweetness. Nathan's hands in mine were cool, despite the warmth of the fire before us.

And my eyes . . . at that moment my eyes saw nothing but Nathan.

'That's very "league of nations" of you,' I said lightly. 'You'd marry me just to negotiate peace between me and my daughter?'

'I'd marry you for any reason you'd have me,' said Nathan with uncharacteristic seriousness.

It was exactly the wrong time to remember Sonny and his marriage proposal years before, but they crept unbidden into my head. Fear had spurred me into handling that situation all wrong. I didn't want to make the same mistake again. But the same old fear was gnawing at my heels.

'I don't know what to say,' I said, wincing at my own triteness.

'Say yes then.'

'Nathan, I—'

Nathan placed his finger over my mouth. 'If you're not going to say yes, don't say anything. At least, not until you've had a chance to think about it.'

'I'm not turning you down, Nathan,' I began.

'But you're not jumping for joy either, are you?' said Nathan, pulling his hands away from mine.

'But not for the reason you think,' I tried to explain. 'My life is a confused mess right now. I care about you too much to drag you into the middle of it.'

'I want to be part of your life, Sephy. No dragging required.'

'Nathan, please give me just a little more time. OK?'

'OK,' said Nathan. 'I'll go and get our coffees.'

Nathan jumped up before I could stop him. I opened my mouth to call him back, but then let him go. The easy, jovial mood between us had been fractured. Words would only make things worse. Restless, I got up and wandered round the room. Should I stay or just get my things and leave? Meandering aimlessly around the lounge, I sought something to do with my hands, my thoughts. I sat down at Nathan's desk in the corner of the room and removed a piece of paper from his printer. I grabbed up a pen and started scribbling, almost before I knew what I was doing.

You remind me of a boy I used to know
Same smile, same easy, laid-back style
And man, could he kiss
Blew my mind the very first time
His lips touched mine.
You remind me

You remind me of a boy I used to like
Same eyes, strong arms, same open mind
And man, could he dance
Arms around me, lost in a trance
I'd hear his heart,
You remind me

I'm scared of you
How did you find me?
Turn and walk away
'Cause you remind me

You remind me of a boy I used to love
Same laughter and tears, shared through the years
And man, how he felt

Made my bones more than melt
He touched my soul.
You remind me

I'm scared of you
How did you find me?
Turn and walk away
'Cause you remind me

'What're you writing?' Nathan asked from over my shoulder.

My cheeks were flaming. 'Nothing.' I tried to cover the piece of paper with my hands. Nathan put down the two cups of coffee on his desk and slowly, deliberately removed my hands from the piece of paper. He picked it up and with a questioning look at me, began to read.

one hundred and one.
Callie is 15

Mrs Paxton, the headmistress, glanced at her watch. The end of the lesson couldn't come quickly enough as far as I was concerned. I usually enjoyed our debating lessons, but not today. Mrs Paxton had posed the question, 'Is an "equal" society possible or even desirable?' And she'd picked Tobey to argue the pros and Bliss to argue against it. At the end of the lesson, we were supposed to vote.

Tobey's presentation was OK, but when he spoke he shifted from foot to foot like he was embarrassed to be up there and speaking to all of us. Bliss on the other hand was confident, spoke out and treated the whole debate as if the outcome was a foregone conclusion.

'Bliss, you now have one minute to sum up your arguments,' said Mrs Paxton once both of them had made their main presentations.

As if we hadn't heard enough of her drivel.

'Thank you, Mrs Paxton,' Bliss smiled, before turning to the rest of the class. 'Equality cannot exist between all people in society because people themselves are not equal. We all have different hair styles or different-shaped eyes and that's the way it should be. It'd be soooooo boring if we all looked the same. So what's the point of saying that people should be equal? That is soooooo unrealistic. And we're not even born equal: some have more money than others, some have more brains than others . . .'

I raised my eyebrows at that bit. Bliss was talking pure, unadulterated twaddle but she'd got that last bit right. When brains were being given out, she was elsewhere having her nails manicured.

'It's pretty silly to say that a person with an IQ of, say, two zillion should sweep the roads,' Bliss continued, showing off her artificially whitened teeth as she smiled her way around the room. 'And it's just as silly to say that a nought could be . . . well, Prime Minister one day. I mean, that is soooooo never going to happen.'

'Time's up, Bliss,' said Mrs Paxton.

Finally!

'Therefore, I'd like to end by asking that you all vote "no" because, well, you know I'm right,' Bliss said on fast forward.

She sat down and not a moment too soon. I'd met paperclips with more insight.

'Thank you for your views, Bliss,' said Mrs Paxton. 'Your turn, Tobey.'

Tobey stood up slowly, without saying a word. And for some reason he was looking at me. He hadn't looked at me all lesson; now all of a sudden, he couldn't take his eyes off me. He smiled, a brief tentative smile. Before I realized what I was doing, I smiled back. As Sammi and some others turned to look at me, my face began to get hot and I could feel myself blushing.

'Tobey, the clock is ticking,' Mrs Paxton reminded him, glancing down at her watch.

'Bliss is making the mistake of thinking that "equal" means "the same". It doesn't,' Tobey began quietly. 'Yes, people aren't the same. We're all different. But we are all equal, or we should be – from the poorest to the richest, from the most intelligent to the likes of Bliss.'

That made me and most others in the class laugh. Bliss, however, failed to see the joke.

'If a decent education is only available to those who can afford it, what does that say about our society? If I get ill and my treatment differs from yours because I'm a Nought and you're a Cross or because I can pay and you can't, what does that say about our society? And if the law won't protect the worst of us, then it can't protect the best of us. You can't say, we'll have one law for the rich and one for the poor. You can't say we'll have one law for Noughts and another for Crosses. The law has to apply to everyone equally or it can't apply to anyone. Equal should mean equal opportunities, equal choices, equal treatment. So is an "equal" society desirable? Yes, of course it is. Is an equal society possible? Well, it's up to us to make it possible.'

'Time's up, Tobey,' said Mrs Paxton.

'That's not fair, Mrs Paxton. I'm sure he had longer than a minute,' Bliss complained.

'No he didn't, Bliss. He just didn't waste half of his summation saying "soooooo" after every other word and making that one word last ten seconds at a time. Now let's have a show of hands. Those of you who agree with Bliss, hands up.'

I looked around as hands began to go up. Mrs Paxton counted.

'And hands up those of you who agree with Tobey?'

I looked around as my hand went up and so did some others.

Bliss won the debate by three votes. I couldn't believe it. We were all supposed to clap the winner but I was damned if I was going to applaud Bliss's views. The buzzer sounded just as Mrs Paxton called out, 'The topic for next week's debate is animal experimentation so I'd like you all to read up on the subject.'

Books were stuffed into bags, chairs were scraped back and already people were heading out of the door and towards their next lesson. I had to say something. I just had to. I turned to Tobey, who sat at the table behind me.

'I'm sorry you didn't win, Tobey.'

'I did win.' Tobey smiled at me.

'How d'you work that out?'

''Cause I only lost by three votes.'

'Huh? That's called losing, Tobey,' I pointed out.

'Matthew Moore in senior year told me that Mrs Paxton runs this debate every year.'

'So?'

'So in Matthew's year, only four people voted pro equality. The rest voted against it. I'd say losing by only three votes is a result.'

I was the last one in the room as I watched Tobey leave.

I wondered what Uncle Jude would've made of his attitude.

one hundred and two.
Meggie

If it wasn't for doors slamming in this house, there'd be no noise at all. Callie Rose won't tell her mum where she really was over the last three weekends and Sephy won't let the matter drop. I'm trying to stay out of it but, to tell the truth, I'm just as worried as Sephy. Just before each of the last three weekends, Callie told us that she was going for a sleepover at Audra's house, then Sammi's, then Rafiya's. By the third weekend sleepover in a row, alarm bells were sounding in my head so goodness only knew what they were doing in Sephy's.

Right or wrong, Sephy phoned Sammi's mum, then Rafiya's mum. Sephy said it was to reciprocate and invite Sammi and Rafiya to spend the weekend with Callie Rose. And of course, then it all came out that Callie hadn't been to any of their houses in months. Sephy swears she just wanted Callie to enjoy herself by having her friends round. But Callie didn't see it that way.

And now the silence has begun. Callie Rose and Sephy don't speak and when Sephy enters a room, Callie leaves. So after lots of shouting, we had lots of doors slamming followed by lots of silent anger and hostility.

And more than a little sorrow.

one hundred and three.
Callie is 15

'I'll take your coat,' said Lucas.

I shrugged out of it and looked around the beautiful hall, which was the size of a room in itself. A grandfather clock by the stairs chimed the hour. Opposite the clock was a small burgundy sofa, next to a telephone table. I walked over to Lucas to give him my coat, my heels clicking on the wooden floor.

Bad idea . . . this was a bad idea . . .

The alarm bells in my head wouldn't stop pealing.

Very bad idea . . .

Lucas led the way into a room almost as big as one in Nana Jasmine's house. 'This is the lounge,' he said.

'I'd sort of gathered that,' I replied. 'The two settees, the walk-in fireplace and the flat-screen TV taking up practically that entire wall were subtle clues.'

'Sarky trout!' Lucas said pleasantly.

'Only 'cause I'm nervous,' I admitted.

Lucas and I had been going out for over a year now – visits to the cinema, the theatre once, the National Art Gallery twice and a number of meals. Plus quite a few kisses and some under- and over-the-clothes groping action. I longed for more, but gladly settled for less. I longed for someone to hold me, but I didn't really like to be touched. I guess I wasn't used to it. So we were hardly 'love's young dream' – not that I was looking for anything like that. Far from it. Being with Lucas was fun, but it was like playing a waiting game. I was waiting for him to jump up and shout, 'April Fool! It was all a joke, as if I'd ever be interested in someone like you . . .'

And what was a 'someone like me'? I was still trying to figure that one out.

There was a huge part of me that was like the dark side of the moon, the part that Lucas never got to see, would never get to know. It meant I could never truly relax with him. What would he do if I told him about me and the

L.M.? Would he think his dad was right about me? Would he turn his back and walk away? Or would he understand? I didn't know. He's a Cross, he didn't have to walk in the shoes of the Nought minority. He didn't have to put up with stares and jeers and biased media reporting and all the million and one other gnawing details that the minority had to put up with, which the majority never saw. And I was biologically in the middle. I had yet to work out my place socially. What did Noughts see when they looked at me – a light-skinned Cross? What did Crosses see when they looked at me – a dark-skinned Nought? I had to stop seeing myself through anyone's eyes but my own. But it made me wonder how Lucas saw me. He'd never said. I'd never asked.

The problem was, I really liked him. He was a strong person, strong enough to make up his own mind about me when his dad was trying to make up his mind for him. I liked being with him. I liked his arm around my shoulders. I liked kissing him. But every time I did so, it made me feel . . . unfocused.

'So where's the rest of your family?' I asked, sitting down at the end of one of the Jacquard-patterned sofas. Lucas sat down at the other end.

'Ella's at one of her friends' sleepovers. Audra, I think.'

So my friend Audra was having a sleepover, and I hadn't been invited. Ironic really, after telling Mum I'd been at sleepovers for the last three weekends. Such a silly lie. I shouldn't've told Mum anything at all. Audra was having a sleepover . . . I wondered why she hadn't said anything to me. I guess I didn't currently have anything she wanted or could use.

'And where're your mum and dad?'

'They've gone to visit friends in the country. They won't be back till tomorrow night.'

'I see.'

Lucas was actually beginning to look a bit uncomfortable. 'I just thought it would be nice to stay in for a change. And you never invite me back to your house,' he pointed out.

'This is fine,' I told him, adding dryly, 'but your dad probably wouldn't appreciate my bum on his sofa or my presence in his house.'

'Sod him!' said Lucas. 'I live here too.'

'What would he do if he found me here?' I asked.

'D'you want the truth?' Lucas said seriously.

I nodded.

'He'd probably be very polite until you left, then he'd tell me never to bring you here or see you again.'

'And you would follow his orders . . .'

'No way. Like I said, I live here too.'

'Aren't you afraid of incurring Daddy's wrath and being cut out of his will?' I teased melodramatically.

But the joke was on me. Lucas stared at me, stunned, for a fraction of a second, then tried to cover it up with a shrug. But quick as it was, I'd seen by the expression on his face just how dangerously close I'd come to the truth.

'You know what, I'd better go.' I stood up.

'No, please don't. It's fine, honestly.'

'Lucas, tell me the truth. It won't make any difference to my being here, I just want to know. Am I only here to antagonize your dad?'

'No,' Lucas replied at once. 'I promise you're not.'

I didn't believe him. No matter. At least I knew now what he stood to gain. Hell, I'd probably do the same thing if it'd wind up my mum.

'So what's the plan?' I asked. 'A couple of microwave meals, a drink or two and then up to your bed or do you plan to shag me here on this settee?'

'Jeez, Callie, you sure know how to kill a moment stone dead!'

I tilted my head to one side, puzzled. 'You did bring me here for sex, didn't you?'

'Well, I thought we might . . . if we both wanted to . . . later. But it's not compulsory.'

'Hhmm! Want to do it first and get it out of the way?' I asked.

'Bloody hell!'

I pulled off my cardigan and dropped it on the settee. 'D'you want to take off the rest?' My body was trembling beneath my white linen shirt and matching long skirt. I just hoped Lucas couldn't tell.

'What're you doing, Callie?' Lucas asked, his eyes narrowed.

'This is what you want, isn't it?' I said.

Why pretend otherwise? I was so sick of pretence and prevarication and lies.

'And you've done this before?' asked Lucas.

'No, but what difference does it make?'

Lucas walked over to me, calling my bluff. My heartbeat was suddenly audible in my chest. Not faster or slower, just audible. Lucas took my hands in his but they remained at our sides. His head lowered. I closed my eyes. And just like that we were kissing. Only this time felt different to all the other times. Slower and stronger and with the promise of much more to come. Lucas was a fantastic kisser. He didn't just plonk his mouth on mine and try to force all the blood out of my lips. He was soft and gentle, like he cared about me enjoying it too. Lucas let go of my hands and his fingers went to the top button of my linen shirt. He started to undo it, still kissing me.

Something inside me froze.

My mind stepped out of my body and watched, detached, from across the room. Lucas's hands moved to undo the second button, but then they stilled momentarily and to my surprise, he stopped kissing me. I watched him, he watched me, then he did up the button he'd just worked so effortlessly to undo.

'Aren't you . . . going to . . . ?'

'Thanks for the kind offer, but no thanks.' Lucas's forehead was a plethora of frown lines. 'I'll go and get us something to eat.'

What was that about? I wandered after him, across the hall and towards the back of the house into the kitchen. Standing in the kitchen doorway, I watched as Lucas took two chicken supreme and rice meals out of the fridge.

'Want some help?'

'No. Thanks,' said Lucas. 'These OK?' He held up the boxes to show me. I nodded.

'Lucas, what's the matter?' I asked, moving further into the kitchen.

'Let's get something straight, shall we?' Lucas threw the two meals down on the work counter and kicked the fridge door shut. 'Contrary to what you obviously think, I'm not going out with you to piss off my parents. And I didn't just bring you here for a quickie before throwing you out the door. Understand?'

'I didn't say—'

'You didn't have to. Your body did your talking for you,' said Lucas. 'I like you, Callie. Very much. But it's like . . . it's like you're watching me, just waiting for me to mess up.'

'What d'you mean?'

'Sometimes being with you is like taking a test where I don't know the questions and I know I'm supposed to fail.'

'Lucas, it isn't like that.'

'Isn't it?'

He turned back to our dinner, ripping open the boxes to get to the contents.

I stood in front of him, forcing him to look at me.

'I like you, Lucas,' I said. 'I really do.'

It took a good few seconds for the resentment on his face to fade. I smiled. At least he wasn't quite so ready to explode any more.

'Ready to eat?' he asked.

I nodded.

'And after our meal, we could watch a film if you'd like.'

'That'd be great.' I forced a smile.

'And then I'll take you home,' said Lucas.

I opened my mouth to argue, but he shook his head.

'And then I'm taking you home.'

one hundred and four.
Jude

Callie Rose was very disappointing last weekend at training camp. I expected her to perform better. I guess I was hoping to see more of Callum in her. When he joined the L.M., he went through training in double-quick time. He could put his feelings aside and get on with the task at hand. He was a good soldier that way. Callie Rose can't do that. Her feelings are part and parcel of anything and everything she does. If she's set a task, she has to believe in it, body and soul. I'll have to be sure to remember that when I use her in the future. I obviously pushed too hard too fast. She phoned me this morning to say she didn't want to go back to training camp. I'll give her time to cool off then start working on her again. I'm not going to lose her now, not after all the time and effort I've put in to get her to fulfil my dreams.

I rolled over onto my back and stared up at the ceiling. It was all coming together. Almost two months ago the election had been called and all my commanders were hard at work, aiming to make this an election campaign no one in this country would ever forget. My gaze moved across the ceiling like a lethargic spider. Dark, hairline cracks weaved like tendrils down the adjacent wall towards the large bay window. The wind blew against the window, rattling the panes. It sounded like the frame might need some attention. Anna put her arm around me and kissed my cheek. Then she snuggled up, putting her head on my shoulder. Her ash-blond hair tickled my nose.

I wasn't sorry I'd accepted Anna Tenski's invitation to come back to her flat. Better her place than my hotel room. I'd give it ten minutes then make my excuses and leave. All I wanted to do was get out of the bed and back to work. But for now I had to lie still, my arm around her. It wasn't terribly politic of me to sleep with one of my regional commanders but she was the one who'd made all the running. And it'd been a long time since I'd been with a woman.

'What're you thinking?' Anna whispered, her warm breath irritating my ear.

What is it with women always needing to ask that question? My thoughts are my own, I thought with annoyance. And if I wanted to share them, I'd tell you without having to be asked.

An image of Cara came into sharp and unexpected focus in my head. What would it have been like to make love to her? Not as mechanical as it had been with Anna, I'd put money on that. She wouldn't've expected anything from me, she wouldn't've wanted anything but me. She had class. And she wouldn't've asked me what I was thinking because she would've already known . . .

'You look so far away,' Anna said softly.

Her voice brought me back to the present with a jolt.

What the hell had I been thinking? I flung myself out of bed and headed naked towards the shower.

'Did I say something wrong?' asked Anna, sitting up.

I turned round. 'No. No, I just want to have a shower. I need to get back to work,' I told her, remembering to smile.

'Jude, you work too hard. You have so much on your plate. I wish I could do more for you,' said Anna.

'You do enough,' I told her. 'And I appreciate it.'

'All us commanders are thrilled to be working with you on this latest initiative,' Anna told me. 'We're all waiting with bated breath for this masterstroke of yours. It sounds like it'll be something people will be talking about for years.'

'That's the idea,' I told her. 'Ironic, really. The election is just a few weeks away and the biggest coup in L.M. history will be thanks to a child.'

'A child?' Anna said sharply. 'I don't understand.'

'You don't need to.' I leaned over the bed and kissed her forehead before heading back to the shower.

The water sprayed like blunt needles against my skin, just the way I like it. I hate showers where the water trickles like limp drizzle. I reached for the shampoo to wash my hair, when the shower door opened.

'D'you mind if I join you?' Anna asked silkily.

She stepped in before I could tell her that yes, actually, I did mind.

Before she could close the door I heard my phone ringing. Saved by the bell.

'Excuse me,' I said, stepping past her.

Anna pouted with disappointment. 'I hope you're coming back.'

'Of course. I haven't washed my hair yet.' I smiled.

Grabbing a towel, I flicked it quickly round my legs and feet to dry them off a bit before heading out into the bedroom. I retrieved my mobile phone from my discarded trousers.

'Yes,' I barked.

'Sir, it's Morgan. I thought you'd want to hear this before the progress meeting tomorrow.'

And I listened with a great deal of interest to what he said next.

one hundred and five.
Sephy

I was curled up on the sofa, my feet tucked under me, Nathan's arm around my shoulders. It was comfortable. Not exhilarating, not nerve-racking, no never-ending fireworks, but very comfortable. There was a lot to be said for contented comfort. Meggie was out visiting my mum and Callie Rose was out . . . somewhere. With Lucas, I think, though I couldn't be sure.

'I've decided I've been doing this all wrong,' said Nathan. 'I should seduce you with wine and roses, make mad, passionate love to you and then ask you to marry me. After all that, you wouldn't be able to resist.'

'You don't think much of yourself, do you?' I smiled.

'Would it work?' asked Nathan.

My smile turned into a grin. 'You'll just have to try it and find out.'

'Is that a challenge?' Nathan asked.

'It might be.'

'I'll try and rise to the occasion,' said Nathan softly.

'Oh, I don't doubt you will,' I replied. 'But why don't you jump to the last thing on your to-do list and see what happens?'

'The last thing . . .' Nathan frowned. His eyes widened in surprise as he worked out what I was suggesting. He went very still, removing his arm from round my shoulders. Had I made a mistake? Maybe, for all his banter, Nathan had changed his mind and I'd called his bluff. After all, he had first asked me weeks ago and I'd kept him dangling all this time. But he hadn't run away when he'd read the scribbled poem I'd written. In fact, to my astonishment, he'd asked to look at some others. He was constantly surprising me like that. I had thought I didn't like surprises, but I found I did when they came from him. Maybe, though, once again I'd left it too late.

I looked away from him. 'It doesn't matter. It was just an idea. A joke . . .' I began, giving him a way out.

Nathan took my face in his hands and turned me to look at him. And what I saw took my breath away.

'Sephy,' he began with some trepidation. 'Will you . . . marry me?'

I smiled. 'Yes, I will. I'd love to.'

'You're joking!' Nathan said, amazed.

He obviously hadn't expected it to be so easy after weeks of me putting him off and asking him to wait for me to come to a decision.

'What made you change your mind?' he asked.

'You did,' I replied honestly. 'But you haven't asked me in almost a fortnight. I was beginning to wonder if you'd thought better of it.'

'No way. In fact, I'm going to see about getting a special licence before you can change your mind.' Nathan sprang up.

'I'm not about to change my mind. Now can we watch the rest of this film?' I said.

'No way. I'm going to . . . I've got things to do! I'll see you tomorrow at the restaurant,' said Nathan.

And he was out of the room before I'd got to my feet.

Oh! Not even a kiss, I thought ruefully.

But Nathan must've read my mind because he came rushing back into the room, swung me round in a movie-star clinch and kissed me until I thought I was going to pass out from lack of oxygen.

'Just something to hold you until our honeymoon.' He grinned at me after putting me on my feet.

He was out of the front door before I could catch my breath. Funny man! Full of surprises. I sat down, still chuckling to myself. I was going to marry Nathaniel Ealing. Mother would be thrilled. But what about Meggie? And what about Callie? My smile faded. The doorbell rang. I looked around, but couldn't see anything Nathan had forgotten. But there had to be something or he wouldn't've come back so quickly. Or maybe he was after another kiss. I know I was! Heading out into the hall, I flung open the door.

'Did you forget . . . to . . . ?' My voice trailed off.

It wasn't Nathan, after all.

It was Sonny.

one hundred and six.
Jude

I listened to Jonathan Kidd, one of my commanders, spew out his excuses until I couldn't stand any more.

'Call this a progress meeting?' I thumped the table in ill-disguised fury. 'Isn't a progress meeting supposed to report on progress? I've already told all of you − failure is not an option.'

I sprang out of my chair and started walking. Try as I might I just couldn't keep still. I forced myself to slow it down to a saunter as I moved around the table. I had the undivided attention of everyone in the room. I stood behind Jonathan Kidd, my hands resting on the back of his chair as he continued to piss me off with yet more pathetic whinging.

'I expected you to be a lot further forward than you are, Jonathan,' I said from behind him.

Jonathan tried to turn round to face me, but I put my

hands on either side of his head to keep him looking forward.

'You're not just letting me down, Jonathan. You're letting down all your colleagues around this table,' I told him, my hands still on his head. I could feel the perspiration on his face beneath my fingers.

'Sir, the Secret Service have arrested most of the members of my two best cells and I'm—'

'I'm not interested in your excuses,' I interrupted. 'By the next meeting I want to hear about the amazing progress you've made. Is that clear?'

'Yes, sir.'

I strolled round the table, listening to Peter MacPhailen recount his division's exploits. His report was more satisfactory. I looked at Morgan, who was sitting in a corner of the room, taking notes. He looked sombre, almost grim as he regarded me. I smiled at him and carried on ambling. Then it was Anna Tenski's turn. I stood behind her chair, my hands resting on the back of it, just as I had done with Jonathan.

'Let's have your report, Anna,' I ordered.

She tried to turn to face me, just as Jonathan had done. I had to place my hands on her face so that she presented the report to the others around the table, not just to me. Then I stroked her hair, to put her at her ease.

'Sir, we've made excellent progress,' Anna began.

Her hair really did feel silky smooth beneath my fingers.

'Carry on,' I urged.

'Well, I've personally . . .'

Placing my free hand under Anna's chin, I gave her

head a quick, practised jerk. A sudden click in her neck and Anna slumped forward onto the table. I straightened up, looking down at her treacherous back. Peter was already on his feet. Jonathan looked horrified. There was a muffled scream and a few gasps.

'Anna was working with the Secret Service,' I told my other commanders.

'How d'you know that, sir?' asked Jonathan.

'I had all your phones bugged,' I replied.

More gasps. Was there a lack of oxygen in the room? If so, then I was the only one not affected. I made my way back to my chair at the top of the table.

'Morgan, could you remove that traitor's body please? The sight of it offends me.'

'Yes, sir,' said Morgan, standing up.

The other commanders looked at me with varying degrees of fascination and revulsion. Morgan lifted up Anna's lifeless body, which flopped like a rag doll in his arms, and left the room.

'That's better. Ladies and gentlemen,' I smiled. 'Shall we continue?'

one hundred and seven.
Callie is 15

'Thanks for meeting me, Callie,' said Lucas.

'It sounded urgent on the phone,' I said.

We both sat down at a less than clean table in the café we'd dined in on our very first date together. Not that either of us called it a date at the time. It was very late and the waitress didn't look particularly thrilled to see us. No doubt we'd scuppered her plans to knock off early.

'D'you want something to eat?' asked Lucas.

I shook my head.

'I'm paying,' he teased.

'I'm not hungry.'

'Two coffees please,' Lucas ordered for me as the Nought waitress approached. He waited till she nodded and walked off again before turning back to me.

'So what is it?' I asked. 'I'm all aquiver!'

The expression on Lucas's face smothered any thought of light banter on my part. Something was really troubling him.

'I don't know how to say this without just saying it,' said Lucas sombrely.

I sat silent, wishing he'd get to the point.

'I know that your dad was Callum McGregor...'
Lucas began.

'So?' I asked.

'I... I know how he died and why,' said Lucas with obvious discomfort.

'Who told you? Tobey? Or your dad?'

'Dad, but—'

'So you're dumping me?' I realized.

'No, of course not. I've known about it since primary school,' said Lucas.

Which surprised me. I'd thought his parents' objections to me stemmed from my dual heritage, not from my dad's history.

'And you still asked me out?'

'I'm dating you, not your dad,' said Lucas.

If only he meant it. But if that was the case, what on earth were we doing here? I regarded Lucas, trying to anticipate just what was coming next. If he'd known about my dad for ages and he wasn't dumping me, why the phone call to say he had to see me? He'd made it sound like it was a matter of life or death – literally.

'D'you know your dad had a brother?'

'Yes. Uncle Jude,' I replied. I could've bitten off my tongue when I said Uncle's name. How many times had I had it drummed into me that I should never volunteer information about anything or anyone in the L.M.? I was behaving like a neophyte.

'Have you met him?' Lucas leaned forward to ask.

Our coffees arrived so he had to sit back and wait for the waitress to move out of earshot, by which time I'd gathered some of my scattered composure.

'Lucas, what's this about?' I asked.

'I've been doing some digging into your dad's family and—'

'You've been doing what?' I said slowly.

'Don't get upset, Callie. I just wanted to know more about you, that's all. I went to the library to read up on your dad and found a lot about his brother, your uncle.'

I sat back in my chair. First Tobey spying and prying and now Lucas. What made either of them think they had the right to snoop into my personal life? 'Why did you go to the library in the first place? What was it you were hoping to find?'

'I don't know. It's just that you've been so . . . off recently. I thought that if I found out some more about you . . .'

'That what?' I prompted.

'I don't know.' Lucas shrugged helplessly. 'You matter to me, Callie, that's all.'

'You've got a funny way of showing it,' I told him belligerently.

'I knew you'd get mad, but I had to tell you,' said Lucas.

'Spit it out,' I said with impatience.

'Your Uncle Jude is wanted by the police. They reckon he's been behind a number of the L.M. outrages that've taken place in the last few years.'

I was about to deny that but I thought better of it. Best not to let Lucas think I knew too much about my uncle's activities.

'What's that got to do with me?' I said.

'Have you seen him? Has he tried to contact you?'

'D'you think my mum would let me have any contact at all with my dad's brother?' I asked disingenuously.

'I . . . I wasn't sure,' said Lucas. 'But I just wanted to tell you that if he did try to make contact, you shouldn't meet him. According to the stuff I read, he's a really dangerous man.'

'But suppose I want to meet him?' I asked evenly.

Lucas frowned at me. 'Then I'd come with you.'

'Telling your mum and dad and the police first?'

'No, never. But I'd come with you to make sure you were safe.'

As if Lucas could keep me safe from Uncle Jude. The notion almost made me laugh out loud. My first encounter with Lucas left him with a bloody nose before he ran off to tell on me. No doubt any chance of an encounter with my uncle would have him racing to do the same again.

As if he could read my thoughts, Lucas said quietly, 'I don't tell tales any more, Callie Rose. You can trust me. I wish I knew what to say to make you believe that. I'm on your side.'

My side . . . A Cross on the side of the L.M.? How far over to my side was Lucas prepared to travel?

'I think your dad would have something to say about that,' I said sceptically.

'And I've already told you, I don't care. I'm not a clone of my dad and one of these days I'm going to find a way of proving that to you.'

'Well, you don't have to worry, Lucas. If my uncle hasn't got in touch with me by now, he never will.'

Lucas nodded but he didn't look totally convinced. I

didn't care. Uncle Jude was the best thing that'd happened to me and I wasn't about to let Tobey or Lucas and their half-arsed snooping change my mind about that. It was a simple choice. Tobey and Lucas and the tedium of ordinary, everyday, pointless nothingness – or doing something with my life, making a difference, being *someone*.

I'd already tried being no one. It didn't suit me. I wanted my life to matter, my existence to matter to someone, somewhere. Working with Uncle Jude, it would. Staying at home with a woman who couldn't bear to even touch me, it wouldn't.

one hundred and eight.
Sephy

'Sonny? W-what're you doing here?' I still couldn't believe it. My heart was swinging around like a skipping rope.

'Can I come in?'

I stepped to one side, holding the door open so he could get past. The years we'd been apart had been very good to him. His black trousers weren't anything you'd get off the rack at the local department store and his burgundy shirt would've looked silly on most men, but it worked just fine on Sonny. His hair was slightly longer than when we'd been together. That suited him too.

'Go through,' I said. 'You know the way.'

Sonny headed into the living room with me in tow. Why on earth was he here? I waited for him to pick a seat so that I could sit opposite him.

'It's good to see you again,' I told him, tucking my legs under me.

'You too,' said Sonny. 'I was in the neighbourhood so I thought I'd drop in and see how you are.'

'I'm fine,' I replied.

'Callie Rose?'

'She's fine,' I lied.

'Where is she?'

'Out with a friend.'

'And Meggie?'

'She's fine. She's out too.'

'And what about you, Sephy?'

'What about me?'

Sonny's expression changed from nonchalance to a kind of self-mocking humour.

'That was a lie, about me being in the neighbourhood,' he admitted. 'I came because I had to see you.'

'Why? What's wrong?' I knew Sonny well enough to know that something was troubling him deeply.

'Have you missed me?'

I frowned at him. 'Is that what you came here to ask?'

'I just want to know if you've missed me.'

'What d'you want me to say, Sonny? The first year after we broke up, I missed you all the time. Sometimes I even cried myself to sleep.' Which was a lie, because it was more than just sometimes. 'Callie Rose blamed me entirely for you not being around any more. I missed being with you, I missed writing with you, I missed talking to you, I missed sleeping with you. I'd hear our songs on the radio and your new ones and wish and wonder. But that was then. I'm doing OK now. Better than OK.'

'So you did love me?'

'Very much.'

Sonny's gaze fell away from mine, his expression twisting as if in pain. When he turned back, his face was unreadable.

'D'you know, that's the first time you've told me that,' he said at last.

I hung my head. Was it really? I thought back, but I couldn't bring to mind a time when I'd said the words to him. My head was beginning to hurt from trying to remember.

'I regret that very much,' I said, looking straight at Sonny. 'You deserved to hear that. My head was still all mixed up when we were together. I thought there was only a finite amount of love in me which had to be shared between Callie Rose and Callum, her dad. So I told myself that what I felt for you wasn't love, but close enough. I did both of us a disservice. And by the time I realized the truth, it was too late. Story of my life.'

'Why did you never try to get in touch with me after we split up?' said Sonny.

I was confused. 'Was I supposed to?'

'I was hoping you would,' said Sonny.

'Why? When you left you made it very clear that you didn't want to work with me or be with me any more,' I said, even more confused. 'Was I supposed to go chasing after you?'

'You never struck me as the type of woman to give in so easily, not if it was something you really wanted.'

'People aren't possessions,' I said. 'And you can't make someone love you. You fell out of love with me and in love with Sherona. What was I supposed to do?'

'Fight for me,' said Sonny.

'Pardon?'

'Fight for me,' Sonny repeated.

The pain inside my head was getting worse, like bony knuckles being rubbed across the inside of my forehead.

'Sonny, this conversation is doing my head in. Have you and Sherona split up? Is that what this is all about?'

'Sherona and I never got started,' said Sonny.

'You've lost me.'

'We went out a couple of times, but she dumped me soon after she caught us in your dressing room at that club.'

'It's a restaurant,' I corrected pedantically. Hell! Who cared what it was? It was as if I was in the middle of a really confusing film and was desperately trying to catch up. 'Why did she dump you?' I had to ask. 'It was only one kiss and if you loved her, couldn't you—?'

'That wasn't the reason,' Sonny interrupted.

'I can't believe she dumped you because of me,' I protested. 'I was out of the picture.'

'But not out of my head,' said Sonny. 'Sherona and I were in bed and I called her by your name. Women aren't too keen on that sort of thing!'

I wasn't sure how I was supposed to feel after that revelation. 'I'm sorry,' I said, aware of how ineffectual my apology was. 'But how come you never told me before about you and Sherona splitting up?'

'The only thing I had left from our relationship was my pride.' Sonny shrugged. 'I wasn't about to give up that as well.'

'So why are you here now, after all this time?'

'Because my pride doesn't make me happy during the day or keep me warm at night. Because I miss you and Callie Rose more with each passing day, not less. Because I want to give us another try,' said Sonny.

Stunned didn't even begin to describe how I felt. Sonny wanted us to start again? 'And you've waited all this time to tell me that?'

'Have I left it too late?'

'Sonny, I've just agreed to marry Nathan.'

'Nathan?' Sonny's eyes narrowed.

'Nathan Ealing, my boss and the owner of Specimens.'

'D'you love him?'

'I wouldn't've said yes otherwise.'

'The same way you loved me?'

'Sonny, don't do this,' I pleaded. 'It's not fair.'

'All's fair,' said Sonny.

'You can't just turn up after all this time and expect us to pick up where we left off,' I said. 'Your life has moved on. So has mine.'

'Do you love me, Sephy?'

'Sonny—'

'Just answer that one question. D'you love me?'

'Sonny, you need to leave.' I stood up.

Reluctantly, Sonny stood up too. I headed straight out into the hall and opened the door. 'Bye, Sonny.'

'I'm not giving up, Sephy. Not without a fight.'

'Bye, Sonny,' I repeated.

'And you never answered my question,' Sonny pointed out.

He headed towards his car. Opening the driver's door, he turned round to look at me.

'I still love you, Sephy.'

I stepped into my hall, quickly shutting the front door. I leaned against it, my eyes closed. And I didn't move until I heard the sound of Sonny's car leaving. This just wasn't fair. Every time I thought I had one part of my life sorted out, something always came along to show me how wrong I was.

one hundred and nine.
Callie is 15

'Uncle. It's me.'

'Hello, Callie. Is anything wrong?'

'No, sir. I just wanted to say . . . I'm ready to go back to training camp. Any time you say.'

Silence.

'Sir? Are you still there?'

'Of course I am.'

'I'm sorry I missed last weekend's session but I'm ready to go back to training . . .'

'That won't be necessary,' said Uncle Jude. 'I want to talk to you about something special. Something only you can do, soldier.'

'Yes, sir.'

'When can you get away?' asked Uncle.

'Any time you say, sir,' I replied. 'And, sir?'

'Yes?'

'I promise I won't bail on you again.' I put down the phone, strangely at peace.

Was Dad watching me now? Was he sad? Proud? Gratified? Did I care? In a perverse way I actually think I did. Dad was evil, but he was committed. He did what he thought was right and he didn't let anyone stand in his way. No sacrifice was too great. Dad didn't set limits on himself. And much as I might detest him, I could still . . . appreciate the part of him I wanted to emulate – that single-minded determination to get what he wanted, by any means necessary. How strange to hate someone as much as I hated my dad and yet, in some inexplicable and chilling way, understand him. My head was seriously messed up, but I embraced my ambivalence towards my dad and his motives. I was no longer a part of what had been before. I wasn't doing the same things as my friends, I wasn't into the same meaningless trivia. I wasn't better than them, just no longer in the same place, occupying the same space. They were then.

I am now.

one hundred and ten.
Jude

I've won. I know exactly which buttons to press to get Callie Rose to do exactly what I want. I've got a mission for Callie which will complete my revenge on the whole Hadley family. It's been a long time coming but the moment has arrived at last. The damage we in the L.M. have already caused to two government buildings and the departure lounge at the country's biggest airport are small fry compared to what's coming. My plan to eliminate the Defence Minister was foiled, unfortunately, but at least we came close. He'll be in hospital for a while so that's something. And the best is yet to come. The election is in three days and our L.M. activities have concentrated the nation's mind on our demands. But what I've personally got planned will ensure that we'll go down in history. No one will ever doubt the resolve of the L.M. or underestimate us again.

Callum, we've won.

And best of all, Sephy Hadley has lost.

one hundred and eleven.
Callie is 15

The late afternoon sky was white-grey, with no hint or sign of the blue behind it. The weather matched my mood and suited my clothes. This would be the last time I came to this park and sat at this bench. This would be the last time I'd just sit and *be*.

And I wasn't sorry.

Uncle Jude was right. What I was about to do was heroic, not to mention momentous. It's going to make a difference. I recalled the pride on Uncle Jude's face when I told him that I'd be honoured to take on the task he'd assigned me. That's when he told me who he was in the L.M. and how hard he'd worked to get there. Then it was my turn to be proud of him. My uncle is the General of the whole L.M. He became General when the previous one was captured and put in prison for life almost three years ago. Uncle Jude says that there is more than one way to serve though, and I believe him. That's why I'm going to go through with this. I'm not going to let him down. I know what I have to do, I just don't know the target yet. But Uncle Jude says my actions will make all the difference in the world. My actions will make life better for thousands and thousands of people – Noughts and Crosses. Surely that's worth something? More than I'd ever dared to hope.

'I thought it was you. Hi, Callie Rose.'

'Just Callie, Tobey,' I corrected, not bothering to look at him properly. I watched the wind dance with the branches above me.

'Sorry, I forgot,' said Tobey, sitting down on the arm of the bench. 'What're you doing?'

'Just enjoying what's left of the rest of the day,' I said easily.

'Mind if I join you?' Tobey asked cautiously.

'I don't own the bench,' I pointed out.

Tobey slid down to sit at the other end of the bench to me. I turned to look at him to find him already watching me. His appearance made me start. When had he shot up like that? And when had he had his hair cut short? How long had it been since I'd taken a good look at him? He certainly looked different to the boy who had stood in my garden all those years ago, his hands full of dirt.

'What're you thinking?' Tobey asked me.

'D'you remember when I was five or six and we argued about something or other and I said the only way I'd forgive you was if you ate horse manure?'

'You were seven, almost eight,' said Tobey.

'You remember how old I was?' I said, surprised.

Tobey shrugged. 'So what about it?'

'Would you have done it?' I asked. 'Would you have eaten that stuff?'

'To get you to be my friend again? Yeah,' said Tobey.

He made it sound like I shouldn't even have to ask. Tobey really was one of the strangest guys I knew. He didn't seem to fit anywhere. He stood out wherever he went, at school, on the street. He didn't try to blend into the scenery like most people. He was a misfit, like me. But once he'd made up his mind to be your friend, he'd be your friend for ever. Lucas on the other hand was Mr Popular. He was friends with everyone, and everyone liked him – except maybe Amyas. But Lucas wasn't losing any sleep over that one. Lucas had the self-confidence that came from being told every day of his life that he was good enough. Tobey had the self-confidence that came from having to work that out for himself.

'So what will it take for the two of us to be friends again now?' asked Tobey.

'What are you prepared to do this time?' I smiled.

'Whatever it takes,' said Tobey seriously.

If I told him what I'd been ordered to do, would he join me? Would he stand by me? Would he try to talk me out of it? Or betray me? Which one? I wondered. I regarded Tobey. He and Lucas were so alike in some ways and so different in others. It wasn't just their physical similarities and differences that made me pause, or even what they said and how they said it. No, the major difference for me came in which one of them I was more inclined to believe.

'Just ask me,' said Tobey.

'It means that much to you?'

'It always has.'

And I could see he meant it, meant every word, but in my constantly simmering anger I had turned away and missed it. Tobey and I were unfinished business.

'Tobey.' I slid along the bench to sit next to him. I offered my hand. 'Friends again?'

'I'd like that, very much,' he said, taking my hand in his.

Then he surprised the hell out of me by kissing me, full on the mouth. And I couldn't help comparing the way he kissed to the way Lucas did it. I pulled away, puzzled.

'What was that about?'

Tobey smiled but didn't answer. We sat in silence, watching the others in the park, watching each other. It took me a while longer to realize we were still holding hands.

one hundred and twelve.
Jasmine

Just look at the swine! He makes me want to throw something at the TV screen. He's got the scent of blood in his nostrils. And look at that smile. Could it be any more smarmy! The General Election is only a couple of days away and he reckons he's going to glide into power on a landslide. I recognize that look. Kamal will never change. He thinks there's nothing to stop him getting back into power — and if the latest opinion polls are anything to go by, he's right. His brand of politics always makes the headlines, the politics of hate.

Our policies are failing? Blame the other political parties — remind the people that we may be bad, but they are worse or things would be worse under the other lot. Or if we can't blame the main opposition, find a new scapegoat — a section of society with no power, no voice. Blame the travellers or the noughts or the immigrants. Cheap, gutter politics to appeal to the lowest common denominator.

And Kamal gets away with it.

If I were to tell just half of what I know about that man . . . all the dirty deals and backhanders and mutual back-scratching that went on when he was a councillor and a junior minister. I know where the bodies are buried, though much good it does me.

The General Election will come and he'll slither into power on a trail of slimy promises and unctuous, oily handshakes.

He's going to get away with it. Again.

one hundred and thirteen.
Callie is 15

Nana Jasmine swallowed two painkillers, followed by three or four other pills, washing them all down with a glass of bottled water. She'd lost so much weight, she looked gaunt. Her skin was closer to grey than brown. I watched her, my mind swimming further and further out in a sea of sadness.

'Nana Jasmine, w-why didn't you tell me you were so ill?'

'What good would it have done?' asked Nana.

'I would've known,' I told her. 'I should've been included.'

'No one was trying to exclude you, darling. I didn't even tell Sephy and Minerva about having cancer until I had to. The first time round, I had my biopsy, a lump-ectomy and a course of radiotherapy and I thought that was it. But I was unlucky and it came back.'

'You still should've told me,' I said, my voice wob-bling. 'I only found out about your . . . about you because I overheard Mum and Nana Meggie talking.'

'Callie, you can say it. The word won't kill you,' said Nana Jasmine.

I didn't want to say it. I didn't want Nana Jasmine to be ill. I didn't want a lot of things. Why did the world hurt so much?

'Can I do anything to help?' I asked.

'Yes, you can talk to your mum,' said Nana Jasmine at once. 'She loves you very much.'

'I'm not an idiot, Nana Jasmine,' I said with im-patience.

'I never for a moment thought you were,' said Nana.

It was sweet of Nana but we both knew the truth, even if Nana didn't want to say it.

'Poor Callie,' Nana Jasmine sighed.

'Why d'you say that?'

'You really have no idea just how many people care about you.'

'Like who?'

'Like whom, dear,' Nana Jasmine corrected.

'Whatever,' I said edgily.

'You are loved by me, your Nana Meggie, your mum, your aunt and all her family and that boy – what's his name? Tobey. And that's just for starters.'

I stared at Nana. 'What're you talking about? Tobey doesn't love me. He's not even my boyfriend. Lucas is my boyfriend.'

'And I really like Lucas, even though you've only brought him here twice. But that doesn't alter the way Tobey feels about you. Every time he looks at you, it's as unmistakable as a bad facelift,' smiled Nana.

'Are we talking about Tobey Durbridge? My Tobey?'

'Your next-door neighbour. Yes,' said Nana Jasmine.

'But he's . . . he's . . .'

'He's what?'

'He's just Tobey,' I dismissed.

'Who is crazy about you.'

'I'm not being funny, Nana, but I think your pills are making you hallucinate.'

'Actually, my pills are helping me to see more clearly than I have in a long, long time,' said Nana calmly. 'Why is it so hard for you to accept that anyone could love you?'

'Because I know the truth,' I replied. 'I went to the library and looked up all the information I could find about my dad and mum. D'you know, when I was born, Mum put an announcement in the paper saying I would take my dad's name of McGregor. She hated me enough to saddle me with a terrorist's name.'

'Nonsense. She loved Callum enough to want the whole world to know who you were,' said Nana Jasmine.

'Then why did she change her mind? It says Hadley on my birth certificate, not McGregor.'

'You'll have to ask her that.'

'I'm not asking her anything,' I dismissed. 'I'm never going to speak to her again.'

'Callie Rose, you are so young. And like all young people you think you've got it all figured out. You think you know exactly how many blue beans make five. But the older you get, the more you realize just how little you know.'

'I know how many blue beans make five,' I argued.

'Oh yes?'

'A bean, two beans, a bean and a half and half a bean. Everyone knows that saying.'

'Now tell me why Sephy, your mum, didn't marry Sonny.'

'Because she's not interested in any man who isn't a murdering, terrorist bastard,' I answered harshly.

'Please don't use that kind of language in front of me, sweetheart,' said Nana. 'Why did your mum have you? She didn't have to, you know. She could've had an abortion.'

'She had me to spite my dad,' I replied.

'To spite Callum? Exactly how did that work?' Nana Jasmine frowned.

'Mum had been bonking my dad for years and then they broke up and she went to another school. So my dad got some of his L.M. friends to kidnap Mum and that's when . . . that's when he raped her and I was conceived. If she'd got rid of me then maybe my dad wouldn't've hanged. But she hates me, because of the way I was conceived.'

Nana Jasmine stared at me. 'Where on earth did you hear that . . . that garbage?'

'It's not garbage. I read it in the newspaper archives at the public library.'

'Oh, then it must be true,' Nana Jasmine said with sarcasm. 'The newspapers of fifteen years ago never wrote about noughts unless it was something negative. And your grandfather made sure that no one printed Sephy's version of events.'

That's when I remembered that I hadn't read that bit. Uncle Jude had told me. That's how I knew it was true.

'So what did happen?' I asked.

'Why don't you ask your mother?' said Nana Jasmine.

That phrase was really beginning to irritate.

'And if Sephy really was raped, surely that was even more reason to have an abortion,' said Nana Jasmine. 'So why didn't she then?'

'I don't know. Moral reasons? A cosmic ray scrambled her brain or maybe she just wanted to piss off my grandad? I don't know.'

'Then why don't you ask her?'

That phrase again.

'Callie Rose,' said Nana Jasmine quietly. 'You think you know the truth, but you don't. The only person who can tell you the truth is your mum.'

'She hasn't so far,' I said.

'She had her reasons for that.'

'Which were?'

'Why don't you ask her?' we both said in unison.

'Look, Nana, can we please change the subject?' I appealed.

Nana Jasmine regarded me. 'The truth doesn't stop being the truth just because you don't want to talk about it or won't face it.'

'Nana . . .'

'All right, darling. But take it from me, don't leave it too long to talk to your mum or one day you'll wake up and find it's too late.'

I shook my head. 'Nana Jasmine, it's already too late.'

one hundred and fourteen.
Jude

'Callie Rose, it's me.'

'Morning, Uncle Jude.'

'I have the final details of your mission, soldier.'

Silence.

'The mission we were discussing, sir?' asked Callie Rose.

'Yes.'

'I'm ready, sir.'

'Are you sure? Because if you have any doubts or misgivings, you need to let me know now.'

'No, sir. I'm ready. I've never been so sure of anything in my life.'

'I'm proud of you, soldier.'

'Thank you, sir. I won't let you down.'

'I know you won't. Your name will go down in history. What you're going to do will be the turning point in Nought–Cross relations.'

'Yes, sir. Thank you, sir.'

'Meet me in the Doppel Hotel on King's Street in exactly one hour. I've reserved a room under the name Allan Springer.'

'The Doppel Hotel. Yes, sir.'

'I've got all the equipment you need. Once I've handed it over, we won't meet again. You'll stay in the room to assemble the device and when you leave you're to take the device and all other evidence with you. Is that clear?'

'Yes, sir.'

'You will also be given the name of your target. It is imperative that you get to your assigned target – by any means necessary. Understand?'

'Yes, sir.'

'I'll see you in an hour,'

'I'll be there. Bye, sir.'

I waited for Callie Rose to put down the phone first. Only then did I allow myself a smile. I allowed myself to *feel* again. I was truly happy for the first time in a long, long time. Everything I'd ever wanted was just a day away.

one hundred and fifteen.
Callie is 15

The rain slammed against the window like tiny knuckles, rapping to get in. The wind rattled the window panes in their ill-fitting frames. But I gave the rain and wind no more than a passing thought before turning back to the olive-green, padded windcheater lying on the bed. Studying it critically, I didn't realize that my eyes were narrowed and my lips pursed until I caught a glimpse of myself in the cracked mirror carelessly attached to the opposite wall. All day yesterday, I'd followed orders and spent hours sewing various-sized pockets onto the inside of the garment where they couldn't be seen. Pockets – breast-high, waist-high, pockets wherever there was a spare amount of space. And now those pockets were going to be put to good use.

'Well, soldier? Any questions?'

'Yes, sir. I did just wonder why I couldn't use an ordinary backpack or a belt for this assignment?'

'Because you won't be able to take your bag with you when you go to see him. Bags and backpacks have to be checked by Security and left in the cloakroom – no exceptions. And a modified belt would be too noticeable.'

Him . . . My assignment was a man then.

'I see.'

'Any second thoughts?' asked the General.

'None, sir,' I replied.

I glanced at the General's face before lowering my gaze to his chin. I watched his gloved hands unconsciously curl into fists and uncurl repeatedly. No way was he nervous, I told myself. Only one person in the room was sweating bricks. And it wasn't my forthcoming assignment that made me anxious, it was the General. He had a way of looking at you, like he was turning you inside out and inspecting every deficient little bit. He always looked at me like that, like he knew what I was going to say and do before I did. Like he was three steps ahead of me and patiently waiting for me to catch up. The General had been leaning against the wall, but he straightened up and handed me a carrier bag.

I took it, bracing myself. My arm flew upwards unexpectedly. I'd expected the bag to be much heavier.

'Is there enough in here, sir?' I queried.

'For your purposes – yes. More than enough.'

I fought to resist the urge to inspect the bag's contents in front of the General. It would appear disrespectful. I gripped the bag more tightly. I held Death in my hands. It was a strange feeling. A kind of calm, deliberate disquiet.

'You know what you have to do?'

'Yes, sir.'

'Are you up to it?'

'You know I am, sir.'

'Good girl. I'm relying on you,' said the General.

'I won't let you down.'

'I know you won't,' said the General sombrely.

He handed me a sealed, blank envelope. 'The name of your quarry and full instructions are in the envelope. Once you've read it, you know what to do?'

'Yes, sir. I burn it then take the charred residue and bag it up before dumping it somewhere away from here,' I replied.

'That includes the envelope as well. On a mission like this, it's the little details that count. It's very important that you don't forget that.'

I nodded. 'I won't, sir.'

'No mistakes, soldier,' said the General.

'No, sir. No mistakes.'

It was the moment I'd been born for. I felt like every breath, every decision ever taken in my life before had been leading to this one moment. The start of the most *relevant* hours of my life.

'I'm so proud of you, Callie Rose.'

'Thank you, sir. I won't let you down,' I replied.

I watched as the General let himself out of my dingy hotel room. He turned at the door and nodded once, before closing it behind him. I didn't blame him for wanting to leave as quickly as possible. The room gave cramped a bad name, with a dingy grey-white, low ceiling and the paint on the walls a clotted-cream colour. The small double bed had a mattress which had seen its best days at least ten years ago. It was made up with two pre-stained sheets and a paper-thin duvet. And the incessant rain outside couldn't make any inroads against the grime on the outside of the windows.

I opened up the carrier bag and peered in. I put one hand in but stilled as I thought better of it. Moving over to the door, I chained as well as locked it. I couldn't take any chances – not now I was so close. Sitting on the bed, I at last allowed myself to take the items in the bag out with careful precision. Nice and easy does it. One by one. No rush. No mistakes.

Detonators.

Connectors.

Wires.

Batteries.

Hand switch.

And two blocks of wrapped-up plastic explosive.

Like the man said, no mistakes. Time to get down to it. I put on my latex gloves and gingerly unwrapped the explosive. Once it was uncovered, I placed it back down on the bed and forced myself to touch it, to feel it. It felt putty-like and cool beneath my tightly covered fingers. It couldn't harm me – not until the detonator caps and switch had been connected – but my heart was still clapping with thunderous applause. Just how much damage would the explosive on my bed cause? I took another deep breath. I could do this. I had to. This wasn't the time to get jittery.

Get it together, I told myself. And keep it together.

Another deep, steadying breath to calm my nerves and steady my heartbeat. This was what I wanted. This was the only thing I wanted. Nothing else mattered. The General believed in me. He didn't for one second doubt that I'd go through with it. I wasn't going to disappoint him. I pulled off the first chunk of plastic explosive.

Quickly kneading and moulding the explosive in my hands into a thin, cuboid shape, I slotted it into the first makeshift pocket I'd so meticulously added to the inside of my windcheater. I forced myself to work with care, slowly and steadily. Bomb-making required a great deal of patience. And whilst I might not have all the time in the world, I did at least have the rest of my life. A few hours to make it, take it and wear it to my last meeting with the person I'd been assigned to kill. I glanced down at the sealed envelope on the bed. My hand reached out towards it, but then I thought better of it. First things first.

At last every pocket was full. Time to try it on for size. Slowly, carefully, I picked up the windcheater and slipped it over my shoulders. The switch was across the bed out of harm's way but my heart was still racing. Would I be able to do this? Would I be able to walk up to my intended victim and stand before him and blow us both to kingdom come? And not just my intended victim. Anyone around us would get more than they'd bargained for too. How did I feel about that? Deliberately, I shrugged. I was part of the Liberation Militia now. We were at war. All wars carried casualties. And as long as the man I was after was killed then it'd be a successful assignment, it was as simple as that.

My thoughts startled me, bringing me up short. Is this how my dad felt when he was preparing to kidnap my mum? Was he scared? Exhilarated? Appalled? Did he feel the same sense of sick anticipation? Or did he force himself to feel nothing at all? Probably the latter, just like me. Like father, like daughter after all. Funny but a couple of years ago the worst things in my life had been homework and not enough cool clothes. And now I look back at my life as it was then and it's so far away from where I am now, it's like remembering a TV programme or a story told to me long ago about someone else.

The windcheater fitted OK even if it was uncomfortable and slightly bulky. I placed a loose-fitting jacket at least a size too big over the windcheater and checked my appearance in the mirror. I wondered about doing it up as opposed to leaving it undone. In the end, I settled for doing up only the middle button of the jacket. Even though the plastic explosive was on the inside of the windcheater, I didn't want to take any unnecessary chances. I checked my reflection again, this time more critically. The explosive wasn't bulging in a really obvious way. I looked pretty shapeless but that was all. I'd wear a coat over the jacket so that I could take that off but leave my jacket on. That should work. I took off the jacket and threw it on the bed, followed by the windcheater, which was placed more carefully.

The explosive was ready. Now it was time to add all the other ingredients to the mix. Time to make the bomb active. I picked up the wires and detonators and got to work. Less than half an hour later it was finished. The only thing left to do was connect the switch. Now to find out who the target was. I pulled off my gloves and opened the envelope.

The card inside left my mind reeling. Of all the names I'd been expecting . . . But why not his name? It made sense when you thought about it; it's just that I hadn't thought about it. The card contained a name, a place and a date:

Kamal Hadley: Hewlett House, Croftways: Tomorrow

I scrunched up the card. My target was Kamal Hadley, Member of Parliament and leader of the Opposition. Kamal Hadley, divorced man and father.

Kamal Hadley.

My grandfather.

one hundred and sixteen.
Callie is 15

'Mum? Nana Meggie? Is anyone home?'

Silence. Good. I was back home with my completed afternoon's work hidden inside the carrier bag I clutched in my hand. I had a couple of phone calls to make and time to kill. First things first though. Get it done. I picked up the phone in the hall and made my first call.

'Hello?'

'Can I speak to Mrs Hadley please?'

'Speaking.'

That threw me. I hadn't expected her to pick up the phone herself. I was sure I'd have to battle my way past a P.A. or a home help at the very least.

'Mrs Hadley, I'm sorry to trouble you. My name is

Callie Rose Hadley. I'm Kamal Hadley's granddaughter,'
I began.

'Ah, yes. I remember you. And call me Grace.'

Didn't expect that. Didn't expect the friendly tone
either.

'Thank you,' I said after a moment. 'I'm sorry to phone
out of the blue like this, but I was wondering if I could
come and see my grandad. I know he's concerned with
the forthcoming election but I promise I won't take up
much of his time. I just need to talk to him,' I said. I mar-
shalled my thoughts, ready to counter all the protestations
she might make.

'I'm sure that could be arranged,' said Grace. 'He's
really busy at the moment, what with the election the
day after tomorrow, but I'll tell you what, he'll be home
tomorrow afternoon at around two but only for an hour
or so. Why don't you come to see us then?'

Was that it then? That was far too easy.

'Is he . . . I mean, I won't get the door slammed in my
face when I turn up, will I?'

'No, that will never happen again. Kamal knows what
he did was wrong, especially after both your mum and
I had finished with him, but my husband can be a very
stubborn man.'

I didn't reply. My silence held uncertainty.

'Callie Rose, I'll make sure you and my husband get a
chance to talk properly, and not on the doorstep either. I
give you my word.'

'Thank you.'

'You can bring your mum as well if you'd like. It's time
for all of us to put the past behind us and move forward.'

Grace by name, grace by nature. But too late.

'I'm sorry, Mum's busy tomorrow,' I lied.

'D'you want to wait for another day when you can both come together?'

'Thanks but I really need to see Grandad as soon as possible,' I said.

'All right then. When you visit tomorrow, maybe we could set another date for the whole family to visit,' said Grace.

'That would be lovely,' I said. 'I'll see you tomorrow then.'

'Looking forward to it. Oh and Callie Rose, happy birthday for tomorrow.'

How strange that she should remember my birthday when even I had only given it a passing thought. I had to force myself to speak. 'Thank you, Grace. Bye.'

I put down the phone, only to immediately pick it up again. I phoned Uncle Jude on his mobile.

'Hello?'

'Sir, it's me. I'm in. Tomorrow afternoon around two.'

'Excellent. Well done, soldier. And just remember, the angels are on our side.'

'Yes, sir.'

'It's been a privilege to have known you.'

'Thank you, sir. I won't let you down.'

'I know you won't. Goodbye, soldier.'

'Goodbye, sir.'

I put down the phone, feeling the calm and peace that the inevitable bring. This time tomorrow, all my pain would be gone.

one hundred and seventeen.
Sephy

I paced up and down my bedroom, the phone in my hand. 'What should I do? Call the police?'

'For your own daughter? Are you mad?'

'Then what should I do?' I asked, frantically.

'Sephy, calm down,' Mother tried to soothe.

'How can I calm down? You didn't hear what they said, Mother. I did.'

'What made you listen in on the extension in the first place? D'you listen every time Callie Rose makes a phone call?'

'No, of course not. I was napping and something woke me up. I thought maybe I'd missed the phone ringing, so I picked it up and I heard Callie talking to Dad's new wife, Grace.'

'She's hardly new, dear. They've been married for over a decade.'

'That's not the point. Callie Rose is up to something terrible and I can guess who put her up to it. After she got off the phone to Grace, she immediately phoned some guy and he congratulated her on getting in to see Dad. Mother,

I'm scared to death. I think . . . I think Callie was talking to Jude and he kept calling her "soldier". Oh my
God! You . . . you don't think Callie had anything to do
with what happened to the Defence Minister? Or maybe
the bombs that went off at the airport last weekend? No,
she couldn't've . . . my baby wouldn't do anything like
that . . . Mother, I'm so—'

'Persephone, get a grip,' Mother snapped. 'Look, d'you
want me to come over?'

'No. Just tell me what to do.'

'You and my granddaughter need to sit down and talk.
Really talk.'

'How? She can't bear to be in the same room as me. I
enter, she leaves,' I said. 'She'd never listen to anything I
have to say.'

'Then we have to find a way to make her listen.'

'How? It's never going to happen, short of locking her
in a room with me.'

'Then that's what we'll do. You come over to my
house tomorrow morning at nine. I'll invite Callie Rose
over at ten and then the two of you can talk.'

'She'll leave the moment she sees me,' I said.

'Then she won't see you until it's too late for her to
do anything about it. You can hide out in my cellar and
when Callie goes into it, I'll lock the door.'

'Why the cellar? It's freezing down there,' I protested.

'It's the only room in my house which has a lock on
the outside of the door,' said Mother.

'How can you sound so calm?' I cried. 'Callie's going
to do something really stupid. Something that's going to
ruin her life. I can feel it.'

'Then, we'll have to make sure that doesn't happen,' said Mother.

'How? Jude has got his hooks into her. If she doesn't do what he wants tomorrow, she will next week or next month. He won't stop till he ruins her life because he knows that's the only sure way to get to me. It's just like him to organize something for Callie's birthday. That man doesn't miss a trick.'

It was very quiet at the other end of the phone.

'Mother . . . ?'

'You just be here tomorrow at nine and leave the rest to me,' said Mother at last.

'What can you do?' I said with more open scepticism than I'd intended. 'Mother, I didn't mean it that way. It's just that you're . . . you're ill and . . .'

'I'm ill, Persephone, not ga-ga. Now, you're going to have to trust me. OK?'

'I—'

'D'you trust me or not?'

'Yes, Mother.'

'When we've finished here, get Callie to call me. I want to talk to her. And do me a favour, Sephy. Stop calling me Mother.'

'But I've always called you Mother,' I frowned.

'Yes, and I've always hated it. Call me Mum.'

'Yes, Mum.'

'See you tomorrow, Sephy.'

'Yes, Mum.'

'And, Sephy,'

'Yes, Mum?'

'I love you.'

Mum put down the phone immediately before I could utter a word. She loved me . . . She hadn't said that for the longest time. Not since I was a teenager. Not since before Callum died. Mum loved me. And just like that, the wild panic I'd felt subsided a little. A very little. But I was still scared to death. I loved Mother . . . Mum very much, but even if her plan to get me and Callie Rose talking to each other worked, she still couldn't sort out our other problem with Jude. No one would be able to do that. Jude was too clever, too powerful. But she obviously had something in mind. One last appeal to Meggie to talk to her son perhaps? Whatever it was, I didn't need sharply honed instincts to know that one way or another, the following day, Callie Rose's birthday, was going to be a turning point in all our lives.

one hundred and eighteen.
Callie is 15

My mobile phone rang for the second time in five minutes. How strange to be so popular this late in the day . . .

'Hello?'

'It's me.'

'Hello, you!'

'What're you up to tomorrow, birthday girl?' he asked.

'Nana Jasmine just phoned. She's having some friends round for lunch tomorrow and she wants me to go round in the morning and help her.'

'What happened to her cook and that other woman, her P.A.?'

'They're both away apparently,' I said.

'So are you going?'

'I guess so. She's not been too well, so she isn't all that strong at the moment. She said she asked Mum but Mum's busy. So that leaves me. I thought I'd hang out on her beach for a while, then head to her house.'

'Want some company?'

'Well, I'm not—'

'Don't say no. I want to see you tomorrow. Please?'

I surprised myself by saying, 'Yes, OK then. But only on the beach. And I can't stay long – I have to be somewhere else in the afternoon.'

'Fine with me. I'll meet you there then.'

'You'll have to go right round Nana Jasmine's house to get to the beach. You still remember the way?'

'Of course. See you tomorrow.'

He rang off. I wondered why I'd said yes. Did I really want to see him on my last day? My head told me no, but my heart knew my head was lying. It would be the last time I ever saw him and I wanted a fresh memory of the two of us together to take with me into the night. If I'd been asked which one out of Lucas or Tobey I'd want with me on my last day on Earth, I would've replied almost without thinking. How strange that when it got down to it, my heart's choice wasn't the same as my head's.

one hundred and nineteen.
Jasmine

✖ ————————————————————

Letter-writing has never been my forte, but no matter. Something tells me this letter will get all the attention it deserves. It's taken me long enough to write, but the tone as well as the information contained within had to be just right. He might be able to suppress the letter at one or two newspapers where he can call in favours, but surely not the whole lot? Of course, the beauty of a computer and a printer is the joy of typing once and then making lots of copies. I did think about emailing the letter to every news desk in the country that published an Internet address, but I'd probably make a mess of that. And emails can be too easily dismissed as being the work of cranks or hackers or malicious coders.

I am not a malicious coder.

I am a mean, malevolent ex-wife.

I'll make sure that if Kamal's lot do come to power, he will not be joining the party. The moment the contents of this letter become generally known, Kamal will be finished. He'll be out in the political wilderness, never to return.

Now I have a few other details to take care of before tomorrow morning. The first thing I need to do is have a heart to heart with Meggie McGregor. I need to find out where her son is and I'm going to need her help.

one hundred and twenty.
Callie is 15

I can't get to sleep. Not that I expected to be out like a light but this wide-awake feeling isn't pleasant. Two-thirty in the morning and sleep is just a memory. I'm never going to be able to drift off now. My mind won't wind down. I keep thinking about all the things I'm going to miss. Both my nanas and Lucas and Tobey and chocolate ice cream and the sea and sunrises and sunsets. And my mum. In spite of everything, I'm going to miss my mum. I think she's my major regret. I wish . . . I wish we could've had something different, something *more*. And now that'll never happen. But as Uncle Jude said, sometimes sacrifices have to be made.

And I'm so tired of all this.

So if I have to lie on my back and stare into the darkness until the morning comes, then so be it.

This time tomorrow, I'll be getting all the sleep I need.

Jude versus Jasmine

one hundred and twenty-one.
Jasmine

I can't do this for much longer. The pain is fiercely intense now, so bad that I want to throw my head back and howl like a wounded animal. I want to flop down onto the hotel bed and curl up into a ball. I want to press the switch and end my torment . . .

But I can't.

I promised Meggie as much.

I took two more painkillers out of my pocket and held them clutched tight in my free hand. I was ready to cram them into my mouth but I'd already given in and taken some earlier. Any more would definitely dull my reflexes and I couldn't afford to give Jude any quarter. One slip on my part and it'd be my last.

'Meggie, what d'you want me to do?' I asked quietly.

Maybe if I lowered the timbre of my voice, I could disguise just how truly vulnerable I was.

'I don't know, Jasmine. I wish I did, but I don't know anything,' Meggie replied. 'Except that I'm staying here.'

'Mum, no,' said Jude, urgently. 'You need to leave. I can take care of myself.'

'Meggie, you can't stay,' I told her, ignoring Jude. 'Sephy is locked in my cellar with Callie Rose. You have to let them out.'

Meggie regarded me with a sad smile.

'You knew I'd want to stay, didn't you?' she said softly.

'I suspected you might.' I nodded. 'You have to leave.'

'And if I say no?' asked Meggie.

'Then we all leave this room.'

'And if I say yes?'

'Then you leave this room alone.'

'I see.' Meggie turned back to her son. We all sat in silence for at least half a minute. 'Jude, tell me one thing worth dying for?'

'Lots of things are worth dying for, Mum,' said Jude, scathingly. 'The L.M., freedom, the cause . . . I know you haven't forgotten what they did to Dad and Callum.'

Meggie's eyes sparkled with unshed tears. 'Now tell me one thing worth living for,' she said.

Jude stared at her. He opened his mouth like a drowning fish. 'I—' Jude managed the one word before his mouth snapped shut.

Meggie nodded sadly. 'That's what I thought. You deliberately went after Callie Rose to turn her against Sephy, and please don't insult my intelligence by denying it.'

'I wasn't going to,' he said.

'That's the first honest thing you've said to me in years,' Meggie told him. 'Jude, tell me the truth, did you murder Cara Imega?'

Jude sat back and regarded his mum, his eyes dark and cold as the bottom of the ocean. 'So we're back to that again? You've already made up your mind, Mum, so why bother asking?'

'I need to hear it, Jude. Did you murder that girl?'

'I didn't murder anyone, Mum,' Jude said with a calculated smile. 'Murder implies I unlawfully took the life of another person. All I did was kill a Cross.'

My gasp of horror was lost beneath Meggie's. The tears she could no longer hold back slid mournfully down her cheeks. Poor Meggie. My heart wept for her. There but for the grace of God went Minerva or Sephy or even me. What must've happened to Jude to make him hate all of us so much? I, in my complacency, was probably part of the problem. I cringed to remember how, a lifetime ago, I'd told Sarah, my personal assistant, to fire Meggie because she hadn't provided me with the alibi I'd needed. Was that when all this began with Jude? If I hadn't fired her, would we all be sitting here now? The hatred Jude had inside was far worse than the cancer eating me up. For him there was no hope, no reprieve, no remission. No act of degradation or violence would ever be enough for him. His hatred fed on itself and the more it devoured him, the more it wanted. And Jude had never seen that. Or maybe he just didn't care.

My heart wept for him.

My heart wept for all of us.

'This bomb you gave to Callie Rose, who was it for?' I asked.

Jude turned contemptuous eyes on me. 'I didn't give Callie a bomb, she made it.'

'Who was it for?'

'As you're wearing the thing, I'd say that was academic,' said Jude.

'It was for Kamal Hadley, wasn't it?' I said. 'You wanted to make a martyr out of my ex-husband.'

Jude turned away from me. He wasn't going to deign to throw another word in my direction. No matter. I could guess.

Jude was a fool. He wanted to deify my husband and his particular brand of noxious politics. What did Jude think would happen if Kamal was murdered by the L.M.? Ah, but it wouldn't be the L.M., would it? It'd be at the hand of his own granddaughter. And what kind of statement would that make?

Meggie stood up wearily. 'Jude, I want you to know something. I want you to remember this. I love you very, very much.'

Jude didn't reply. He didn't know how. Meggie bent down to kiss her son on his cheek, before straightening up. Turning to face me she said, 'I'm leaving. Alone. I'm saying yes.'

She headed for the door.

'Meggie,' I called after her without looking away from her son. 'Tell Sephy and Callie Rose . . . explain this to them. And tell them I love them very much.'

The door of the room opened. Moments later it clicked shut with a symbolic finality.

Jude and I were alone again.

one hundred and twenty-two.
Jude

Mum left me. She's really left. She's more or less given Mad-Bitch Hadley her blessing.

Mum . . .

Well, I don't need her. I don't need anyone. Jude's number one law will get me through this: *Never, ever allow yourself to feel. Feelings kill.* I came into this world alone, travelled through it alone and that's the way I'll go out. But not today. I'm not ready to go yet. I still have things to do.

Get to your knife, Jude. It's now or never.

I was just reaching down for it, under cover of scratching my leg again, when the sound of the fire alarm made me jump. Damn! I'd been so close. And now the hotel was on fire – with a little luck. 'Cause that meant the fire brigade would be here soon, and they'd go from room to room . . . We sat in silence as the alarm warbled on and on, its high-pitched whine continuous and piercing. Doors further down the corridor opened and slammed. There were shouts and cries and the sound of foot-steps running. But soon those noises died away. And throughout the whole thing, Jasmine sat perfectly still and never moved.

'We have to get out of here,' I told the mad bitch. 'Unless you fancy burning to death.'

Jasmine sighed and stood up. 'There's no fire, Jude. Your mum set off the fire alarm to get everyone out of the hotel.'

I stared at her. My mum had done that?

'We arranged it all last night and this morning,' Jasmine told me. 'We agreed that if she left this room by herself, if she said yes to what I planned to do, she'd set off the fire alarm to evacuate the hotel. I'm not a murderer. I don't intend to kill anyone but you.'

'Isn't this murder?'

'No, it's putting you out of my family's misery.'

'No, wait. Stop. You mean, Mum could've saved me?' I asked.

'If she'd stayed,' Jasmine nodded. 'All she had to do was say no. There's no way I would set this thing off with Meggie in the room. She knew that. Besides, how would my daughter and granddaughter have got out of my cellar if she'd stayed?'

'I don't understand.'

Jasmine smiled. 'You don't have to. Any last words, Jude?'

Any last words? Did she think this was the end of some war movie? Last words? How about − *I'll see you in hell*? They were fine, final words.

Jasmine didn't take her eyes off me as she said, 'May God forgive me but this is for my daughter, Sephy, and your brother, Callum, and their child, Callie Rose.'

Jasmine took a step towards me. That's when I knew my last moments on this sorry earth had come. Jude's law number fifteen sang in my head: *If Heaven is full of Crosses, I'd rather live in Hell.* And there was one person in my head. Only one. Not Mum or Dad. Not Lynette. Not even Callum. The very last person I expected.

Cara . . .

I started to laugh. Louder and deeper than I'd ever laughed before.

CARA . . .

I raised my eyes to heaven. Cara, I know you're watching. Come and take my hand and lead me down to—

one hundred and twenty-three. Meggie

God, forgive me. Please God, forgive me.

I want to turn round and run back to the hotel. I want to . . . I want to run into that hotel room and scream STOP . . . I don't want this. He's my son. My one remaining child. Don't force me to give him up. I love him so much. Please don't take him from me.

I can't do this. I have to go back to the hotel.

But I can't.

After walking so far, so fast just to get away, I can't take another step. I'm standing on this pavement, frozen to the spot, unwilling to go forwards. Unable to go back.

Jude, forgive me . . .

No, I can't do this. I have to stop Jasmine – if it's not too late. Turn round, Meggie.

But what about my granddaughter? Callie Rose is the future. And how can she exist with Jude's hatred poisoning her every breath? I know he's told her things, shown her things that no one should ever see, never mind a child like Callie. He's been doing it for years.

I just couldn't see it, didn't want to see it.

Jude wants to fill up the whole world with the pain he feels. He could've let it go. He had that choice. I wish, oh how I wish I could turn back the hands of time. I'd hug Jude to me and stroke his hair the way I used to and I'd say the words I was never able to say except in my heart.

Jude, I love you. I'll never leave you. I'll always be here for you.

But how can that be true? I left him in that hotel room with Jasmine, knowing what she plans to do. Why am I being forced to choose between my son and my granddaughter? I can't make that decision, I just can't.

Turn to the past.

Turn to the future.

Which way?

Jude needs me. So does Callie Rose. It's not too late for Callie Rose. She's young. I can show her what I was never able to show my son. I thought I had to be tough because Jude was going to have it tough, a nought boy in a Cross world. I thought I was preparing him for what was ahead. But I know better now. So I'll tell Callie Rose I love her every day, every hour. I'll hug her and hold her and love her. She needs me. It's not too late to show Callie Rose that love is real, that love exists. And with love inside, nothing is impossible. I'll help Callie Rose and her mum come together again. I'll do whatever it takes. Whatever it takes.

Oh, Jude . . .

It's not too late for Callie Rose.

It is too late for my son. He breathes in bitterness and breathes out hatred. He has no faith in the future, so he has no stake in the future. He doesn't believe things will get better. He has no trust. He has no hope.

But he's still my son.

Walk forward, Meggie. One step at a time. But it's so hard, and it hurts so much.

'Are you all right, love?'

The words lift my head. I have to blink several times before I can see the face of the man who spoke. An elderly nought man selling newspapers looks at me with concern. His hair is more grey than brown, but his eyebrows are still dark.

'Are you OK? Is something wrong?' the man asks.

I open my mouth, but there are no words.

'Look, d'you want to sit down for a moment?'

I can hear sirens screaming around me. Two, then three police cars race past. And they're all going in the direction of the Isis Hotel.

'I wonder what that's about?' the nought vendor says softly as we both watch the police cars turn the corner.

Jasmine hasn't done it. Not yet. Surely not yet? Not so soon. An ambulance flashes by. Jasmine couldn't've done it yet. I hadn't heard anything. No flash, no blast, no boom. There's traffic all around me and a pneumatic drill sounds further up the road. I can hear car horns and people shouting, laughing, talking – but no explosion. I would've heard it, wouldn't I? Surely, I'm not so far away yet that I wouldn't've heard something? Something I know I tried to shut my ears and close my heart to, as I left the hotel. But thoughts and fears and sorrow and tears don't drown out the sound of something like that, do they? I look up at the sky. Where's the rain? I heard a single clap of thunder before, but there's no rain. Shouldn't there be rain? Maybe the noise scared Jasmine into changing her mind? Maybe Jude managed to stop her, to persuade her not to . . . ?

Jasmine couldn't've done it yet . . .

Please, God . . .

'It's all go today, love, isn't it?' smiles the vendor. 'Mind you, it's a good day for us, isn't it?'

I don't understand. The vendor's grin broadens. He holds up the first edition of the evening paper. I look at the headline: KAMAL HADLEY IS OUT!

'Stitched him up nicely. Hell has no fury . . .'

I still didn't understand.

'His ex-wife!' the vendor explains. 'Jasmine Hadley sent out a letter plus proof positive that Kamal Hadley took backhanders, made dodgy deals to get into power, did favours, even interfered to make sure a couple of his political mates didn't come to trial for fraud when they should've done. So he's stepped down. He says it's because he doesn't want his party to suffer before tomorrow's election, but I reckon it's too late. There's no way his party will win now. Thank goodness.'

Only the previous evening, all the news reports had Kamal's party ahead in the opinion polls. It was almost a foregone conclusion that Sephy's dad was going to be the next Prime Minister. But not any more.

And Jasmine had done that?

Another ambulance roared past.

The vendor smiled at me. 'Cheer up, love. It might never happen!'

I nodded, unable to smile back, but so grateful for his kindness.

Walk, Meggie. Just keep walking.

Callie Rose needs you.

And so will Sephy.

Callie Rose and Sephy

one hundred and twenty-four.
Callie Rose

Were we never going to get out of this ruddy cellar? My bladder was beginning to say hello! I glanced down at my watch. It was almost four in the afternoon. Grandad Kamal would be long gone from his house by now. Not that I cared about him. I still had so many questions for Mum. Nana Jasmine was right. There were things that only she could answer.

'Mum, were you and Dad . . . lovers before you were kidnapped?'

'No, love. That night in the cabin was our one and only time together.'

'And you got pregnant first time?'

'Yes, thank God,' said Mum sincerely. 'Because I got you.'

'Why . . . didn't you have an abortion like Grandad Kamal wanted?' I had to ask. 'You and Dad could have been together . . .'

'You really don't know?' Mum asked softly.

I shook my head. I had battled for months and months

to try and figure that one out, but each possible reason was assessed and dismissed.

'Callum was . . . my present. You are the future. Callum was love. You are . . . hope. Callum was my other half. You are Callum and I as a whole. And there was no way Callum would have wanted to live, knowing you'd died for him. I know that like I know my own name. Your dad loved us both too much to put an end to something started with so much love.'

'So Dad never . . . raped you?' I had to look down as I spoke.

Mum placed her hand beneath my chin and lifted my face until my gaze met hers. 'Never. Never, ever. Your dad would've died before he did such a thing.'

'And that letter you showed me was real?' I asked. 'Dad really did . . . love you – and me?'

'He loved us very much, Callie Rose. I'm going to keep telling you that until you start believing me. If you doubt it, read your dad's letter again.'

So I did, slowly, carefully, letting each word of love wash over me. All at once I felt strangely lighter than air. Like something had been pressing me down, something heavy and malevolent. And now it was gone. I felt so strange, like a window had been thrown open inside my head and my heart, where there had been closed shutters before. And the light and the bright were filling me up so fast I could hardly breathe. A weird and wonderful feeling flooded through me as I looked at Mum. A feeling stronger than concern and as enduring as love. It took me more than a few seconds to recognize what it was.

Hope.

For the first time in, oh, so long, I had hope for the future. Hope that Nana Jasmine would get well again. Hope for Tobey and Lucas and school and my friends. Hope that Mum and I might get to know each other, might be friends, might even one day find something more.

Hope tried to flutter up within me. Doubt tried to squash it back down again.

'Mum?'

'Yes, love.'

'Why d'you believe Dad's first letter and not his second? Maybe the second one was the one he really meant?'

'No, he meant the first one,' Mum told me emphatically.

I needed more than words. I needed Mum's conviction to sweep away my fears.

So I asked again, 'Yes, but how d'you know?'

one hundred and twenty-five.
Sephy

'Callie Rose, I know because now I trust my heart and I trust my memories and I trust Callum. He was always there for me – always. And when I was kidnapped, your dad was the one who helped me escape. He loved me.'

I closed my eyes and snapped back to a time in a bare room, in a cabin in the middle of nowhere. Back to one of the happiest moments of my life. The one and only time Callum and I had made love.

Callum's kisses burned against my body, almost as much as his words, whispered against my skin, had indelibly burned their way into my mind. He kissed me like he was a drowning man and I was his oxygen. I didn't even have to think to remember all the things he'd done to me before his body moved over mine, his legs parting mine.

'Sephy, I want you . . . so much . . .' Callum told me, his grey eyes burning, blazing bright.

'Callum, you've got me,' I whispered back. 'Always and for ever. Don't you know that?'

We watched each other for countless seconds, until I smiled, making no attempt to hide what I felt for him. Maybe he just couldn't wait any more, or maybe it was my smile that did it. His mouth covered mine, his tongue thrusting between my lips as his body joined with mine. The breath caught in my throat and I was immediately still. Not because he was hurting me, but because in that second when our bodies melted together, it was like . . . like touching heaven. Callum was right. There was no other way to describe it. Like touching heaven.

'Sephy . . .' Callum looked at me then, all regret and concern, mistaking the reason for my stillness. He was going to pull away and leave me. I held him tight inside, just as my arms held him to me. Then I cupped his face with my hands.

'Don't stop,' I whispered.

Callum took one of my hands in his, our fingers linked

together. I smiled at our fingers together. How I loved the contrast in our skin colour, alternating brown and pink, Cross and Nought, me and Callum. I kissed his fingers as Callum moved very slowly further into me. I could feel every part of him and it was like we were born for this moment. Like he was me and I was him and we could never go back to being two people.

Callum pulled back slowly and then moved forward again, just as slowly. It was a pleasurable torture that was almost too much to bear.

'I love you, Persephone,' Callum said softly, still moving within me. And then he kissed me so long and so hard. And I didn't even realize I was holding my breath until I gasped not just from what Callum was doing to me, but to drag air back down into my lungs.

'I love you,' Callum said again. 'Only you. For ever.'

But I hardly heard him. My skin was almost unbearably hot, my insides were hotter, melting me from the inside out. I rocked against him, wanting to make our time last for ever but desperate for the increasing tension in my body to be released some way, somehow. 'Kiss me,' I pleaded.

Callum's lips worked their way up to my neck and nibbled on my ear and across my cheek until his mouth was against mine. My arms were wrapped round him, pulling him closer, ever closer, always closer. His arms were wrapped around me. It was kissing and touching and belonging and being, all at once. There was something deep inside me coiling tighter and tighter like a key in a wind-up toy. But I didn't break. Instead my body became a fireworks display. I held onto Callum for dear life, my eyes wide open as I stared at him, stunned. I gave myself up completely to this new sensation overwhelming my body. It was like nothing

I'd ever experienced before, like nothing I'd ever imagined. And Callum looked just as stunned by the wonder of it as I was. He closed his eyes and groaned his release.

We'd lifted off from Earth and touched heaven all right.

But heaven burned.

And freefalling back down to Earth brought with it a new kind of reality. The fantasy was over. I clung to Callum, trying to hold onto the moment, trying to make it mine for ever, but it wasn't working. I couldn't make it work. Until Callum started to make love to me all over again, with even more love and tenderness than before. And the second time I was so sure we'd always be as one, stay as one, that it was a shock to come back down to Earth and the truth. So the tears had started . . .

'Mum, what're you thinking about? Mum? Mum?'

I looked up, emerging from my vivid memories on a wave of heated embarrassment.

'On second thoughts, don't tell me,' said Callie, dryly. 'I'm probably too young to hear it.'

I laughed.

'Were my thoughts that obvious?'

'Not until you blushed.'

'How did you know I blushed? My cheeks are too dark to go red like yours.'

'The tips of your ears went red,' Callie told me with relish. 'What were you thinking about?'

'Your dad,' I smiled. 'To answer your question, Callie, there are no guarantees in this life. Some things you just know in your heart. And some things you have to take on faith. That's how I know your dad meant the first letter he wrote and not the second. That's how I know Callum loved both of us more than his own life.' Then I remembered something else. I beamed at Callie.

'What?' she asked immediately.

'There was a prison guard called' – I had to concentrate for a moment to remember – 'called Jack. Jack Labinjah. He was with your dad on the day he died.' My smile faded with the memory but inside I felt strangely peaceful. 'Your dad told Jack that he meant the first letter, but he wanted me to move on with my life so he wrote the second. Dippy git!'

Callie tilted her head to one side, looking so much like her dad that my heart leaped. She said, her tone straightforward, 'You loved Dad very much, didn't you?'

I nodded. 'Very, very much. For a long, long time I thought it'd be impossible for me to love anyone else.'

'Did you love Sonny?' Callie asked me seriously.

'Yes, I did,' I said. 'I tried to convince myself that our relationship was one of . . . mutual convenience but I was wrong. Sonny loved me. And if I hadn't been so afraid, I could've loved him as he deserved.'

'Afraid of what?'

'Afraid of falling in love with anyone but Callum. Afraid of being disloyal to your dad if I gave my heart to someone else. And I was convinced I brought nothing but bad luck to anyone who dared to love me,' I said sombrely. 'So I refused to put my whole heart and soul into our relationship. And Sonny knew that.'

'D'you still love Dad?'

'I'll always love him.'

'How can you love Dad and take up with someone else?'

'Ah, Callie, your dad will always have a special place in my heart. A place that will always be his and no one else's. But it's unrealistic to think that there's only one person in this world whom any of us can love. Some lucky people get to fall in love with one person and spend the rest of their lives with that person – but they are few and far between.'

'I don't get it.' Callie shook her head.

How could I put this so she'd understand?

'Callum and I were like a fire that couldn't burn itself out. We were all-consuming passion and intense emotions. If we'd had the chance to be together, I think we would've spent the rest of our lives blissfully telling the rest of the world to go to hell. But we didn't get that chance. And when I got that venomous letter from Callum after you were born, I thought I was . . . unlovable. Sonny came along to show me that wasn't true, but our timing was off.'

'And what about Nathan?'

'Nathan and I understand each other,' I said. 'It's not all fiery passion, but it's caring and sharing and comfortable.'

The unimpressed look on Callie's face made me laugh.

'I don't mean it's boring. It's not. But we share the same sense of humour and the same values and I like him very much. It's very important to like the one you're with as well as love them, Callie Rose. Don't you forget that.'

one hundred and twenty-six.
Callie Rose

I had an awful lot to think about. Too much to take in all in one go. But this much I knew for certain:

My dad was Callum Ryan McGregor.

My dad loved my mum.

My mum is Persephone Mira Hadley.

My mum loved my dad.

I was conceived with love, not hatred.

My dad loved me.

That's all I know so far.

But it's a pretty good start.

'So what happens now?' I asked Mum.

'I don't know,' replied Mum softly. 'What d'you want to happen now?'

I wanted to snap my fingers and make the world and Mum and me right. But it wasn't that easy. I tried to tell myself that nothing worth having ever was.

'You and me,' I sighed. 'We still have so much between us.'

'A lot behind us,' Mum agreed. 'But a lot more ahead of us.'

'I wish I'd heard the truth about Dad from you, Mum,' I told her, unable to let it go completely.

'I know, love. I know.'

'No more lies?'

'No more lies,' Mum promised.

But the past clung to me like a scratchy shirt sewn to my skin. How wonderful to be able to cast it off, but that would take more work – from both of us. We both sat for a while, but the silence was calm rather than uncomfortable.

'Mum, how do we . . . how do we forget the past?'

'By embracing the present and looking forward to the future,' said Mum. 'It's what your dad wanted more than anything. I believe it's what he died for, to give us both a future.'

I nodded. Mum believed all good things about my dad. She held onto only the good things. I'd try, but it would take me a little while longer.

'What else do you believe in, Mum?' I needed to ask.

'I believe in love and forgiveness. I only have to look at you to believe in God. I believe in friends and family and friendship. I believe in second chances and the present. I believe in lots of things,' Mum replied.

There was something about the present I needed to know.

'Mum, are . . . are you going to marry Nathan?'

'Why d'you ask?'

'Nana Meggie says the two of you are very close. And you seem happy with him.'

'I am.'

'So will the two of you get married?'

'He asked me, but there's a problem.'

'What's that?'

Mum's smile faded into a sigh. 'Sonny's come back, and he wants me to marry him too.'

'Sonny came back? When?'

'Just recently.'

'So which one will you choose?' I asked eagerly.

Mum smiled. 'Which one d'you think I should marry?'

'The one you love,' I said at last.

'Good advice,' said Mum. 'And what about you and Tobey? Or is it you and Lucas?'

'You knew about Tobey too?' I asked, surprised.

'Callie, everyone knew about Tobey – except you.'

'Well, I know now,' I said. 'They've both said they want to be with me.'

'And which one will you choose?'

'Which one d'you think I should choose?' I asked.

'D'you love either of them?'

I frowned. 'I didn't think so, but this morning I was with one of them on the beach . . .'

'And?'

'And when I thought I'd never see him again, I realized how much I really did care . . .'

I could feel myself begin to blush, so I stopped speaking. I thought Mum might laugh or have an indulgent look on her face, but she didn't. She took my hands in her own and we sat side by side, just watching each other. I hadn't looked at Mum, really looked at her, in so long. She was so beautiful and her eyes just blazed with love. Love for me.

For the first time in a long time, I didn't know what to

say, what to do. I didn't know how many blue beans made five. I searched for something to say but the words wouldn't come. As if Mum knew, she smiled at me and opened her arms. And there was such peace and welcome in her eyes that my jumping heart was instantly still. I moved into her arms and they closed around me, soft and warm and much, much more – slow enough for me to back away if I wanted to, I think, but firm enough to hold me for the rest of my life with love. And then I remembered something which drove the last vestige of any doubt from my head.

'Mum, you know when you told me that if we crashed on a mountain and you died, I could eat you?' I said with a smile. 'Well, I get it now.'

Mum laughed softly and stroked my hair. There was no uncertainty left in me. My heart grew until it threatened to burst out of my chest.

'Happy birthday, Callie Rose McGregor-Hadley,' said Mum. 'I love you with all my heart.'

But I hardly heard her. My cheek was wet. I knew I was crying but the tears on my face weren't mine alone. Mum hugged me so tight, tighter than anyone had ever hugged me before. I could smell her soap and the faint residual trace of her perfume. I could feel every breath she took, every sob she made. I could hear her heart – or was it my heart, thumping with joy?

Across the cellar, the door slowly opened – and there stood Meggie. Momentarily startled, she started to smile at us. Mum and I smiled back. I turned to Mum. My mum – who loved me more than anyone else in the world. Who loved me so much, she gave up her first love for me. Who loved me so much she was prepared to give me up to keep me safe.

'Callie Rose, I love you,' said Mum.

Another fact to add to my list of things I knew for certain.

'I love you too, Mum,' I whispered.

I'd never tire of hearing it. I didn't want to stop saying it. And even though the cellar door was open, this was a moment in time no one could take from us. I didn't need an open cellar door to know that I was finally free. Dad's letter hadn't really solved anything between Mum and me. We'd have to do that for ourselves. We'd only taken the first few steps, but at least we were hand in hand, both heading in the same direction. And Dad's letter of love was paving the way.

Dad, can you see us? Can you see how much Mum loves me? Can you see her holding me tight? Can you see us, Dad?

And I swear I could feel my dad's arms around both of us, and in my heart he was smiling.

Read on for a preview of the fourth
electrifying story in the
Noughts & Crosses series.

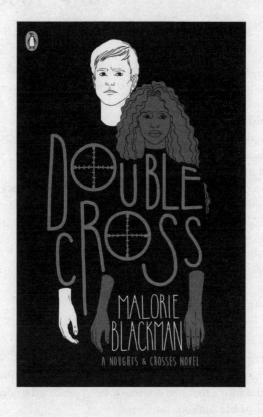

'Powerful'
Sunday Times

And continue this incredible series with:
Crossfire

one. Tobey

'Tobey, I was er . . . thinking that maybe you and me could . . . er . . . you know, go to the pictures or go for a . . . er . . . you know, a meal or something this weekend?'

Godsake! Couldn't she get through one sentence, just one sentence, without sticking umpteen 'er's and 'you know's in it first?

'I can't, Misty. I'm already going out.' I turned back to my graphic novel − a humorous fantasy that was better than I had thought it would be when I'd borrowed it from the library.

'Oh? Where're you going?'

'Out.' I frowned, not bothering to look up from my book.

'For the whole weekend?'

'Yes.'

'Out where?'

I turned in my chair to look at her. Misty tossed back her brunette hair with blonde highlights in a peculiarly unnatural move that had obviously been practised to death in front of her bedroom mirror.

'Out where?' Misty asked again.

This girl was stomping on my last nerve now. She'd

been asking me out all term and I'd always found some reason to turn her down. Couldn't she take a hint? Miss I'm-too-sexy-for-myself leaned closer in to me, so close that I had to pull back or she'd've been kissing my neck.

'I'm going out with my family. We're visiting relatives,' I improvised.

I'm too nice, that's my trouble, I thought sourly. Why on earth didn't I just tell her that I wasn't interested in a date or anything else for that matter? For one thing, hugging her would be like trying to cuddle a chopstick. I liked curves. And even if I did fancy her – which I didn't – there was no way I'd ever get it on with an ex-girlfriend of my mate, Dan. That was a definite no.

'Maybe the er . . . erm . . . following Saturday, then? We could maybe . . . er . . . go out then if you'd like?' said Misty.

Rearrange this sentence: hell – freezes – over – when.

The classroom door swung open and Callie Rose strolled into the room. She stopped momentarily when she saw who was sitting in her chair. Scowling, she strode over to Misty.

'D'you mind?' Callie asked.

'I'm talking to Tobey.'

'Not from my chair, you're not,' Callie shot back.

'Er . . . can't you find somewhere else to sit until the lesson starts?' Misty wheedled.

Uh-oh! I held my breath. Callie let her rucksack slip from her hand to the floor as her eyes narrowed. She was one nanosecond away from moving up to Kick-arse Condition 1.

'Misty, you need to get up off my chair,' Callie said softly.

'I'd shift if I were you,' I advised Misty.

Much as I found the thought of a cat-fight over me appealing, I didn't fancy Callie getting into trouble and then giving me grief for what was left of the term.

Misty huffed and stood up. 'Callie, I'm going to remember this.'

'Remember it. Take a photo. Break out your camcorder. I don't give a rat's bum. Just move.' Callie stepped aside so that Misty could squeeze by, before flopping down into her now vacant seat.

'Damn cheek!' Callie carried on muttering under her breath as she dug into her bag for the history books required for our first lesson. She turned to look at Misty, who was now back in her own chair.

'If looks could kill, I'd be seriously ill,' Callie said as she turned to me, annoyance vying with amusement to colour her eyes more hazel than brown. Every time she was upset or angry, her eyes literally turned greener. It was one of the many things about her that got me going. She had the most expressive eyes I'd ever seen. Chameleon-like, they changed colour to reflect her every mood.

'Every time I want to sit down next to you or be within half a kilometre of you, I can't move without tripping over that girl first. What's up with that?'

I sucked in my cheeks in an effort not to chortle. One snicker and Callie would bite my head off. I tried for a nonchalant shrug.

'So what did Miss Foggy want this time?' Callie asked.

'Why d'you insist on calling her Miss Foggy?' I laughed.

I know it was mean, but 'Miss Foggy' really suited Misty.

'That's her name, isn't it? Besides, I'm not the one who chose to name her after a type of weather, and if the shoe fits . . .' Callie said pointedly. 'And you haven't answered my question.'

'She was inviting me out this weekend,' I replied.

I watched keenly for her reaction.

She shook her head. 'Damn! Misty's got it bad.'

'Are you jealous?' I asked hopefully.

Callie's eyebrows shot up so far and so fast, she got an instant face-lift. 'Are you kidding? I just think it's pitiful. She's been chucking herself at you all term and you haven't exactly been rushing to catch her, have you? In fact, most of the time you just fold your arms and let her drop on her face over and over again. You'd think she'd have got the message by now.'

'So you are green-eyed.' I grinned.

'Tobey, I don't know what you're taking, but you need to get yourself to rehab – quick, fast and in a hurry.'

'My girl is jealous.' My grin broadened. 'It's OK, Callie Rose. There'll never be anyone for me but you.'

'Go dip your head,' Callie told me.

'I mean it.' I crossed both my hands over my heart and adopted a ridiculously soppy expression. 'I give my heart . . . to you.' I mimed placing it carefully on the table in front of her. Glowering, Callie picked up her pen and mimed stabbing my heart on the table over and over again.

I burst out laughing, but had to smother it as Mr Lancer, the history teacher, entered the room. Callie started muttering all kinds of dire threats and promises under her breath the way she always did when I got under her skin.

And I loved it. It was music to my ears.

Callie quickly suppressed a laugh as the buzzer sounded for the end of the lesson. I'd spent the last fifty minutes passing her silly notes and making *sotto voce* remarks about Mr Lancer's newly bald head with its deep groove down the middle. It now resembled a certain part of the male anatomy and there was no way I could let that pass without comment. Callie had been in smothered fits of the giggles throughout most of the lesson. I loved making Callie laugh. God knows, she'd done little enough of that since her nana died in the Isis Hotel bomb blast. Callie was reaching for her rucksack on the floor and I'd barely made it to my feet when we had company.

Lucas frickin' Cheshie.

Misty wasn't the only one who couldn't take a hint. OK, so I still wasn't quite sure what to call my friendship with Callie, but I knew what Lucas and Callie weren't – and that was an item. She wasn't Lucas's girlfriend any more, so why did he persist in sniffing around her? Being older than us, he wasn't even in our class. But he must've seen Callie through the classroom window – and now here he was, lingering like an eggy fart. Smarmy git.

Completely ignoring me, Lucas said softly, 'Hi, Callie Rose, how are you?'

Callie's smile faded. She was instantly wary. I was grateful for that, if nothing else.

'I'm fine, Lucas. How are you?'

'Missing you.' Lucas smiled.

Callie searched for something to say, but unable to find

anything, she merely shrugged. I glared at Lucas, but he wasn't going to give me the satisfaction of acknowledging my presence.

'Ignore me all you want, but if you think I'm leaving you alone with Callie...' I projected my hostility towards him through narrowed eyes.

'I'm so glad to see you smiling again, Callie Rose. I'm glad you're getting over the bereavement in your family,' said Lucas.

The light in Callie's eyes vanished, as if a great, dark cloud had swept across the face of the sun. Callie's grandmother had died two months before, but Callie wasn't over it. Sometimes I wondered if she'd ever be truly over it.

'And you were so close to your nana Jasmine, weren't you?' Lucas continued.

I glanced at Callie before turning back to Lucas. A Cyclops with a pencil in his eye could see that Callie was getting upset. Lucas would have to be stupid not to see the effect his words were having. And Lucas was a lot of things, but stupid wasn't one of them.

Callie said nothing.

'Callie Rose, if you ever need to talk about your grandmother and how she died or anything, then I'm here for you. OK?' Lucas smiled. 'I just want you to know that I'm your friend. I'll always be your friend. If you need anything from me you only have to ask.'

Dismayed, I turned to Callie again. With a few well-chosen words, Lucas had not only knocked Callie to the ground, but then danced all over her. Her face took on the haunted, hunted look she always wore when thinking about Nana Jasmine. Her eyes glistened green with the tears she desperately tried to hold back. Callie hated for anyone to see her cry. My hands clenched into fists at my side. I had to hold myself rigid to refrain from smacking Lucas a sizeable one.

Lucas put his hand under Callie's chin to slowly raise her head. He was still ignoring me. 'Just think about what I said. I mean every word.' He smiled again, then sauntered off to join the rest of his crew waiting in the doorway for him.

Callie and I were alone in the classroom. I chewed on the inside of my bottom lip. What to say? What to do? I was so useless at this kind of thing.

'Callie . . .' I turned to her in time to see the solitary tear balanced on her lower eyelashes splash onto her cheek.

'Callie, don't listen to him. He was being a git,' I began furiously.

Puzzled, Callie turned to me, her eyes still shimmering. 'He was just trying to be kind.'

'Kind, my arse. He did that deliberately . . .'

'Tobey, what's wrong with you?' Callie whispered. 'You know what, I can't cope with this now.'

'Callie, can't you see what Lucas was up to? He was . . .'

But I was talking to myself. Callie was out the door, leaving me in the classroom.

Alone.

MALORIE BLACKMAN

A KNOCK AT THE DOOR, A VISIT FROM AN EX,
LIFE CHANGES IN AN INSTANT . . .

BOYS
DON'T
CRY

'Extraordinary . . .
Malorie Blackman
at her best'
Guardian

You've got it all planned out. A summer of freedom, university,
a career as a journalist – your future looks bright.

But then the doorbell rings. It's your ex-girlfriend,
and she's carrying a baby. Your baby.

You agree to look after it, just for an hour or two.

Then she doesn't come back – and your life changes for ever.

'An extraordinary book'
Guardian

Go back to where it all began.
Read the very first story in the
Noughts & Crosses series.

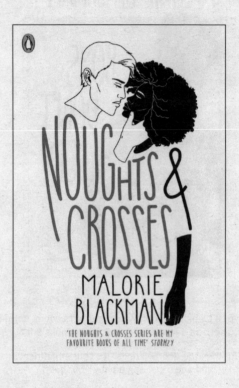

NOUGHTS & CROSSES
MALORIE BLACKMAN

'THE NOUGHTS & CROSSES SERIES ARE MY
FAVOURITE BOOKS OF ALL TIME' *STORMZY*

Sephy and Callum – friends from childhood – have fallen in love.
But theirs is a violent, hostile society, where the Noughts are
ruled by the superior Crosses.

Callum is a Nought. Sephy is a Cross.
The world is determined to keep them apart. They are
determined to be together . . . at whatever cost.

'Unforgettable'
Guardian

Introducing a new adventure from
Malorie Blackman.
Now available in paperback.

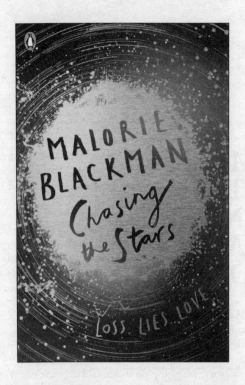

Olivia and her twin brother, Aidan, are heading alone back
to Earth following the virus that completely wiped out
the rest of their crew and family.

Nathan is part of a community heading in the opposite direction,
when their lives unexpectedly collide. Nathan and Olivia are instantly
attracted to each other – like nothing they have ever experienced.

But surrounded by rumours, deception – even murder – is it
possible to live out a happy-ever-after . . . ?

'A thrilling love story'
Mail on Sunday

BOMB BLAST VICTIM IDENTIFIED AS JASMINE HADLEY

Jasmine Hadley was yesterday finally identified as one of the victims of the bomb blast at the Isis Hotel. The former wife of Kamal Hadley, ex-MP, was killed five days ago, but it has taken this long to make a positive identification. A source working for the forensic science division of the police force stated, 'The damage to her body was so severe that a combination of dental records and DNA testing had to be used to conclusively identify the victim.' One other unidentified Nought male was also killed in the hotel explosion. The police are making strenuous efforts to establish the identity of this Nought in an effort to ascertain his connection, if any, to the blast. This latest outrage is suspected to be the work of the Liberation Militia, although as yet no one has claimed responsibility. Jasmine Hadley's ex-husband, Kamal Hadley, whose party crashed so ignominiously in the general election held last week, was unavailable for comment.